Praise for *In the Memory of the Forest*

"Powers's sense of place is astounding. . . .
In the Memory of the Forest with details . . .
Powerful enough to evoke . . . *For Wh*. . .
    —*Los Angeles Times*

"A brilliant novel . . . a fast-paced, thought-provoking, well written
mystery."   —*The Rocky Mountain News*

"Powers's writing is nothing short of masterful. Whether he is detail-
ing the ancient rhythms of daily life on a small Polish farm . . . or the
deepest feelings of one of his many, warmly-drawn characters, he
writes with an eye, a voice, and a clarity rarely seen."
    —*St. Louis Post-Dispatch*

"A good story, rich in action and character."
    —*The Atlantic Monthly*

"Has the authentic poetry of native born narrative, but loses no
poetry in translation. Powers renders the gnarled forests of modern
Poland accessible to anyone who's ever wended down the lush
wooden paths of his own head, only to trip on the roots of his past."
    —*The Philadelphia Inquirer*

"An extraordinary portrait."
    —*Pittsburgh Post-Gazette*

"Images of the remote village, as well as the fears, hopes, and pride of
its residents are beautifully portrayed in this captivating novel."
    —*Polish American Journal*

"*In the Memory of the Forest* is entirely absorbing, entirely satisfying,
a powerfully observed and structured novel that renders a post-
Communist Poland haunted by criminality, by complicity, by surveying files on its citizens and most of all by what those files omit."
    —Joan Didion

PENGUIN BOOKS

IN THE MEMORY OF THE FOREST

A native of Missouri, Charles T. Powers (1943–1996) was a journalist for the *Los Angeles Times* for more than twenty years. A former Nieman Fellow at Harvard University, he served as the newspaper's Eastern European Bureau chief in Warsaw from 1986 to 1991. For the last five years of his life he lived in Bennington, Vermont, where he completed *In the Memory of the Forest*, his only book.

IN THE
MEMORY
OF THE
FOREST

A NOVEL

CHARLES T. POWERS

PENGUIN BOOKS

For Rachel

PENGUIN BOOKS
Published by the Penguin Group
Penguin Putnam Inc., 375 Hudson Street, New York, New York 10014, U.S.A.
Penguin Books Ltd, 27 Wrights Lane, London W8 5TZ, England
Penguin Books Australia Ltd, Ringwood, Victoria, Australia
Penguin Books Canada Ltd, 10 Alcorn Avenue, Toronto, Ontario, Canada M4V 3B2
Penguin Books (N.Z.) Ltd, 182–190 Wairau Road, Auckland 10, New Zealand

Penguin Books Ltd, Registered Offices: Harmondsworth, Middlesex, England

First published in the United States of America by Scribner,
a division of Simon & Schuster Inc. 1997
Published in Penguin Books 1998

10 9 8 7 6 5 4 3 2 1

THE LIBRARY OF CONGRESS HAS CATALOGUED THE HARDCOVER AS FOLLOWS:
Powers, Charles T.
In the memory of the forest: a novel / Charles T. Powers
p. cm.
ISBN 0-684-83030-2 (hc.)
ISBN 0 14 02.7281 X (pbk.)
I. Title.
PS3566.0836815 1997
813'.54—dc20   96–36664

Printed in the United States of America
Set in Adobe Garamond
Designed by Erich Hobbing

A NOTE ON PRONUNCIATION

This novel is set in Poland, with Polish characters. Although a compromise with the spelling of Polish names—daunting to many readers—might have simplified the issue of pronunciation, it would have compromised more seriously the sense of reality. In any case, it is not the pronunciations that are so difficult, but most often the unfamiliar arrangement of consonants that are puzzling to the English reader's eye. Here is a simplified guide:

The Polish *sz* combination is pronounced as the English *sh*
The Polish *j* is equivalent to the English *y*
The Polish *w* is pronounced as the English *v*
The Polish *l* is pronounced as the English *w*
The Polish *e* is pronounced as the English *en*

As in:

Leszek = Leshek
Jola = Yola
Powierza = Povierza
Jadowia = Yadovia
Walesa = Vawensa

IN THE
MEMORY
OF THE
FOREST

PROLOGUE

Our forests are dark places, secretive, yet well-trodden. You perhaps would not realize their measure, given the prevailing notion of a country so planted with steel mills and coking plants and factories devoted to the manufacture of tanks and heavy machinery. The forests are, in fact, extensive, and their brooding, meditative gloom is so suggestive of isolation that it is not easy, in some of them, to imagine that a human foot has touched their layered leaves before. Of course, this is not true, for Poland is an old country in an old Europe.

In one of its eastern border regions, I once visited an ancient forest, said to be the last primeval woodland left in Europe. In this deep, hushed forest, untouched by blade or saw, with its towering oaks and huge fallen pines that lay rotting for decades upon the ground, are smoothly contoured and perfectly circular mounds, some rising as high as six or eight feet above the surrounding forest floor. From the top of one of them, an oak tree has grown, reaching a height of perhaps 140 feet. Its age is between six and seven hundred years. Its location, on the exact crown of the mound, amounts to a small mystery: Did the acorn fall here and take root by chance, or was it planted? For beneath this mound and protected within the encircling roots of this giant rest the now-powdered bones of a few of my most ancient ancestors, nameless chieftains of the Slav clans who walked or hunted or fought not only in this forest but in the woods closer to my home, the ones I know, or thought I did. I consider this often now: There was always someone here, always some token, some footstep left in the soft accumulation of seasons, in the generations of leaves and decay. In this empty, rustling, inviting stillness, always, there was someone here.

CHAPTER ONE

LESZEK

I wish I could tell you a tale of espionage and international intrigue, the kind of story I once liked to read, set in places I liked to imagine, but I'm sure I would get the details wrong, put croupiers at the blackjack table and tumbleweeds in Miami. So I won't do that. This is a story about a little town in Poland and intrigue on a narrower scale, about minor corruptions for dubious profit, retribution and forgiveness, and the accounts of the past that we live by or fear. My father once told me that our history is like a force behind us, pushing us along, unacknowledged or even unknown, but dictating the way we live our lives. As with many things he told me when I was young, I accepted this notion as simple and unassailable, an adult concern, like his way of reading the weather by the mist around the moon. Only later was it troubling, a warning I had failed to notice. And so the events that occurred here, small as they might seem, became for me—and maybe for all of us—a struggle against both past and prophesy, history and future. My father, with his muddy boots and his face to the wind, was never wrong about the weather.

The village where I live is called Jadowia. The name derives from an archaic Polish word that means "venom" and possibly refers to the snakes that may have inhabited the place in the Middle Ages, or, more likely, to an odor of mold and dampness that rises sometimes from the decay in its lowland marshes or waterlogged fields. There is no geopolitical intrigue here, although through the centuries a number of armies have fought back and forth through our forests and bogs, as though our poor soil were a prize in itself instead of a line of defense against greater losses. Here we have no owners of numbered bank accounts nor keepers of sleek women; no patrons of glittering casinos nor barons of teak-paneled boardrooms. These diversions I merely read about in the Western thrillers that now come my way in translation. Our instruments of death, while sometimes cunning, are not technologically advanced. I will work with what I have.

My name is Leszek. Along with my grandfather, who is seventy-four and has a tumor the size of a walnut on his right thumb, and the ghost of my father, who died of cancer, I am a farmer. Together, we have twenty-six acres, scattered, in the Polish manner, in six locations, the farthest of them—planted in rye last year—set six miles from the house. We own twelve cows, fourteen pigs, a horse, a tractor, and a newly bought used combine. By local standards, we are reasonably prosperous and on good terms with our neighbors, among whom we have lived since further back than my grandfather can remember. I am twenty-six years old and in need of a wife.

My mother, Alicja, who lives with us and shares in the work, as she always has, worries over this wife problem considerably. Of course, she does not know about Jola, and, so far as I know, no one else does either. So I see my mother in the village on market days or in church, scanning the dwindling population of young women for a potential daughter, a partner for her son. "He reads!" she wants to announce. "He is sober." She is right, but this is not the decisive factor, for in fact her survey, across the shadowed benches of the church and the few quiet streets of the village, is a dismal one. There are not many prospective brides here. A lifetime of watching their mothers and grandmothers riding to town on market days in wooden wagons pulled by a horse or tractor, sharing space with a load of potatoes or a penned hog, has planted its potent warning. Much of our climate, excluding a short golden autumn and the blossoming of spring, is sodden and gray, and our nights are inno-cent of the faintest trace of neon. Even grimy Warsaw, a hundred miles distant, takes on a powerful allure. I know, because for a time it drew me as well. So, simply, the young women flee.

But my mother retains her hopes for me, and for some unspoiled and unfound flower of the countryside. Her energy is considerable and undiminished despite the blow from the loss of my father a little more than a year ago. Although she is getting heavier now, I can still see in her face—especially when she laughs, perhaps at one of my grandfather's jokes as she sits in the kitchen after supper—a hint of her youth, a reminder of the gentleness of young girls, the soft and knowing Slavic width of their faces, a suggestion of what she seeks for me or I for myself.

She does not mourn much, or does so only in a quiet, private way. It is our national nature, I think, to grieve publicly, at appointed times: the anniversaries of death, on All Souls Day, at cemeteries on Easter or Christmas. Our women shed tears easily, as if on cue, onto the cold stones of March or November, but the private mourning is hidden, as it is with her. I have not spoken with her about my father's voice, but I am not sure she hears it as I do. To me, it is distinct, heard while I am busy hitching the harrow or tossing hay or stirring bran and potato mash for the pigs. I am not sure I believe in ghosts, but I do believe in a kind of knowing, an awareness, that is part imagination, extrapolation, or maybe eavesdropping by intuition. I am persuaded that my father, as he once promised, or rather predicted, is a presence, and much of what follows—how much I cannot precisely say—comes from him and because of him. My father and I, I always used to think, were close; perhaps we still are.

His name was Mariusz. Before illness seized him, he was thickset and strong. He seldom drank more than a ceremonial glass of vodka, and I never saw him drunk, which accounted for one difference between him and most of the men in the countryside, for whom heavy drinking amounts to a purpose in life. He had black hair, another oddity in our region, and, still more oddly, eyes of different colors, one (the left) hazel-brown and the other a pale blue. This curiosity unnerved many people. We are country folk among other country folk, and familiar enough with maladies resistant to our home cures—seizures, cancers, problems with the skin, not to mention farmyard maimings; any count among ten grown men will yield no more than ninety whole fingers. Even so, a man with eyes of two colors was remarkable, and I used to see people looking into his face with a special intensity, as though they were drawn into a spell of wonder or speculation just below the surface of their conversations with him. My father was a listener and quiet-spoken, and people shared confidences with him. Neighbors and others from the village came to him for advice. He seldom actually gave any, as nearly as I could tell, but he always offered his time and his patient, direct way of listening, and his visitors usually went away with a lighter step, unburdened if not enlightened.

When I was a boy, seven or eight, he served for a year on the village council, along with about fifteen others, and for hours each month he sat with them in glacial consideration over the priorities for road repair and the clearing of drainage ditches. They elected him chairman, but he passed the job on to someone else after a few months. When his term was over, he refused to allow his name to be put up for the next election. It was a bad time for us then, and that was probably the reason he quit. There were other reasons, too, although I did not know about them until later. But his withdrawal from this token public office, with its rote approvals of plans handed down from above, had little bearing on his standing in the village.

I said these were bad times for us, for we had an ordeal of our own, but they were grim days for everyone. The country had fallen under a peculiar blight. I was not sure then what it was about, or what caused it, exactly, but even as a child I could feel it, a kind of malaise mixed with tension, an endless uncertainty. Farm people were better off in some ways than most; we could always eat, although not necessarily well. The meat shop sold only hog fat. People lived on cabbage and potatoes. We had no money, nor did our neighbors, which meant that animals had to be sold for cash and not killed for food. Not that the cash came to much, and, of course, there was nothing to buy with it. You couldn't locate a bag of cement or a hundred bricks or a pound of nails. You couldn't find a new milk bucket. When sickness descended, as sickness always did, there was no medicine to buy even if you had money for it. Most people couldn't afford a pair of rubber boots; they traded old sweaters with holes in them for twenty eggs. In the village, when new goods were delivered to the "home economics" store—a consignment of socks, or underwear, or lightbulbs—my mother would wait in line for her rationed allotment of whatever was being sold. When she returned home she set her purchases on the table in the kitchen for our admiration, like trophies of the hunt, small packages tied with string and wrapped in gray paper.

And yet, no one starved, I suppose, or froze to death from lack of clothes. And, God knows, the nation had been through worse, and the memory of it was still vivid. But the country, and the countryside as I knew it, seemed suspended in ice. The winters, then, stretched on forever, in years of gray. In the mines—somewhere in the south, I remember being told—and in the shipyards on the sea, there were strikes, soldiers on alert, and stories of police firing into crowds. Our neighbor, Powierza, was detained and fined for felling firewood in the forest. Another was jailed for a month for selling a pig to a man from Warsaw, the city man having been stopped in a highway police check and interrogated on suspicion of black marketeering. My grandfather, sullen and furious, began raising rabbits, which he sold to our neighbors for a pittance. He struck them on the head with a split stick of firewood, stuck them in a bag, and stalked off with them through the pine woods, following the same paths he used when he was thirty-five and thought a handful of men like himself could fight off the Communists with German pistols and Springfield rifles. He fought them again, now, with a cloth bag of slaughtered rabbits. I remember him stomping out through the drifts of snow at the back gate, early in the afternoon, and returning after dark, entering the house noisily and striding about the kitchen with such satisfaction that half an hour would pass before he could sit down to the soup that my mother put on the table for him. "By God," he would say, "you should have seen Dubiński's face. He and that old woman of his haven't seen meat in two months."

Of course, none of the authorities would have cared about his rabbits even if they had known, which, in fact, they probably did. Grandpa's action was symbolic and ineffectual, and his gloom would settle upon him again in a day or two, as the gloom settled over the whole of the village and the land. The winter sky descended, in fogs and mists that erased the tops of the trees in the forest and brought the horizon close, yet indistinct.

The sky has importance in a land as flat as this, or so it does to me, and my recollection of that time is that the sky seemed to have vanished, blended with the earth. It cannot have been so implacably bleak, of course, but my memory and imagination mingle, like the clouds I used to watch then, lowering from above and dissolving into the mists of the fields, erasing the line where they met.

This was years ago, a very different time. Many large changes have come. There are American detectives now on our television screens, and serialized melodramas of Texas families rich with oil. We wonder if our lives, too, will be different. We have a new politics. A new time is upon us. Many of us have to work at believing this, and many will not, many cannot. My grandfather cannot. He spent his life running a plow through the fields as though he were laying open Russian entrails. He does not believe the Bolsheviks have gone away, nor their local hirelings, who, he says, have burrowed in like ticks on a sick dog. You can pull them off, he says, but their heads are still there, below the skin, where they will infect and fester.

So history hangs on, and has a way of doubling back on us. The fog thins slowly, perilously, and gives way, finally, to still more fog, clinging perpetually in the distance.

But I think of this as a wasteful bitterness. And I promise myself that this fight will not be mine.

I don't know why this should be true, but on a day when someone you know dies, the sunset glows red and lingers a long time. The first time it happened I was eight and my two-year-old sister Marysia died. She was born with a defective heart. This was the bad time I mentioned, filled with her spells of crisis, the house hushed and overheated in summer and winter, sounding with the footsteps of my parents up in the night and walking with her, the whispered conversations, the panicked efforts to get to a hospital or doctor, the confusion of neighbors arriving with horses and wagons piled with straw and blankets. Usually the neighbor was Staszek Powierza, who lived just to our left and, then as now, had the emotions and a heart the size of a barn. He burst into the stilled house like a thunderclap and jolted us all into movement. I did not go on these journeys to the doctor. I figured mostly among the shadows of my parents' worry, which cast a lantern's twilight over me and the house. I stood to the side and I watched. Of course, I worked, harder than I might have had it not been for the calamity that had fallen on the house. I did chores my father might have performed alone, and work that was usually my mother's. I milked, I hauled water, I cleaned, I even cooked in a simple way.

One day, when Marysia was about a year old and in the waning stages of one of the crises that wracked her and all the rest of us, I lay down next to her on my parents' bed and saw what my parents must have seen. I saw, in the pinched and wrinkled skin that gathered unnaturally at her temple, that she was not growing, that whatever was defective, the valve that refused to open properly or pump sufficiently could not repair itself. She would not survive. She died in the hospital a year later, early in the morning. A man from town drove my father and mother home. I heard the car stop in the road. I ran around the corner of the house, saw the branches of the apple tree bending over the gate, saw my father, in his rubber boots and brown jacket, supporting my mother, whose eyes were closed and whose feet moved as though she had aged thirty years.

The sunset that day—it was early March and tattered snow still lay across the fields—filled the sky with red, and I studied it for a long time and in a new and different way. This was death, it had made its subtraction from the world, and I was watching for all the signs that accompanied an event so large. I remember helping Powierza and his boy Tomek, who was my age and went to school with me, when they came over to do the milking for us. Powierza clattered about noisily, banging the buckets and milk cans, as I fed the chickens and geese, and carried armloads of hay to Star and Piotr, the horses we had then. I remember going about these chores and the animals being easy and quiet, in a way they are not always. Amid these muffled noises, I stepped outside the barn, pails of steaming milk pulling at the sockets of both shoulders, and looked up into a towering, cloud-streaked sunset. I still see it, I think, with every fleck of gold and purple edge in place. And this: my friend

Tomek, appearing soundlessly (which was not his way, either), arriving as though he swam up through an aquarium of tears, to lift the buckets from my hands.

Several years later, when my grandmother died, I saw the same fiery sky at evening, though it was high summer and the sunset lasted until ten o'clock at night. She was severe, church-bound and older, somehow, than her years, and she died quietly and painlessly in her sleep. Grandpa, dignified and tearless throughout the day, received friends, drank a few glasses of vodka, and was in bed before dark. My father and I milked and did the chores together. After supper, after the priest and my grandfather's friends had left, my father and I lingered outdoors a while. He sat on an upturned bucket and smoked a cigarette. We could cut the rye in four or five days, he said, if the weather held, and if we could lay our hands on some cement in the meantime, we could start putting down the floor to extend the pig barn. On the gatepost the funeral banner left by the priest, the sign of a house in mourning, swayed in a light breeze. I wondered if my father would speak of her dying, but he did not. Having buried a child, he seemed to find the death of a parent easier.

Years later, my father became ill. From the beginning he was quiet and calm, and readily accepted the hospital's verdict that there was nothing to do. He showed no sadness or fear, and seemed sure that when his death approached he could meet it without agony. My mother was terrified. My grandfather, although he said little, was haunted and remote and given to a solitary, distant idleness, standing with his elbows on the wooden gate that led out of the barnyard, staring off toward the forest. I, too, was afraid, but I spent more time with my father than anyone, even more than my mother did, who could not sit with him for long without tears trickling down her face. When I sat with him neither of us would cry. We spoke mostly about the farm, deciding whether to take two calves to market or three, and speculating over whether Kowalski, one of our neighbors, would sell us the six acres my father had wanted to buy for the last three years.

"Keep after him," he said. "He'll come around. It's good land for you. And a good place for a house, the north end of it, on the rise."

"I don't see myself working that land without you around," I said. I startled even myself with those words; they sounded too charged, too direct, so I softened them. "I mean, that's a lot for Grandpa and me."

"I'll be around, don't worry," he said.

I glanced at him quickly, for he had always spoken of his nearing death directly, with no false hope or argument.

"Don't worry," he repeated. "When I go, I'm not going very far. I'll be around."

It was sometime around then, I suppose, that I began to think seriously of that field—the yellow field, I called it, for that was the color its fallow grasses turned in August. I found myself stopping to look at it as I passed by, and I sensed what its soil was like before I thrust my hand into it: a deep, rich brown. It lay on a slope that rose gently, south to north, and caught the warmest southern light of spring and late into fall. The crown was bordered with a line of plum trees where the sweetest fruit in the vicinity ripened every September.

Although he was long past farming it himself, old Kowalski had resisted selling it. I had seen him rebuff my father with that special knack for insult that sometimes passes for banter among rough-spoken men of the country. He grinned his broken-tooth grin, slapped my father on the shoulder, and told him, "I'd give it to my fool children or turn it over to the Bolsheviks before I'd sell it to you, Maleszewski." My father changed the subject to something neutral; better not to push at the wrong time. Kowalski, limping along, whacked my father again on the shoulder. I wanted to see it as a good-natured poke, but I was walking just behind the two of them and I could see the hand had hit with force. My father felt it, too, but he said nothing as Kowalski rattled on.

"Oh, no, Maleszewski, not to you. A fellow with one brown eye and one blue." He cackled again. "How do I know what color you see when you look at me, eh? The color of a fool?" He spat heavily. "Yes," he said, "damn cold weather for April. Fool farmer weather." He was still laughing when we left him at the gate.

I had never heard anyone speak to my father in such a manner, and I'm not sure I ever heard anyone mention his eyes before, unless it might have been Powierza. He seemed to disregard the comment, as he shook off the blow against his shoulder. A few minutes later I broke the silence. "He's crazy, Papa."

"Old," he said. "He is from old people. Poor people."

I knew what "old" meant in his lexicon. Old as in medieval, old as in the time of the *szlachta,* the manor house, the peasant farmer, the tenant on the land, old as in the idea of a population locked in superstition and ignorance, the paralysis of religion or drink or laziness. "Old" meant old Poland, old Slav, the plum brandy that no one made anymore, and women in dresses so dirty their bellies shined, but who made the best pots of *bigos* in all of sorrow-ridden Christendom. Kowalski, his name as common as the smithy his ancestors once tended, was a relic, an artifact, stubborn, temperamental, and—this always—demanding of respect. Given time, perhaps, he would relent. I had a chance.

So, uninvited but not without hope, I walked that wide breast of land, my fingers spread against the tassels of ripened grass and the golden heads of the barley growing volunteer from the patchy field across the border thicket. I walked the slope and felt the rise of the land beneath my feet as a living presence, as though the earth breathed and I could feel its lift, feel its possibilities in the muscles of my arms and legs. Sitting beneath a plum tree, I admired its slow and gentle descent to the tangle of linden and willow that hid the narrow stream folded below.

I went there one evening with a short-handled hoe and cut away a patch of grass, shredding it back with soft strokes, opening the soil to the air, and in the dirt I scattered seeds of barley, rye, and some grains of wheat from the handful in my pocket. I would watch them and see. Afterward, I sat as the light faded and I listened, as to music, as the soft wind rustled the grasses and pushed the clouds toward a crescent moon.

My father died in the month of September, the season of burning in the Polish countryside, when the air is heavy with the smell of smoke from the fields, as the drying husks of summer are raked into serpentine rows and set to slow smolder. These fires are an old habit, part purification, since they rid the fields of pests, and, part, I'm sure, a ritual observance of things ending and beginning. Our fields, too, offered their lines of fire and smoke. On the afternoon my father died, Grandpa and I were out with our rakes amid the smoke and the pale autumn sunlight. Mother walked the mile out to the field to fetch us home. The sunset, hours later, was as I expected it would be, huge and deep red, but feathered over with the smoke that shifted across the sky in bands of gray and rose. I stood once more in the barnyard (dusty now, at the end of summer) and watched. I did not feel alone.

We lived side by side with the Powierzas, the back wall of their milk barn nearly butting the back wall of our pig shed, leaving enough space for cats to hunt and bear their litters every May. We worked together often and sometimes shared equipment, good enough neighbors to each other, but no one would have had difficulty seeing that the two barn lots and houses were owned by different people. Powierza's place was a maze of tools and interrupted projects, pieces of equipment tilting around on their axles or resting on a pile of bricks, waiting for a spare part and the time to install it. His woodpile fell in a loose tumble, the hinges on his barn doors were forever broken, possibly useful trash accumulated in piles, shards of iron and rusted tools hung by nails from the walls. Staszek Powierza was my father's age, and the two got along well, although their temperaments were far apart. Father liked him, but knew when to keep his distance. "He's like Poland at war," Father would say, "Brave and crazy." His complexion was fair and always raked red by the wind or sun. A big man, thick and tall, by turns lamblike and volcanic, he was stubborn and bloody-minded about the things that mattered to him, and when he was arrested for cutting firewood in the state forest years ago, he never repented and in fact sought out a forester to bribe in order to continue his small larceny—which, of course, he did not see as larceny in the first place. "This is supposed to be the people's forest, goddammit," he said, "and the people are cold."

I grew up with his son, Tomek, who had inherited most of his father's contrary nature. Predictably, the two of them fought from the time Tomek was a teenager. The boy knew, instinctively, how to infuriate his old man. The technique that produced in me a willingness to work—praise from my father—was, to Tomek, a license to stop working, a holiday earned. He would pedal into town on the rickety family bicycle to have the plow-hitch welded, or to buy a bag of nails, a task his father might have given him as a reward, and he would stay all afternoon and not return before the milking was done. Powierza fumed, hollered, and scolded. He loved the farm and he loved the boy, and he wanted the boy to love the farm. Powierza had two older daughters, quickly married and gone, and so it would fall to Tomek to maintain the house, the land, the name, the line. Tomek understood this, and leadenly resisted.

Powierza tried, vainly, to wring some spirit of ambition or competition out of Tomek. Once, when we were kids, Powierza asked me, in front of Tomek, about my marks in school, and when I told him, I suppose with some pride, he said Tomek could do as well except that he was lazy and that if he had to work harder around the farm he might find that doing his lessons was easier. Then he tossed a pitchfork to Tomek and told him to muck out the barn. A little later, when Powierza had left us, I walked into the barn and smack into a shovelful of cow shit. Tomek stood there, shovel in his hand, its blade green with manure, his face crimson. "You're a sonofabitch, Leszek," he shouted.

He bulled into me and we wallowed in the stalls, pummeling each other. He walloped me in the face, bloodied my nose, and ran out the barn door. When I told my father about the incident—this was unavoidable, since he caught me crossing our barnyard smeared with blood and fresh manure—he shook his head. "Christ, boy, it's a wonder he didn't bury you in cow shit."

I must have looked stricken again, but he took me gently by the shoulder and led me to the barn to clean me up, out of sight of my mother. "Your grades aren't any better because Tomek's are worse," he said quietly. I was not happy with the injustice of this. "Tomek is your friend, Leszek. You have to get along with him, not his old man." My gushing nose throbbed with grievance, but I could understand the sense of what he was saying. Days later, my wound healed, and I made it up with Tomek somehow, telling him I was sorry without saying it in so many words. In a similar fashion, Tomek both ignored and accepted it.

And for years that's the way we were with each other. We some-

times worked together side-by-side, and we never fought again. We
went to school together, but, as naturally as he sat in the back of the
classroom and I sat at the front, we went our separate ways—
myself, I admit, toward convention and conformity, and Tomek
chafing at confinement and dozing over books. He hated school,
the farm, and the village. He wanted out. When he was old enough,
he enrolled in the technical school in a town nearby but he did not
perform any better there than he did in grade school. He drank and
caroused around in the larger towns away from the village on weekends. He luckily escaped injury in a car wreck that sent a pair of his
carousing friends to the hospital for weeks; he had a scrape or two
with the police. He began to disappear from the farm, gradually at
first, so that I never knew if he was around or not. After a couple of
years, he went to the city.

I could not imagine Tomek going there to take on heavy work. He
had enough of that on the farm. A long time went by and I didn't see
him. Once, when I ran into him in town, he told me he was thinking of "business." By now a lot of people in Poland were thinking
about "business," which usually meant simply buying and selling,
using a variety of connections to obtain merchandise in short supply—
anything from jeans to canned peanuts—to sell on the streets. Very
few of us had any idea of what it meant or how to do it.

"I know a guy," he said, "brought ten thousand disposable diapers from Berlin, made five hundred dollars in one day. Anyone can
do it."

"But you have to have the money to buy the diapers in Berlin," I
said, "and you need a truck, or a car."

"Sure, you need a car. You need to pay a bribe or two at the border, so you don't sit there for two days. But there are ways."

I was impressed with this knowledge, with the breezy way the
idea of bribery was approached and surmounted, effectively accomplished, in the space of a breath. I wasn't sure I would know how to
do this. It wasn't a question of moral qualm; just lack of know-how.

"I don't think it's so simple," I said.

"It's easier than staying here digging potatoes."

"What about the money? To buy the diapers, I mean?"

"You get yourself a partner."

I don't know if he found one. When I asked Powierza about Tomek, he never had much information. He spoke as though Tomek had definite, though shifting, employers, and I think he envisioned an office or a warehouse or a certain address. By this time, I had my doubts, for I had spent some time in the city myself. I understood its attractions, even the allure of its darker sides. Part of my time in the city, Tomek was there as well. Our paths never crossed, although I once went looking for him at a broken-down apartment building on the east side of the river in Praga. I could find no Powierza listed on the mailboxes, and no one, among the few I questioned, who knew him. I supposed he had moved on, fulfilling his goal to be lost in the city. In that way, at least, he was no different from most of our schoolmates, whose first ambition was to leave the village.

It was natural enough. We had spent our lifetimes in Jadowia, a place where nothing ever happened during all that time, and maybe never would, a junction of two main roads, meeting in an offset cross in the town's center—which happened to be at the doorstep of the wretched "fourth-class" restaurant and bar where the town's cast of alcoholics staggered out each day looking as if their faces had been boiled. Three or four narrower streets spliced off the main roads, withered into rutted tracks by the gates of the last of the houses, then stopped altogether or proceeded as foot trails into the forests. It was a village, as the expression goes, of a hundred "chimneys," but that count was generous. Among the stokers of those coal fires there was not a name nor a face that was unfamiliar to us, not a chained dog whose bark surprised us as we walked past. But for all that we thought we knew, for all that we saw as numbingly familiar, our memories were short, incomplete. We could only know what we grew up to see with our own eyes. History commenced here after the war, in the decade before we were born. What more we heard was distant. There were houses here that were Jewish shops before, whose front shutters had opened once onto counters where fresh loaves were stacked, meat was trimmed, clocks repaired, cloth cut, heels nailed on boots. Few who lived now under these same roofs, long ago patched and expanded, had lived here before, and the people who once occupied those houses and shops (their doorways now guarded, inside, by a crucifix) left behind no archive nor, so far as we knew, any descendant.

Of course there were newer houses now, scattered among the old ones of rough and weathered wood, but even those newer ones, built mainly of brick and cinder block, had required so many years in their fitful stages of construction that they seemed as old as all the rest. For a generation that craved newness, that yearned for novelty, nothing bright and shiny existed here, and there was no sign of it coming soon. Poland's novelty, if any, resided in the city.

I left for all those reasons, and because it was something that had to be done, a kind of ritual. I was just shy of my twenty-first birthday. My father was well then and had no thought of dissuading me and evidently no apprehension that I might not someday return. I found a job as a house painter for a state construction company, and lived in a workers' hotel in a rough Praga neighborhood, across the river from central Warsaw, with two roommates from other distant regions of Poland. One spent all his pay on beer and vodka, was drunk most nights and all weekends. The other had nightmares and often cried in his sleep. When I wasn't working I explored the city. I rode trams to the last stop, stepped off, and walked for hours, until I tired myself out, then asked my way onto other trams that ferried me back to the center. I wandered in neighborhoods I'm sure I could never find again. I drifted in and out of shops, stood watching beside crowded street corners and towering apartment blocks, peered in store windows under buzzing neon signs until I realized that colored lights did not automatically signify novelty or quality. Warily I studied the city girls, their makeup and hair and city clothes, which were, without doubt, different, more energetically varied. They worked harder at it here, made more of an effort to stand out. I listened to them talk and heard, often enough, the accents and grammar of the country. If I felt brave, now and then I would try talking to one of them. And now and then, if I was lucky as well as brave, they would talk back. But luck and courage arrived together like an eclipse of the sun. Girls in the city had distinct goals, and a housepainter, smelling of turpentine and living with two other men in a workers' hotel, did not figure among them.

"You know what we are here?" asked my roommate who cried in his sleep. "Crap. Just crap."

A few days before, I had met a girl on a tram. She had dark eyes and dark hair, and bit her lip with beautifully white narrow teeth. When she promised to meet me the next day, my head swam. She named a coffee shop on Nowy Świat, near the university, where she was a student and where, I was sure, many young men pursued her. I hurried to arrive at the appointed time and waited for an hour. She did not come. I walked through the university gates, thinking I might see her with a handsome student. I returned to the coffee shop and lurked around the bus queue near the door, but she did not appear.

"We're all crap," my roommate said.

So I worked and saved what money I could. I read in the public reading rooms, or, wearing my best trousers and a new sweater, in coffee houses. I roamed the city. I saw dirty rooming houses where dreadful, foul-mouthed whores quarreled in the hallways. Sometimes I went to the better hotels, ordered a coffee in the bar, and ventured to watch as other prostitutes, prettier and more polite, adjusted their skirts over their dark stockings, smoked their cigarettes, and waited, while I wondered about the money in my pocket and what it might buy me should I be so foolish and courageous. A few times I went drinking with men from work, and stood at chesthigh tables in outdoor beer gardens designed like pens to separate a species of antisocial animal from the ordinary population. Most days, the number of fallen bodies around these places after closing time would suggest a bomb had exploded, flinging victims face down on sidewalks and weedy lots.

I did not angrily dislike the city, the way both my roommates did, but it was no more my place than it was theirs. I tried to think of the city as a new (to me) kind of natural world, with its own set of noises and smells and rhythms. When I heard the whine of the trams through an open window in the spring or summer, I thought I would always associate the sound with the approach of warm weather. When I heard the same noise, but more muffled and rumbling, in winter, I thought of cold streetlights, of people standing bundled, their breath steaming, surrounded by blackening snow and the high, lighted windows of the apartment buildings. I would see the stalled cars and feel the stress and snarl that formed the atmosphere of city life. My shared room, no more than a cubicle with three beds, three shelves, and a table, stank most of the time of dirty clothes and remains of food left over from the communal kitchen where we each, individually, boiled our sausages or heated our soup. In the summer, with the windows opened, it was better, our own sweaty odors diffused and mingled with the air of the trees, the buses' breath, the smells of the kitchens in the next building, the disinfectant swabbed along the stairwells. This, I thought, was city-nature, and I thought that if I had grown up with it, it might be conceivable to miss it. But I grew up in the country, with the smells of a barn, of milk warm in the pail, the tang of raw wood and harness leather, the sweetness that sprang out of the earth behind a plow's blade. The city smells issued from a different earth, one rank with garbage and congestion and sour breath in enclosed places.

One day on the street I bought four tomatoes and carried them up the four flights of stairs to my room. It was spring. The window was open. Flowers and trees were blooming. I had taken off from work early and my roommates were not home. I set the tomatoes on the table and cut one open. The smell of the vine struck me like a dropped hammer. I put the tomato on a chipped plate and sat down, a book open before me, while the smell of the halved tomato rose in my head. After some time, I ate it, then sliced the other three and slowly, ceremoniously, ate them. My roommate, the drinking one, came in then and searched, muttering, under his mattress for his dwindling envelope of money, and my trance was broken. But I knew then that it was time to leave. The next day I gave my notice at work and a week later I arrived home. I had been gone a year and a half.

I did not make any conscious resolution about the farm then. My resolution rejected the city. As I worked again in the real earth, I began to understand—because I was watching more closely without even realizing it—how hard it was to be a good farmer, how hard it always had been. Now the system was changing; suddenly, out of nowhere, there was a revolution of sorts, and talk of new possibilities. And more suddenly, as lightning snaps a tree, my father got sick. Almost as quickly, he died. My choice—unexpected, rapid, final—was made. I would stay and farm our acres as seriously and as well as I could.

Powierza helped me in many ways in those months, offering sound advice and even instruction, and often we worked together. Somehow, I brought in three fields of rye and most of a fourth before a burned-out magneto halted the tractor and a two-day rain mired the field. Powierza and I, using the horses, salvaged what was left when the worst of the mud dried.

For what seemed like weeks, I dug potatoes with my mother and grandfather in the fields. It was a task I had performed all my life, but now there seemed both a pressure and a sense of accomplishment in the daily yield, the year's last harvest, that was something new to me. Some evenings, when the rest of the chores were finished, I would stand at the end of the growing storage mound, the potatoes buried in straw and earth, a triangle as high as my chest, thirty paces long. I was caked with mud. My fingers were raw. I felt my muscles ache as deep as the bone, yet the ache was pleasing, rich and strong, like a voice. Still more potatoes waited in the field, enough for at least another mound as long as the one in front of me, but I felt not so much tired as eager for the morning. And when the morning came, out in the fields with a spade in my hand, or my knees pressing into the damp earth, my hands piling potatoes into heaps, I found myself thinking ahead to the next day or the next week, or even to the spring, and whether I would plant this field again in potatoes or rest it a season and gamble on wheat. Could a good harvest of wheat earn down payment on a potato harvester? Was this field drained well enough to sustain wheat in a wet year? I imagined my father, staring up at a ring around the moon to forecast rain in two days, or predicting a dry spring because the forest oaks were holding their acorns. As for myself, in his absence, I had taken no time to walk in the forest. Now these were my decisions, and I employed a hard logic, trying to attend to details, to stay ahead of things. A farm is a process, and undone work stalls it. I worried, of course, but I was confident. Powierza, Grandpa, Mother, all listened to my plans and notions, and gave me their counsel. But I decided matters, and I liked that. The future was mine to choose.

Winter approached. I began to see Tomek linger around the farm more, although he would still disappear for days at a time, returning sometimes with a pocket full of money, a new leather jacket or a handsome sweater from a city shop, or sometimes more quietly, his face bruised from three days of drinking. He appeared once with a beat-up car, its back seat filled with bananas, still a commercial novelty, which he sold, proudly, to the grocer in town. For three straight days of cold rain and spitting sleet, Tomek, Powierza, and I labored together. We repaired the roof on the Powierzas' barn first, then hauled in the winter coal for both our houses. Tomek, flush with banana profits, made it clear that his appearance on the farm would be short-term. In a bouyant mood, he kept us laughing and bought bottles of beer, clanking in a plastic bag, for us to drink while we waited in line for the coal. A string of wagons, mostly pulled by horses, waited with us. As usual, the loading of the coal took less time than the paperwork, performed by the ancient Mr. Norbert, whose seamed face was etched in coal dust. His fingers trembled as he inserted the carbon papers upside down in his receipt book.

"I could get you a computer, Norbert," Tomek said.

"Yeah?" said Norbert, not bothering to glance up from his receipt book. "Could you get me a stiff dick instead?" Another draft horse pulled an empty wagon onto his scales. Its driver leaned over the side and blew his nose onto the ground. We rode home then and spent two hours shoveling our coal, joking about how much easier it would be if Tomek could get a computer to help us.

And life went on, in its wheel of colors and seasons, the mud of winter passing to the green of spring, summer's yellow, the old gold of autumn, and in this time I found Jola, or she found me, glimpsed first in the village street, then in the forest at the edge of a field. Perhaps it was only time, but it seemed that the air of loss or grief dissipated and a new existence commenced, that life had a forward tilt and a future, even if I could not see through all its turns and new complications.

Then winter rode in again, and one day, late in the morning as fine sleet gathered in ruts in the barnyard, two cars pulled up in front of Powierza's house. I was on the way to the barn, and I heard a bellow that rose over the rooftops of the sheds, the house, the last brown leaves clinging to the poplar by our door. I had never heard this sound before, but I knew it was Powierza; an anguished protest that roared out as from the mouth of a cavern. Only something awful could cause it. I knew, instinctively, it was Tomek.

He had been found, in a forest not far from the village, his head smashed in by a heavy blow.

This was in December. The season's first snow stole in behind the sleet, from a bank of livid clouds, and night dropped suddenly, like a thrown blanket.

No lingering sunset marked Tomek's death.

I should have taken that, I suppose, as a warning.

CHAPTER TWO

Some two hours before the two cars—one belonging to the village police station and one to the village physician—halted before Staszek Powierza's house, Father Tadeusz Król was finishing his midmorning meal in the rectory of St. Bartolomeo's in the center of Jadowia. As was his habit, he took a bowl of kasha and warm milk, a single poached egg, and a slice of toast. He was sipping his second cup of tea when old Pani Jadwiga, the housekeeper, shuffled into the dining room, where Father Tadeusz sat silently, patting his lips with a napkin, his bald head reflecting the gray light from the windows. The dining room, fitted out with a table large enough to accommodate the retinue of an archbishop, was the centerpiece of a grand rectory, the largest building in Jadowia, excepting only the church itself next door, which, with its double brick towers, was clearly the tallest. The parish house contained eighteen rooms and was evidently, as nearly as Father Tadeusz could discern, the career masterwork of the indefatigable pastor before him, who had served here nineteen years and died in one of the upstairs bedchambers. Miss Jadwiga, the heels of her felt slippers slapping on the floor, made for the dirty plates, but paused in her reach to tell Father Tadeusz that someone had called to see him.

"Andrzej," she said, scowling. "The plumber."

"We have a plumbing problem?"

Jadwiga picked up his bowl and saucer. "Last week he was here. For the kitchen. Perhaps he wants money."

"Tell him I'll be there in a moment." He raised his teacup and held it halfway between the table and his lip. "I think we paid him last week," he said.

Jadwiga, her gray smock fastened loosely across her thin back, left the room without answering. Father Tadeusz distinctly remembered paying Andrzej. The plumber had reappeared at the rectory in the afternoon, after the kitchen drain had been unstopped, and asked to be paid, and admitted forthrightly that he wanted money to go to the bar. Andrzej was already a little drunk, but then he always was, as far as Father Tadeusz had observed. He was, however, the only plumber in town, and reliable enough, considering his habits. In fact, he was often paid in vodka, since his clients assumed, with forgiving practicality, that the work went better and cheaper that way. There was probably no house in Jadowia—at least one with plumbing—to which Andrzej had not paid a professional visit. He was ubiquitous, Father Tadeusz noticed, visible on the streets of the village at all hours, on the way to or from some errand, or huddled with a group of men by a woodshed or a broken tractor or the collapsed wheel of a wagon, passing a bottle and a chunk of fat sausage. What was it about broken machinery, Father Tadeusz wondered, that attracted drinking men? Father Tadeusz drained his tea and went to the cramped office off the rear entry of the parish house, where all visitors waited.

Andrzej stood by the scarred desk, cap in hand, reddish blond hair stuck to his forehead where his cap band had pressed.

"Andrzej," Father Tadeusz started, "I thought I paid you last week."

"You paid me, Father, thank you. It's not that. Krupik sent me. He needs you."

Krupik was the town policeman. "Yes?" Father Tadeusz said, his eyebrows raised. "Now?"

"Yes. There's been something. Some trouble. They need a priest."

"An accident?"

"I suppose an accident. Not a car accident. Something in the forest."

"Well?"

"A deceased person, you could say," Andrzej said, almost apologetically, as though the ears of a priest were too delicate to receive such blunt information.

"Accident, you say?"

"Well, Krupik said I should bring you."

Father Tadeusz retrieved his galoshes, his coat and gloves, and tugged his black wool beret over his head. He picked up his bag of sacramental oils and returned to the office. Andrzej led the way across the churchyard toward the street. It was a gray day, a fitful snow adding to the thin covering that had fallen through the night. No one had yet swept the walkway.

"Where are we going, Andrzej?"

"Out the Łachów road. West. Krupik sent his car."

Father Tadeusz was sixty-two years old, tall and thin. He had spent a career in the priesthood in small parishes, despite a lifelong desire for an assignment in a city, with libraries and museums and theaters. The closest he had come to a city parish post was in coal country, on the fringes of Katowice, and he thought of his career as a priest—as measured against his early ambitions—as a lackluster disappointment, if not an outright failure. He had lived in Jadowia barely two years, and he had not, he was aware, put his weight down here. He thought it possible that Andrzej, who was striding now two paces ahead of him and who knew everything, was among those who referred to Father Tadeusz as the "invisible priest." Unlike Father Marek before him, he wasn't everywhere in the town, at all occasions. He didn't bless the new photocopying machine in the town office. He was not seen circulating on market day, buying oranges and squeezing the tomatoes and hefting the squash and praising "God's bountiful earth," the way Father Marek, a relentless fund-raiser and baby-kisser, always did.

By contrast, Father Tadeusz's service in Jadowia seemed almost cloistered. No one saw him on his solitary daily walks in the forests. He took them for exercise, not inspiration, striding briskly and never for less than an hour. He slowed his pace only when he heard ravens in the forest. They were strange and cautious creatures, and when he heard their ominous croak through the trees, he would stop and peer through the canopy of limbs. They seemed far more interesting to him than the human life in Jadowia. He knew this was wrong, and felt guilty about it, but it was reality for him, and he surrendered to it, as to the process of aging. He *was* aging—no, he thought, he was old already. Nearly forty years a priest, near to retirement, and now serving out his time, here in Jadowia, undoubtedly his last parish. Had he stopped caring? Stopped worrying over the matters that were supposed to concern priests? Counsel to the old: that's what it came to in Jadowia, a parish of the aged. And what counsel could he offer them? That they were rightfully unhappy? That their village showed every sign of dying? What they needed, of course, was their children, who had fled for bigger places and seldom returned, even for visits. Just there, crossing the street on her cane, was old Pani Daniszewska, a widow for thirty years—and mass every day of those years, Father Tadeusz assumed, no matter that she was sick or bent double with osteoporosis like an old playing card. And the younger woman, just passing on her way to the greengrocer's? Did he know her? Was her name Szymanska or Stepanska? Kasia or Krystyna? No matter, he thought, noting her clumsy, bright-striped athletic shoes; she had one foot out the door already, leaving the village to the decrepit and the priest who said their funeral masses. Last year he conducted three funerals for every wedding, four funerals for every baptism. He had looked it up. In the first week of his arrival he discovered that Jadowia was a town that he could walk from one end to the other in five minutes, but it could support three carpenters who advertised their services as coffin makers. He noted their signs, creaking on hinges in the wind. Except for bootleg vodka sellers, there wasn't three of anything else in Jadowia.

Father Tadeusz and Andrzej climbed in Krupik's old Fiat, Andrzej respectfully opening the door for him. The air in the car was choked with cigarette smoke. They rode in silence out the west side of the village.

"Accident," Father Tadeusz muttered, half under his breath. No one answered him. The word conjured the image of an electrocuted child in a parish many years before. Spilled water and a frayed lamp-cord: a frozen blond toddler and a stricken family. They lived only two doors down from the parish house or he would never have seen it. He had rushed there, arriving before the ambulance, and later had said the funeral mass, but the sight that paralyzed him still was the slow-breaking portrait of horror and grief on the face of the baby girl's mother as she returned from a trip to the market and entered her flat. He prayed then, and often since, that he might never see such a sight again.

Andrzej steered off the main road, then made two more turns and soon they jounced along a wagon track through the forest. Tracks of other cars were braided over the thin snow ahead of them. Then Father Tadeusz saw the town's police jeep, olive drab, and another car, hazed in the mist. As soon as the car stopped, Krupik and his deputy materialized out of the woods.

"This way, Father," Krupik said. He pushed past low pine boughs, and stepped into the woods. Krupik, a short, fat, red-faced drinker, halted abruptly and Father Tadeusz almost bumped into him. Then he saw a pair of muddy boots, toes down, blue jeans, a green jacket. He stepped cautiously around Krupik and saw the rest.

He was puzzled first by the sight, and then, after a pause, felt a heave of his stomach. He gulped, looked away quickly, and then down again. There was not much blood, but it was the thickness of it that startled him. It puddled up, like melted ice cream, heavy, pink, not red except in the thin mat of snow. Then he realized that what seemed to have been melting was part of a man's brain. He noticed the yellowish fragments of broken skull.

"Have a closer look," said Krupik with a salacious leer. Father Tadeusz recoiled from the sour fumes of vodka on the policeman's breath.

"Who is it?" Father Tadeusz said.

"Should you do anything, Father?" Krupik said.

"Yes, of course." And for a few minutes Father Tadeusz busied himself with the solemn ceremonies, the oils, the missal, the words, the folding and unfolding of ribbons of cloth. Then he stood and walked out of sight behind some trees, away from Krupik and his assistant. He glanced up at the sky through the latticework of pine boughs—a fleeting, infinite series of crosses—and gulped lungfuls of cold air. There was a strange and ugly smell in his nostrils. The air steadied him.

He stepped back through the trees, folding his handkerchief into his pocket.

"Do you know him?" he asked.

"His name is Powierza," Krupik said. "Tomek Powierza."

Krupik could see the name meant nothing to Father Tadeusz.

"His mother and father come to church," Krupik said. "I'm not sure you would have seen this one, though."

Zbigniew Farby woke up late that morning, to the sound of the radio from the kitchen. His wife was already up. The radio was tuned to a program that dispensed news, music, and tips to house-wives on home management. A caller advised putting a handful of salt in rinse water, now that winter was coming, to prevent under-wear from freezing on the clothesline. Farby listened, opened one eye to the gray light intruding through the drawn curtains, then realized he had a meeting with Jabłoński and that he was going to be late. He hauled himself from between the covers, stood uncer-tainly, and threaded his way between the bed, the bureau, and his wife's sewing machine, still with one eye shut to help his focus, until he reached the bathroom. The lethal spirit of the distillery still fogged his vision and his brain. His stomach felt raw. He dressed, hesitated by the kitchen table long enough to bite off a piece of sausage and wash it down with a bowl of tepid coffee. He hurried out to his car, pulling on his coat, and left his wife to shut the door after him.

Farby was the *naczelnik* of Jadowia, a position that corresponded roughly to the post of mayor. It was not an elective post, though it would be soon. He was short, plump, with a round face and thin-ning dark hair, and always seemed to have traces of bacon grease around his mouth and evidence of recent meals spotting his cloth-ing. Roman Jabłoński, the head of the village Farmers' Cooperative, who was at once Farby's benefactor and his nemesis, always noticed the grease on Farby's face and once remarked to him that it was Miss Flak's "slime trail" that coated his chin. This caused the *naczelnik* to blush, because, indeed, he was in love with Zofia Flak, his secretary in the town office. For Zofia he had taken to wearing the cologne he bought at the Russian market in Węgrów one day. It was labeled "Tuscan Musk" and he kept it in the belly drawer of his desk, beneath a jumble of dried-up stamp pads, loose papers, and bottles of pills. His wife, alarmingly, had noticed its bouquet before Zofia did, and for a while, worried over his wife's suspicions, Farby stopped dabbing it on his cheeks. But then he would see Zofia in the office, bending over to put on her galoshes or retrieving some documents from the bottom drawer of the filing cabinet, the flesh of her behind swelling tightly against her brown skirt, and Farby would stir in the drawer for the little bottle of pale liquid as though it were smelling salts.

He daydreamed over Zofia Flak, her blond hair, her large, businesslike bosom. He dreamed of escaping with her for a weekend in Białowieża. Or to a cabin in the forest. He thought of feeding her grape leaves and pomegranates (he had never seen a pomegranate, but he had read that this was done), strawberries and haunch of wild boar. He envisioned her, in turn, cooking for him, feeding him pierogi and morsels of sweet sausage, her fingers dripping with sweetness and love. Farby had to admit that Zofia was a demure young woman, outwardly and properly modest, but he sensed in her a great depth, a capacity she did not recognize herself. He could almost taste it. One day, he was sure, he would make all this clear to her, and thus arouse her deep appetites. He was thinking of this as he arrived at the Farmers' Cooperative. He went in and took a seat in front of Jabłoński's desk. Jabłoński was signing papers and issuing orders to his own secretary, a woman with glasses and prominent teeth whose face reminded Farby of an onrushing Zastava dump truck.

"You have bacon grease on your face again this morning, Mr. Naczelnik," Jabłoński said. This was becoming a regular greeting. He had not even looked up. Farby reflexively drew a sleeve across his mouth. There cannot be much more of this, he thought. The secretary gathered her papers and left the office, disregarding the standard protocol of offering coffee to a visitor. Farby recognized he had become too familiar here. He decided to assert himself. "Is there coffee this morning, Mr. Chairman?" he asked.

"You had problems last night, Mr. Naczelnik?" Jabłoński asked, ignoring his request.

"What problems?"

"I don't know. Problems. Did you have problems?"

The secretary pushed open the door and reentered with a handful of files, which she thumped down on Jabłoński's desk. Farby watched as Jabłoński leafed through the documents. He had a bureaucrat's well-practiced thumb for turning over papers. A lifetime in offices with pale buzzing fluorescent lights had blanched his tissues colorless, his skin nearly translucent, his sparse hair somewhere between blond and gray, the same tone as the flesh of his scalp. A decade ago, Jabłoński had held the job Farby had now. In fact, Farby owed his position to Jabłoński's patronage, but things were changing now in ways that were uncertain to both. Jabłoński was as keenly aware of this "instability," as he sometimes referred to it, as Farby, but he operated as though his superior position were obvious and invulnerable. Farby, forever an appointee, by habit and instinct a creature of the hierarchy, burrowed in and hoped his place was secure.

"Mr. Naczelnik could use some coffee, Grazyna."

"With milk?" she asked, as if she hadn't served him coffee a hundred times.

"Please."

The door closed again.

"So?" Jabłoński said.

"There were no problems," Farby said.

"Our friends were happy?"

"They weren't complaining." Farby wasn't sure "happy" was a word to be applied to Russians. "They seemed okay."

"Our young colleague was there?"

"Yes."

"I haven't seen him this morning. Unusual for him."

"It was a late night. Maybe he got drunk with them."

Farby's burning stomach reminded him well enough. Of course he had gotten drunk with them.

Farby had not wanted to spend half the night at the distillery. The place exhaled an evil breath to him, the by-product, he supposed, of the process. The distillery manufactured alcohol from rye, or sometimes potatoes. It was located two miles outside the village in an ugly, square building, dark as the Middle Ages but dating from sometime in the last century. Vodka for a partitioned Poland. It was not "finished" vodka, however. Its big vats, boilers, condensers, fermentation tanks, its cooling tower, the coils of pipes, gauges, and valves rendered, finally, a clear liquid that bubbled up, springlike, from a dark, upward-pointing spigot enclosed in a glass case behind an inspector's official seal. Like a museum's treasure. Czarnek, who managed the place, called it "unrectified" alcohol. From there, it was shipped to another plant which produced the vodka. Or at least some of it was. "Ninety-two percent pure," Czarnek told Farby once. "You can drink it, but too much of it, you'll go blind."

Of course the state owned it, but Czarnek ran it, had run it for years. As usual, Czarnek disturbed Farby. He was stocky and strong, his hair and brows a lusterless black, his cheeks stubbled with a dark two-day beard. As far as Farby could tell, Czarnek's only mood was a strapped-down anger, like a boiler about to blow its rivets. His age was indeterminate to Farby, but Czarnek's experience seemed to reach back before Farby through a succession of village officials. As usual, Farby remembered, Czarnek had taunted him.

"So Jabłoński makes you come out here on Friday night at midnight," Czarnek said.

"It's no problem." Farby did not want to dwell on this fact. Everyone had his role to play, he thought. "You're here, too, Czarnek."

"Yes," he said, "but I work here. This place doesn't operate without me."

"Some things don't operate without Jabłoński."

"Or without Mr. Naczelnik to grease the gears, if that's what you do. You grease the gears, Farby, or you just stand around and watch? Lot of watchers we have. Half the system is watchers."

They had been outside, resting their rumps on a fender of the Russians' car, waiting for a holding tank to drain. It was cold. The three Russians were inside with young Powierza, drinking some sweet concoction Czarnek made to cover the taste of the alcohol. A faint mist fell through the glare of the lamp hanging on the corner of the building.

"We all have our little place, don't we, Farby?" Czarnek went on. "Or we have two places."

Farby wished he were some other place, with Zofia in a warm

bed, or even at home in front of his television set. It was a pleasurable puzzle to him to think of these two worlds that were intertwined but irrevocably separate. "Yeah," he said, "two places."

"Two places, two jobs," Czarnek went on. "An official job and another job as officials. One job for the system, another job for the people who run the system."

Farby had stopped following Czarnek closely. He was wondering if he should ask Zofia to work late one night next week, and what he might do if she agreed. He sighed. "Life is complicated, Czarnek."

"No, not life, Farby. Only the bookkeeping."

And that was all, really. The two of them returned inside, finally, and drank with Powierza and the Russians. The Russians were new to him, although Powierza seemed on familiar terms with them all. Beyond the office came the subterranean murmur of fluids circulating through valves and vats and pipes as big around as milk buckets. There was no gleam of stainless steel or polished copper for relief, but rather a predominant mud-brown corrosion and puddled rust, an atmosphere sour with yeast and fermentation, a floor gummy with residues that released the shoe soles with an audible tick. Czarnek's dog lay beside the table while they sat drinking for an hour, then two hours. Farby took the money from the Russian they called Misha, and tucked it into his jacket pocket.

It was still there, folded in an envelope. He handed it across the desk to Jabłoński.

Jabłoński picked it up, looked quickly inside, and slid it into a desk drawer. He glanced at his watch.

"Find Tomek Powierza for me," he said. "I need to talk to him."

The door opened and the secretary entered with a cup of coffee on a plastic tray.

"Never mind, Grazyna," Jabłoński said. "Mr. Naczelnik is in a rush this morning."

Czarnek's house was set only thirty yards from the distillery building he commanded, but was nearly obscured by a thicket of gnarled poplars, grown shaggy with branches that sprouted from old prunings like whiskers. Dark and shadowed even in winter when the enveloping limbs were bare, the house fended off the eye's penetration, and the corrugated iron brow of its roof, glowering low over a peeling, soot-streaked facade, resisted intrusion. For the nearly twenty years he had lived in the house (which came with the job), Czarnek had lifted no hand to lighten the effect.

But for his dog, he lived alone. There were stories, persistent enough but still only rumor, of a woman who visited him sometimes. Beyond this uncertain surmise, Czarnek's hospitality was not known to extend beyond the distillery's official domain, where he was hale enough, in his gruff way, among the farmers whose potatoes and rye he bought, signing in and weighing their loads, joking with them, and handing over not cash but receipts on chits to be converted in some state office, or traded for credits on the spent mash the farmers later hauled back to their farms and fed to hogs.

The farmers knew him perhaps as well as anyone in Jadowia, and that was little enough. Some of them who lived on adjoining land were used to sighting Czarnek out walking with the dog, a dark, nearly black Alsatian of startling size, skirting the margins of their fields, or they glimpsed him disappearing into the forest, a finger of which ran nearly to his house and crooked along one edge of the distillery yard. Czarnek had a car, a grimy old Czech Skoda, that he only rarely ground to life for his well-spaced provisioning runs to town. There his stolid form, his soiled and quilted black coat stretched shiny across his broad back, moved efficiently through the two or three shops required to buy sugar, salt, flour, coffee, or a cabbage, or the meat shop where he purchased oxtails and beef for stewing. In the shops he stood silent, unruly black hair curling over his collar, just patient enough with the old women in front of him as they eyed the scales and counted out their tattered money. He was not uncordial as he made his own payment, but he was brisk and invited no conversation. The few men on the streets during these trips, standing and chatting in pairs, he passed with no more than a nod, and was never seen to enter the bar, the one seriously male domain on the square, with its thick air of mumbled plans and incoherent argument. Returning home, Czarnek would find the dog where he left him, stretched across the plank of the front step, and the shadowed house secure under his guard.

In the morning—still dark, now that it was winter—the dog left his pallet and batted the side of Czarnek's bed with his tail until Czarnek rose and let him out to sniff the stillness, nose through the tangled grass, and spurt at the flimsy back fence where the deer had foraged or wild forest pigs rooted in the night.

Czarnek, stiff with sleep, kindled the stove, put coffee to boil. Carefully, he folded the Book, open from last night, the little boxes, carried them to their place in the notched compartment in the wall, behind the hanging woven rug from Zakopane, the same one that had hung on Danusia's wall, and hid secrets there as well. Old Danusia, with her saints, her fears, her hiding places in the walls, in the barns, under piles of manure, her lifelong protection and denial. There were still secrets walled into the foundations of houses, in the very stones, their graven faces hidden. It was December now, and spirits surrounded Czarnek in December. He felt a part of them, a ghost here too, a half-life like them. The memory of certain dark December nights had begun to return to him. He could not say why they recurred to him just now, again, so insistently that he dreamed them the way he had years ago, when he was a teenaged boy waking, soaked, amid his twisted blankets. As the blood-roar in his head subsided, Danusia's little house would be silent but for her snoring from the other bed. Now again, he saw himself running over furrowed and sodden fields in the dark, the pale line of the forest refusing to draw nearer, his feet clotted and heavy with mud, his legs weakening with the weight. Now he was no longer a boy running in the dream, but his adult self.

He wanted to shout, in the dream, but his voice failed him.

He finished his coffee. A trip to Karski's farm, for a bag of fresh eggs, would take twenty minutes. Czarnek locked his front door, circled to the rear of the house, and entered the forest. The dog trotted ahead of him. The frost-stiffened leaves rustled under his feet. For a time, he followed a path that he had worn himself, but after a few minutes the path crossed the first of the narrow and mostly unused roads cut at intervals through the trees. He walked quickly, turning first right, then left, then choosing an oblique cutoff to another footpath that divided a grove of ash and oak, then pressed on through thickets of bare-limbed hornbeam and hazel. The dog paused once as a trio of roe deer and a yearling fawn snapped their heads upright, ears flicking, then silently sprang away. Czarnek kept his steady pace.

The forests around Jadowia sprawled like a great patternless maze, a shape like liquid poured onto a floor, with no apparent plan, stretching from sweeps to narrow bands and small isolated islands. Stands of pine mixed with birch at the edges, gave way to old oaks and ash at the deepest centers, then tapering again to link with other broad stands. Between the fingers of forest, framed through breaks in the trees, lay the farms—clusters of houses and tilting unpainted barns— and sometimes only the flat fields, empty and remote, isolated from the dwellings of the farmers who mowed and plowed the fields in other seasons. The woods wound on in this formless, random way for mile upon mile, so that whole villages, including Jadowia and its closest neighboring hamlets, the scattered houses, barns, sheds, the broken open fields, all seemed near in the same way to the embracing forest. Czarnek's path steered him well away from its edges. Amid the trees a soft vapor rose off the dusting of snow.

It was the low moaning growl from the dog that brought him to Tomek Powierza's body.

It was not far off the margin of one of the shallow-rutted forest roads, the sort of road that farmers used, in their wagons and horses, as a shortcut between fields. He had seen car tracks, maybe more than one, when the dog stopped, ears pricked, then bounded off the road and froze in a crouch, a growl of warning or alarm in his throat. Czarnek halted at the road's edge, looking first to his dog and then just beyond. He immediately recognized the boots, the stone-washed jeans, the bulky pale green jacket. He stepped closer, saw the wound, the congealed yellow that had gathered like cheese amid the blood.

For some moments, he remained motionless, rooted, bent over the body. The dog crept closer, sniffing toward the wound. "Back," Czarnek ordered, and stood upright. "Back." He glanced around him, at the mat of leaves and pine needles on the ground, the thick forest ahead of him. There was no noise except the rustle of the dog's feet as he nosed in the leaves around him. Czarnek backed up slowly to the road, looked up and down, and headed back the way he had come to the distillery.

Two farmers, Ratyński and Piwek, were waiting on their wagons, one in front of the other, to load barrels of mash for their pigs when Czarnek crossed the yard. The fine snow, although clinging to the yard's tangled grass, was melting in the black-cinder mud of the drive. A wind had picked up, the temperature was falling. Czarnek heard Ratyński yell something at him. To hurry up, probably.

Czarnek did not acknowledge him. To hell with Ratynski. He would have to wait a few minutes. He unlocked the distillery door and went in. Gray light filtered through the high smudged windows. He started the pump for the mash tank, listened as it shuddered, heaved, and stopped, then jammed a thumb onto the starter again. It caught this time. He opened a set of valve wheels, then ran water into a teakettle and switched on the hot plate. Through the window, he could see Ratyński, hunkered on his wagon seat, jabbering to Piwek, his dullard peasant face twisted, the flaps of his cap dangling loose, like a dog's ears. Ratyński beat his wife and he beat his horse, and he was a foul-tempered shit. Let him wait. Czarnek pulled on his coveralls. He had been wearing them for three weeks now, and they were stiff with dirt and sweat.

He filled the barrels for Ratyński, then Piwek, entered the figures on a ledger, then, when Ratyński had left, he stepped outside to the mash tank. Two bottles of alcohol bulged in his coat pocket.

"Can I trust you to do me a favor, Piwek?"

Piwek's dog, a short-legged, bright-eyed cur, perched on the wagon seat. Piwek was in the back, fastening the lids on his barrels. He looked at Czarnek doubtfully.

"I promised Jacek Kozub I'd give him this for the weekend. He's having a christening." Czarnek held up the two bottles and watched Piwek's eyes fix on them. "You live near him, don't you?"

"Two miles is not near, Czarnek." Czarnek knew where both men lived, anticipated the resistance.

"Take the forest road then," Czarnek said. "Straight to the old pines, where they cut last year, left on the second road. You come out three hundred yards from his place. Come on, Piwek, he'll give you a drink for your trouble. It's Saturday." Czarnek lifted the bottles higher, as if to hand them over.

Piwek, his eyes entranced, leaned down from the wagon and

clutched the bottles. He stuffed them into the straw on the wagon bed, then climbed over the bench, sat down, and slapped the reins on his horse's back. "Ho," he said. "See you, Czarnek."

Czarnek watched the wagon roll out of the yard, hoping that Piwek could both follow directions and resist sampling the bottles on the way. If he did as he was told, either he or the dog would spot the body and report it.

Czarnek went back to his office. It was as plain and battered as a rural gas station, unchanged for years, except for the wads of stuffing that pushed through the ripped coverings on the chairs. Czarnek picked up the telephone on his desk, just to make sure it was working. Sometimes it went dead for days. Then he waited. It was another three hours before Jabłoński called.

Roman Jabłoński sat in his big plastic upholstered easy chair, a cone of lamplight falling across his shoulder. His wife had fallen asleep watching television, and hours ago he had roused her and sent her to bed. A ledger book splayed open on his lap, and a bottle of vodka and a glass stood on the table at his elbow. The bottle was half empty.

He could hear the wind rising in sharp moaning gusts. Sleet rattled against the windows. The radiator ticked and groaned, and somewhere in the basement of the building the constricted steam pipes protested winter's first demands for pressure. The furnace room below leaked like a cave, dripping a stain of sulphuric deposits on the floor. Jabłoński and his wife were relative newcomers to the apartment, the sole dwelling located in the back corner of a building that had once housed the Party's offices in Jadowia. It consisted of four cramped rooms, including the kitchen with its encrusted stove and wheezing Soviet refrigerator. The walls were a dreary green and unpainted for years, the floors a hard linoleum over cold concrete that Anna Jabłoński had tried to soften with shaggy dun-colored rugs they had brought from their previous quarters, a larger and warmer apartment upstairs from the town clinic. She had cried when they had to move here, and she told her husband she could see the way things were going. She was frightened and confused. They owed him, she said. They couldn't treat him this way.

She meant the system. They. Them. All-purpose pronouns of villainy, Jabłoński reflected. He stared at the dim green wall opposite his chair, his lips moving soundlessly. He supposed that enough people through the years had included Jabłoński, along with his wife, as part of "them." After all, he had served the system all of his life.

The system, what was it anymore? He had a clean, clear conception of it once, but that seemed to have gotten lost in the day-to-day business of nursing it along, adjusting to the endless crises its managers inflicted upon it. For years it had been like a broken-down car, its last miles wrung out, worked over by incompetent mechanics.

God, the patience it required. He removed his spectacles, rubbed his nose where the frames pinched, then emptied the bottle into his tumbler. Yes, decades of patience. He remembered, from years back, his friend Żurek. How many hundreds—thousands—of hours had he and Żurek sat through these meetings? Plenary sessions of councils, committees, commissions; local, regional, provincial, national; droning speeches and circular debates that after three days arrived at recommendations and resolutions that were already policy dictated from the top and would not have altered short of a declaration of war.

Jabłoński remembered meetings in which the debate droned on for days over issues of local autonomy in accounting procedures in district road department offices. Lenin was quoted. Polish poets were quoted. Stalin (after Khrushchev) was vilified. Attacks were launched on mismanagement and bureaucratic tyranny. Small stage-managed rebellions were permitted, mostly for effect, or perhaps entertainment. In the end, the locals won the right to maintain certain methods of petty theft at the village level. That's what it was always about, more or less. Stay out of our goddamned hair, you people in Warsaw, with your special shops for meat or television sets. You have no idea what it takes to operate out here, no idea what you have to do to obtain a load of coal for a village of two hundred houses when November has arrived and every bin in town is empty. Jabłoński and everyone else knew what it required. It took a gift here, a favor there. Half a pig. A summer dacha for free. A prostitute. A case of vodka.

He had been a relative youth when he started going to these meetings, a studious underling in a district office, learning his trade. He watched, listened, went drinking with his elders, learned, as the saying went, to "work with his liver." Now, he thought, his liver worked him. He accepted sloppy thirds with whores in hotel suites in Lublin at the Matopolska meeting of district energy supply officers. He fornicated and drank and sat through three days of verbal gear-grinding so hung over he could not eat and his brain felt like it was wrapped in hot tinfoil. In the morning sessions, he would survey the horseshoe arrangement of tables, watching the hands tremble as the participants lit their cigarettes. A whole career, he attended meetings with men whose faces in the mornings looked like pounded meat. Livid purple bags sagged under their eyes, their cheeks glistened with the cold sweat of their exhausted livers. The odors in the toilets, at break time, might have been piped straight from the fuel pits of hell. In the meeting rooms, some men got up to speak (for one was more or less expected to contribute something) and made no sense whatever. It was all jargon to begin with, of course. Some could use it to good bureaucratic-political effect and others just mouthed the phrases currently in fashion. "Rightist opportunism," "Luxemburgism," "adventurism," "utopian thinking," "materialist provocations," each term a sort of shorthand strung together in a cryptology of nonsense, half-understood terminology straight from the Party's theoretical journal, which probably didn't understand it either.

What Jabłoński acquired from these affairs—a session, say, of the provincial representatives of the All-Polish Committee of the Front of National Unity—was connections. Connections, he was to learn, were vital. He had met Żurek at one of those two-day meetings in Kraków when he was twenty-nine. It was instructive. Żurek was two years younger than Jabłoński but was already a deputy Party secretary in a farm province in northern Poland. Jabłoński had heard him in the meeting. Żurek knew how to talk the party talk. They were introduced, finally, in a smoky hotel suite while both their bosses, on the oversize couches across the room, were nuzzling a pair of women generously provided by the hotel managment. Jabłoński's boss was whispering in the ear of one. The other was kneading Zaremba's crotch (to no visible effect) with one hand and sipping her vodka with the other. Zaremba was Żurek's superior, his guide. His head lolled back. He was on the verge of passing out. The prostitute with the glass knocked back her vodka and shifted her attention to Żurek, sitting with Jabłoński at a coffee table laden with glasses, bottles, and overflowing ashtrays. Żurek was handsome and had the additional attribute of being reasonably sober. But Żurek had tractors on his mind. Jabłoński found it hard to focus.

"Could you use two?" Żurek asked.

"Two what?" Jabłoński said.

"Tractors. Two of them, brand-new. I mean immediately, next week they're yours. What I want from you is eight tons of cement."

"Where do I get eight tons of cement?"

"I don't know. Borrow it. That's your problem. You want tractors, I need cement."

The woman sat down on Żurek's lap. Zaremba was now soundly asleep. Her colleague had relinquished her labors and leaned against the wall, applying her lipstick. Jabłoński's boss had also nodded to sleep. After another glass of vodka, Jabłoński led the woman down the hall to his own room and rolled around with her on his single bed. She was pudgy and soft and he felt the white anklets on her feet when she wrapped her legs around him. The next morning, when he looked at his wallet, he thought a few bills were missing, but he wasn't sure. Maybe he had overpaid the waiter, he couldn't remember. Well, whores had to eat too.

Żurek, at the meeting, bent confidentially over his chair to remind him about the tractors.

"I'm telling you, they're straight from the factory," he whispered. "Call me next week. Eight tons I need, Portland 150. Here's my card."

Back home, a couple of days later, Jabłoński sent a truck to the town warehouse and ordered four tons of cement, in two-hundred-pound bags, to be loaded from the supplies reserved by the town council to shore up the Piwko Creek bridge. Then he commandeered two more tons from Siwa village the next day when the village leader was out of town—attending a meeting, of course. He wheedled two more from Danko in Grówek town with a promise to hire Danko's halfwit nephew as a night watchman when he was released from jail the following month. It was a valuable lesson, and much easier than he thought. Ten days later, Żurek sent the tractors down. Jabłoński's boss, who had the job of allocating the tractors, thought Jabłoński was a magician.

He was pleased, but deflected the compliment. He could see, even then, the danger that lurked in too much praise. That, too, was a part of the system. Look at Żurek now, a near non-entity. High ambition was easily cut down to nothing, a lesson against rising too fast or reaching too far. No, the system required caution and a keen peripheral vision. It meant casting the faintest of shadows.

Instinctively, Jabłoński dressed in the colors of a city pigeon and trod the twilight corridors of higher authority on the whispering treads of crepe-soled shoes. He was pale and thin-lipped and chose eyeglasses with transparent plastic rims. He could pass through any crowd unnoticed, a quality he valued as the protective coloration of a survivor. It was, he thought, a function of natural selection, like life in a wilderness.

As the guiding principle of a career, it worked well enough for him. For nearly ten years, he had presided as Jadowia's *naczelnik*. He practiced the exercise of power, but kept his own head an inconspicuous target. True, this was not the Politburo, it was only Jadowia. But he persevered, he survived. He had more than enough influence to appoint his own pliant successor, the reliable forty-watt Farby, and to orchestrate a sufficiently comfortable job for himself as head of the local Farmers' Cooperative.

He might have done more, he thought now. Surely he had the brains for it, but brains guaranteed nothing. No, he had chosen for safety, security. He dwelled in the great muddy middle ground where the strongest assets were caution and obscurity.

Or stealth, he thought. That was another word for it. He finished his glass, stood slowly, put his ledger aside, and went to the kitchen cabinet where he kept his vodka. Two bottles stood in the pale dark, labels lined up like the breastplates of soldiers on guard. He was dipping into the Sunday supply. He twisted the top slowly. Stealth, caution, self-preservation. Yes, it had served him, so far.

But his wife was right. Nothing was sure any longer, the great pyramid of power was crumbling, visibly notched and chunked at the top, reduced to uncertain sand at the bottom, not so far from where his own feet strove for a solid hold.

And now what? What the hell had happened to Powierza?

Czarnek knew nothing he would talk about on the telephone, and Jabłoński had decided against going to see him right away.

He had called the police office and offered the idea to Krupik, who owed him a favor or two, that perhaps Powierza had met with a hunting accident. If Krupik detected any hint of suggestive thinking on Jabłoński's part, he ignored it.

"Yeah," Krupik said. "Maybe some pissed-off husband was hunting for him with an iron pipe." Besides, Krupik said, there was no gun, and Powierza was not known as a hunter or woodsman. "His head was split like a squash," Krupik went on. "Whoever did it, we better find him before the old man does."

"Who?" Jabłoński asked.

"His father. Staszek. He's going nuts. He's been here three times already."

Jabłoński flicked off the light and dropped into his chair. He settled back in the darkness, listening to the wind.

CHAPTER THREE

LESZEK

I could not follow all of Staszek Powierza's frantic motion in the first days after Tomek's death. The merging of farm and household chores, forced by the crisis, sent my mother and grandfather and me in and out of the Powierza house several times a day, amid the comings and goings of neighbors, both sympathetic and curious. A murder! It unleashed a thousand speculations, morbidities, and fears. Among most of the neighborly visitors, the assumption commonly voiced was that Tomek had been a victim of robbers. Much harder to explain was the mystery of what Tomek might have had in his possession worth stealing, much less why any simple robbery would have required such a devastating blow. No one I talked to could imagine the crime as stemming from Tomek's relations in the village, which were, as far as we knew, uncomplicated. It was not that Tomek was well liked particularly, or, on the other hand, disliked. In fact, there was not much to say of him, which seemed only to deepen either the mystery or the unlikeliness of his death. Why Tomek, and not, say, Mr. Żukowski or young Krzysztof or Pani Hania here? the visitors asked. Was no one was safe? Newspapers from the city, one or two of them at least, printed a paragraph about the death, and the Warsaw papers were commonly quoted for their descriptions of a nationwide outbreak of lawlessness, mostly in the cities. Police, it seemed, no longer did their jobs, or were overwhelmed. The moral disintegration, the newspapers suggested, had accelerated. Now, the crime wave extended even here, as a distant weather pattern sends its ripples across a continent.

Tomek's sisters arrived, first the one from Warsaw and then the younger one, from Sopot on the Baltic. They both seemed puzzled, vaguely disoriented at being home again, and anxious to leave. Basia, from Warsaw, arrived with her two children but not her husband, who, she said, was on a business trip. She argued often with her mother, whose sobbing voice I heard one afternoon complaining. "It takes something like this to get you to set your foot in this house again," she said. The younger sister, Teresa, spent her time trying to negotiate peace between them.

At the funeral, I helped bear the coffin. It was nearly a week after the death. The authorities held onto the body for days, waiting for the postmortem examination. Father Tadeusz said the mass. The church appeared unusually full, for a week had not dissipated the curiosity, the outright novelty, of such a death or its possibilities for spectacular bereavement. Old women attended who would not have recognized Tomek on the street, and I heard one remarking to another outside the church that it was a shame the coffin had to remain closed. "Because of the state of the face," she said. Of course, she would have liked to have seen it, and I could imagine her, with her companion, halting their tears long enough, passing by the coffin, studiously appraising the corpse. I had looked at it myself and would rather have been spared, but I had been with Powierza two nights earlier at the mortician's and was invited, if that is the correct word, to view the remains.

"Do you want to see him, Leszek?" Powierza asked.

I was hanging back, my hands clasped, in that attitude of submission so naturally adopted in the presence of the formally arranged dead. I had, after all, been here before. I thought of my sister, my father, waxen and somehow remote from the beings they had been to me. Powierza watched me expectantly, and I felt I had no choice. I stepped forward and looked. I could not look long. Of course, it was Tomek, that was the first thought, the full mouth, the rounded chin like his father, but from the cheek upward, it was a matter of bad reconstruction, like chipped plaster, rough and misshapen, covered with a paint of makeup that seeped a tinge of blueness, the hair missing or somehow strangely combed. I backed up quickly.

Powierza remained there as I sat down. This was Tomek. I realized I had been holding my distance from this fact, this event that had ravaged my neighbor and my friend, whose eyes for days had been haunted and furious. By now he had seen the body many times, had been summoned first, of course, to identify it, had accompanied it from the morgue to the mortuary. The initial shock was gone, and now he could not seem to remove his gaze from it. Now, having seen the violence done to him, all the worse for its caricature of repair, I felt some of the same anger and helplessness. I could not say Tomek was close to me, though we had grown up, in a way, side-by-side, and I could honestly say that I knew everything about what he was and where he came from. In truth, though, I was closer to his father, this hulking, slope-shouldered, often-angry, and always generous neighbor whose pain knifed into me. He left the coffin, finally, and sat down hugely beside me, his hands heavy and inert on the arms of the chair.

"If I knew who did this, Leszek, he would not live out the day."

I said nothing. It occurred to me that once he would have spoken to my father this way; my father would have been his natural confidant and ally. My father might have known what to say, but I didn't. I suppose I could have said, "That won't bring back Tomek," but I could not bring myself to speak the words. Priests were supposed to say this. I knew that Powierza had a capacity for anger and determination that no platitude would dissipate. I heard the springs of his chair popping under his weight, and I felt the hard stone of his resolve.

"I wouldn't care what happened to me," he went on. "It wouldn't matter. If I knew who did this, there would be another murder."

The church, that funeral day, was cold as usual, and the funeral mass crept forward. A special prayer was offered by Father Jerzy, the new assistant to Father Tadeusz. His words bore a vaguely cautionary message, veiled in metaphor, the political double-entendre of the committed activist priest, which caused Father Tadeusz to frown quickly and busy himself with the folds of his robe.

Powierza was mute during the funeral and the procession afterward. His round red face, like a painted moon, was expressionless, but I could see the film of tears in his eyes. He walked to the grave-yard behind his wife and daughters, towering over them and staring straight ahead. I stood near him at the grave, saw the polished grooves of the pickax in the frozen clay. Poweierza held himself in. When people approached him to whisper their condolences, he nodded solemnly. People drew back quickly, as though sensing the fury tamped down inside him.

The next day we met again, at my house. We were in the kitchen. Mother and Grandpa were both out. He sat at the table while I boiled water for tea. It was midmorning, same time yesterday, I thought, that we lifted Tomek's coffin off the wagon and shoul-dered it to the edge of his grave, easing it onto the stripped pine poles above the open hole. Powierza laid his cap on the table and looked at me.

"What have you found out?" I asked.

"Nothing. The police know nothing. Krupik is an idiot. Everyone knows he is an idiot. He says they are thinking it was a robbery. I heard from Andrzej that they think it must have been something over a woman. Do you know anything about Tomek and a woman?"

"They mean a married woman?" This I could not imagine. Surely this was not something that was going around, like the flu. "No," I said. "I can't imagine that."

"He never said anything to you about a woman?"

"This is a small place, Staszek," I said. "Who could it be? No, that's crazy."

"I know. That's Andrzej talking, but Andrzej gets around."

"But Krupik didn't tell you that?"

"No. He says maybe Tomek was drinking and someone robbed him. They don't know about alcohol yet. Alcohol in his blood. The medical examiner's report hasn't come back."

The notion of Tomek drinking, even of Tomek falling-down drunk, was not hard for me to imagine, nor, I'm sure, for his father, though I know it troubled him. But what would Tomek have had with him that was worth stealing? The idea of Tomek with as much as a hundred dollars in his pocket was unlikely.

He had left for Warsaw on Friday morning, the day before his body was found. He simply announced to his father he was going to

Warsaw and would be back in one or two days. Powierza assumed he had walked to town and rode the bus to the city. There were five buses a day to Warsaw, and, considering the time he left the house, he could have taken the midmorning bus and arrived in Warsaw by early afternoon.

Powierza had reported this information to Krupik. Krupik shrugged. So what? Maybe he went to Warsaw, but he wasn't dead in Warsaw, he was dead in the forest near Jadowia. Krupik said he could hardly be expected to travel to Warsaw with a photograph of Tomek and run around asking passersby if they had happened to see this man in town.

"Krupik says it looks like Tomek was killed right where he was found," Powierza said. "So he says their investigation is here."

This "investigation" seemed to have exhausted itself quickly. Powierza was right about Krupik. He was no policeman, not in the usual sense, but rather a town constable, a relic of the system, appointed through the usual old network, so far as I knew. He was around all the time, as common as a lamppost though perhaps less useful. A major investigation for Krupik would most likely mean filing a report when kids threw rocks through the school windows. He probably reported to the next-higher headquarters in Węgrów, fifteen miles away. Powierza had journeyed there too, troubling a gray-faced, chain-smoking inspector who jotted notes on a pad and told Powierza it looked like a "difficult" case. Meaning they had no suspects and no prospects for finding any.

"Do you know why Tomek was going to Warsaw?" I asked.

"He didn't say." Powierza avoided my eyes, gazing toward the window, and I could see the emotion crowding him. He quickly shook it off. "No, he never said. He never told me anything he was doing. I was mad at him. He was going to help me build some rabbit hutches to sell to a guy in Łachów, but then he said he was going to Warsaw and couldn't do it. So that was it. He left without saying anything."

I had no trouble imagining this scene, Powierza's sullen anger and Tomek's defiance. Their old contest.

"You don't have any idea who he was seeing in Warsaw? Did you look though his stuff?"

"Yeah, I went though his things. I couldn't tell anything from it. He didn't have much." From his pocket he pulled a handful of papers, just scraps, some phone numbers on the back of receipts from cafes, a couple of business cards. There was nothing Powierza recognized, and they meant nothing to me. The business cards gave the names of companies. Ogród Impex, agricultural products, one said. Wymiana Kulturalnu, said the other. Cultural Exchange. Five numbers listed. In these times it was anyone's guess what these businesses did. Peanuts from Senegal, computers from Singapore, gym shoes from Yugoslavia, stolen cars from Holland; anything was possible as long as it was cut-rate. Powierza had not gone to the post office in the center of the village to try any of the numbers. Neither of us had a telephone, and service at the post office was intermittent at best. The business cards didn't suggest much. In the new climate of breakneck commerce, people distributed business cards like handshakes. I handed the wad of papers back to Powierza.

I guess I could see then what ought to be done. I'd read enough detective stories. I could picture it, the shamus in his seedy office with palm trees out the window. He would be working the telephone, dialing the numbers, driving his coupe into the back streets of San Francisco or Hollywood, climbing stairs, knocking on doors. But I knew that was just entertainment and fantasy. Here, when bad things happened, the telephones didn't work, there were no palm trees, and no car to drive. People were robbed or killed and no one was ever caught for it. In the real world, I had two sick calves in the barn, and I needed to walk across town and find the vet. The tractor wouldn't start. I had errands at the hardware store and the welding shop, and I needed to clean about a ton of manure out of the barn. I had a farm to take care of and an apprehension about work piling up, of things put off. It was a worry that had come to reside alongside my independence, the other side of its coin. Powierza's red fingers held the papers gleaned from his son's possessions, held them frozen the way I had handed them back, as though his son's existence had been reduced to this sad bouquet. I stared for a moment at Powierza's thick hand, the raveled and dirty sleeve of his coat, the bits of paper. I reached out and took them back.

"Look, Staszek," I said, aware of my irritation, perhaps with him, or maybe with myself, "have you checked to see if he actually got on the bus?"

"How would I do that?"

"Why don't you ask the bus driver?"

I did not want to accompany Powierza on his errand. It would be good for him, I thought, to keep busy, to get it out of his system. Maybe it was my time in the city, maybe some fatalism I sensed in the life there, but I could foresee no solution to the mystery of Tomek's death. I knew better than to try to tell Powierza that finding the killer would not bring back his son. The Polish taste for revenge runs deep. But Tomek could have been killed just as easily in a car wreck—he had narrowly missed it once, he told me—and who would have been the target of Powierza's quest for justice then? He could have done nothing. He was using his anger as mourning now, and maybe in a few days, maybe a few weeks, he would find relief.

I thought of Tomek's death as senselessness, like a lightning strike. It wasn't an idea to satisfy most people. I thought of something the priest—Father Jerzy, the young, pudgy one—had said at the funeral. I could tell from his accent, from the way he used the language, that he had come from some little town, like this one, probably, but closer to the East, where priests saw themselves as campaigning against the Communists or the Russian Church, an immemorial feud. They saw themselves in a patriotic fight for the Fatherland. Standing over the coffin, he said, "The culture of the totalitarian gives rise to the totalitarian solution, to force, to murder." No one in the church had the slightest idea what he was talking about. Robbers? Father Jerzy was born five years too late, I thought. He missed most of the battles of the revolution, or observed them from the seminary, back in the days when the MSW, the secret police, harassed outspoken priests and even murdered a few. How would Father Jerzy explain crime and killing in another five years?

I thought of my father and his feelings about the church. "Religion is politics," he used to say. He would go to church, but dutifully, it seemed to me, rather than from any deeply felt impulse to take part in its rituals. He always said he believed in the basic rules spelled out by the Old Testament, by the Commandments. He told me that most all religions shared certain principles, contained similar prohibitions of bad behavior and encouragement of the virtues, and were therefore part of the human struggle to set down rules for survival. Beyond the shared principles, he said, the differences all reduced to politics, sometimes old politics, ancient revenge, and competition, but still just politics. I could hear his voice now, as though it sounded from behind my ear. I was in the barn, lifting the pitchfork from its rusty hook.

The calves had diarrhea. I mucked the mess quickly and forked in clean straw. I imagined Powierza, in the village, standing at the bus shelter, his crimson face staring down the road, waiting for the bus in company with his timorous, sympathetic neighbors, who would be silently curious and glad for the diversion. Let him ask his questions. It would be good for him. Let him wear down his rage. He had a farm to run, too, and in the end, this was what was important, to get on with it.

Tomek's scraps of paper were still in my pocket when I started for the vet's clinic, in a hurry, for the calves seemed to be weakening, their noses dirty, their eyes glittery. It was some fever, perhaps, and not serious if I attended to it, but the vet was not always in his clinic and a wait for him was not unlikely. Nor, for that matter, unwelcome. Jola was there.

My secret, my problem.

I walked quickly, skirting the village center on the worn path that crossed the field behind the bar and the bakery, then followed the cobbled road that ran by the town equipment shed, its corroded machinery sitting idle in the yard. Some of it had been there, as nearly as I could remember, since I was a child.

Already the look of midwinter was here, lacking only the snow. The sky was dull gray, there was mud between the cobbles in the road, brown water in the hoofprints of draft horses. The poplars were wet, black, leafless, the soaked fields blurred with mist. To my left was the village, a half-mile distant. A horse and wagon rattled up the road from town, two figures on the wagon seat, one of them listing sideways: a drunken husband fetched out of the bar by his wife.

Most likely, the vet was at the bar, too, which was why I avoided the center of town. He would be returning home soon, but I wanted to arrive before him. I had developed, I realized, an awareness of his routines, a depressing admission, for Karol Skalski was not a man whose activities should have interested me. But he was married to a woman who had begun to obsess me. I was exhilarated by this, but I was also worried, perhaps even frightened. It had been going on for months now, even though I tried first to deny it, to think of it as a kind of lark or passing adventure.

I believe Jola thought of it the same way at first, but then, somehow, it changed. Now I felt like a man at sea in a rowboat, the tides poised, a bright fog enveloping me, the beach vanished. I was no longer sure what she thought.

She was beautiful, a small, quick woman with dark eyes that could by turns be sly and shrewd, then soft—hazed almost—with an expression of gentleness and surprise, as though pleased by some discovery she found within herself, something she could not quite share. She held back much of herself, and it was this reserve, this mystery I sensed in her, that spurred me on, that made me want more of her. Of course, she had many surprises she did share, a combination of innocence and worldliness in shifting balance. It was the worldliness, and its newly discovered pleasures (new at least for me) that gripped me first. I was, no doubt, naive, stricken, mildly deranged. I did not appreciate the obstacles before her, before the both of us. I could not imagine myself ending it. True, she was a married woman, but miserably married, bound to a man who spent most of his days and nights drunk, a man who mistreated her. Though I am not a particularly religious person, I considered the Commandments, and I decided I had not coveted my neighbor's wife *because* she was my neighbor's wife. I could not say this excused me, if indeed an excuse was needed. To my mind, it had not happened between us in that way; it had not been calculated, planned. We found each other in the wilderness—the forest, actually. I could not claim to be sure of anything in my life, and my experience with "love" was, well, limited. And yet the fact that I wondered over it so much told me, I thought, something. For as much or as little as I understood it, I loved her.

The clinic was flat-roofed, utilitarian, two-storied, a rectangular box, mud-stained at the foundations. It was no more than fifteen or twenty years old, which made it one of the newer official structures in town. Jola and Karol Skalski, and their two children, lived in an apartment on the second floor. As I drew closer I could see that Skalski's car was gone. His vet's cow-squeezer cart stood beside the drive. The clinic door, as always, was unlocked, and I rang the bell and went inside. It was a dim, tidy office, unheated to save on coal. Porcelain basins lined one wall. A green metal desk, a cast-off from army supply stocks, was bare except for a folded newspaper and an old microscope, black with brass fittings, which Skalski used to inspect samples of slaughtered pork for the local farmers, who required a veterinarian's inspection stamp to sell meat in the new free markets that were springing up. I lingered in the half-light. The side door to the office opened.

"Come here," Jola commanded. "Now."

I followed the tug of her hand. The door led into a hallway, and off the hall was a small room with a washing machine and the clean, chemical smell of soap, a close, dusky atmosphere of warmth and damp. She pushed me gently, backward, into an old overstuffed chair.

"Where are the children?" I asked.

"Sleeping."

"Your husband?"

"Drinking."

"What are you doing?" I tried, weakly, to lean forward. Her hand pressed against my chest, pushing me back.

"Sh-h-h . . ."

Some minutes later, I had the glancing, nearly dazed thought—and also not for the first time—that perhaps I had simply become an addict. I displayed the most revealing symptom: I could not stay away. My knees still felt weak. She, meanwhile, had gone briskly upstairs to fetch tea, and I was back in the clinic office. I flicked on the light, which ignited in pale, fluorescent bursts then buzzed gently. She returned with the tea.

"He'll be here soon," she said. I looked at her with wonder. Steady, casual, she sipped her tea, standing, then with her toe she spun around a tattered office chair, its wheels squeaking, and sat at her husband's desk as though she were about to go to work. I watched her, feeling physically soothed but psychologically jangled. Minutes ago she had taken me as though she were dying to present me with a gift of herself that seemed a step beyond intimate. And now she seemed almost oblivious, as if she had done the easiest thing in the world; had simply entertained herself by the exercise of her power over me. I felt I had been worshipped, momentarily, then, as easily, dismissed. I had a sudden impulse to pick her up in my arms and carry her home. I wanted to capture her. I said to myself: We have stolen time long enough. She rummaged in the desk drawer and found a cigarette.

"How are you?" she asked.

"Impatient."

I think she understood what I meant, but she didn't say so. "He'll be here in five minutes. I predict." She smiled at me. "I'm glad to see you. It's been a week. What have you been doing?"

I told her about the Powierza funeral, about Staszek's anger and grief. She had heard, of course. Because of her husband, who was always circulating in the village and the countryside, she was usually in on the earliest gossip. Anyway, you'd have to have been dead in Jadowia not to know about the murder or the funeral.

"The medical examiner said Tomek was probably drunk," she said.

"Yes?" This was new to me.

"Karol heard it somewhere. Farby, maybe. I don't remember who he said told him. Anyway, that's no shock in this town."

"What else did Karol hear?"

"That's all he said. I think he said someone told Krupik that Tomek had been in town that evening, the night he was killed. Earlier, I mean."

"Who saw him?"

"Don't know. I don't think he said."

I remembered the papers in my pocket. Skalski had a telephone in the office, one of the few in town that was reliable. I sorted through the papers and selected out one of the cards.

"Can I use the phone?"

"You can try."

The phone, an old office model with buttons for multiple lines, stood on a counter between the basins. Stray superfluous wires, sloppily spliced, ran into it from a junction box on the wall. When I lifted the receiver, it gave back nothing.

"Wiggle the wires," Jola suggested.

I heard a tone, lost it as I dialed, then wiggled the wires some more and got it back again.

"Dial slowly," she said.

I dialed the codes for Warsaw. Slowly. Then the numbers from one of the cards. Ogród Impex. There was a distant rattle and ping from the mechanical switching center in Łachów. Then, from far away, several rings. There was no answer.

I hung up and was searching for another number when I saw headlights pull in the drive. It was dark now.

"Here he is," she said. I folded the papers back in my pocket. Skalski pushed the door open.

"Hello, Leszek," he said. He smiled at Jola. She smiled back, but did not move from her chair. He carried a couple of envelopes and a small box, indicating he had stopped at the post office. Skalski was thickset, bulky without being fat, although he had a heavy face and full, thick lips. There was an adolescent's physical clumsiness about him. He dropped the box on the counter, but too close to its edge, and it toppled into the basin. He left it there, and pulled up the second chair, sat down, and sighed wearily. The smile was still there. In fact, the smile seldom left Skalski's face. It was one reason people liked him. I could see he had reached a stage of mellowness from his hour or so in the bar.

"Hope you didn't have to wait too long," he said to me. He sighed again and shook his head, as though he understood that we appreciated the trials of his day.

"Busy?" I said.

"Very. A cigarette, Jola? Very, very." He lighted up and let the smoke coil up into his nostrils, the way actors did in television dramas. "These people," he said. "They want you to come right now, but they always complain about paying you. They don't know things are changing."

"I was going to ask you to come right now too," I said. "I'll even pay you."

"Oh," he waved his hand. "I didn't mean you. You know how people are, they want to talk. They want to get their money's worth, so you're always late. That's all. What brings you?"

I told him about the calves. "I think they've got some fever. They're not eating. It's only been a day or two but I thought you ought to look at them. I don't want to lose them." I saw, while I spoke, that he had directed a long, unsmiling look at Jola, who returned his gaze for an equally unsmiling moment. It didn't last long, but it seemed to be questioning, perhaps even accusatory. There was a second or two of silence after I had finished.

"All right," he said. "Just let me go upstairs a moment and we'll be off. Jola, there's a package of meat in the car." Farmers sometimes paid him that way. They stood up at the same time, Skalski teetering off-balance as he rose. He shut the hallway door behind him and I could hear him lumbering up the stairs. Jola stood at the outer door before stepping out onto the driveway. "Good-bye," she whispered, and pursed her lips in a kiss. She reentered the house through another door. I waited a few more minutes for Skalski. He was looking fresher, his hair dampened, and I imagined him upstairs taking a grateful piss and splashing his face with cold water.

"Okay," he said, "to the barn."

His car was a worn-down red Fiat. Like the house, the car was assigned with the job. The village vet position was a state-paid job; every village-level community in the countryside had to have a vet, and the only way to lure them was the clinic, with the apartment attached and the car part of the deal. Some vets were good and responsible and a help to the surrounding farmers, and some were lazy as thieves. Skalski was okay, neither the best nor the worst, when you could find him and he was sober. He was prone, however, to binges. As with all local vets, he was a part of the village establishment, such as it was, vets being as important, in their way, as the regular physicians. He had been the vet here for eight or nine years, married to Jola for four years. She had been married before, and her daughter had come from the first marriage. By now they had a child together, a boy, a year and a half old.

Skalski slammed the tinny door of the Fiat, hit the starter, and hunted in his shirt pocket for a cigarette. The smoke quickly filled the car, mingling with the mashed-grass smell of the vodka on his breath. The car was loose and worn to fit him, like an old shoe. He was more at home in it than in his office, and however rocky he might have been on his feet, behind the wheel he seemed unimpaired. He headed up the road, steering adroitly, almost gracefully, threading the smoothest course around holes and ruts. He had driven this road thousands of times, as I supposed by now he must have driven every road in the district to perfect familiarity. I watched the headlights bouncing over the road, for I was avoiding an impulse to watch him, the husband of my—my what? What was she? My lover? My love? I had trekked all the way to his clinic to see her, on the excuse of summoning him, although I knew full well a visit to the bar would have been more efficient. In my nervousness, I suspected he must have realized this too. Whether he felt it, I could not say, but I was aware that he was driving rapidly and not talking. He was, normally, a voluable talker.

No other car was in sight as we drove through the center of town. The evening bus, though, was waiting at its stop, its engine on fast idle and blowing a haze of diesel smoke we could smell as we passed. I saw a figure, halfway up the stairs of the bus, conversing with the driver. Skalski, slowing as he eased around the corner, craned his neck to look.

"Powierza," he said. "Poor bastard. He's driving himself crazy."

"It's hard," I said. "It was his son."

"It's just the one boy he had, was it? People had bigger families once."

"He has a couple of daughters."

"Not the same for him, is it? The girls go away. Women don't want to live here. Hard enough to get the boys to stay. How does anyone find a wife here?" He glanced across at me as ashes spilled onto his lap. I left the question unanswered while he slapped at the ashes on his pants. We were nearly there. "Next right," I said.

Grandpa was in the cow barn, irritated that I was late to help him with the milking, but he was happy to see Skalski, whom he disdained in a mild, teasing way, as he did anyone he associated with what he thought of as the structure of Socialism.

"Where did you find him?" he said to me and stuck out his hand to greet Skalski, his swollen, tumored thumb rising like a balloon over their hands as they clasped.

"He found me the hard way," Skalski said. "He went to the clinic."

I led him to the calves. They were both down, feet drawn under. In the first stall, he whacked Frieda across her flanks and shoved at her until her hind legs shuffled sideways in the straw. Her head swung down, turning and watchful, and Skalski stayed close to her side as he knelt to look at the calf. He was good with animals. He knew a cow has a hard time kicking you if you're standing close to her.

"Pretty calf." He felt her nose, gripped an ear, pulled back an eyelid. He was quick, sure. He fumbled through his bag, found a syringe and serum, administered the shot. Grandpa had gone on with his work, bending now over the milk cans, grunting softly as he lifted the buckets, murmuring to the cows as he moved among them, twelve broad-backed Friesians, big healthy animals with good milk, bought year-by-year, one-by-one. The soft rustle and stir of their eating and breathing filled the barn to the rafters, where pigeons cooed, roosting down for the night.

"Give the mommas some more molasses in the feed," Skalski said. "I gave them some mild antibiotic. They should be okay in a day or two." He stood up and his gaze wandered down the barn, at the backs of the cows rising above the stalls. There was a steamy, soft glow from the dangling lightbulbs. I had hung those lights with my father. "No mastitis in the last year?" Skalski asked.

"No," I said.

"Good. That should do it," Skalski said.

I walked out with him to the car, paid him what he asked, and thanked him for coming.

"That's Powierza's place, isn't it?" he jerked his thumb toward the barn lot beyond our shed. Of course, he knew that. I nodded.

"It's a bloody shame, you know, but don't let your neighbor drive himself nuts over it," he said.

"He's okay. He'll settle down."

"He's asking questions all over town, you know."

"He's just trying to figure out what happened. He's not getting much help from Krupik."

"What's he expect Krupik to do? Krupik's just a village police-man, he isn't going to do anything." He shrugged, dropped his bag into the back seat of the car, and shut the door. "It's tragic, I know, but these things happen."

"They don't happen here, do they? People getting killed?"

"Yeah, well, you don't count on anything anymore, do you? We got crime now. Somebody broke in the hardware store in Łachów the other day. Just smashed the front window and went in. Middle of the night. No one saw a thing."

It was true. Everyone complained about crime now. Robberies, break-ins, car theft. Even tractor theft, for God's sake. Murder, though, warranted a higher order of concern, it seemed to me.

"Young Powierza was probably dead drunk when he got it," Skalski said. "That's what the postmortem said."

"How do you know?"

"I got a friend who's got a friend who knows. Blood alcohol point two-zero. Be a wonder he could walk. Be a wonder he could even breathe."

"Tomek liked a drink."

"Don't mind one myself. Sometimes a few. Two-oh is quite a few. Two-oh'd fell a horse."

"Hear anything else from your friend?" I tried not to sound sarcastic about Skalski's friends.

"That mashing he got on his head?"

"Yeah?"

"They think he got hit somewhere else, then dumped."

I was trying to absorb this as Skalski opened the car door and climbed in. He rolled down the window.

"Wait a minute," I said. "Do they say where?"

"That I don't know. Maybe they don't know." He revved the engine, flashed on the headlights, and began backing out of the drive, but he stopped and leaned out the window.

"Next time you want me," he said, "look in at the bar. That way you won't have so far to walk." His regular, thick-lipped smile was fixed on his face. I looked at him to see if there was something more registered there, but it was dark.

He reversed past the gate and pointed the car toward town. There was a pause and the flame from a match flared yellow light onto his face, and then he left.

By accident I met her. If I had met her when I was in Warsaw, riding on a tram, meandering the streets looking, for all the range of my curiosity, mostly for someone like her, would it have been more by accident? If her luck had been different—better, let's say—it could have happened. I have no trouble imagining her there, on the streets, the buses. I have studied my worn map of the city and I think I can picture the district where she told me she lived during her time there, an area built for steelworkers at Huta Warszawa, where cranes had hoisted prefabricated slabs into place so that the walls of the apartment buildings looked like something made from children's building blocks, their balconies crowded with tricycles and fluttering laundry, and the land all around treeless and brown and dotted with the leftover piles of construction rubble.

But our accident was here, or near accident as it was. In the center of town, on a market day—the most we know of traffic in Jadowia. Cars wheezed in from surrounding farms, impatient with the horses and wagons and tractors. Russian hawkers of underwear and tool kits and refrigerators, bought cheap off Belorussian factory foremen and hauled across the border. They halted at Jadowia's market as though they had run out of gas or food and could go no farther. Jola was in the bread shop, her daughter with her, and the little girl ran into the road just as a bus rounded the corner on its way out of town. And I was there and simply stepped into the road and scooped her up. It was no daring rescue—the bus had ample time to stop—and if I had not plucked her out of the street someone else would have. I carried her to the sidewalk and set her down and glanced up into her mother's exasperated, embarrassed face, and, for just a second, it took my breath away. There are some things you know instantly, upon impact, as it were. It was summer. She was lightly dressed. Her face, under the gaze of the usual clusters of people who congregated here on market days, was flushed, her brown eyes glittered. I could not place her face; it was new to me, but she did not look or act like a newcomer here.

"Thank you," she said, and then, several times, "excuse me,

excuse me," and gave the girl a soft swat on the seat of her pants. The child seemed untroubled by this, and smiled up me, as though charmed to have made my acquaintance.

And that was all, at first. No other words were spoken and no introductions were offered. I spotted her a week later, again on market day, from a distance. The market lot, an open field a block off the square, was crowded. Through the shifting shoppers, I could see her buying oranges, and I watched her as she paid, extended her hand for change, and moved on with her bags, out of sight, behind the wagons and trucks and milling people. I stood at the far end, where the farmers sold fodder or feed grain. I was buying feed for the horses, but I was in no hurry. Old Zeus, a bearded trader from Węgrów, was offering me a price. "You won't do better, young man," he said. I told him I would be back and walked away as he let a fistful of grain trickle back into the bag.

I followed her, maintaining a careful distance. I just wanted to watch her. She bought apples, she waited in a short line and added bananas to her bag. There was some lightness, a grace or economy of movement, that was not like other women. She was small, her arms and wrists were thin, and as I drew closer I could see, as she bent to cushion a paper bag of eggs among her other goods, her hair fall away from her collar, showing her slender neck and the fine hairs that whorled there against her pale skin. I must have been lost in my absorption, for in quick succession I collided with a man carrying a load of potatoes on his back and a fat farm woman who nearly knocked me down. "Wake up," she growled.

Jarred back to my senses, I returned to old Zeus and bought my bags of grain.

But the image of her, the pale flawless skin, the dark hair and eyes, lingered in my mind. It did not take much effort to find out who she was. I asked Andrzej, the plumber.

"The vet's wife," he said, simply.

"She came from Jadowia?"

"Yes. Her father works in the machine factory in Łachów. They live out on the schoolhouse road."

Then, with the sort of oddity that later makes a thing seem preordained, I saw her when I was working in the field. It was haying season, hot but crackling with the threat of rain. I had completed half the field and stopped to adjust the cam roller on the mower blade, the sweat pouring off my face as I knelt on the ground amid the hopping bugs and the thick swirl of mowing dust. When I got the roller adjusted, I mopped my face and made for the cooling shade of the trees that bordered the field. As I stepped across the low raspberry thicket at the field's edge, I saw her, walking on a path through the forest. She strolled as her daughter ran ahead of her. She carried a basket in one hand and a wilted forest flower in the other. She looked right at me.

"Hello," she called. "It looks hot out there."

I cannot remember how I responded, but I moved on through the sudden cool of the trees and accepted her offer of a drink, and she produced a jar of apple juice and wiped a cup, from the basket, for me to use. I asked her name and told her mine. "Yes," she said, "I know." She looked straight at me, so directly that I felt my face flush.

"Yes," I said. "I knew your name, too."

"It's a small town."

"Yes."

"I didn't know this was your land. I walk here often. It's cool."

"It's a nice forest."

"I pick mushrooms here in the autumn. Beautiful mushrooms. I've never seen you here before. In the field, I mean."

"I was mowing."

"Yes, I saw. You've been working some time now."

"I'm trying to get it in before it rains."

"Yes."

"I'll have to rake it in a day or two."

"Mmmm."

And so it started. I waited two days and came with the tractor and side-delivery rake. She came to the forest again on that day with her daughter. The next day she came alone.

And for many days afterward as well. We talked, walked in the forest. She was soft, funny, and was curious about such things as farming and farm animals, about which, to my surprise, she knew almost nothing. She was, she pointed out, the daughter of a factory worker, not a farmer. She wanted to know why all the cows in

Poland seemed to be black and white. "Aren't there brown cows sometimes?" she asked.

"Yes, but mostly they're Friesians in Poland."

"German cows? That would be typical. We get it from the Germans in black and white."

"No, they're a Dutch breed originally. The Germans probably claim them. They make lots of milk, but not much butterfat."

She wanted to know about the wild pigs in the forest. One day she noticed the rooted-up leaves all scattered around. "It looks like someone's been raking here," she said.

"Pigs," I told her.

"How did they get here?"

"They live here."

She looked puzzled. "Whose are they?"

"No one's. They're wild. You've never seen them?"

"No."

"Haven't you heard of people hunting for wild boar?"

"Of course. Is that the same thing?"

She asked if we could see them. I led her deeper into the forest. At the edge of a small glade, thick with fern, we sat on a fallen log and waited silently.

"They come here?"

"Just wait. Don't talk."

She watched the trees, the sky above, and I could see her eyes absorbing everything, as if seeing the forest for the first time. For myself, I suppose I began then to see her and think of her in a different way, as though I were watching a flower blossom. The air was warm and soft, summer poised at its end. Sunlight flickered across the forest floor, filtering through the high pines and thick-limbed oaks. I watched the pulse in her throat. Her mouth was slightly open, the faintest of smiles lifting the corner of her lips. She looked contented, happy. "What's that?" she whispered.

My eyes followed hers. A sow, with her spring pigs, parted the thicket at the clearing's edge. The piglets had grown their wiry hair by now and were foraging on their own, yet never out of their mother's sight. We were downwind from them and they don't see well, so they continued their foraging and rooting. They snuffled their way to within thirty yards of us before the sow scented us. Then she hurried her family along at a brisk trot, out of sight.

Jola said they were wonderful. "Are they always here? In this place?"

"Not always."

"How did you know they would be here today?"

"I guessed. There was a storm last night. Did you hear the wind?"

"No. What does that have to do with it?"

"Those are oak trees. See. They like the acorns. They know the wind blows the acorns off the trees."

"They're smart?"

"All pigs are smart."

"How did you know that?"

"That pigs are smart?"

"That wind makes the acorns fall off the trees and that makes the pigs come."

I wasn't sure I knew the answer. My grandfather? My father? I know I had walked here with them both, and I could remember seeing pigs in the forest when I was a small boy, wandering by myself amid the trees that rustled in the soft air as they did now. The forest brought a feeling of peace, a sense of being at home. I felt this way now, sitting on this log beside her, my elbow touching hers, and feeling from this pressure a comfort, a permission. And so I kissed her. She did not stop me.

We continued meeting. One warm, cloudy afternoon, the kisses were longer and harder, and her cool fingers unfastened the buttons of my shirt. My own fingers, thick and fumbling, struggled with the buttons of her blouse until her hand reached up to mine, moved it gently away, and she unbottoned the blouse herself, her eyes fixed intently on mine. We made love on the blanket she brought with her picnic basket. I remember, afterward, how we laughed, laughed for no reason but sheer pleasure, for relief and release, for the conspiring current of gentle breeze that soothed our sweat-filmed bodies.

The summer went on, and we in it.

I found things out about her, in bits and stages. That she could curse with vivid proficiency. That she had no idea which mushrooms were fit to eat, and picked them all indiscriminately. That she had a scar on her abdomen commemorating a surgeon's stab at emergency appendectomy, and a birthmark resembling a tiny leaf on the back of her right thigh. She had a glorious behind. She liked to laugh, and had no hesitancy about laughing at things I said that I didn't intend to be funny. I liked that, after a while. And yet there was a dark side to her, a mood with no perceptible transition beyond an abrupt physical stillness. I would speak; she would not answer, her eyes fixed on some infinite point.

She would say little about her earlier marriage or the time in War-saw, where she had gone to seek for work, except to brand it all a miserable period. She shuddered, as though she was recalling an escape from prison. The marriage was foolish, she said, a mistake. Her former husband had gone abroad; she didn't know where. She had fled the city with her child and returned to her mother and father in Jadowia. Here she met Skalski and married him six months later. With hindsight, great mistakes seem so obvious, so clear, that we amaze ourselves later that we could have committed them. Jola was duly amazed. But she had been trapped in her parents' home, with a child to raise. Skalski was persistent. And he was a way out. By now they had a child together, a boy, a year and a half old. "I wonder sometimes," she told me one day, "if I am prone to making these mistakes one after another. If I will ruin my life, step by step."

She asked me then if I knew of Pani Słowik, an old woman who lived to the east of the village, in a tiny house, a shack, really, at the edge of abandoned farm fields. She was in her nineties, a widow for thirty or forty years. Jola brought her food sometimes, particularly in winter, when snow drifted the fields and the old woman never left the one room she lived in except to empty her slop pail, leaving a narrow trail of packed footprints to the privy. All day she sat by her stove feeding small lumps of coal to the fire, living on bread dipped in the bacon fat she melted in a blackened skillet.

"Do you see yourself like this?" she asked me. "No, you see, men don't. Men don't see this as a future for themselves even when it is. Why I don't know. I think most men don't care. I think of them as solitary creatures. You are creatures, all of you, in that way. I don't mean beasts. Just that there's an animal self-sufficiency men have, or they can fall back on. Men can live in huts, and they know how to make it okay. If they live like that, it's just that they're eccentric, maybe even crazy, and it's okay. Somehow they take care of themselves. Even if you feel sorry for them, it's different. For a woman, it's pitiful. I look at Pani Słowik, and it's terrifying. She can hardly get her firewood. Her hands are black with coal dust."

"You see yourself like that?"

"Yes. Not as fatalism, not a foregone conclusion, just a possibility. A distinct possibility. Maybe every woman does."

"But you have children." I wanted to add that she had a husband. Or that she had me. But I didn't say it.

"Pani Słowik has children, you know. Three of them. They're all gone, two in Canada, one a seaman. They don't know she exists, or don't care. It's useless to blame them. She would love to see them, and if they showed up tomorrow, she would be overjoyed and would never suggest they owed her anything. It wouldn't even be a question of forgiving them, you see? She wouldn't think of it like that. Probably I wouldn't either. If I were her and my children came back, I'd only be sorry I had no place for them to sleep. You see what I mean? I'd be ashamed I hadn't had a bath in two weeks, or that I had no food in the house to feed them. Do you understand? Men would never be like that. Men feel, well, that's the way it is. They're harder, stronger. They even die younger, don't they usually? You see? I think that's a blessing for them. When I go to see old Pani Słowik, I go because I know she needs things, but I also go because I want to learn from looking at her."

"Learn what?"

"Always keep your coal near the door."

"Pardon?"

"Well, that's it, isn't it? The meaning of life, what it all comes down to in the end. Your four walls, your little fire. Yourself." She smiled at me, as if to say she were joking, and yet when she talked like this, it was never fully a joke. "So I'm figuring out how to prepare my own hut, for when the time comes. I pick up a few ideas." She laughed. "Always keep your coal near the door."

This was part of what she was for me, this current of dark observation, sadness and humor. I had never heard these things talked about in this way. Not among the girls I grew up with, much less the boys. Not around the table in my own house. I found the hardness in her mixed with a tenderness, a sweetness I could not have imagined before. I wanted, all at once, to protect her from the things she feared, and to feel her protection, for a woman who saw the world in such hard terms, I knew instinctively, would fear nothing that frightened me. What frightened me was not destitution, not the future, but the lack of a strong voice in my ear. It was not that I had to agree with her—that was impossible sometimes—but she was always, in herself, a point of view, my bell in the void.

Now, months later, at the beginning of winter, I stared from my bed into the darkness, the wind whistling outside, and thought of that season scented with the sweetness of mown hay and dry dust and the softly acid odor of sere pine needles. There I rested beside her, contemplating the colors of her skin and hair, at the genius of nature's harmony of hues, eyelash and lip, iris and brow, and the earth beneath, the soft symphony of color in a chance piece of shredded pine bark caught in a black tendril of her hair. I did not expect for all this to happen. How could I have known how impossible it would be to walk away from it? Or how hard to plead innocence?

Powierza brought his report to me as though I were a lieutenant of detectives and knew what to do next. He had been dogged and thorough. For two days, he had questioned every bus driver who pulled to a stop in the village square. On some days there were six buses en route to the city, on some days five. Sometimes there were breakdowns. The buses always halted for a few minutes, so there was time to talk to the drivers. Some were brusque and sarcastic when Powierza asked them if they remembered who got on the bus the night of December 8. They looked at him as though he had asked them if they could name the capital of Peru. One of them told him that for all he knew his bus might have been boarded by "a flock of three-legged chickens." Powierza didn't laugh. He put his large hand on the driver's back, not hard but with a certain weight, and, leaning over the driver's shoulder, produced a photograph of Tomek. "This is not a three-legged chicken," he said, "this was my boy, and now he's dead. And I want to know if you saw him on this bus."

Not surprisingly, most of the drivers claimed not to have worked on that Friday. He would have to check with the Friday drivers. Then one of the drivers clarified further and told him they worked shifts of two days on and a day off, and the easiest way to tell would be to go to the bus yards in Węgrów and check the schedules and find out who was assigned the route that day. So he took the bus coming out of Warsaw and headed back to the depot in Węgrów. He sat on the front seat by the door and spent the forty-five-minute journey chatting up the driver, who, however reluctantly, allowed him to ride from the last stop in Węgrów to the garage and the yards. There, in a greasy office decorated with posters of nude women, he found the foreman, sitting behind a glass-topped desk with a cup of stale coffee. He was not inclined to help.

"But I persuaded him," Powierza said. "He showed me the logs."

Five Warsaw-bound buses passed through Jadowia on that December Friday. Powierza wrote down the names of each operator. The driver of the early afternoon bus was named Rybnik. He lived in Węgrów. Powierza walked until he found Rybnik's address, an apartment block at the edge of town. He climbed the steps to the third floor and found Rybnik at home. Powierza described him as a wispy man, "thin, like a sick sparrow," who would have seemed larger in command of a bus driver's seat than he did standing in his apartment doorway, felt slippers on his feet. Although hesitant, he offered no real resistance to Powierza's entrance. Two small children sat watching television. Rybnik's wife was out, apparently. Rybnik switched off the television and shooed the children from the room.

"He was scared," Powierza said. "You know, most ordinary folks are when strange men come asking questions. They think everyone is from the MSW. I told him I was looking for my boy. I didn't want to tell him Tomek was dead. It'd scare him more. I said he ran away from home and left his wife and baby and I was trying to find out where he went. I said they lived with me, and we had an argument and it was my fault and I had to find him. I asked him if he minded if we had a little drink and if he could get us a couple of glasses."

They had a drink. Men from the MSW did not usually provide drinks with their interrogations, and Rybnik relaxed a little. They talked about the usual things, escalating prices, how bus drivers' wages were awful and unfair, how the farmers were struggling. After a while, Powierza showed him Tomek's picture. Rybnik looked at it a long time and handed it back. It was not, in fact, a good likeness of him. "I couldn't say," he said. "I don't recognize the face."

Powierza described him. Thin, blond, blue eyes, jeans, green jacket. "He would have got on your bus in Jadowia. Got off in Warsaw, probably."

"Green jacket," Rybnik said. It was not a question, but a sort of musing. "Green jacket. A shiny green jacket?"

"Nylon," Powierza said. "Yeah, shiny, I guess. Kind of jacket you buy in the city."

"Skinny kid?"

"Yeah."

"Let me see the picture again."

He looked at it and said, "Maybe I remember him."

"On your bus to Warsaw?"

"Yeah, but he didn't go all the way to Warsaw."

"No?"

"That's why I remember him. He wanted off on this side of the river, in Anin, where the road splits off and continues to the Poniatowski Bridge. There's a signal there, where I have to make a left turn. There's no stop for another quarter of a mile—it's a big highway. He wanted down there. He asked me to let him off. I said no. It's against the regulations, you see. You can't let someone off in the middle of an intersection, in traffic. He should have got off at the stop before. You let someone off there, they take your license or they give you trouble. So I said no. I told him to keep his pants on. I see why your boy's a real problem, Mr. Powierza. He's trouble."

"Why?"

"Because he reached right in, right beside me, and threw the door release. Just like that. The door opened and he jumped out while I was waiting for the light to change. He turned right around and said 'Many thanks.' If I had seen a policeman, I would have stopped the bus and had him fined right there. Yeah, I remember him. The green jacket. Sound like your boy?"

Since the visit to Jola and the clinic, I had not tried any of the telephone numbers Powierza had retrieved from Tomek's belongings.

After Powierza told me about the bus driver, I went to the post office to use the public phone and try again. The number I had tried before rang again, distant and brokenly, still with no reply. Another number from one of the cards yielded no ring at all in three attempts. I tried the second business card.

"Hello?" A woman's voice.

"Hello," I said, "I'm calling about Tomek Powierza." I suddenly realized I did not know what I was trying to find out, exactly, or what too ask.

"Who?"

"I'm calling about Tomek Powierza," I said, feeling stupid.

"You must have the wrong number."

"No, please, just a moment." She sounded impatient, and I was afraid she might hang up. "Does anyone there know Tomek Powierza?"

"Just a moment." I heard voices in the background and then nothing, and I had the impression of the mouthpiece covered by her hand. After a few minutes a man's voice came on the line.

"Hello," it said. "Is this Jabłoński?"

"Jabłoński? No, I'm calling about Tomek Powierza."

He leaned away from the phone and I heard him ask, "Who is this?" I didn't hear a reply. He spoke again into the phone. "Who is this?"

I told him my name. "I'm looking for someone who knows Tomek Powierza. Does he work for you?"

"You've got the wrong number, friend," he said, and hung up.

CHAPTER FOUR

Leszek's grandfather liked to think of certain of the farm's fields as his own, and he preferred to work them, when he could, in his own way. Leszek was content to maintain them as meadows. A few were narrow strip-fields planted with fodder grain, a mixture of barley, rye, and oats that provided winter feed for the cattle. The old man plowed with the horse and cut hay by scythe, although he would defer to Leszek if the "young man," as he sometimes spoke of him, seemed in a particular hurry. "All right, then, go ahead," he would say to Leszek, distractedly, as if he had other important matters to attend, and he would let Leszek cut the hay with the mower, watching his grandson hurry through the work, handling the tractor with an undeniable expertise. But Grandpa always chose to set off on his own for the fields, the scythe on his shoulder and sharpening file stuck in his hip pocket. He might complete a quarter of it before Leszek would arrive to finish it off, the tractor and its blade devouring the field in eight-foot strips in the space of two hours in the afternoon, before milking time. The tall grass fell under the mower like a sea magically becalmed, but it brought the old man no pleasure. The scythe cut and cast the hay in a way that suited him better—slower, yes, but the hay, tossed in irregular waves, dried more evenly, if it was done right, the way he had been taught by his father and grandfather. To him, the old ways moved in a harmony with the seasons, the sun, the weather. He knew it was less efficient. But it had another quality, too, that pleased him: it was solitary.

Being alone followed what he thought of as the natural course of his life. Most men of his own age, those from the village and the surrounding farms, were transplanted here from somewhere else, and he had never been close to them. His own people had been on this land for so long that no one knew exactly when they had arrived. Records of marriages and births, now secured in an old, cracked leather box, traced back 150 years, then faded, like the browned margins of the parchment. The faded ink whispered to him from the brittle papers, their folds now tenuously held by weblike fibers that separated and fell away with each unfolding. The penmanship, in the curling Cyrillic of the old Russian administration, was indecipherable to Leszek. Back then, the old man would explain, Count Zamojski owned this land, part of a territory that stretched as far east as the reach of outriders from Lvov and almost as far north as Lithuania. The name on the paper, which Grandpa had no trouble reading, was Zygmunt Maleszewski, his great-grandfather and namesake.

Four generations later, as the senior surviving Maleszewski, he held in his mind a history, where others saw none beyond their own time, the time of their arrival here. The old man saw the land, the forest, as connected to him by the blood of his ancestors. How many here could say that? A handful. One or two men. A few widows, women left by themselves for years—decades now—still hanging on, addled by age and living in rooms in the villages, the farms and land they once possessed with their husbands broken up and gone, like their families, their vanished children. And replaced, the old man saw, by those without histories, those from outside, from backgrounds of no consequence, people without a sense of responsibility, without a sense of place. It was not a matter of position, strictly speaking, or a question of status by birth. His family had not been a noble one by any stretch. Gentry, perhaps. Of course that meant nothing today, but it was a recognition of a sense of order, a system of responsibilities and obligations—the responsibility of the state toward the individual, and the individual's obligations to the state. Or was it the other way around? He was no longer sure. What mattered was the belonging—to a history that attached to a stretch of land, its shallows and hillocks, its solitary crowning oaks and hushed forests, to struggles won and lost there; to its silences and its secrets.

*   *   *

As usual, he was out of bed and outside before anyone else, assessing the day's weather from a slowly lightening sky. The horse's yellowed teeth crumbled the carrot from his pocket, a noise like old bones breaking. No tissue as soft, he thought, as a horse's nose. He harnessed Star to the wagon, steered her out the gate, listening to her break wind as a rattle-voiced flock of crows flapped from the line of forest at the edge of the village. The wagon's tires slowed in the forest road's sand ruts, but Star, strong in the morning's cold, pulled against the drag of the wheels without urging, through the dark canopy of limbs. After a half-mile of forest, the road grew firmer and wound through a clearing of fields. Grandpa leaned forward on the wagon seat, chin out-thrust, the reins slack in his hands.

Through the morning he loaded cut lengths of pine logs, stacking them so that they filled the wagon's narrow bottom. He worked deliberately, never straining beyond his strength. He could have loaded the wagon in half an hour had he wanted to, but he had no reason to hurry. The sun bore through a soft cloud cover and retreated again. It was cool and windless, and the brown border of the woodland ticked with the sound of the last leaves dropping from the oaks. When the wagon was full, he sat on the smooth tread of one of its tires. He drew a chunk of bread from his pocket and chewed pieces of it slowly as he looked toward the forest. Then from under the seat of the wagon he pulled a wad of hay and dropped it on the ground for Star. He went to the rear of the wagon, reached into a hollow beneath the load of timber, and, holding the wood back with one arm, he tugged with the other hand until a weight gave and slid toward him. A stone slab emerged, gray-green, flat, partly covered with a feed sack. He balanced it a moment on the lip of the wagon bed, then heaved it onto his shoulder.

He carried it without pausing for some four hundred yards into the forest before he stopped to rest beside a tree, leaning the stone against the trunk, balancing it against his shoulder. When he caught his breath, he wobbled on under the weight, following an undulating ridge on the forest floor. He rested again, listening to the breath whistling in his chest. Twice more he went on and stopped to rest, until he reached a point in the forest where the ground descended in a wide swale, the center of which was marked by a depression some ten feet across, its bottom blanketed with fallen leaves.

He dropped to his knees at the edge of the depression, leaned forward as if in a bow, and let the stone slide from his shoulder and into his waiting arms. He eased the slab carefully to the ground, felt his way backward into the depression, then allowed the slab to slide down after him. He cleared away a space among the leaves, slid the stone there, then replaced the leaves over the stone.

He stood up then and looked around. It was perfectly still. With his shoe, he probed into the drift of leaves, feeling around the depression's sloping edge, and detected the chunk of other stones beneath his toe. He raked more leaves over his new deposit, so that no sign of disturbance was visible. He climbed out of the depression. It appeared untouched, except by the wind. He backed away, smoothing the marks where he had knelt and dropped the stone, and inspected for signs of his footsteps. Satisfied, he returned through the forest to the horse and the load of wood waiting in the field.

Father Tadeusz happened to be looking out the office window in the rectory when he saw Father Jerzy hustling into the Sunday School building across the road. He was followed, in quick succession, by a group of men. One or two looked familiar, although, as usual, Father Tadeusz could not put names to the faces. Except for one: Aleksander Twerpicz, the wiry, furtive-looking man who had formed the Citizens' Committee chapter in town. His busy public activities had penetrated even to Father Tadeusz. The Citizens' Committee was the new wave, the voice of liberation, long years in the making. What was Father Jerzy up to now?

Father Tadeusz wondered if he should look into this, and decided, reluctantly, that he should.

He waited until evening, after his meal of watery soup, toast, and cheese. Jadwiga had gone. The parish house was still, and the only light burning in its entire eighteen rooms was the lamp in his bedroom. As he often did when he was deep in thought, Father Tadeusz walked up and down the darkened corridors, his eyes well adjusted to the gloom. Sometimes he stopped, still as a newel post, silent on the hallway carpet, then resumed his march, back and forth. Sometimes he entered the spare bedchambers or meeting rooms, walked to a window and peered out through the parted veil of curtains at the sparse evening life on the street. Seldom did the view include more than one moving soul at a time. A woman in a lumpy nylon parka hurried past, clutching a plastic bag of food from the corner store. A solitary man walked unsteadily from the bus stop. One of the short-legged cur dogs that populated the town trotted past. He liked these dogs, all homely creatures of improbable mix, as though a blend of German shepherd and dachshund: squat, thick-coated, and clever. They seemed to Father Tadeusz to be dogs with a purpose, moving smartly up the street as if they were out on specific errands, dogs with jobs to do, business to conduct. He wondered why he had never gotten a dog. Though he knew of no specific prohibition, it seemed as if priests were not supposed to have dogs, pets of any kind. They had, after all, the human flock to tend.

He did not confront Father Jerzy that night. He waited a day to see if Father Jerzy approached him, but of course he did not. The following afternoon, he happened to see, as he walked from the side door of the church to the parish house, that Father Jerzy was standing across the street talking with Twerpicz. Jerzy, from this distance, was a round, emphatic black shadow over Twerpicz, who looked, by contrast, like a piece of rusted pipe in dirty khaki pants, his scrawny neck rising from the collar of a mottled brown jacket. Father Tadeusz wondered if Twerpicz was a plumber, for he appeared suited for fitting himself around intricate obstacles in close spaces. As Father Tadeusz observed, it was Jerzy who spoke while Twerpicz listened.

That night, after his supper, Father Tadeusz crossed the street and rapped on Jerzy's door.

"Come in. I've been expecting you."

Already, Father Tadeusz felt he was beginning at a disadvantage, one step behind. Jerzy held the door ajar. He wore a T-shirt that said "Cleveland Indians." Tadeusz had seen him in another one reading "New York Mets." On one wall was a picture of the pope, on another a magazine photograph of Ronald Reagan.

"Why were you expecting me?" Tadeusz asked.

"I was sure you did not approve of my message on abortion at vespers service on Friday. You seemed uncomfortable with it. So I expect you've come to suggest, ah, more restraint. Correct?"

"Oh, no, I have no objection to the message," Father Tadeusz said. "Perhaps it was somewhat graphic." Tadeusz remembered the words "living tissue gasping in blood and membrane in hospital trash receptacles," but did not want to flatter Jerzy by quoting him now. Tadeusz did not approve of abortion, to be sure, but he could not accept it as the obsessive and lurid issue it was becoming these days. He said, "Perhaps there may be more positive messages now."

"What could be more positive than ending the murder of living souls?"

Father Tadeusz did not relish being drawn into an argument, a confrontation. A softer approach would be better. "Of course you are right," he said. "I just wonder if perhaps it is time to get back to some sense of the normal, the constructive. In forty years, people have been warped enough."

"Normal?" Father Jerzy leaned back in his easy chair, his hands relaxed on its arms. "Constructive? Is it normal or constructive that fetuses are dumped in the incinerators at Węgrów Hospital?"

Father Tadeusz shook his head. No, he thought, this is not the argument here. Nor would he win it, he realized.

"Of course, this is horrible. Please, say anything you want about abortion. I have no objection."

"I'm glad to hear that, Father."

"But I wonder if there are everyday concerns worth addressing as well. Is it normal that people, for example, don't know how to work anymore?" Father Jerzy opened his mouth to speak, but Tadeusz held up his hand. "People need to begin doing things for themselves, learn some initiative. The town needs many things. It is a poor community."

"It is a poor *country*," Jerzy said. "It is poor because the Communists robbed the people for forty years. Suppressed the church. Encouraged the collapse of the family. Sent Bolshevik Jews and Stalinist tyrants to rule over our lives, to remove religion from the schools."

All of this Jerzy recited as though from a tract, a zealot's speech from a soapbox. Father Tadeusz realized he had not paid much attention to Jerzy in the six months since he had arrived, with his single suitcase and boxes of books. Back then, their only discussions had been matter-of-fact outlines of schedules and duties, routines of the parish. After a week, when Jerzy announced he would prefer his living quarters across the road from the parish house in the spare room of the school building, Father Tadeusz could feel the implicit assertion of independence, perhaps even rebuke, but he chose not to dwell on it.

"We are not going to let them get away with this any longer," Jerzy said, breaking the moment's silence.

"Who?" Father Tadeusz said.

"The old orders."

"What old orders?"

"The ones who ran everything."

"Are they getting away with anything?" Tadeusz asked mildly. "It seems to me they're finished."

"Is it possible you are being naive, Father?"

Father Tadeusz didn't speak for a moment, genuinely considering the question, although without much inclination to answer.

"Oh, yes, it is possible I am naive," he said finally. "Still, I think their time is over."

"I wish it were so simple. You must know they're preparing their intrigues. They changed the name of the Party, and shed their skins, that's all. They look for new opportunities while then can. They scheme to make their return. But we must to stop them. We are *going* to stop them and reveal their secrets and their crimes."

This again, Tadeusz thought, sounded like a speech.

"I imagine," he said, "their secrets would be a waste of time. Their crime is incompetence. Stupidity. I think it would best be forgotten."

"They were abortionists and atheists. They destroyed the social fabric, and they should pay."

"How? You can't prosecute Lenin. Or your schoolteachers."

"Yes, too bad about Lenin," Father Jerzy smiled. "No," he went on, "just the guilty."

"Who then?" Tadeusz asked.

"The responsible ones. The ones who ran everything."

Father Tadeusz felt an unaccustomed heat of argument rising to his face; he suppressed it. The young man facing him reclined in the chair, relaxed now, evidently enjoying himself. His face was pale and smooth, like dough rising in a pan. Tadeusz felt heavy in his own chair. He had not inquired about Twerpicz or the meetings in Jerzy's room, but now he knew.

"So, Father," Tadeusz said, "where do you plan to start?"

"We start here. Now."

"With whom?"

"How about the naczelnik?"

"Who is the naczelnik?" He realized he was exposing his detachment from the place, another weakness revealed. Of course he had met the naczelnik, although he could not just now recall the name. He also realized that Jerzy had maneuvered around considerably here, that he was, in fact, miles ahead of him.

"His name is Farby."

"Oh yes, Farby." He remembered: the fat one in the town office, the one with the razor burn on his plump cheeks. "A small bureaucrat."

"Yes, a bureaucrat, and possibly a criminal."

"Maybe he took bribes. They all took bribes."

"Perhaps a bit more than that."

"Yes?"

"Well, surely we can all point to the rise in crime. You yourself administered the sacraments to one victim."

Father Tadeusz looked back at him, startled.

"Maybe they were stupid," Father Tadeusz said. "Maybe they took bribes. I can't see them as murderers."

Father Jerzy held his gaze, his eyes unblinking in the yeasty fullness of his face. "I don't think," he said, "I should say any more. Except, of course, that your assistance, perhaps your blessing, would be welcomed." A faint smile played on his lips, cold as a sharpened wedge.

Father Tadeusz turned away from the younger priest, staring into a corner of the room, where the wall met the ceiling. Stains from leakage, like an antique map, held his eye. When he turned back to Jerzy, he saw the young priest's eyes still fixed on him.

Father Tadeusz took his leave then. He shut the outer door carefully behind him, politely lifting the dragging door across its jamb until the latch clicked. He picked his way slowly across the muddy path to the parish house and went to his room, where he turned out the light and sat on the edge of his bed in the dark. Father Jerzy's moonish face swam before him, mouthing the words, "I don't think I should say any more."

But of course he would. There would be no stopping him.

Staszek Powierza shoved open the gate in the splintered fence that tilted crookedly in front of Krupik's house. The policeman's car, filthy with road spray, sat in the drive, so Powierza knew he was home, even though his knock on the door went unanswered. He walked around to the rear of the house. It was one of the older dwellings in town, quarters for a succession of village policemen. Powierza could not remember when Krupik had assumed the post, arriving from some other job in some other village, but it had been, he believed, five or six years. The windows of the house, settled with age, were cockeyed. A dozen filthy chickens scattered across the packed mud of the side yard at his approach. At the rear of the house were two outbuildings, a shed and a small barn, both unpainted and deeply weathered, with green moss creeping up the boards from the ground. A muffled voice sounded from inside the barn. A door, at one end, hung ajar, suspended by one rusted hinge.

"Krupik."

"Whore! Sonofabitch! Who is it?"

The barn was dark except for the daylight from a smeared window at the opposite end. At first Powierza could not locate the voice amid the jumble of garden equipment, boxes, old tires, and assorted junk. Then he saw Krupik, a squat figure in a black coat. He held a shovel in both hands.

"It's Powierza."

"Yes? What do you want?" Krupik turned away and glowered at the foot of the wall. Powierza's view was blocked by the dim tumble of barn objects. He could not detect the object of Krupik's wrath.

"Just a minute," Krupik said. "I'm coming."

Powierza stepped outside and lighted a cigarette. The chickens picked around the bordering fence. The bare limbs of an ancient pear tree dripped with mist. Some of the window panes in the back of the house had been replaced with cardboard. A stain of kitchen slop-water streaked the ground between the coal shed and the back door, marked with curling pieces of orange peel. For a second, he saw the pale shadow of Mrs. Krupik's face behind one of the windows. Then he heard Krupik emerge from the barn behind him. "Jesus," he said.

"I hope I'm not bothering you," Powierza said. His tone was not quite peremptory, although his regard for Krupik's schedule, whatever it might be, was minimal.

"No. What do you need from me?" Powierza read the comment as a bureaucrat's dread, some demand for paperwork, the curse of semiliterate officialdom.

"Do you have anything new?"

Krupik looked at Powierza in puzzlement. New what? his lips said silently. Then he recovered.

"No, I don't." Krupik's constricted expression eased toward its normal plumpness. "Nothing more. Nothing at all, unfortunately."

"I found out that Tomek went to Warsaw that morning."

"What morning?"

"The morning before," Powierza said. "Before they found him."

"I see. Well, I'll put that down."

"Put it down?"

"In my report." Krupik seemed to be gazing at the button on Powierza's jacket pocket, as though he were staring off at the sky. Powierza reached into the pocket and offered a cigarette to Krupik, who accepted it wordlessly.

"Are you doing anything else?" Powierza asked.

"It's being looked into, Mr. Powierza."

"Did you know he had gone to Warsaw?"

"Yes, you told me that," he sighed. "Maybe we can get Warsaw to look into it."

Powierza, towering over Krupik, stared at him in silence.

"Jesus, Powierza, I'm sorry, but I told you I can't go interviewing people on the street in Warsaw."

"Do you know if Tomek was working for Jabłoński?"

"Jabłoński? I never heard that. Why don't you ask Jabłoński?"

"Why don't you?"

"If Mr. Jabłoński wants to tell me anything, he will." Krupik pivoted back toward the barn, but after two steps he turned again to Powierza. "When I see Jabłoński I'll mention it, okay?" He dragged on the cigarette. "For whatever good it will do. Hey, come here and look at this, will you?" he said. "Something's got into my barn. Dug a hole right through the foundation, right through the stone."

Krupik motioned Powierza to follow him to the rear of the barn. Tall dead grass was mashed down by footsteps. Halfway along the wall, at the foundation, was a shallow hole and a pile of dark foundation stones fallen loose onto the ground. The boards of the upper part of the wall, weathered and mossy, were undisturbed.

"What the hell did this?" Krupik said. "Some kind of animal?"

"Is anything missing?"

"No. There's nothing in there worth stealing. If there was, you could carry it out the door. It's never locked." Krupik studied the shallow hole, stabbing at one of the fallen stones with his shoe. "Could a dog do this?"

Powierza inspected the lumps of dirt lying nearby in the grass. A couple of clumps bore the smooth edge of a shovel's blade.

"Doesn't look like a dog to me," Powierza said. "Looks like a shovel had to do this. Maybe somebody's trying to make your barn fall down. Kids or something."

"Why not just burn it? Why pull the stones out of the foundation?"

Powierza had no interest in Krupik's barn. He left the policeman staring slack-lipped at the collapsed foundation stones and raw dirt. The sight of the upturned sod sickened him. He had gone back to Tomek's grave twice since the burial, and had returned the second time with a shovel to tidy the work of the grave diggers, whose efforts had been as sloppy and careless as village road crews. He raked up the loose clods around the loaflike mound, smoothing them into the earth beneath which his only son rested. His wife had made her own solitary trips there too, and left flowers from the shop in town, a pair of trumpet-shaped lilies that had frozen and collapsed onto the brown earth. Hanna Powierza, now that her daughters had returned to their homes, seemed to have receded into the shadows of the house.

Powierza, standing with the shovel at the edge of Tomek's grave, could think only of the silence, the weight, the darkness he imagined would be felt from below. Funerals, graveyards, the ceremonies of death—these had never cut him before, and he wondered at his inability to understand bereavement. Tomek, what would he have been? The boy, he had decided, would have returned to the farm; was, in fact, already on his way back. He had been exploring, that's all, as youth must. He would have been married, someday, and fathered children bearing the family name. Powierza had as much difficulty as anyone imagining his family vulnerable to tragedy. To the extent such a calamity was possible at all, he could have conceived of Tomek dying in a car accident, could imagine police cars arriving at the house with the news from some highway or hospital. It was his first impression when Krupik appeared at the house, saying there had been an "accident." His bellow of protest had burst out at the vision of a crumpled car, a bloody stretcher, of long-haul truck drivers and farmers smoking cigarettes at the side of a wet road while traffic crept past. Powierza had not comprehended what Krupik had told him. He still could not understand why Tomek's body was below this fresh clay. Nor could he escape the suspicion that there were those who did understand and would not tell him.

From Krupik's place, Powierza headed home though the village center. It was midmorning. The usual floating collection of standers loitered in front of the shop that sold bread and vodka. He saw their heads swivel, one by one, to look at him, as though he bore some physical mark of catastrophe. He glanced up at them and away, just as one of the men waved a greeting. He chose not to see it. Those men never seemed to move, he thought, although he knew in fact the cast of characters here shifted constantly through the day, as though some secretly enforced rule decreed a minimum presence be on duty through all daylight hours. It was naturally an all-male gathering, since the level of obscenity and intoxication among them discouraged the presence of women. Powierza heard footsteps running after him: Andrzej, the plumber, had detached himself from the standers. They shook hands.

"Do you hear anything?" Andrzej asked.

"About the investigation? No."

"They'll never find anything," Andrzej said. He fell in stride beside Powierza. "They never do."

"No."

"Strange. And your wife? How is she?"

"She'll be all right."

The Warsaw bus careened around the corner, blowing black smoke across the street.

"The pump I fixed for you last summer? It's okay?"

"Yes. Fine."

"Good. I was wondering, have you spoken to Karol, the veterinarian?"

"No, why?"

"I heard him talking the other day about something."

"What?"

"I'm not sure I understood it. Something he heard somewhere. He gets around, the vet. An intelligent man, although he's a bit of a drinker. But very intelligent. Some intelligent men are like that, you know. Especially in a place like this. It's the way they cope."

"Yes, Andrzej. What did he say?"

"I'm not sure, but it was something about trucks. Russian trucks maybe."

"Yes."

"Someone has been seeing them. I don't know when. But someone saw them, maybe a few times, on the old quarry road. By the distillery. At night, I think is what he said. You know Karol. He's hard to understand sometimes. But he hears things."

"The quarry road? There's nothing there, is there?" The quarry was a small one, once a source of road gravel, and unused for twenty years.

"The distillery is not far."

"The distillery?" As he walked along the path, Powierza felt Andrzej's gaze in a beat of silence. Andrzej shrugged.

"I don't know," he said. "I know that where your boy, uh, passed on . . . well, that's not far from the distillery. Pretty close, anyway. I just heard this, so I thought . . ."

"Thank you."

His backed away, feet shuffling. "Okay, so, well, I've got some work to do."

"Andrzej, did my boy do work for Jabłoński?"

Andrzej thrust his hands in his pockets, his shoulders hunched against a quickening wind. It had turned colder.

"Well, I couldn't say exactly."

"What do you mean?"

"I saw him there once. I was fixing the boiler. At the Farmers' Co-op. I just saw him there."

"What was he doing?"

"Nothing. He seemed to be waiting. Maybe to talk to someone. It was some time ago. I didn't speak to him."

Powierza's encounters with Jabłoński were fleeting and rare, for he made a point of knowing as little as possible about official matters of the town and the surrounding district. The guardians of the state's interests, as far as he was concerned, were most notable for their absence in any emergency and their ineffectiveness in dealing with any matter of civic need. They couldn't even manage to install a public privy off the market square to shield women and children from the spectacle of town drunks pissing against the trees on market days. Powierza's own general observation matched the public perception that only a boot licker or mental defective or both held an office where Communist Party membership was required. His own arrest, years ago, for cutting firewood on his own land, was the result not of an official campaign against profiteering (although that occurred, too), nor the erroneous assumption that he was selling the wood. As nearly as Powierza could read it, he was arrested so that some official could win recognition as a vigilant public servant, the sort of Party loyalist who would tolerate no suggestion that the village coal supplies—yet again—were inadequate. In the Party's view, you burned coal or went cold. The arrest provoked exactly the sentiment it was designed to forestall, namely that the country was wracked by shortages and managed by incompetents.

Jabłoński, he knew, was different: not incompetent—not quite—and canny. He had been the Party leader in town a dozen years, relinquishing the post only when the Party itself was dissolved, as it happened, beneath him. In his heyday, Jabłoński's presence at town meetings brought about a muted acquiescence on whatever issue was up for the day, and he had only to appear in the room for the usual windy argumentation to cease. His reputation as a man who fired the recalcitrant and struck for revenge seemed to go before him, like a cloud. He was known as ill-tempered, even vicious with his staff, and was famous for an incident, years back, in which he actually kicked his secretary in the behind, an indignity which won her no sympathy, since she was as mean as the man she worked for.

Powierza had never feared him, merely ignored him. Now he could do neither.

Jola sat in the kitchen, a book open on the table in front of her. The children, Anna and Marek, were asleep, and the house was still, except for the television's murmur in the living room, where Karol slept in his big chair, his snores interrupted by fits of coughing. Jola left the television on to cover the noise he made and to keep him asleep, as a sort of lullaby. She feared he would wake up soon, as he almost always did on a day like this, when he reeled home at midafternoon, already well on his way, and continued drinking until he fell asleep. Today he drank until he emptied most of a bottle, bellowed for his supper, ate messily, and sank into his chair. Some days—lucky ones, she felt—he slept in the chair all night. More often, he woke up after an hour or two. Withdrawing from the vodka, he began again with fresh determination and the temper of a starved dog. Jola tried to be in bed before that, to be out of his way. Sometimes, even when she turned the lights off and feigned sleep, he lurched in, found the light switch, and insisted on picking a fight.

She could not concentrate on her book, a gloomy Polish novel, plucked virtually at random from a shelf in the library. She felt, as though she sensed a shift in barometric pressure, that a storm was moving in. He would awaken soon, and she was wondering how much longer she could take it. She could not go to bed an hour after dark, and she resented that she should consider it as an escape, pulling the covers over her head like a frightened child. She had been trying to devise a strategy, a plan for leaving the house, but every possibility was frought with complications. The home of her parents was one, but the situation there was hardly an improvement. She had been there earlier today, and so had Karol: drinking with her father, who was in no better shape than Karol. Worse, possibly, although her father did not possess her husband's deep streak of meanness when he drank. But Karol was, depressingly, one of her father's principal drinking companions.

What would Karol do if she left? She feared he would go crazy. She feared trying to banish him from her parents' home. Her mother, of course, would side with her. But she could envision the scenes of rage, in the center of town where every neighbor would watch and listen while Karol shouted and crashed down doors, her mother wailing and her father half-drunk and ineffectual, and Anna cowering in fear and confusion in the upstairs bedroom. There seemed no safe place to take the children.

She sat at the table, her head in her hands, her fingers pressing into her scalp. And here, she thought, in the village, had she simply reduced herself to grasping for adventure? Poor Leszek, sweet Leszek. He was an innocent, too young. It was her voraciousness, she knew, that had hit him with such force. The desperation in her was beyond his comprehension, something she was not sure she could talk about or explain to him. She wanted him to understand. He was full of hope and plans. The future was all brightness to him. His voice rose with optimism when he talked about the field he wanted to buy, as though it were an answer for everything. Most likely, Leszek would eventually come to his senses. He would see things more realistically. And she would wind up the way she had always seen herself in her darkest moments: with nothing. She thought of old Pani Słowik in her shack behind the splintered, broken fences, in the room that seemed like a cave, black with soot.

She heard Karol coughing in the other room, his foot banging against the table, stirring himself awake. She waited, heard another thump of a deadened leg falling to the floor, a muttering groan. Music trickled from the television, then voices. He was awake now, muttering back to the television. She heard him lumbering toward the bathroom. She didn't look up as he lurched past the door. She thought, once more, of turning out the kitchen light and hurrying to the bedroom, but instead she sat. Karol's footsteps thumped again, and she could feel his shadow, his breath, at the door.

"So there you are," he said. "Face in a book." He entered into the kitchen, his feet shuffling. "So smart and getting smarter." He clasped a fresh bottle in his hand. Where, she wondered, did he keep them all?

This was always the way it started, the two of them locked into this cycle, and so she sat, in resignation, facing her bout of anger and fear.

She glanced up at him for the first time. His heavy face looked more swollen than usual, his large lips reddened and his eyes puffed.

"I read," she said, "so I don't have to think about this place."

He dragged a chair out from the table and sat down heavily. She could smell his breath; she thought there was nothing quite as horrible as this sour chemistry of toxins and blood, alcohol and tobacco, this liverish digestion. He tilted the bottle upside down, smacked the bottom with the palm of his hand, and unscrewed the top. He poured a shimmering glass. "Have a drink."

She looked at him with as much contempt as she could muster.

"Okay. Read your book. Be smart. See if you find any answers in it." He threw back the drink. A bead of vodka glistened on his lower lip. He licked it away.

"The town is going to go crazy now," he said. "Did you know that?"

"What do you mean? This house is crazy. Why should I worry about the town?" Karol poured another shot of vodka in his tumbler. "Jesus, Karol, don't you ever get enough?" she asked.

"I'll need more than this before it's over."

"Before what is over? What are you talking about?"

He said nothing, absorbed momentarily by the task of fishing a loose cigarette from his shirt, then standing to cross the kitchen in search of a match. Trailing a sheet of smoke, he dropped again into the chair. He had her attention now, and she felt apprehension tightening like a violin string in her spine. Was he talking about her, about Leszek and her? They had been too careless; Karol was bound to find out. When she spoke, her voice sounded taut with fear, wind across a wire. "What do you mean, Karol?"

"So fucking smart," his words were slurry, stalling, trapped in mental backwash. She wondered now, as she sometimes did, what was happening to his mind. She imagined regions of his brain that would go soft with alcoholic decay, or were rotting already. The thought projected a picture of his deterioration that terrified and saddened her, that shunted even her anger aside.

"Karol, you can't even talk."

"I can talk just fine, my pet. Oh, I can talk and I can listen, too, and I've been hearing things."

"What are you talking about?" But she suspected, with his words, that whatever it was had nothing to do with her. Surely Karol would not wait on that. He would not drag it out. Or would he? Would he taunt it out of her by slow stages?

"They're going to get Jabłoński," he said. He belched, pulled on his cigarette. "They're going to get him, and Farby and God knows who else. Stupid bastards."

Jola sighed, relieved, and for the first time in the conversation, for the first time in an hour (the muscles in her back told her), she relaxed in her chair. She listened, almost idly, as she listened to gossip.

"Who are 'they,' and why are they going to get Jabłoński?"

"The new boys. The righteous reformers. Twerpicz and that fucking priest, what's-his-name, Jerzy. The snot-nosed fat one. And the rest of them. They're going to get him because he's there, because now they can. The temper of the times. And then they can run things."

"So what? They're all shits."

"So what?" He snorted. "Somebody should ask them so what." He toyed with the glass in his big fingers, his heavy head down. "So what and then what? Once they get started, where do they stop, huh? There's a question for you." He looked up at her, silent momentarily, then reached out toward her book with his thick index finger. "Your book tell you about that?"

"What do you care if they get Jabłoński? He's a bastard, and everyone knows it. Who cares?"

"Your books don't tell you?" He riffled the pages with his thumb, leaning over the table toward her. His voice was soft now, and thick. "No answers there?"

She stared at him, and saw, in the redness of his eyelids, in the mortified pouches of flesh beneath his eyes, some vulnerable zone she had not glimpsed in a long time.

"Sweetheart?" he said. His bloodshot eyes fixed on hers.

"Yes?" She felt something for him she could not identify. Sympathy? Sorrow? Love?

"My sweetheart," he said.

She sat motionless, waiting, but he seemed, as she watched, to have sagged, wound down, his energy spent.

"No, no, no," he muttered, and he seemed, now, far away. "We all feed from the same slops here." He wiped his mouth with the back of his hand. "Everyone gets splashed in the same trough. Even your fine young friend. What's his name? Leszek?"

"Leszek?"

"Leszek."

Jola stared straight back at him, her face as near to a blank as she could make it. Karol put his head on the table and in a moment was asleep.

Jabłoński's lumbago was acting up. As he bent over the cardboard boxes, his right fist, balled around a faulty ballpoint pen, traveled automatically to the small of his aching back, knuckle pressing into muscle. Grimacing, he peered into the packing material, trying to count the plastic dolls inside the containers. It was the bending and straightening that nagged him. He knelt down, finally, tossed the papers on the filthy floor, and pawed through the mess of foamy pellets that attached themselves, with a maddening defiance of gravity, to the back of his hand. He studied the numbers on a sheaf of papers in his left hand. So, he thought, it's come to this. Not just accountancy—he was used to that—but the demeaning cop-work of inventory control. People stealing him blind. No, stealing themselves blind. They'd been pilfering for so long it was second nature to them; or easier, like breathing.

He was alone in the storeroom and muttering softly to himself.

Two dim lightbulbs hung from long cords, throwing his doubled shadow in his way. Around the walls, floor-to-ceiling bins that once held spare parts for tractors and hay rakes and grain augers sat in greasy cobwebbed dimness, mostly empty. The Farmers' Cooperative didn't deal any longer in spare parts. The offices, in the adjoining building, were also empty now. He was used to that, too. All his working life, Roman Jabłoński was a man who stayed late.

He thought he heard, from the office side of the building, the slap of a closing door. He listened for a moment, then went on with his counting. He picked up the paper, holding it toward the light to read the numbers. Four dozen, it said. When he turned back a figure was standing in the doorway: Czarnek, from the distillery, motionless in the shadow, scowling. Jabłoński straightened up, startled, one of the rubber dolls dangling from his fist.

"What are you doing here?" Jabłoński said. He pushed his glasses into place, dropped the doll into the box, and shook off the white pellets that still clung to his sleeve.

"Don't worry. I didn't come to rob you, Mr. Chairman."

"It's late," Jabłoński said. "And don't call me Mr. Chairman."

"We need to talk."

"Let's go to the office."

Czarnek surveyed the cardboard boxes, feet planted as if he did not want to unblock the door, even as Jabłoński approached and waited for him to turn. "If you please," he said, switching off the light behind him. Czarnek wore boots, but moved without a sound, almost languidly, like a cat curling into a room. Jabłoński pulled the door shut and fastened it with a heavy padlock. He could feel Czarnek behind him, like a shadow.

Once in his office Jabłoński removed a bottle from the bookshelf and poured two small glasses.

"Cheers," Jabłoński said. "Now why do we need to talk?"

"Are you worried, Mr. Chairman?"

"Why would I be worried? And don't fucking call me Mr. Chairman."

Czarnek drank and for a moment stared at Jabłoński without speaking. His deepset eyes seemed darkly threatening. He thumped the glass solidly on Jabłoński's desk.

"All right. Romek." He used the given name, Roman, in the diminutive, the "R" richly and sarcastically rolled, a form of address Jabłoński had not answered to, perhaps, since childhood. "You know where our friend was the night he was killed."

"So?"

"So, a few other people know, too."

"Such as?"

"Farby."

"Why should you worry about Farby?"

"Because someone's going to start asking questions, and if it gets to Farby, I'd be stupid not to get worried. I don't know what happened to Tomek Powierza. I don't want to know. But I know where he was, and if someone finds out he was at the distillery, what am I supposed to do then?"

"Relax, Czarnek. Have another." Jabłoński refilled the glasses. "I'll protect Farby."

"It's not like the old days, Jabłoński. You don't control this place anymore. If he's relying on you, he might as well be lost in a marsh. You guys say 'trust me,' it means 'fuck you.' And if you think it's going to be me left standing there with shit on my hands, Jabłoński, I'm warning you, there's going to be trouble."

"I'll take care of Farby, Czarnek, don't worry. That's what I do. I take care of this place. It's what I've always done." Jabłoński rotated the vodka bottle in his hand, studying the label. Yes, he thought, I looked after this benighted shit hole in the middle of nowhere while a government of spineless compromisers minced around in Warsaw begging for a chance to kiss George Bush's ass on satellite TV and inviting the Great Electrician to beat them in an election. And here in Jadowia, while the standers on the street corner bellyached about the price of bread, and Jew money-lenders in Washington made sure it kept going up, it was me, Jabłoński, who kept the place running.

"I see how you take care of the place," Czarnek said. "You open little shops all around and fill them with junk from Berlin. And the Farmers' Co-op tractors rust out there in the rain. You think the people love you or something. Have you been unconscious for the last year? Nobody gives a shit what you say."

Jabłoński stared back at Czarnek. He had always been difficult—

it was in his blood, he supposed. But, still, he thought, this was not the way discourse used to proceed in the old order, this foul-mouthed disrespect. Once he would not have put up with it, but he resolved to keep his voice calm.

"All right, Czarnek, you're right," he said. He drank his glass and swiveled back in his chair, an executive, explaining the elementary. "People have short memories. Or they think they do. A new order is what we're supposed to have here. The information age is upon us. Did you hear of that? They mean high technology, computers, things like that. Information's the key. Information is everything. Information is power. Do you understand that, Czarnek? Information is never obsolete, as long as it remains information. You, especially, should appreciate that."

He rocked gently in his chair. Czarnek stared at him through narrowed eyes.

Jabłoński smiled placidly.

"I may have to get some computers in here soon," he said. "Stay up with things."

Czarnek said nothing.

"You follow me?"

"It's right what they say, isn't it?" Czarnek said.

"About computers?"

"That old Communists never change. Why is it you think your secrets are so powerful? You think you're the only one around here with secrets? People aren't afraid of that anymore."

"We'll see, Czarnek," Jabłoński said. "But no one is going to bother me." He clasped his hands behind his head, his chair creaking as he leaned back. "Besides, they have no reason to bother me. I'm a small, ordinary person, that's all, and I do what I can to survive. I have working for me now—how many is it?—thirty-four people, putting food on the table for their families. So I contribute. I do my part. Everything changes, and I am a part of the changes. I perform a service."

He suddenly rocked forward in his chair and stared at Czarnek evenly. His voice lowered to nearly a whisper.

"Go and do likewise, sir. Run your alcohol factory. Mind your own business. Don't come tiptoeing here in the night and threatening me.

What do I know about Tomek Powierza's visits to your little operation? There is no connection between us. He did a little work, that's all. Ran errands. I told his father that today. Yes, he came to see me. A big simple man, like bread and salt, the very guts of Socialism, he seemed to me. Or should be. So I was very sympathetic. Yes, Tomek delivered some things for me, disposable diapers, boxes of shampoo, things like that. Very sorry for him, and so on. A nice man."

Jabłoński picked up the bottle and poured.

"No," said Czarnek, and stood up, looming above the desk. Jabłoński looked at him over the rims of his spectacles.

"I would not say much, Czarnek, if someone visits you to ask." His gaze shifted to the clear liquid in his glass.

"Well, it was you who found him, wasn't it?" Jabłoński went on. "No, don't say anything. Officially it was old Piwek, I know. Of course, Krupik asked him how he came to be there, since he couldn't have been doing anything but stealing wood or on his way to somewhere other than his house. Krupik's ambition as a public servant is by no means dazzling, but he gets along, in his way. He asked. Piwek said you sent him that way. That's all. And the tracks of a dog."

Czarnek's face darkened.

"A big dog. Like yours, perhaps. Yes? Now there's information for you, Czarnek. A small example. So I'd be careful, my friend. No one knows where Powierza was before he was killed. Perhaps it was you who found his services dispensable, perhaps he rubbed you the wrong way. Your temper is well known, isn't it? You are a less than deeply loved local businessman." Jabłoński sipped from his glass. "Perhaps even less loved, given your, shall we say, your dubious history."

Czarnek leaned forward, both fists on the edge of the desk, so that Jabłoński was aware of a vibration, a faint tremor, transmitted through Czarnek's arms to the desk.

"Never mind, Czarnek." Jabłoński drew back slightly. "Don't let your temper show. And I am grateful for your reminder that Naczelnik Farby is not, perhaps, the most reliable of pillars to lean on. We should both watch our step."

Czarnek stood over him, glowering. Slowly he moved to the door. Jabłoński noted again the big man's curiously liquid movement, the silence of his footsteps. He felt a chill.

"Good night, Mr. Chairman," Czarnek said. "Enjoy your bottle."
"I plan to."

Yes, he planned to enjoy his bottle. Not the one on the office shelf, but one waiting across the road at his flat in the basement of the old Party building. Lined up in the cabinet like a willing soldier. But first he went through the offices extinguishing the lights, and thinking, naturally enough under the circumstances, of old Marcin, his mentor and guide, teacher and protector, dead now for ten years. Marcin had been Party leader here for seventeen years before he died. Jabłoński remembered him shriveling at the end, his face like a drying apple. The yellow light that once glowed from the deep sockets of his eyes flickered out, too, before the end, and he jabbered nonsense—regressing to childhood, kites, fishing, bicycles on summer paths. But Jabłoński fancied, as he saw him the last time, just hours before he died, in fact, a spark of that hooded light returning, a final glitter of cunning. His voice rattled softly, like the crumpling of tissue paper. "Take the boxes, Roman," he said.

"I have them. Already. As you said." The old man had forgotten; he was, after all, dying. Jabłoński's own eyes had filmed with tears.

"Ah yes. Good. Protect them, Roman."

So the papers in the boxes resided now deep in a closet across the street, in a small two-drawer file cabinet of military issue, the keys hidden. It had been years since he looked at them.

CHAPTER FIVE

LESZEK

I went to Warsaw on the train, packed in with shifts of factory workers and nightwatchmen, the sort of laborers who did shifts of two days on and two days off, carrying forty-eight hours' worth of rations in battered shoulder cases or plastic shopping bags. It was morning, the mood among the passengers sour as a growling stomach. From the power stations along the river, coal smoke spread its dark wings over the city, shrouding buildings in a gray-brown gauze, giving them a spectral flimsiness, suggesting a city of mirages, stretching infinitely from the center. The impression of sprawl was no illusion, for massive buildings were set at the city's perimeter, great clustered hives of high-rise apartment blocks containing thousands of people pressed into tiny rooms, generation impinging on generation. From the train window, the city seemed unchanged, dressed in its winter mud and construction muck, a poor *babcia* in her tattered coat, ceaselessly repaired, year after year.

The Central Station spilled us into a maze of underground corridors lined with peddlers and pickpockets and squealing Gypsy children. I had worn my gray sweater (which I thought of as my city clothes) and my best coat, which was plaid and had the unmistakable look of the country. I imagined the news vendor, when I bought a newspaper, appraising my coat and my haircut and my shoes. Of course he paid no attention at all, but this was the feeling that always afflicted me in the city, a self-consciousness coupled with a tinge of excitement, and a suspicion that the place tapped out a steady code I would never decipher. I followed the flow, gripping my small bag and my newspaper, and emerged onto the street.

The red-and-yellow trams slid along Marszałkowska with their low electric moans and their cargoes of indistinct faces. I was unsure where to go, but I needed lodging. Places in the city's center would be too expensive. I would have to cross the river to Praga, the only district I knew to harbor rooming houses or hostels for working men. But it was still early in the day, and I was in no hurry. I stood, deciding this, in a tram crowd in the center of the avenue, feeling the crush around me, jostled back and forth by people shoving on and off, people who lived here and knew where they were going, who were used to pushing obstacles aside. It was my way of acclimating myself to this urban atmosphere of human breath and murmur, the smells of electric tram motors and car exhaust, the fragments of conversation. Finally, I shoved back myself and pressed on across the street to the Palace of Culture, a bespired Stalinist skyscraper, planted like a totem in the center of the city. Around its base the tented kiosks of peddlers were scattered like a circus encampment. The place had become, in my absence, a huge open-air market. I threaded my way through it, among the hawkers of denim jackets and skirts and fake leather coats, perfume and cosmetics, soaps and shampoos made in the West, radios, tape recorders, computer parts, and toys.

Polish traders claimed the prime real estate, the kiosks at the center, driving the Russians to the periphery, to peddle cheap tools, combs and hair brushes, little piles of screws and bolts, pocket knives, kitchen knives, socks, children's underpants, pots and pans, plumbing fixtures, even scalpels and surgical tools, a virtual wonderland of junk. The itinerant Russians were forced to travel light: they laid their stuff on fold-up tables, or on towels and strips of plastic sheeting spread on the pavement, and sat cross-legged behind their displays, squabbling mildly with each other in Russian. An endless parade of muddy boots shuffled past them. With thick red hands, the women ceaselessly adjusted their little piles of goods and scowled up at the passing faces with expressions bordering on contempt. Russians and Poles didn't like each other very much, an enmity that stretched back centuries. Most Poles believed they could hear a small whine of sarcasm in the way Russians pronounced the Polish formal address, "Pan" and "Pani," which mean, literally, "lord" and "lady." It was, admittedly, a far cry from "comrade." It cut both ways. I have heard my grandfather tell a joke: If you were in a foxhole and you were being attacked on one side by Germans and on the other by Russians, which would you shoot first? "The Germans," he would say. "Business before pleasure."

I paused once, to look at an electric drill and set of bits. "It's good, Pan," said the man squatting behind it. He clenched a fist. "Strong." I asked how much for the drill. It was not cheap, after all. Soviet equipment like this was supposed to be of good quality. Heavy but indestructable. It was one thing they could manufacture, although back in the village no one would be likely to show off some acquisition of Soviet origin. Were it American or West German, then you could invite your neighbor over to watch it drill holes.

At the market's far edge, near the base of the building, Russian men presided over goods of military issue: binoculars, sniper telescopes, packs, belts, pistol holsters, army greatcoats. These attracted a solidly male crowd, from school boys upward, who tested the points of the bayonets and lifted the field glasses to peer around the crowd. The sellers operated from tables draped with gray-green army blankets. The smell of black tobacco from their cigarettes scented the air. The men stood in small groups, sometimes handing a bottle back and forth, speaking quietly and shifting from foot to foot, keeping a vigilant eye on the fascinated and sticky-fingered schoolboys. I could not resist the fascination myself, for these strange martial items, the web belts, the compasses, the flattened field packs and sniper scopes, were accessories of a force that, according to the teachings of our childhood, was to command our respect and gratitude. It was Soviet might that saved us from Hitler, that put Gagarin in orbit, and then, of course, clutched us in less-than-grateful submission. The first part we learned in school, the second around the supper table. It was not much more than a year ago that a hawker of Soviet military field glasses might have gone to prison for spying or sabotage or peddling state secrets. Now such stuff was being sold openly, like pieces that had fallen off the iron hide of some mighty machine, and an illicit air still hovered about the whole area, overseen by men who had the watchful expression of prison inmates.

I had a look, trying out a pair of binoculars. I would have liked some field glasses, although I'm not sure why. A toy, I suppose. They did not seem so powerful when I tried them, their tiny circles of light through the lenses dancing evasively in a tunnel of darkness. I set them down. "How much?" I asked. "Seven-hundred-fifty," the man said. He shot me a dismissive look.

"Thousand?"

"Of course." We both knew I was not serious.

For an hour I wandered through the marketplace, then walked to the margin of the Old Town to catch the tram across the river. Eager to be rid of my bag and get on with my task, I needed now to find a room. I had agreed with Powierza to try to find the office whose telephone number we had called. Powierza had talked with Jabłoński and learned only that Tomek had received or delivered goods that Jabłoński sold in his shops. But according to Jabłoński, Tomek had done no work for him in several weeks. He claimed that he couldn't recall where Tomek had gone on his errands. It was too long ago, he said, and there were too many wholesalers who came and went. The market, he claimed, was confused, full of operators who were in business one week and vanished the next. They went broke, or used their profits to move another notch up the commercial chain. Everything was new, he said. People who started by selling soap advanced to perfume and then to leather jackets or television sets, always eyeing a higher profit and a faster turnover. No one stayed in the same place for long. Jabłoński might have been lying to Powierza, but he was right about this, more or less. The country was wide open. The Wild West reborn in the East: businesses started and quickly vanished. Crooks and swindlers abounded. Money changers and fledgling bankers had absconded the country with millions and headed off to South America.

I rode the tram toward Praga, a part of town always notorious for its criminal population, now supposedly the turf of organized gangs, where Polish thieves joined forces or fought with a traveling arm of the Russian mafia. Praga had escaped much of the destruction of the war, so its buildings were older, more dilapidated, chunks of brick and masonry crashing regularly from facades of neglected buildings. It was the poorest part of Warsaw, its streets close and crowded, winding through clogged neighborhoods where washing hung from windows. I imagined that streets here looked like the streets of Warsaw before the war, only choked now with cars and trucks, rather than horses and wagons. Here the aged and infirm were more conspicuous, characters in long coats sorted through the trash barrels, more old widows hobbled to the market for one turnip and one carrot, counting out their crumpled hundred-zloty notes, careful to save back enough for a few ounces of pork fat to melt for dipping their bread. These were the ones hardest hit now, the ones whose tenuous presence on the street called to mind the principle which Socialism was supposed to have erased and which now rushed back: the survival of the fittest. The old people seemed to be dying out before one's eyes.

My former quarters in Praga were no longer a possibility; those rooms were let out to companies that rented them to their workers. But I knew of several nameless rooming houses in the area. I headed for the nearest, and found signs behind the desk in Polish and Russian. When I asked if rooms were available, a woman with purple lipstick and hair bleached to the color of straw named the price without glancing up. I said I would take it for two nights. I paid and received a key attached to a wooden block by a dirty string. The room was on the third floor—toilet down the hall. Dirty curtains hung over a grimy window that offered a view onto the backs of other buildings and other dirty windows. I tossed down my bag, fished out my bits of paper and phone numbers.

An out-of-order sign was taped to the coin phone in the lobby. The desk phone, the woman behind the desk said, was not for use by guests. I hurried to the telephone office three blocks away and waited in line ten minutes for my turn, and called the number that had yielded Jabłoński's name before.

A woman's voice answered, a simple "Hello," no company name.

"Pardon me," I said, "but what company is this?"

"This is Rapid Trading," she said.

"I am coming from Węgrów," I said.

"Where?"

"Węgrów."

"Yes?"

"I am opening a shop," I said. "I was given this number. I'm looking for goods for my shop."

"What kind of goods?"

"Various things." I tried to picture items on the shelf of a country shop, while the line hummed. "Soaps, perhaps."

"No, we don't deal in such things. Where did you get our number?"

"From an acquaintance. Perhaps it is the wrong number. You are a trading company?"

"Yes."

"Dealing in . . . ?"

"Light industrial goods."

"I see."

"Probably not what you want." Her voice lightened. "No soap."

"No soap," I laughed with her. "No disposable diapers?" I remembered Jabłoński had told Powierza that Tomek had delivered diapers from Warsaw.

"No diapers, no soap," she said. "Not anymore. Not for some time now."

"But you did once?"

"Not for some time. We handle industrial products now."

"What industrial products?"

"Various components. Various things. Not interesting for your business, probably. I'm sorry."

"Where are you located?"

"In Anin."

"Your address?"

"Ummm," she hesitated. "Feliksowa Street."

"The number?"

"There's nothing here you could want," she said.

"I have friends that might be interested. What products do you sell?"

"Machined steel products. For factories, for industrial equipment. Gears, bearings. Steel products." I could hear her patience evaporating. "Things like that. Is that all?"

"The number. On Feliksowa?" I gave her a laugh. "I'll send you a card when I open my shop. What's your name?"

"Irena," she said. "Number sixty-five. Good luck." She hung up.

It was late in the day now and nearly dark, but I wanted to find Feliksowa Street and locate Rapid Trading. I doubted there would be much to learn from a building, but I supposed that's what a detective would do, and my call to the place was making me feel like a private eye.

Since I had no idea where Feliksowa Street was located, I went back to my hotel to retrieve my old map of Warsaw from my bag. But the map included only the fringe of the Anin district, and no Feliksowa Street was listed in the index. I would have to take a bus to the area and find my way by asking. At the bus stop on the street that was now called Avenue Solidarity, I waited, buffeted by the eastbound traffic roaring off the bridge from central Warsaw. A light mist was falling and the streets were hissing and wet. The bus stops along Targowa Street were thronged, the buses late and over-loaded. Finally, I shouldered my way onto a bus for Anin.

I got off near the railway station and asked for directions. After three inquiries someone pointed me in the direction of Feliksowa Street. The instructions were none too precise, but the woman who guided me was sure the street was in an area where new houses and buildings were under construction. It was now fully dark. The railway station was in a neighborhood of old houses, small and poor, with cluttered yards and gnarled untended fruit trees, the sort of houses that were once nearly rural, with old collapsing grape arbors and barren rosebushes. The streets were of rutted black cinder, but at least were signposted at every corner. I followed a zig-zag course, and the intersections grew farther apart. There was no traffic on the streets, no one out walking, or no one close enough to ask directions. At last I noticed houses under construction, the cinder streets rutted more deeply by the trucks that hauled in bricks and lumber. In front of one building site I saw a man loading tools into a van. When I approached him he jerked upright, startled. He told me Feliksowa was one or two streets farther east.

It was an older street, but with a mixture of newer buildings finished in white stucco. Some of these were evidently businesses, though their outward appearance offered no clue as to what sort of commerce they carried on. At last I found a number on the pillar of an old two-story house. I marched on. Number 65 was a newer building, with a balcony on the second floor, where dead plants drooped from window boxes. A low wall ran around the front, with a wrought-iron gate and an intercom buzzer glowing on the pillar. There were two buttons on the box: the name Patek and Rapid Trading. I assumed Patek occupied the upstairs apartment. No lights were visible in the downstairs half of the building. The street was dark, but several cars were parked nearby on the street, including a dirty black Mercedes, several years old, a Russian Lada, a Skoda, and a baby Fiat.

What had I expected to find out here? After pushing the buzzer for Rapid Trading, I stood in the silence of the street and then ventured to look into the cars. Through the Lada's window, I could see a rumpled map on the back seat, along with some newspapers and a cloth cap. Except for a full ashtray, the Mercedes was empty.

"What do you think you're doing?" The voice barked from the gate behind me, and I nearly fell over backward as I stood up straight from the window of the Mercedes.

"If you don't back away from that car, I'll shoot you."

I backed away and turned around.

He was a stocky man in a leather coat. I couldn't see his hands, but I had no doubt he could shoot me.

"Pardon me," I said. "I rang the buzzer."

He swung the gate ajar. One hand was bunched in his pocket. He stared straight at me, menacingly.

"You rang the buzzer and then you look into the car? Who are you? What are you doing?"

"I was looking for Rapid Trading."

"It is closed now, of course. Why are you looking for Rapid Trading after working hours? You have some business in the middle of the night?"

"I spoke to Pani Irena today. By telephone."

"Yes, and she told you to come here at night?" He glanced up and down the street, and seemed to relax, apparently deciding I was no threat to him or, now that he was present, to the cars either. I realized that he had good enough reason to be suspicious: car theft was rampant everywhere.

"I am making an inquiry for a friend," I said. "I wanted to see where you were located."

"At night?" He stepped closer.

"Yes," I said quickly. "I just wanted to find your office, that's all."

He looked hard at me. "So you found it. Now go away and come back during business hours."

"All right. Thank you."

"What is your inquiry?"

"It's someone who worked here once . . ." I wasn't sure what I was asking.

"I see," he said. "You're a driver . . . you want to drive?"

"Ummm." A noncommital mumble. "Maybe," I said. "Maybe, yes."

"You have a car?"

"No. Or maybe. Soon."

He laughed. "I see. Not yet."

"Yes." It seemed to be the right answer.

"Come tomorrow. After eight."

"All right."

"Then good night."

I walked up the road, north, not the way I had come, but back toward the station. I glanced back, when I was safely up the street. He was still standing where I left him, watching. After this, his vigil would probably bring him to the gate every half hour until dawn. He said he'd shoot me, a preposterous idea, but I didn't dismiss it. Once only the police had guns. The "militia," they were called, because it evoked the idea that there was no domestic crime, only subversives working on us from within. It was more or less true; the absence of crime was a mystery of Communism. Now weapons were sold in the market, gas guns with CO_2 cartridges that fired pellets and were not supposed to be lethal and therefore fell outside firearms laws. But firearms changed hands now too, and stories in the newspapers recounted sensational shootouts with police. Probably the new traders sold guns, Soviet army pistols brought across the border wrapped in baby clothes and hidden under the faked-up icons and the electric drills, and swapped among truck drivers at roadside rest stops. Yes, the man at the gate probably did have a gun.

In the morning, the hotel awakened early. The hallways creaked with footsteps. I could hear the occupant of the room above mine pacing back and forth, three steps this way, pause, two steps back. I lay listening for a while, thinking of my time here, my small room and my roommates. I thought about going to see them. Did Czesław still cry in his sleep? Did the girl in the tram, the dark-eyed angel, ever alight to search for me at the coffee house across from the university? Did she ever walk in and survey the room to see if the boy from the country was sitting there waiting for her?

I crawled out of bed, dressed, got coffee and a slice of bread across the street, and headed for the tram stop. It was cold, windy, and gray. Even the school kids, clambering aboard the bus, were hushed by the raw weather. I changed buses once, and rode directly to Anin. Now, in daylight, I could see that the neighborhood had transformed itself into an enteprenurial district. Plots were cleared and under construction, piles of sand and concrete blocks isolated the aged houses, the ones with chickens in the yards, and coops in back for pet pigeons—a hobby of old men. Late-model cars eased past me, their drivers cautious with these proud acquisitions, not wanting to scrape the undercarriages on the cinder street's heaved surface. More cars lined the wall now in front of the Rapid Trading building. The Lada was gone; the Mercedes was parked on the opposite side. I pressed the button on the intercom. As the buzzer sounded, I pushed the gate and walked to the door at the side of the house.

The impression of polished crispness offered by the small brass plaque on the gate dissolved in the interior: an anteroom with walls of dull green, like a hospital corridor, dimly lit by a flickering florescent tube, three straight-backed metal chairs with chipped paint, a half-closed door leading into a hallway. I stood for a moment, coughed, scraped my feet on the linoleum floor to announce my presence. I could hear voices. A middle-aged woman, balancing a cup of tea on a saucer, leaned through the door.

"Can I help you?" she asked.

"I'm from Jadowia town," I said.

"Yes?"

"Where Mr. Jabłoński lives . . . ?" I could see no reaction in her face. What to say next? I wondered. Improvise, stall. "I thought," I went on, "I might see Mr. . . ."

Still no reaction. She was letting me stammer on.

"Mr. . . ." I rubbed at my forehead, giving my impression of a failed memory. What was I doing here?

"Mr. Bielski?" she offered.

"Yes," I said, relieved to get something out of her. "Yes, I think. Maybe Mr. Bielski."

"Have a seat."

She left, the door closing after her. I sat and listened to the ring of telephones, but no voices penetrated the door. A man in a leather coat bustled in from outside, entered the offices, and closed the door behind him. He was not the man I had seen the night before. He seemed to give me the once-over as he passed, and I was conscious of looking out of place. I did not want to feel conspicuous. Tomek had come back from the city once wearing a leather jacket. It wasn't a long leather coat like this man wore. My own fake wool plaid coat was the product of some state-run factory, a peasant's coat to go with my farmer's outdoors face, my shaggy haircut. My shoes were black, round-toed, heavy-soled. Farmer shoes. I was a bumpkin in the city, from a country village where the houses had coal stoves and no telephones, and I slopped pigs and milked cows and had big nicked-up farmer's hands to prove it. I looked at them—thick fingers, chipped nails that remained grimy no matter how much I washed. I shoved them in my pockets and tucked my feet under my chair so I couldn't see the round toes of my shoes.

After about fifteen minutes, a secretary stepped out and beckoned me to follow. She led me to an office where a broad-shouldered man with a high forehead and thinning black hair was talking on the telephone. "He can go screw himself," he said into the telephone. "Listen to me. Don't worry about it. He'll know what's good for him." He motioned for me to sit down, while he kept nodding into the telephone. "Just get started and I'll take care of it. I'll speak to you later." He hung up.

"You came to see me?"

"Mr. Bielski?"

"Yes, I'm Bielski. You want a job, or what?"

"Maybe," I said. "I'm from Jadowia. My name's Maleszewski. I think a neighbor of mine worked for you."

"From where?"

"Jadowia."

"Oh," he said. "Jadowia," he said. "I suppose Jabłoński sent you."

"I know him."

"You have a car?"

"I don't know if . . . I don't know what the job is."

"Where in hell . . . ?" he said. He was looking for something on his desk, barely paying attention to me. "You can drive? You have a license?"

"Yes."

"I don't have a goddamn fleet here, you know. It would help if you had a car. I told Jabłoński that."

The secretary stuck her head around the door. "Berlin," she announced.

He stared at the phones on his desk—there were three of them—then excused himself and left the office. I could hear his voice echoing down the hall, but not clearly enough to make out what he was saying. I sat there, studying his desk piled with papers and notepads. A couch filled the wall behind me, and a set of dirty coffee cups was spread on the table in front of it. The furniture was new, along with the desk, done in black-painted pine, the sort of office furniture that was newly on the market. The room still smelled faintly of fresh paint. I wanted to rifle the papers on the desk, but I was afraid Bielski or his secretary would catch me doing it. I was about to lean forward to see what I could read upside down when Bielski appeared in the door.

"Can you come back tomorrow?" he asked. "I've got to go out now, but I may have something for you. You're sure you have a license?"

I started to show him, but he waved this off. "Never mind. I have to go. Where are you staying?"

I told him.

"There's a place on Brzeska Street," he said. "Cheaper. Near the market. Sometimes my people stay there. Give me your name again."

I told him, then asked, "Did Tomek Powierza work for you?"

"Who's he?" Bielski was gathering up his papers, not really listening to me.

"My neighbor," I said. "From Jadowia. Maybe he worked for you."

He pocketed a ring of keys and plucked a pack of cigarettes from his desk drawer.

"He was killed," I said.

"Killed?"

"Yes. Did you know him?"

Bielski scanned his desktop as though he had forgotten something. "Never heard of him. What's his name?"

"Powierza. Tomek Powierza."

"Never heard of him." He slapped the desk drawer shut. "Come back tomorrow, okay?"

He hurried to the door and held it open.

I found the place Bielski mentioned. It wasn't a hotel, strictly speaking, more a cross between a rooming house and the worker's hostel where I lived before. It had survived the war, a four-story building of dark crumbling brick at the lower end of Brzeska Street, south of the market. Brzeska was a legendary street in Praga, the habitat of thieves and bootleggers. A dirty yellow sign in the building's front window advertised rooms. A gray-faced man wheezed over my money— half the price of my other room— and slid a key toward me. The hallway he guarded like a troll exhaled the odors of sausage and boiled cabbage. I found my third-floor cubicle, barely larger than a closet, equipped with a table, chair, and sagging bed covered by a foam-pad mattress.

Exploring, I found downstairs a common dining room with bare green walls and four tables, and behind this lay the kitchen, where a deep sink was draped with drying rags and a four-burner cooker stood streaked with stains. It was midafternoon, and the kitchen stood was empty except for its medley of odors. I knew later it would fill up with the building's lodgers, each preparing his own supper. I had purchased no food, so I went up the street to the market, bought a chunk of cheese, some sausage, and half a loaf of bread. It was cold and windy, and ice was glazing the street. The mood of the market was foul, quarrelsome, like the weather. Two ranks of Russians faced each other with their trinkets, gadgets, strange collections of tools. I purchased a pair of wire cutters for the price I paid for my bread. The Russians argued back and forth, stoic in their bleak setting, used to harder times and harsher cold than this. Back in my room, I sprawled on my bed and fell quickly asleep. I dreamed, the way I do sometimes if I sleep in the daytime, as though floating in an unaccustomed space, and not entirely surrendering my weight to the bed. I dreamed of Tomek. I saw him standing in a rank with the Russian peddlers, wearing, like them, a fur cap that disguised his features, so that at first I did not recognize him, nor he me. He seemed older and gaunt, his nose red with cold, eyes a bright, glittering blue, his face darkened by whiskers. He was selling a selection of hex wrenches and feeler gauges, spread out in both hands like fans, and I pressed forward, trying to approach him, trying to shoulder aside the crowd swollen around him, frantic to purchase his wrenches and gauges. As soon as one buyer departed, two others moved into the vacant space. I could not reach him or make him hear me.

I awoke in darkness and noise, not comprehending for a moment where I was. Light from the hallway leaked in under my door. Footsteps sounded on the stairs, loud Russian voices approached and receded.

I fumbled for the light, a dim yellowish bulb on a shaky table by the bed, and collected my provisions from the market. The hallway smelled of fresh cooking, and I followed the scent and the voices down the stairs to the kitchen. The tables were all occupied, the air thick with cigarette smoke. Conversations quieted as I entered, but only for a moment. I spotted two empty chairs at one table and approached, nodding at the two men already there. A torn loaf of bread, an oily tin of sprats, and four bottles of beer were arranged between them. One of the men motioned, palm upward, toward the empty chairs. I sat. After a watchful pause, they talked on in

Russian. I supposed they were trading together, sharing room and food. I unwrapped my sausage and bread, found a knife on the shelf near the sink, and sliced the kielbasa. The Russians finished their sprats, dabbed bits of bread into the oil, and drained off their beer. One of them, his face fleshy, his eyes red and stricken as if by the distance from his home, gazed at the slices of sausage on the paper in front of me. His eyes met mine and then flicked away. I slid the paper toward him. "Please," I said.

"Nie," he said, "Thanks." He used the shortened form of the Polish, the way Russians always said it.

They got up then, picked up their things, and departed, leaving behind crumbs from their bread. Conversations around the room continued. I ate slowly and watched. Bottles materialized on two of the tables, the smoke thickened. One table in the corner—it was graced with two bottles of vodka—seemed to radiate the largest influence and the loudest talk. Men from the other tables found reason to stop over and accept a splash from one of the bottles. One man there, large-chested and loud, clearly commanded some authority from the others. He was the talker among them. The others listened, nodding, murmuring *"da, da,"* then burst out laughing as he finished his story and hoisted his glass, deadpan, like a comedian. Vodka was poured all around, and cigarettes were lighted up. Finally, as the bottles were emptied, only this table, with the thick-chested talker and one companion, remained occupied. It was then that I heard the phrase "Feliksowa Street," and I realized, at the same time, that I had heard the phrase earlier in the conversation as well, although I had not recognized it in the welter of Russian. Bielski, after all, had sent me here from Feliksowa Street. Were these his people? I wadded up my paper, swept up my crumbs, and carried the knife back to the sink to wash it, passing slowly and close to the table.

"Good evening, sir," said the thick-chested man. He spoke in Polish.

"Good evening to you," I replied. Deliberately, I washed the knife. When I finished, he was watching me. He seemed voluble, flush-faced, conversational, a little drunk.

"How is Poland?" I asked.

"Expensive."

"Full of Poles," said the man—small, sharp-faced and blond—across the table from him. He leaned forward on his elbows, swirling the silver liquid in his smudged glass.

"Sit," said the big man. "My name is Valentin."

"Leszek. Thank you."

"Yuri," said the other one. We shook hands.

"Drink?"

"Okay." He poured.

"To freedom," he said, and laughed. "To perestroika."

"To free trade," said Yuri. We drank. The vodka caught my breath. I coughed, nearly spraying the table.

"You don't like?" Valentin asked. My throat burned.

"Is Polish vodka," Valentin said. "Better than Russian shit. No vodka in Russia now. Very expensive."

"Gift of Gorbachev," said Yuri.

"Like gasoline now," Valentin said. "Russian vodka is like gasoline. Cleans out your valves."

Yuri laughed and slapped his palm flat on the table. Valentin smiled faintly. I felt the heat in my stomach.

"Where are you from?" I asked.

"Near Moscow," Valentin said. "Have you been there?"

I told them I had never been anywhere in the Soviet Union. Yuri said I was lucky.

"How long have you been here?" I asked.

"Two weeks," Valentin said. "This time. But we come often. For trade."

I said I had heard them mention Feliksowa Street. Did they work for a company there? I asked. They glanced at me, then at each other, and I hurried on.

"I saw a Mr. Bielski there and I might work for him," I said. "Do you know a Mr. Bielski? From Feliksowa Street?"

"Mr. Bielski. Yes, Mr. Bielski," Valentin said.

"What do you do for him?"

"Help make him rich," Yuri said.

"Various things," Valentin said. "Trading. Have another drink." He poured.

"I will take some Polish vodka home," Yuri said. "And kielbasa. Many kilos of kielbasa. Almost as good as money. But harder to carry."

"Russians make shitty sausage now too," Valentin said.

"They forgot how," Yuri said. "My grandfather used to make it but that's when he had pigs. My childhood. I last saw a pig in my childhood."

"Now your grandfather makes tractors."

"You can't eat tractors," Yuri said. "Anyway, he's dead now."

Yuri filled the glasses again.

"I'm ready to go home," he said. "It's a shithole, but home. I want to raise pigs, make sausage, like my ancestors."

"You're drunk," Valentin said. "You don't know which end of a pig to feed."

"Is okay," said Yuri. "The pigs know. Your health. To pigs."

I drank. It went down better this time. The alcohol warmed its way to my stomach and seemed, once there, to glow, like a liquid coal. All right, I thought, I would take my time. I had been drunk once in my life. Ironically, it was with Tomek. He had stolen a bottle from the blacksmith's coal shed, and we drank it in a barn, with another boy from the village. I remembered summer sunlight slanting through the boards of the hayloft. For a while I had felt like I could fly; then I threw up.

Yuri rambled on, waxing sentimental, talking of pigs, his grandfather, Russians and their land, memories of mushroom hunting and birch forests. Valentin egged him on, then debunked the sentimentality.

"They're all radioactive now, your mushrooms," he said. "They give you cancer."

"Drink," said Yuri.

"Your health," Valentin said to me.

"To mushrooms," said Yuri.

"To pigs."

"Free trade."

They jibed on that way, and I listened, not quite staying with them shot-for-shot, but close. After an hour or more, the gray-faced old clerk flicked the lights, and we tottered up the stairs to their room.

Packed duffel bags were piled in the corner, and Valentin kicked dirty clothes out of the way. He pulled another bottle from one of the bags. There were two beds in the room, sagging cots like mine, and a chair. Valentin offered me the chair. *"Pozhalzta,"* he said.

We sat. Yuri poured. My legs felt numb.

"So," Valentin said, "you driver? For Bielski? Is interesting work."

"You have gun?" Yuri asked.

"No. I need a gun?"

"No," Valentin said. "Yuri likes toys. Is not necessary."

"Can get you gun," Yuri said. "Is better to have gun. Insist on gun."

"Why would I need a gun?" I asked. "Is this dangerous work, driving?"

"Well," Valentin said, "you are on the roads, sometimes at night. It is a precaution, but not necessary. Yuri is dramatic."

I asked them what it was they delivered, driving for Bielski.

"Small machined units," Valentin said.

"Components," said Yuri.

"Of what?" I asked.

"Various steel products," said Yuri.

"For reexport," said Valentin.

"For reexport where they are wanted."

"They are always wanted," said Valentin.

"There is always a demand," said Yuri.

"You talk like you deal opium," I said.

"Is like opium, yes," said Valentin.

"That's good, opium," said Yuri. He laughed loudly. "You have it, you want more. But you don't smoke it, you don't inject it." He laughed again.

"You put it straight into the bloodstream," said Valentin. They were having fun with this now, playing with their riddle for my benefit. My brain, by this point, was nearly as numb as my legs. Valentin refilled the glasses. Yuri was still laughing.

"Straight in the bloodstream," he said. His face was red as he laughed and coughed at the same time. "In the belly." He reached for the cigarette in his mouth, but it stuck to his lip and dropped straight into his vodka glass. "Fuck," he said, in English.

"The skull is good, too," said Valentin. Yuri fingered the butt out of his vodka and quickly slogged back the glass, ashes and all.

A wave of nausea overtook me. The dirty brown carpet and yellow walls threatened to whirl. I fixed my eyes on the lamp and held them there while they rattled on. The nerves in my face tingled. I thought I might vomit. I clutched the sides of the chair and held on.

"You don't look well, my friend," said Valentin. "You need some sausage. Do you have some sausage, Yuri?"

Yuri rummaged in a bag. When I looked up again, he was holding out a slice of fatty sausage between his thumb and the blade of his pocket knife. Pig fat with vodka, a country custom. I ate it. What was I doing here? I sat for a while as Yuri and Valentin conversed in Russian. I did not try to pay attention. After a while Valentin lifted the window. My head cleared and the surge of nausea ebbed. What *was* I doing here? Yuri and Valentin seemed to be arguing about something, almost quietly, as though out of deference for my reeling head. I thought of my grandfather's joke about shooting at Russians. I liked these two men. They had been friendly to me. The chill air from the window braced me.

"Do you know Tomek Powierza?" I asked, interrupting their conversation.

"Who's he?" Valentin asked.

"A friend. Maybe he worked for Bielski. He was from my village. A Pole. Did you know him? He might have delivered things for Bielski."

Both expressions were blank.

"Many people work for Bielski," Valentin said.

"Did you ever hear of anyone who worked for him who got killed? Murdered?"

The two Russians looked at each other silently. Valentin shook his head no.

"Insist on gun," Yuri said. "If they don't give you, come see Yuri. I fix you."

"You never heard of him?" I insisted. I looked from one face to the other; their lack of recognition seemed genuine.

"No," said Valentin.

The medicinal bacon fat had ceased working its magic. All I wanted now was to lie down, to sleep. Unsteadily, I rose to leave, and my hosts steadied me to the door, murmuring encouragement and friendship. I managed the stairs with their help, unlocked my door, and, once inside, threw open the window and thrust my head outside: cold air tinged with coal fumes but free, at least, of cigarette smoke. A thin slice of street gleamed icily four floors below. A taxi passed, then a police car. Then nothing. It was late. A cat pressed itself into a doorway, and grainy snow swirled across the wedge of pavement. My breath plumed into the darkness. The clatter of a garbage can rattled somewhere, echoing along the walls of the alley below me. The whole city seemed asleep, except for police and taxi drivers and men coughing in smoke-filled rooms like the one below me. Deal-makers. I wondered if, somewhere across the river, the new president was still up, wishing to have a drink with his old intellectual friends, or with drivers of forklifts from the shipyards. President Lech, grown portly, yearning to drive the roads at night, the way he used to, or drink a vodka with George Bush, his new friend. Or reliving his toast to the Queen of England, his speech before the American Congress. Imagine! An ordinary Polish man, born in a bog. They liked that in America, a president born in a swamp, at home in the country, in forests, beside rivers, fishing. He liked fishing.

But not hunting.

Only Communist presidents went hunting. Brezhnev. Zhivkov. Gierek. In the ancient forest, Białowieża, with a retinue of assistants, sighting down on the bison, the wild pigs. Guns blazing.

Could it be guns?

Slowly, my head cleared.

Of course, it was guns.

It would make sense: they would go east from Poland.

Probably from a small-arms plant somewhere. It was well known they were going broke. It had been in the newspapers. Old customers were now off-limits. They wanted to manufacture sewing machines now, but they had no customers for those, either.

From Poland into the confusion of the Soviet republics, where anything was possible and all borders leaked. Armenia. Azerbaijan. Or on to Croatia. Sri Lanka. To the Kurds. Who could know? Maybe Belfast. Yuri was right, there were never enough. There would be always buyers. And here, in Poland, whole factories full of guns with no place to sell. Except perhaps to Valentin and Yuri. Or Bielski.

But Tomek? It was easy enough to imagine him in an activity that might, strictly speaking, skirt the law, in some small way. Smuggling a case of liquor, slipping deutsche marks into the expectant palm of a border guard. But something truly dangerous? Something as serious as guns? That was a new leap, and my head swam with its implications.

I crept into bed, too far gone to shed my clothes.

Valentin and Yuri had vanished in the morning, at least by seven o'clock, when I got up. I wolfed down dry bread and tea on the street by the market, then headed directly to Anin. A moment after I walked in the door at Rapid Trading, Bielski emerged from the inner office with a group of men. One of them, I thought, I might have seen at the hotel the night before, speaking with Yuri and Valentin. I didn't have long to study him. When Bielski saw me, he told the other men to go ahead. Then he turned to me.

"I spoke with Jabłoński," he said.

"Yes?" I answered.

"He knows who you are, but he did not send you here. You don't work for him."

"I didn't say I did."

"Well, you don't work for me either. Go back to your farm."

He held the door. For a moment, I didn't move.

"Did you know Tomek Powierza?" I said.

"All I know, my friend, is that you're leaving. Right now. And don't come back."

The man in the long leather coat slid into the room behind Bielski and stood watching. I edged through the door.

"I just want to ask you about my neighbor," I said.

"Good-bye," Bielski said.

My retreat was accompanied by the percussion of slamming car doors. At the hotel, Yuri and Valentin were not in their room. When I asked the old man downstairs, he said they had left.

I picked up my bag and hurried to the station to catch the train home, feeling strangely fugitive, perhaps even embarrassed. I had found out next to nothing. And now, obviously, my clumsy inquiries had been reported back to Jabłoński. I didn't consider that an advantage. The train was late and crowded with men who looked defeated by the city. I was fitting company for them.

CHAPTER SIX

Naczelnik Farby reserved for the meetings of the village maintenance council his full attention and paper-distributing seriousness,
but he always made a point to arrive five minutes late, bursting into
the drab meeting room at the back of the village "cultural center"
with a brusque, businesslike rush. Zofia Flak, reliable as usual, had
alerted him so that he had plenty of time to walk across the square
from the town offices. He had been sitting at his desk leafing
through a magazine that interspersed articles about cars—how to
repair and tune them—with photographs of nearly nude women.
The captions under the photos identified the girls as Polish, but
Farby suspected the pictures were really of girls from Sweden or
Germany or some other place where the women were decadent and
blond, because he didn't believe there were that many women with
such large breasts in all of Poland. Of course, he mused, Zofia's bust
would qualify for inclusion, but she would never consent to such a
thing. The thought inspired a moment of daydreaming which
Zofia herself interrupted to announce that it was time for the council meeting. So he killed five more minutes going to the toilet,
pulling on his coat and hat, and then returning to his desk for the
necessary papers. He crossed the square, slowly at first, then quickened his pace so that he would arrive with the requisite air of harried authority.

The regular members were present: Barski, the druggist, on the
front row, whispering to Klużewski, the greengrocer; three farmers,
Hajnek, Halski, and Halek, the three Hs, who sat on the third row,

as usual, with one seat between them. There was Mrs. Gromek, the retired secretary to the main village council, whose short, iron-colored hair and fierce eyes made her look like Stalin without a mustache; a veteran of such meetings, her expression was an advance rebuke for every procedural error. Behind her slouched Niechowski, the hardware store manager; and, next to him, Ortowski, who worked at the Farmers' Co-op and was, effectively, Jabłoński's ears at the meeting. Farby marched briskly to the front table and immediately sensed an unusual quiet among the members. He dropped the bulging folder of papers on the table and sat down to face the group.

"We have a long-standing situation here to dispose of," Farby said. He scanned the room, saw that Barski and Klużewski had begun whispering. "If we're ready to open our business."

"The minutes," Mrs. Gromek interrupted.

"Oh, yes, the minutes. Mr. Barski, the minutes."

Barski read the minutes from the last meeting.

"Okay," Farby said when he finished, "now the drainage ditches on the Węgrów Road." He opened his sheaf of papers, walked along each row of seats, and, licking his thumb, counted out the sheets.

"You will find—is Korczak here today? No? Okay, you will find the previous action summarized here for your reference."

The sheets traveled down the rows and the members scrutinized them, finding nothing they could exactly remember, although it was true, as Farby said, hours had been consumed in discussions of the drainage ditch along the Węgrów Road and, possibly, resolutions to commend the matter for further study.

"Węgrów Road drainage ditch passes Sunshine Marsh and the Słowik Creek," Farby recited. He had resumed his place at the chairman's table and replaced the extra copies of the "Summary of Action" onto the piles of documents arranged in front of him. He continued reading. "Due to heavy rains last summer, and the burdensome workload of the village crews, the work was not completed. That is, it was not started. The work was inspected by the crew supervisor—I believe the inspections were done in July and again in August. In July, it was said the ditches were too wet and in

August they had insufficient personnel because of commitments and the work-crew holiday schedule."

"Mr. Naczelnik." This was Klużewski. "Why are the works department supervisors always allowing their people to go on holidays when there is important work to be done?"

Klużewski's term of service on the maintenance council extended back to the days when Farby was in secondary school. He knew the answer very well: Holidays were holidays, and the crews were paid whether they did their work or not.

"Yes, Naczelnik," insisted Halek's voice from the farmers' row. "Klużewski has a point. And why are we talking about this now, when winter is just arriving and the weather is cold, and the works inspector will just say the frozen ground prevents them from working?"

A murmur of assent swelled in the room. Farby was taken slightly aback. This was only routine stuff. He was not used to voices being raised at this meeting. "We cannot manage to change vacation schedules," Farby said. "These, as you know, are set far in advance." He bent over his file folder, searching for something.

"The bastards don't work even when they are not on vacation." Farby didn't respond, but he could recognize Niechowski's voice. Jesus, he thought, what's got into these people today?

"All right, all right," Farby said. He found the piece of paper and straightened up, holding it in front of him, aware, meanwhile, of a general titter flitting over the room. They were, he realized with a pinprick of alarm, having fun at his expense.

"You will see by my memorandum," he announced, eyes squinting as he studied the page, "that the council, on my motion"—he paused to let the reference to his initiative sink in—"on my motion, duly approved, complained about the ditches not being cleared in July, when the kilometer of road between Kowalski's barn and the Sunshine Marsh was flooded. A copy of the motion was forwarded to Korczak at the maintenance office." Farby stared at the room over the paper's edge. "I have noted that Korczak is not here today." Why not let Korczak, he thought, take this heat? He hastened on.

"As a result of the action of this council—and my further personal inquiry on this matter—as a result of this, and my own order, another inspection was done in August." Farby dropped the paper to the table and regarded the assembly with an expression of satisfaction.

"But in August it was dry!" This was Halek again. He lived out by the Węgrów road and remembered its flooding well. Based on past experience, he had every reason to expect the road would become virtually impassable again this spring, as soon as the clogged ditches backed up again.

"Yes, it was dry in August," Farby said. "The inspection report so states it was dry." He could not suppress the note of counterattack in his voice. What, he wondered, was going on here?

"So did they think it would never rain again?" Niechowski asked.

"If it was dry, why didn't they do the work then?"

"Motion!"

"One moment," Farby said, holding his hand up, palm outward, like a stop sign.

"It's time to get rid of them!"

"Hear, hear!"

"Just a moment! The work crews have to have their holiday time. August has always been their holiday time."

Laughter erupted from several voices at once—barking, derisive laughter.

"Motion!"

"He ought to be reprimanded."

"Fire him!"

Farby, feeling the blood of anger pounding at this temples, held fistfuls of paper, reports, old motions, in both hands, glaring at the council members, who all seemed to be talking at once. He thought, for a panicked moment, they meant him.

"Fire who?" he said.

"Korczak!"

A flood of gratitude, of relief, washed over him. Of course, this council could not fire a town *naczelnik;* he knew that. But they could always make trouble, and these were not times to be courting trouble. Korczak! Yes, Korczak, of course! A reprimand! That should do it.

"Is there a motion to enact a formal reprimand to forward to Mr. Korczak as head of the maintenance department?" Farby's voice, gathering composure after a shaky start, assumed the tone of a judge asking the accused to rise for the jury's verdict.

"Fire him!"

"Is there a motion?" Farby intoned.

"Motion!"

Jabłoński, he thought, had to have been behind this. Mrs. Gromek, the old troll, would not have joined in this anarchy without a cue from Jabłoński. Farby, still flushed and wondering how he would draft a meaningless reprimand to Korczak, walked back across the square to his office, now genuinely hurrying, mostly out of anger. As he rounded the corner approaching the office, he saw Twerpicz dart out the door and set off briskly in the opposite direction, away from the center of the village, as though he wanted to avoid seeing anyone. Was this absurd? As Twerpicz scuttled along, Farby saw him glance back over his shoulder. Farby resisted the urge to shout at him, the way he might shout at a thief. "You little bastard," he muttered. He hurried on to his office. Zofia was standing at her desk, a puzzled look on her face. She clutched a piece of paper in her hand.

"What is it, Zofia?"

"Twerpicz was here," she said. "He's demanding to see some records."

"What records?"

"He brought a letter. From the Citizens' Committee."

"He did?"

"He says they demand to see the records on the village road department. Specifically, it says, 'contracts with and bills from suppliers.'"

"To hell with him."

"And records of production at the distillery."

Farby tried to speak, but his cottony throat allowed only a feeble croak. He tried again.

"Zofia," he rasped, "I love you."

Later that night, thinking of it for the tenth time, reliving it in every detail, he saw her seem to melt before his eyes. She had dropped the paper from Twerpicz on the desk. She walked toward him, took his hand, and led him to his own office. She closed the door, still holding his hand, and, as the latch closed, she pressed herself against him. She was softness and amplitude, generosity and goodness. He could feel her warmth through the fine wool of her sweater.

The moment did not last long—someone bumbled into the outer office, coughing loudly—but it sealed everything. He had looked down at her eyes. They filmed with tears, tears of happiness, and he thought he could feel the rapid beat of her heart. She composed herself and stepped outside to confront the altered world.

Now, at home, sitting alone while his wife slept in the bedroom, Farby tried to think of what he must do. It was clear that Jabłoński was going to sacrifice him. He had not spoken to Jabłoński; that would gain him nothing. He would have no more humiliation. Now he would protect himself. Most of all, he would protect what he had begun to think of as his "new" self, his new life, his life with Zofia. He could take Jabłoński's betrayal. He was worried, yes, but he felt a new energy. Strength! Courage! In the near darkness his chest expanded, his jaw firmed. For the first time in years, he thought, he began to feel—almost—happy.

When it was quiet enough in the distillery, Czarnek could hear the barley sprout. He had discovered this years before, down in the malting room—a damp, warm space, hazed with light filtering through the dusty basement windows, an enclosure with a clean concrete floor spread over with germinating grain that released a smell like earth. The odor was like bloom and rot mingled, a scent like the forest floor when you raked back the leaves with your fingers and exposed the dirt below. It was a smell that was thick with process, not clean, not dirty, but imperative, necessary, real. Czarnek thought that if some great natural force, like gravity, had a smell, it would be like this, something both complicated and yet fundamental. An ancient process, described (he was once told) in the Egyptian Book of the Dead: the barley spread, dampened, sifted by shovel. And so here. Starch to sugar to enzyme. Cells dividing, building, layer on layer. If he watched carefully, as now, sitting motionless on the floor with his back resting against the wall, he could see it happening, the minute movement, like spots before his eyes. The sound he heard was like the ticking of a tiny watch.

A bushel of barley transformed itself here to nearly two bushels of germinated seed. Diastase enyzme malt added to potato starch converted to simple sugar, mixed then with yeast for fermentation in vats of five hundred gallons—and twenty-four hours of its self-generated boil, throwing off yards of carbon dioxide that rolled up out of the tanks, an invisible cloud whose atmospheric weight caused it to fall and accumulate at the floor, forcing the oxygen above it. The fermentation room had no trouble killing a cat, locked in all night, and would kill a cow as easily.

Ferment, boil and flow, hydraulics and chemistry, molecules broken down, reformed, chains with new links, water and ethyl alcohol, first cousins related by an interchange of atoms, carbon and hydrogen. Who ordained it, this reshuffling? Was it decay, or growth? Czarnek sat in the middle of it, an alchemist by virtue of controlling the levers, surrounded by processes in which one particle of matter fed on another, became something new.

At the end, there was the product: spirit, as in a thing that has a life or a being beyond its physical aspect. Finished, it bubbled up from a spout the size of a child's finger, gently rising and falling, clean and clear as a mountain spring, locked in its glass chamber, as if venerated.

It was produced from stuff that looked, at one point, like mud. Or floor wax.

Mostly, it was poison. Another cycle of breakdown and decay.

He rested his head against the wall, closed his eyes, and breathed deeply.

If a job description existed for Czarnek's position, or were he to compose one, included under a heading such as "auxiliary procedures" would have been measures for going along and getting along with Jabłoński, the evil old ferret Marcin, and all the rest who would surely follow through the years and decades. Humor them, remain quiet, and remain employed. A tested method, whether you made vodka, tractors, or tanks. In the special genius of the system, nothing ever failed, it was merely reassessed. No one ever lost a job, except for gross insubordination. Czarnek followed the rules as he saw them, insolent on occasion, but not disobedient. And yet the system was benign only until it perceived a threat, at which point anyone was disposable. Czarnek sensed that now.

A disaster happened; he was ripe for sacrifice. A body is discovered in the woods, the "reassessment" unravels, and loose threads lead back to the distillery. To him.

Jabłoński would cover his own tracks, as usual. No piece of paper would ever lead back to him. Jabłoński had said as much, and on this matter Jabłoński's word could be relied upon. It didn't matter that half the town might regard Jabłoński as a crook; there would never be any hard proof.

Czarnek was not worried about being accused of murder, not directly. Such a possibility, he thought, stretched far beyond the realm of the plausible. In a way, the murder of Tomek Powierza was virtually irrelevant. He doubted that Jabłoński was behind it, but he would bet the distillery, if it were his to bet, that Jabłoński knew what it was about. Whatever had happened to Powierza, he was almost certain, was a matter between him and the Russians. They would not, he was sure, venture close to Jadowia again. These days, Russians were like outlaw gangs in American Westerns, riding across the border in their patched-up cars, then beating it to safety. Who could count the rackets they had their hands in?

Jabłoński's greed ran in a different direction. It was power that mattered to Jabłoński, influence, his name, his ability to be a player in the village. It didn't matter to him how small the pond was. Jadowia was simply his playing field, his little arena. He had been involved here most of his adult life. If conditions changed, he would change with them, maybe even ahead of them. He would prosper, if that was to be the new measure of success. Surviving had been the skill that his elders in the Party passed on to him, like an inheritance. Jabłoński saw himself as the personification of the old regime, as well as its victim, undermined by its softness, its weak will, its avoidance of hard decisions.

Czarnek smelled the danger. Jabłoński would not tolerate being blocked now. If a random murder—assuming that's what it was—sparked an investigation of the distillery, then Jabłoński would help point the way, but be sure to stand clear himself, a champion of justice and an enemy of corruption. He would lead the charge, rally the forces of law and public opinion. Jabłoński would distance himself from him and Farby, let them be led off to the dock and even prison. The town would applaud. Farby was a fool. As for himself, Czarnek had no illusions. Most people, he assumed, regarded him as a dubious loner, an object of suspicion, a virtual hermit. Probably he was disliked by all who dealt with him. Their dislike was reasonable enough, Czarnek thought, for in truth he disliked all of them first, not in the specific so much as the abstract. He had disliked them since he was a child, and they him. The difference was, Czarnek knew why.

Well, it would not go according to Jabłoński's plan. Not this time. Czarnek would not let it happen. If they pursued him, he would force the whole town to remember, and that's what it disliked most.

He had begun to appear more often at this place in the forest. A hush always prevailed here. The stand of old pine, fringed by linden, hornbeam, and birch, was guarded by thickets of bare red-caned berry bushes that clawed at his sleeves as he brushed through them. Once past the thorns, there was a stillness; a predominant hue of pale blue-green he imagined as the colors of the ocean floor. The lichen that clung to the pine bark grew out from itself, layer after layer, in the sea's soft blue; the moss on the shaded sides of the tree trunks a vivid green, verging at the ground to olive. From above, watery winter light shifted though swaying needles. Wavering and remote, wind sang through the boughs. Distant sounds, the growl of a truck, a rooster crowing, arrived from no discernible direction, confused by the wind, then blown away. The hush remained.

The ground in front of Czarnek was uneven. Hummocks and depressions undulated beneath an even carpet of frost and dry pine needles in a way that was undisturbed and yet suggested the touch of a human hand; random, yet too uneven for nature's work. At the edge of the pines, Czarnek gazed over it, hands slack at his sides. His dog trotted to his side and sat.

The stones nearest him glistened, wet with melted frost, no higher than his boot tops, like dwarves under shrouds. Old men, he imagined. He saw them in black, conversing at the margins of muddy streets. They would have known each other, would have visited here many times in each other's company as, one by one, they proceeded to stay. Then back to the street, nodding, talking, arguing. He could see them in his memory, walking away, heads shaking, then pausing for another word, a closing point.

The buildings were all wooden then, with busy painted signs above and beside the doors. Shoemaker, tailor, baker, candle maker, butcher. His father sold pots and pans, lanterns, metalware, parts for coal stoves, aprons, long wooden spoons, kerosene from a tank with a brass cock worn bright by his hand, crocks and jars, nails in barrels, milk pails, shovels, pitchforks. There was a narrow door that warbled three notes on its hinges when it opened and two when it closed, a window that lowered outward and fastened with a hook to make a street-side counter in summer. On warm days the village would be quieter than usual because the farmers and their families were busy in the fields, days when all the shutters on the block would be open, and his father would be out, circulating, talking, his eye on the door for the important customer, and his mother inside behind the counter, sitting usually, for this hour or so of her husband's conversations in the street. She sewed, mended socks, waited on customers, and instructed her son as he dusted the shelves and swept the floors, the broomstick two feet taller than he was. She wore a scarf over her hair, and sometimes he would look up and catch her, watching him, her hands motionless in her lap. Then, as though apprehended in her admiration of him, she would correct. "Sweep in the corner, Chaim," she would say. "Sweep."

Chaim. His lost life. He remembered the bottom shelves, where he would crouch out of her sight, lining up the small shiny cans of paint on dark wood shelves, imagining them as towers and battlements, fortresses, each shelf partition dividing a rival kingdom. "Rebecca, Chaim is lying on the floor," a customer would say. "Is he well?" "He is dreaming," his mother would answer. "Chaim, get up and go find your father."

And he would go out, the door hinge singing its bird's call

behind him. His father would linger up the street, in front of Gutzel's, the baker's, with Meir and Belzer and Szuster, and they would be talking business and taxes, or maybe of a traveling merchant who troubled them with news from Germany. Short men in black gabardines. Meir would leave off twisting and worrying bits of his beard and pinch his cheek when he ran up. "Momma wants you," he would say to his father.

Short men in black coats. His father had wiry, reddish hair. His mother's hair, as he remembered it, was soft and black, luminous as the bolts of satin he saw in Meir's shop. Her skin was pale and clear.

They were not here, under the pines. Nor Meir, Gutzel, Belzer, or Szuster. The squat dark stones, cloaked with wet on the forest floor, were their fathers, grandfathers, uncles, the oldest here where Czarnek stood, at the western border. Czarnek stepped father inward, the ground sagging like sponge beneath the pressure of his boots. The later stones had a more defined shape, less like low, rounded lumps, but higher, flatter, like tablets. He could not read the inscriptions. Some had fallen flat over the years and decades, and all had tilted, settling in the sandy, pine-needled earth, some mossy or etched with the flat blue spread of the lichens, drying or thriving with the seasons. The ground rose and fell. Depressions, some nearly knee-deep, marked the collapse of the box within, and the old stones leaned in on themselves, sinking toward the ground. Czarnek moved slowly among them, recognizing their arrangements like constellations, like families.

Then he stopped. There were four stones in front of him, three of them listing sideways, one fallen.

And one was missing. A dark indentation marked its place, moss and pine needles outlining a damp, empty bed of mud, pocked with the clean holes of burrowing insects, where it had lain flat for years. The stone had been picked up, removed. He inspected the ground to see if it had been heaved somewhere nearby. He did not see it. Slowly, he walked on among the stones, back and forth beneath the pines, to each corner and back again, systematically, and he did not find it. Instead, he encountered another gap, another impression of a missing stone, one of almost the same size, that also had lain flat on the ground. The mud here was drier; it had been taken before the first one. Beyond the grove of pines he saw nothing, no sign. No stones, no marks, nor tracks of wagon or truck. He searched for footprints, but then realized his own had left no trace in the fallen leaves and needles.

He stalked to the edge of the grove and stood surveying the blue-green stillness and felt a chill, a sensation approaching alarm or anger, as if he had returned to his house and discovered it had been entered and robbed.

Christmas and New Year's came and went; January settled in with its mists and murky skies. Father Tadeusz considered the holiday celebrations in the church strangely muted, as if the village were preoccupied, fretful. It seemed concerned for the future in a way he had never quite noticed before. Perhaps, he thought, the "former days," as some called them, at least simplified life. The church was a refuge then, like a great tent raised against the overarching atheist ideology, and brought out a simpler devotion. He could anticipate Father Jerzy's reply to this observation: The people had nothing else. Often these days he debated Father Jerzy in his imagination. Strange how Jerzy could not see this result of politics, that the freer people were, the less they would rely on the church, the more they would fall away. Already in the cities, they talked about it, how the church was losing its influence, even when it worked harder to push its power in every walk of life. Priests were photographed in the national newspapers these days sprinkling holy water on new fire trucks. Father Tadeusz even checked the records against his impression that there were fewer communicants for Christmas and New Year's Mass. He was right. Attendance was down nearly 20 percent. Fewer bouquets of flowers were brought to decorate the church, and though offerings were up, this only reflected the devaluation of the currency. In real terms, they had declined almost 30 percent. Partly it was because everyone was poorer. But there was something more, too, he sensed. The people's minds were somewhere else.

"A reckoning is coming," was old Pani Dąbrowska's warning. She clasped his arm and pulled him close to her, so that her whiskery chin brushed his cheek, causing him to shy back sharply. Her breath smelled like sour milk. It was after church, New Year's Day, as he stood by the great wooden doors between the dark bell towers. "It is a tragedy of the Polish people," she said, her voice high and cracking, the rasp of a starling in a pigeon's gray coat. "They don't know the meaning of thanksgiving." She rapped her cane on the stone floor. "But it's not your fault, Father."

Until then, he hadn't supposed it was his fault. But he thought it a gift of the priesthood that wisdom approached from all corners, from the juvenile and the senile, from such riddles as chance meetings in the street, from the message that leaped out to him from a prayer book parted at random. Maybe it *was* his fault. Maybe he *had* been too complacent, too assured that the people would always find God and the church at the center of their lives, and that all he, as a priest, would have to do was administer the sacraments, unlock the doors, and wait, an occupation requiring no thought, no action, no contemplation of problems at hand. He had been absorbed, for too long, in his own ambitions for culture, for quiet scholarship, and too long nursing his disappointment at never drawing the assignment or the parish of his hopes. He stood, stock still, as Pani Dąbrowska hobbled down the steps and along the walk between the trees, the last person to leave the church (and the first to arrive). Today's messenger, he thought. Yes, he had been marking time here, sleepwalking through his last assignment. He had left no footprints. He had been daydreaming, barely conscious. He thought everything would go on as it always had, and he with it. But it wouldn't, and neither could he.

The rattling at the door caught Andrzej just as he was pulling on his sweater, ready to head toward the square. He was supposed to begin a job at the grade school, a project he had put off as long as possible. It would be nasty labor: mud, corroded pipe, and tight crawl spaces stinking of sewage; a three-day ordeal that would require another man to help—and good luck finding him, since no one wanted to work these days. The banging at the back door persisted as he struggled with his boots.

"Mr. Andrzej!"

It was Mrs. Skubyszewska, from two doors down the street. She was a white-haired woman, very old, and she lived with her husband, a victim of multiple strokes who could barely walk and whose words, when he spoke, were intelligible only to his wife. They were poor pensioners, like almost all old people, and lived surrounded by mementos of their years as teachers. Her coat was pulled tightly around her throat, gripped by one fist, and her expression was alarmed.

"Mr. Andrzej," she said, "you must come. Something has happened to our house."

Andrzej was relieved. He envisioned a frozen water pipe. An excuse to delay the school job again. He felt sorry for Mrs. Skubyszewska. His own father had been one of her pupils. Her blue-veined hand worried at the collar of her coat. Andrzej smiled at her, trying to soothe her agitation.

"All right, Pani Skubyszewska, don't worry. A broken pipe? Don't worry. I'll fix it for you."

"No pipe, Andrzej. It's our house. The what-do-you-call-it, the bottom of the house."

"All right. Let's go see."

They walked through the neighbor's back garden, Andrzej ducking under a pear tree's bare limbs, and entered the Skubyszewskas' gate.

"There," she said.

The house was a one-story wooden building with a roof of corrugated metal that appeared in the country after the war, the paint long ago flaked from its walls. The foundation was native stone, rough and rectangular, like thick flattened loaves, aged to a dark deep green, like the back of a carp. But the pattern of the old foundation was broken. Stones had fallen onto the ground, and above them was a hole, big enough for a man to crawl through. The hole appeared just above the joint in the sill, and though the wood was firm, the weight above the joint had caused the floor joists and the weatherboard to sag several inches. The window above—it was the kitchen window, Andrzej remembered—had caught in the warp and had shattered one pane of glass.

"Andrzej," Pani Skubyszewska said, "someone is making our house fall down."

Andrzej was on his haunches, peering at the hole in the foundation. "Pardon?"

"Last night," she said. She was nearly crying, and her hand continued to flutter at her coat collar. "Łukasz," she said, referring to her husband. "He heard it. Last night. Heard someone digging. He woke me up, but I thought he was dreaming." She hesitated, stifling a sob. "Andrzej," she pleaded, "what is this?"

Three days later, Karol Skalski drove to Janek Piwek's farm to inspect hog carcasses, an activity that was consuming more of his time now that farmers were allowed to sell their meat at whichever market they chose. As Karol sorted among the carcasses, gutted and splayed under a dirty canvas in Piwek's wagon, Piwek complained about something that had happened to his dairy barn.

"I don't think it was a badger," he said. "We don't have badgers here anymore, do we, Doctor?" Karol snipped off sample bits of hog flesh to examine under his microscope. Piwek jabbered incessantly, and mostly to himself.

"No, I don't think so," Karol said.

"That's what I thought too. Old Kurski, you know, he was my father's age. Been around here since Piłsudski was a pup. He ain't seen a badger for thirty years. So I told Marek, Marek, this ain't no fucking badger. Something with two legs done this."

"Done what?"

"Dug stones out of the foundation. Dug 'em out and took 'em, far as I can tell. About three of them, I think. Just carried them off. Now why the hell would anyone do that?"

Karol finished the inspection, washed off his slides under the well pump, and zipped the microscope into its canvas bag. Then he walked around the barn with Piwek to view the hole in the foundation.

"How old is this barn, Piwek?"

"Oh, hell, I don't know." Piwek scratched his whiskered chin. Two fingers were stubbed on his left hand, an accident with a milling saw. "Must be forty, forty-five years."

"You mean after the war?"

"Yeah, that's right. After the war. I don't remember much about it, except it took a long time because you couldn't get anything to build with. And my old man got drunk when he was building it and fell off the roof beam one day and broke his collarbone."

CHAPTER SEVEN

I watched as the village soaked up the sullen winter weather, its temper matching the season. Barnyard ruts were skimmed with morning ice that dissolved in the daytime drizzle. It was chill and damp, not cold enough for a cleansing blanket of snow to fall, the days remaining simply bare-limbed and dark. The bleak mood was common enough for this time of year, with the holidays past and winter stretching dully toward a distant Easter. Everyone complained. Prices were going up, the buses didn't operate, or they broke down on the way to Węgrów or Warsaw; wages were frozen. And yet along with the season's usual grumpiness and unfocused general complaint ran an undercurrent of uneasiness.

There was the business of the foundation stones, which in a few days was identified as a pattern and then as a phenomenon. As I heard it from Andrzej, the plumber, Krupik was among the last to realize that the odd discovery in his own barn had been more or less duplicated at three other places. It was Andrzej, naturally enough, who informed Krupik one morning after he had helped him push-start his police car. It had been stalled for two days. To celebrate this little success, Andrzej pulled a bottle from his canvas tool bag. As they drank, Andrzej told him about the foundations at Piwek's barn and the Skubyszewskis', and, since then, a similar discovery at the storehouse behind the bakery. Krupik was astonished.

"The same thing happened here!" Krupik said. "To me! It happened to me!"

"I know," said Andrzej.

"Come look," Krupik said, and led Andrzej to the hole he had filled in loosely with old brick.

"This happened a week ago," Krupik said. "I must have been the first victim!"

"Victim?"

"The first one it happened to." He hurried ahead of Andrzej, back to his car, its engine racing under full choke out on the road. "Excuse me, but I must now visit the other scenes."

So Krupik rushed to the Skubyszewskis, to Piwek's, and to the bakery, where he could be seen pacing around each site as he scrawled notes on a clipboard. He walked through the backyards, shook the posts of rickety fences for signs of disturbance, peered at muddy flower beds for footprints, and squatted heavily beside the damaged foundations, meditating on the mystery. He canvassed nearby houses, at least in town, but evidently failed to find anyone who could remember seeing anything remarkable or hearing an usual noise, except for old Skubyszewska, whose impaired speech required his wife's translation. For several days Krupik strode through the village, halting here and there to look up driveways and alleys. His detective work was the object of some mirth among the vodka drinkers at the bar, and the standers on the street corner in front of it, but the mystery impelling Krupik's activity became, in time, a more absorbing focus of speculation.

Karol Skalski, who refueled at the bar several times a day between his errands to surrounding farmers and his appointments at the clinic, heard much of it, which he passed on to Jola, and Jola to me. Vandalism, in the form of kids playing pranks, was the first suspicion, but then no one could figure out which of the village's teenaged boys (a small group at that) might muster enough energy to do the work involved. Digging at the foundations of old buildings seemed an odd entertainment for bored teenagers.

Animal behavior was the next suspect. Bears were mentioned, until Karol—called upon as an expert on the behavior of beasts—argued that brown bears, while now and then sighted in the forests, were unlikely to wander into towns and, if they ever did, would be more apt to root about in garbage. Wild pigs were suggested and similarly dismissed.

A two-legged culprit, or culprits, seemed the inescapable conclusion, which sparked more interesting speculation. Theft was an intriguing possibility at first, but theft of what? Even Krupik, who continued to attach high importance to his own position as the first among victims, could not seriously claim a loss among the broken tools and discarded objects in his barn. He conducted as much of an inventory of the place as his memory would allow, and dubiously listed an ax as a possible loss, although he could not explain why any thief would go to such trouble when an unlocked door was available. Among the other sites, not a single object could be identified as missing.

Clearly, it was decided, someone had to be looking for something. Something hidden. Buried money? Gold? Jewelry?

"Ghosts!" This barked declaration, or warning, rang out in the bar from gaunt Marek Bartowski, seventy-four years old, stubble-cheeked, palsied, who had possibly three teeth and a voice like chalk squeaking on a blackboard. He had been a stone mason, years ago, and had helped build the twin belfries towering over the church. Tobacco had yellowed his fingers, ruined his lungs, and shortened his once famous rants to breathless bursts. An unaccustomed stillness pervaded the smoky room, like a spread sheet falling slowly, settling in folds.

"Spirits," he croaked. "Coming back."

It didn't take long for the jokes to start up, but they were less dismissive than even Bartowski might have expected. The humor was superseded by the more prevalent question, the one that had lingered in the air after Bartowski's wheezing outburst. The silence was a slow-dawning, sinking-in kind of silence. For the mention of treasure sent the collective mind of the barroom searching back, asking the question: If it was treasure, whose was it? The answer hung there, unspoken.

Jola told me she had laughed when Karol told her what Bartowski had said, but Karol, his eyes blurred but his voice sober, had warned her. "I wouldn't laugh too hard," he said.

*   *   *

I heard this as from a distance, for Jola's head lay on my bare chest, and I was drifting, daydreaming, content. Our bed was a straw-filled mattress overlaid with one of feathers, spread on a platform of planks in a neglected hunter's shed. The light of an overcast noon, through grimy windows, concealed us with these minimal improvements. Moss and yellowed grass sprouted on the rough-sawn planks and rotting thatch of the cabin roof; dormant spider webs clung to the underside of its splintered eves, trapped dried leaves, and last summer's dead flies. This shed was our cave, for weeks now, and we curled inside it, within our own heat. The blanket, darkly red and wintry, cocooned our intertwined bodies. In the chill of the cabin I could see my breath against the light from the window, but I was thinking of spring. And summer.

In summer I led Jola to the sloping yellow field, a soft September afternoon when the leaves of the willows swayed luxuriantly over the stream and the poplar leaves flickered like mirrors in the sun. She lay back, eyes closed, her arms behind her head, as I sat beside her. The grass around us formed a hollow, hiding us. I watched a ladybug crawl up her arm and imagined, someday, a house rising from the field's crest behind us. I wondered, would it ruin the perfection of this as a producing field? Yes, she said, it is perfect, a beautiful field. Her voice was soft, sleepy. A perfect field, she said. Don't spoil it.

Wheat or rye? I asked.

Why not rye? she said dreamily.

Or wildflowers?

No, she smiled, her eyes still closed. Rye is fine.

The rye we grow produces a heavy loaf, not the light white bread of wheat flour favored by most of the world. Our bread has the weight of a small brick and a sourness that strikes the taste at the back of the tongue. Dense and earthy, it chews; made by God and old Slav kitchens to go with the gravy of pork, roasted slowly, with celery root, garlic, and onion.

In July the rye stands thigh-high and green, then, in two weeks more, with sun and dry weather, it ripples yellow in the wind. In a perfect summer you watched the sky while the ripening advanced, gold on gold; watched the clouds pass while the interest grew on the gold in the field—not in the price, which was unchanging, but because there was a time, a perfect time, an optimum day, perhaps even an optimum hour, for the cutting. I see my father, and my grandfather beside him, hip deep in the field. Grandpa would bend the heads of the rye down upon themselves, placing the tip of the head on its base, and if it broke, it was the day, the hour, the exact moment—Grandpa would declare it—to "bring the steel to the stalk." We would work together hard and without talking, intent and steady in the sun and the dust.

The arch of her foot caressed the calf of my leg. I had been asleep, dreaming.

"I'm hungry," I said. "Are you?"

"No," she said. She stirred beside me, shifted her head to the pillow.

"I was dreaming about food," I said. "And the field."

"The field?"

"Yes. About sitting there with you. Remember?"

"I saw Pani Kowalska in the bakery the other day. She said her husband was not well."

"She told you this?"

"No, she doesn't know me. She was talking to a neighbor. Complaining about him. She said he was sick and very much trouble. He cursed at her all the time, she said. The neighbor said, 'Well, maybe he'll get worse,' and they both laughed."

"He curses at everything," I said. "He's probably driven her crazy." I wondered how sick he really was. He might have been a little crazy before, but he seemed as strong as a twisted old oak.

Jola stared toward the window, that distant expression overtaking her.

"You know, his mood is strange," she said. "I think he knows something."

"You mean Karol?"

"Yes. He knows something. I don't know what."

"Has he watched you, followed you?"

"No. He would never. I don't know what he knows, but I feel he does. I would know. Don't you think you would know?"

I couldn't say. I thought I did not care if he knew.

"He is sad, Leszek."

"Yes."

"I mean there is a sadness in him."

She was right, of course, though I did not want to acknowledge this, or to think too much on the nature of it, or what it might mean to the both of us. And yet I had sensed a conversation like this coming, as I might have felt a tremor through the boards of a rickety footbridge.

"I don't care, Jola."

"Probably not." She sat up, her bare back to me, covering her breasts with the blanket. "It's not so easy for me."

"What do you mean?"

"I mean this is difficult. More than I thought."

"Then leave him. Leave him."

"To go where? To you? To your house? Your family? They would never accept this." She turned to me, her face drained. "Be realistic, Leszek."

"I am."

"No, you're not. Think about this little town. Just think about it for a minute. It has too much memory. It doesn't forgive. You can get lost in a city, but not here."

"It doesn't matter."

"But it does matter. I've made so many mistakes already, Leszek, a string of mistakes, one after the other. Is this just another one?"

"I hope not."

"What do you know? I'm older than you. You should find some nice young girl, marry her, and make your life from the beginning. When you say you love me, do you know what you're talking about? What do you compare me with? Were you ever in love before? Did you ever lose your head over a girl? No! You've told me that and I believe you, but that frightens me a little. I wonder if you know what you're doing. I've made too many bad judgments already, and now I have the responsibility not to make another one. I don't want to hurt you. I'm afraid to hurt you."

"Why?"

"Because it would spoil you. It would damage something nice about you."

"Then don't do it. Make me happy."

"Maybe I would hurt you worse if I did what you want."

"You're talking in circles."

"No, Leszek, I'm trying to tell you something."

"That you don't love me?"

"It's not that. I don't want to say that. There's more to it than that."

She lowered her head. I had just told her it didn't matter, and yet, in some purposely ignored closet of my mind, I knew her concerns did matter. Jola was not irrational.

I pulled her to me. She did not resist, and we seemed to plunge downward, as though whirling, into a pool of warmth and muted color. Her eyes went soft, smoky. Her arms enfolded me. For a while the world reduced itself to this circle of breath and light, and I could not imagine ever having to surrender this gift.

We lay motionless a long time then, not speaking. Later, dressed and wrapped in her coat, she faced me at the open door, the forest behind her silent and misted.

"I have to hurry," she said. "We have to think about this now. Both of us, but especially me. Please understand that." She put her fingers to my lips, then squeezed the lobe of my ear. My eyes followed the red of her scarf, the single splash of color in the fading light. Then the trees swallowed her.

The old rusted padlock I had salvaged from a tool chest in the barn rested in the palm of my hand like a stone, still rusted but its workings oiled within, smooth to the key's touch. I fastened it to the hasp and kicked loose wet leaves against the door, for we were always careful that the cabin should appear abandoned and unused. I turned back to look as I walked away. The cabin's edges seemed to fade and disappear, and I went on, not unconcerned, and yet almost confident, as though possessing a jewel plundered from a castle.

In the days that followed I stayed close to the farm. I had agreed with the manager of the tractor factory in Lechnow to build forty storage pallets. He offered a decent price, and I had a mountain of sawed pine boards for the job. It was cash in a slow season, and I set about the job in a cleared space behind the hay barn. I constructed a new set of sawhorses and spent the first day cutting boards and the second nailing them together. I sawed and hammered, slowly and steadily, and tried to think things through. I didn't make much progress, but I told myself that some things do not get solved with thought, only with feeling and with time. The pallets piled up, one by one, and I liked the feel of the rough-cut pine under my fingers, the solid sweet chunk of the hammer driving the nails home. The question of Jola, of what to do, nagged me. I thought of approaching Karol, but to do that would amount to cutting her out of the decision, of forcing an explosion she seemed unprepared to handle, at least not yet. Nor, perhaps, was I. I had no idea when I would see her again, only that, ultimately, there would be a way.

She was right, too, about my own family, which was to say, my mother. In the end, of course, she would accept Jola, but I could hardly imagine the ordeal of telling her, of explaining, of winning this acceptance. Her mood lately had been distant, pensive. Finally the cause dawned on me: It had been about this time, two years before, that my father's illness, and its awful prognosis, had been revealed to us by the doctors, and it marked the beginning of his steady decline.

As I worked, Kowalski's field began to lure me with fresh insistance, like a beckoning mirage. My father had seen some significance in it for me, had understood, without saying it in so many words, that it was a step toward creating my own life. "Do something," his voice told me. By now I thought of the land as a present to Jola, a promise to us both. It was a declaration that the world was not closed anymore, that all things were possible.

I decided to pay a visit to Kowalski. But first I finished the pallets and delivered them in two trips to the factory in Lechnów. The manager sorted through them quickly, was pleased, and paid me on the spot.

"You want a job?" he asked.

"Here?"

"Yes. I need people who want to work."

I declined. I said I had a farm to run.

"Come see me when you're tired of it," he said.

I had not seen Kowalski since my father's death. I was not sure I would be any more welcome, or even if he would be well enough to see me. I remembered the old ways: I was a suitor, a supplicant. I walked there with a pound of good coffee in my hand.

I could hear him inside arguing with his wife, even over the noise of the dog as it barked and leaped against its chain. The door jerked open. Mrs. Kowalska stood looking at me without recognition until I said my name; then she motioned for me to enter, and led me through the kitchen. I was surprised at Kowalski's appearance, for he seemed to have aged and weakened sharply. His skin had gone sallow, his hair had taken on a yellowish film, and spittle glistened on his worn shirt. His wife, fierce in her silence, nodded when I gave her the coffee, then disappeared without a word.

"Your father is gone now," Kowalski said.

I could not tell if he was asking or needed reminding, or was stating facts as his imperfect memory assembled them. "Gone now. Where?"

"Yes. Passed on."

"Rain. Fucking whore weather. Aghh." He sagged into his chair. "Whore of a horse. No horse can work in this whore weather. Passed on, eh?"

"Yes. Some time ago now."

"Well, that's it then. Never get the work done. Never finished."

For a while the broken circle of conversation dragged on: horses, crops, weather. Kowalski, though, had no horse and no crop, and the weather had not been particularly bad. Another poor climate had descended upon him. Along with his wife reciting her prayers, his children gone and lost, his animals reduced to a few chickens and a chained dog, his life boiled down to a residue of incapacity, anger, and incomprehension. Or near incomprehension, for he righted himself after swallowing some tea from the glass at his elbow. I wondered whether he was eating. Although he was not wasted away in his face and chest, he had become as insubstantial as gelatin. In the corner of the room the old porcelain stove stood cold, its top encrusted, a dented enamel pan resting there on its side. Kowalski's feet shuffled on the floor within layers of unraveling wool.

"No," he said. "I don't think so."

"Excuse me?"

"Not yet. I won't let you have it." His eyes narrowed, as though he had come back to the world, no longer dreaming of the horse he no longer had. "That's it, isn't it? The high field. My field. The field everyone wants. I know. Magda!" He was shouting at his wife. "Magda, give the gentleman tea! Tea, goddamnit!"

A mutter issued from the doorway of the adjoining room.

"Goddamnit."

Feet padded near, a saucer and glass hit the table, then a thin, gnarled hand poured. The tea was as black as coffee.

"Are you a good one?" Kowalski raised himself off the back of the chair. "You don't have your father's eyes, do you? Let me see."

I would not look at him. I had all I could take. I started to stand, but his hand clutched my arm.

"You look like a Pole," he said. "Blue eyes. Not Jew eyes, not fucking Bolshevik eyes." He sagged back again. "Whores, fucking Bolshevik whores." He was seized by a long, phlegmy cough. "Damnable weather. No one can plant in this weather."

My father used to say that people who are stubborn, who are fiercely adamant in their arguments with you, are most often arguing against themselves, against some doubt of their own, and if you can muster the right patience and understanding, you can simply wait for their minds to change. I was not sure that reasoning applied here, but I seemed to see my father's face, calm and melancholy, as though instructing me.

"Pan Kowalski," I said, "I want to make your field the way it was once. A working field." His feet shuffled again, as though to warm themselves on the smooth floor. He peered into my face once more. "I will try to give you a good price," I said.

"Oh, we've paid the price," he said. "Oh, yes."

"Pardon me?"

"It rained this morning," he said. It hadn't rained at all. "What color does your father see the rain, huh, with his eyes? That whore of a horse. She's too old, that horse. Not in this weather. On her last legs, that's what." His hand smacked the arm of his chair, releasing a cloud of dust from the ragged upholstery. It floated in the light from the window. "I will think, young Maleszewski. Come when I am not so tired. Don't change the color of anything, all right? Good. I will see. Fucking whore of a horse. Magdusiu! Goddamnit!"

I left then, with that voice still in my ears. Old Kowalski, mad and not caring, could pass on his land to his lost children if he could find them, or to the state, or to his wife. She would live out her years in that house, attending church and lighting candles to her saints, while the field she had no use for lay empty and sprouting with the blown seeds of the poplars.

Perhaps I had a chance, although it was hard to understand what it depended on—was it his superstitious rattling about my father's eyes? I did not want their house. The money I would pay them, if I could borrow it from the bank, would be enough to provide them, or her, a solid living for a while. But I sensed in her manner especially—the abrupt clatter of the glass and saucer she placed before me—a resistance as strong as her husband's. She offered no smile with that tea, or at my token gift, or upon seeing me at her door, only a croaked syllable as I intruded upon her kitchen-world of salt pork and cabbage soup, and she dismissed me the same way, the door slamming sharply behind me as the dog resumed its snarling struggle with the chain.

The following Sunday my mother asked me to go to church with her, which was something I had done less and less often over the last year. We walked there together, and settled into the rustle of the church, the creak and crack of the pews sounding against the organ's sorrowful whine. Entering a church service always sounded this way to me, perhaps since my sister's funeral, a prelude to sadness, the thinly weeping organ like tears without release. These faces had been around me all my life, most of them, and yet I was struck this morning by how little I knew of them. We visit our neighbors' barns or their kitchens, see the same broken plows and chipped crockery, but know nothing of their trouble.

In the third row to the left of the aisle I saw old Pani Urban, gaunt and weary, birdlike with her scarf and hollowed cheeks and twitching glance. I remembered a scene at her house. A widow—her husband died drunk in a snowbank, frozen on the way home from town—she lived with her son, now grown and following his father's footsteps to the same snowbank. The son, Janek, had sold off all but one of their cows. They kept bees and sold honey harvested from pastel-painted hives, and I had paused to buy some one day, as my father used to do, on my way home. I could see smoke from the chimney; the chained dog yapped at my approach. The barn loft door, hanging by one hinge, groaned in the wind. Janek was lying face down on the ground on a patch of grass. He rolled his eyes when I tried to rouse him, but he was dead drunk and couldn't see anything. I saw movement in the kitchen window, so I knocked on the door. When Pani Urban finally, reluctantly, ventured to the door, I saw both her eyes were blackened, one nearly shut. "I fell," she said when I asked her if she was all right. As to Janek, still prone on the grass behind me, no discussion was necessary. I got the honey myself, using a jar she thrust out to me through the crack in her door, her cold hand closing around the money I pulled from my pocket. I was back on the tractor, bumping along the road, when I realized with a jolt that Pani Urban's bruises had not been inflicted by a fall, but by her own drunken son. By now, I had heard, the last cow was sold and Janek Urban, only three or four years older than me, looked like a man about to die. Perhaps that is why our church draws us in with such sadness. Is it everywhere the same? Surely not, I thought, and surely not forever here, either.

The younger priest, Father Jerzy, conducted the service. I paid little attention at first, but as I began to listen, it was evident that this was one of his "service for the Fatherland" political sermons. It seemed to have taken hold, for I saw others also alert and listening raptly. I noticed, for the first time, Aleksander Twerpicz, no great churchgoer himself, as far as I knew, sitting just across the aisle and slightly in front of me, shined up in his Sunday best. He sat with his arms folded across his chest, as though he felt unprotected here in such unfamiliar surroundings.

"They will not flee, nor will they hide among the flock," Father Jerzy said, his voice reaching a piping pitch. "They will be marked, not by the florid trappings of position, but by the stain of their iniquities, and be called out, for all to see. It is time that the truth, which is spreading throughout our country, spreads through our town as well."

My mother, shifting beside me, nudged me with her elbow. I

glanced at her, and she nodded, not taking her eyes off the priest. He was speaking of corruption, although I seemed to have missed the exact thread, but he spoke of "collusion between elements of the village leadership to sell materials at inflated prices to our own public enterprises." A stir, like wind, fluttered across the congregation.

"This is what we know," he went on, "and we can only begin to imagine the corruptions that lie below the surface, under their glaze of brazen arrogance, so sure were they of never being called upon to explain their actions and accounts. We have lived too long with their arrogance and venality, their grip on petty offices, their profits at public expense. We have had enough of crimes"—he paused— "enough of violent death." A low murmur rippled through the church. Father Jerzy's plump face was flushed and shining.

"The end for them has come," he said, "for at last cleansing manifestations are moving among us." His hand gestured toward the center of the church, and his eyes fixed directly upon Twerpicz. It was the public announcement, if one were needed, of the young priest's ally. It was meant for all to see, this benediction of the priest's gaze, but it seemed to catch Twerpicz by surprise. He sat noticeably taller in the pew, reddening in the face, but with a smile playing on his lips.

The effect was electrifying. I felt the excitement. Powierza was not likely to be in church, but I nevertheless looked around, hoping somehow to see him. Father Jerzy had stopped just short—or was it short?—of apportioning blame for Tomek's murder. Was that what he meant, or was it his sermon's metaphorical extravagance? And what did he intend to do with his accusations of corruption?

Vaguely dazed after the service, Twerpicz attracted a small group of greeters, few of whom engaged him seriously in conversation, but they evidently wanted to shake his hand, to peer beyond his smudged glasses at the visage of a "cleansing manifestation." He became a kind of curiosity, as though he were a prizewinner in the national lottery.

At the same time, the buzz in the church in no way indicated unanimous approval, and I could plainly see worry in the faces of some who stood apart, watching Twerpicz and whispering quietly to their friends. Who knew what disruptions of old arrangements were in the offing if some great civic housecleaning was about to take place?

The stir continued after church, as people dispersed through the village streets and lingered at their gate posts to debate it with their neighbors, exchanging their exclamations on a day that had warmed and brightened suddenly, like a burst of high spirits. Halfway home, Mother lingered to gossip with her friends, and I hurried on, anxious to find Powierza, but I could hear them talking about the priest as I left them.

I found Powierza in his barn. When I told him about Father Jerzy's sermon, he sat down on a milk can, absorbing the news. He looked haggard, his eyes deeply circled.

"Jabłoński's still missing," he said.

"You think he's run away?"

"No, no. Not him. They say he's still on his business trip."

Jabłoński had been gone for days now, apparently having departed a day or two after my return from Warsaw. Powierza and I had decided there was little we could do about Bielski's call to Jabłoński from Rapid Trading in Warsaw. My flailing about in Warsaw had confirmed only that Bielski and Jabłoński knew each other. It also seemed likely that Tomek's errands for Jabłoński had brought him in contact with Bielski's operation, whatever it was. But beyond that we remained in the dark. Powierza and I had discussed my conversation with the Russians, and my suspicion that they were trading in weapons, but this remained only supposition and still provided no direct link to Tomek or Jabłoński.

Powierza stood up and paced the length of the stalls and back again.

"Jabłoński's in on this," he said.

"What do you mean?"

"With the priest."

He went outside and stood blinking in the sunlight. "I bet he doesn't know anything, the priest," he said. He had been, in his manic, emotional way, depressed in recent days and seemed, now, to be quietly seething.

"You know what it is?" he said. The flush of anger brought the normal color back to his heavy face.

"It's politics," he said. "That's all."

*   *   *

Late the next morning I walked in to the village center. It was market day, so the streets were crowded, but there was a rare feeling of excitement in the air, and larger groups than usual had clustered in front of the bakery, the bus stop, and the doorway of the bar.

It took a while to piece it together, but I had clearly missed the morning's main event.

Just after the town offices opened at eight, a group of men had arrived in two cars, a red and a blue Polonez, both bearing government license plates. They emerged from the cars armed with briefcases and file folders, and huddled uncertainly before Twerpicz and another man who had bustled from the town offices to greet them. They shook hands and filed inside.

Several curious observers from the steps of the bar contrived errands or inquiries at the town offices, but all found the door locked. Repeated knocks summoned a stranger's face through a narrowly opened door, announcing that the offices were temporarily closed. The door shut sharply.

After an hour the men left. Zofia Flak, town secretary, went with them, locking the door behind her. Naczelnik Farby had not been seen. The two cars wheeled around in the middle of the street, heading out of town the way they had come, avoiding the town's main intersection where the curious stood watching.

Someone, I heard, had hurried out to the Farmers' Co-op to relay the news to Jabłoński (or to report his reaction to it) but found that he was still away on business.

I went to the bar, waiting a moment at the door for a sweating woman to tow her reluctant husband outside. He resisted, like a ship with its boilers burst, but she prevailed. It was likely to be that kind of day in town, full of staggering men by midafternoon. The bar had a crowd worthy of market day, smoke-filled and loud. Agnieszka, the owner's wife, and her daughter Helena, both red-faced from exertion and harried by the shouts around them, handed out jugs of beer from loaded trays. The windows were steamed over and the odor of sweat mingled with the smoke.

"Hey, Agnieszka, has Janusz found it yet?" someone yelled, bringing a chorus of laughter. Janusz was Agnieszka's husband and the official owner of the bar, though his wife and daughter did all the work.

"We'll know when the walls fall down," someone else shouted. More laughter. Agnieszka, her jaw set, ignored them.

"Hey, take one to Janusz. He's working too hard." This was Górski, who grabbed a mug of beer from Helena's tray and lurched to the back door, sloshing beer onto the sticky floor as he went.

"What's Janusz doing?" I asked.

"Digging," Górski said. "He digs. His first work in years."

I followed. Górski, a mug of beer in each hand, shouldered open the door, then toppled through it, barely managing to keep his feet while losing half his beer. I leaned out and saw Janusz on his knees in a shallow trench at the foot of the building. He held a pickax halfway up the handle, poised to strike at the foundation stones.

"Get your ass out of here, Górski," he said. Górski, eyes rolling, plopped heavily backward on a freshly dug pile of earth. I looked down at Janusz, his face streaked and his hands caked with mud.

"What are you doing, Janusz?" I asked.

"What's it look like?"

"You're putting in plumbing?"

"Fuck you," he said, and chunked his pickax between the stones. "Go away." He jerked out the pick, growling like a dog.

Back inside I saw Karol Skalski, his vet's case in one hand and a glass of vodka in the other. He had just come in, for I had not seen him when I entered, and his eye caught mine instantly. In the beat of a second, less than a second, we stared at each other with no flicker of greeting or welcome, a flat quick moment that suggested a recognition of something that transcended acquaintance. How this sensation was transmitted I cannot say. Was it from my expression, or his? He headed toward me. I seized a beer from Agnieszka's tray.

"Janusz is digging," I said.

"I know," he said. "He's not alone."

"Not alone? What do you mean?"

"There're others digging, too."

"Where?"

"Their houses, barns."

"What in heaven's name for?"

"Loot."

*   *   *

That night the first of the doors was assaulted. Or, more precisely, the doorjambs. With a hammer and a crowbar and a loud, splintering crack, the old dried wood split away in shards, leaving a bright yellow scar against weathered exterior boards and revealing, under this fresh gash, a hollowed square like a box, a niche the size of a child's fist, well worn and dark as the shingles of the oldest houses in the village.

Chapter Eight

Radom at night. Neon-stained fog clung to the square below the hotel window. Jabłoński had not been to Radom for years, and, after two nights here, wondered why he had stayed away from cities for so long. No money, of course. It required money to have a good time in a Polish city. How much had he spent the night before? He didn't want to think. The girls absorbed enough, but then you had to expect that. It was the hotel bar bill that jolted him. Żurek had accounted for at least half of it, but it was Jabłoński's treat, under the circumstances. Be reasonable, he told himself, it was a bargain in the end. And it was business. In America, they would call it "deductible."

"It's been what, nine years, Roman?" Żurek said.

"Seven, I think. The congress in Tarnów. You were in Płock then."

"Christ, yes. Płock. Fucking Płock. You look the same. Lost a little hair. How's the easy life in the country?"

They were in the bar at the Hotel Warszawa across the street from the nearly identical hotel where Jabłoński had booked a room. It was Żurek's suggestion. He was known at the bar, of course, a cavernous room with numerous dim corners (and where the lights were dimmed further after 10 P.M.). It was the chosen rendezvous for both resident and traveling deal-makers. Jabłoński had arrived early and posted himself with a view of the door, not sure he would recognize Żurek immediately after so long. The room had an air of anticipation, evident in the gales of loudly forced bonhomie. The

German visitors, mostly young and on their way up in the acquisition departments of their firms, packed heavy wallets in their jacket pockets and blank contracts in the briefcases they had left back in their hotel rooms. Jabłoński had never seen Radom look quite like this. He remembered it mostly from nearly twenty years earlier when the cheerless hotel lobbies smelled of disinfectant and their loungers were mostly informers and secret policemen in gum-soled shoes, spying on the faithful, on each other, like cats watching their own tails.

Now the groups bustled in, four or five on the Polish side, meeting two or three on the German side, or maybe a few Italians, with back-slapping and whoops of laughter as they crossed the room to order their first rounds of drinks, bottles of vodka (Polish) plunked down before them, followed by a tray of beer (German) and small bowls of broken potato chips. Money was accumulating here now, Jabłoński thought. You could see it in the shoes, the gray gum soles replaced by tasseled loafers, especially for the younger Poles, who favored white socks, as if to accentuate the new soft leather. Never mind the mud outside. The Germans were more stolid—weren't they always?—but sported gold on their wrists under starched white cuffs, and handed over their light, soft-shouldered overcoats to a Polish retainer. Where were the gray synthetic suits of old? Jabłoński scanned the room. Well, there was his own; he'd been wearing it a good dozen years now, not a natural fiber in it. Held to a match flame, it would more likely melt than burn. A few others, too, here and there. Not quite dinosaurs yet, not quite dead. Perhaps it was an advantage, in a way, the look of the past. The young hustlers in the white socks and the soft shoes dismissed them or ignored them. The young men liked to travel on business to Italy or Switzerland and jet home laden with gifts in large plastic shopping bags that were like gifts in themselves, stamped with the insignia of famous stores.

Through narrowed eyes, Jabłoński watched the groups lift their drinks, light each other's cigarettes. Fuck them. Their wives could use the bags to lug home onions from the market.

They were supposed to be building a new economic order, these opportunistic brats. They acted as if the old order had ceased to be of use, but what did they know? It had taken forty-five years, the building of this country since the war. In the space of a year, all that history was deemed worthless. Bankrupt. And those who built it, who willed it to work, who fired the furnaces and poured the concrete and mined the coal, they had been designated as scrap along with the rusted machinery. He had seen them here, as he could see them in any city of consequence, their faces white as milk, their hair faded beyond gray to a dirty yellow, eyes downcast. The new fashion had painted them as agents of repression and despoilers of the earth, that is, to the extent it paid them any attention at all. Let them think what they want, was the counsel Jabłoński offered to himself. We ran the factories, he thought, we pushed the steel out the door, and if a succession of incompetent governments and spineless mendicants sold out the best efforts of those people who, like him, were supposed to be managing the state's business, well, then those who were sold out could hardly be blamed for making their own way. Over the rim of his spectacles he watched one of the young Polish hustlers spring up to greet a pair of arriving Germans. The young Pole slavered over them, waving a waiter over to collect their order.

"Don't worry, Roman," Żurek said. "The Germans will eat them for snacks."

"And have the whole country for dinner."

Żurek shrugged. He sipped his vodka. "Better to be exploited by Germans than by no one at all."

"This time they'll take the whole country without firing a shot. They'll just buy it at salvage prices. Much cheaper than raising an army."

"You liked the Russians better?"

"I like them better now. They're more fucked up than we are, and I thought that was impossible."

"Don't tell me about it," Żurek said. "I could use some German business, myself. My plant is on the verge of collapse."

Żurek, for the past three years, had been deputy manager of a factory that manufactured machine bearings for the Soviet market. Bearings for lathes, for drill presses, for oil-field equipment, for clutch assemblies in giant cranes. Now there was no Soviet market.

There was a Russian market, a Ukrainian market, a Lithuanian market, all of which had run out of money. Two years ago, the Bulgarians, the Slovaks, and the Hungarians dried up, too. Now the Russians couldn't pay for what they ordered last year, stuff that was crated and ready to ship. Żurek did not have to explain the details. Two years ago, the state would have made up the losses. Everyone would have kept working. Now, after a noble history and thirty years of production, everyone was supposed to fight through to the lifeboats however he could. Sink or swim.

"Half our people are on voluntary holiday," Żurek said. "The other half shows up to sweep. We have a very clean factory."

"And no Germans? Swiss? Italians?" Jabłoński could not resist the tease. Żurek had not yet become white-haired or pale as a winter cabbage. He still had his hair, and it was mostly dark, and, if he saw a way, he would be with the soft-shoe boys in two seconds. But he had fallen in that gap; his factory produced nothing of any use west of the Oder-Neisse, and his alliances were welded in. For two years he had even been on the Central Committee, a junior associate in a gang of four hundred. He had his ticket in hand, but the train never left the station. His plum of a factory, which had squeaked out a modest-but-real profit for three decades, was standing idle.

"I have a prospect for you, Żurek," Jabłoński said.

"I'm listening."

"You have deliveries for your former clients?"

"We have no deliveries now. No payment, no delivery."

"But you have goods you could deliver?"

"Half a year's production, on pallets, stacked to the ceiling."

"But you have trucks. And your crates full of bearings. And your old customers, who have ordered but cannot pay."

"Can't and maybe never can, or never will. Who knows what goes on over there? It's chaos."

"But you could deliver them? Theoretically?"

"Theoretically. Frankly, I don't know if we could buy the fuel."

"But your trucks run? If they had fuel, of course?"

"Why not? The mechanics have nothing else to do. The trucks may be the only convertible asset we have left."

"You have customers in Georgia? Tbilisi, perhaps?"

"I have customers wherever there's a smokestack."

"Should we have another drink, Żurek?"

"Let's get a bottle," Żurek said.

"My treat," said Jabłoński.

Zofia Flak flung open the cabin door and threw herself into Farby's waiting arms. She gave off a distinct heat of exertion and excitement. As always, Farby could feel her heart pounding against his chest. The sensation thrilled him.

"I thought you'd never get here," he said.

"I came as soon as I could."

"They didn't follow you?"

"They don't know anything."

"You're sure?"

"Yes, I watched."

"It's late. I was very worried."

It was around 7 P.M., but it had been dark for three hours, and Farby had paced the small house like a prisoner in a cell. They were in the country, thirty miles from Jadowia. He had been here three days, never leaving since his hasty arrival Monday evening, hours after the district authorities sealed his office. He had been late to work by the sheerest luck: the float valve in the toilet tank had stuck, and his wife insisted that he fix it before he left home. He had answered the phone with both arms wet to the elbow and heard Zofia's warning. "Go to Rutno," she said, "and wait. At the store. Just wait. I'll be there." She paused. "And Zbyszek," she whispered, while he stood dripping with rusty water, "I love you."

For Farby, at that moment and since, it was as if all other concerns were secondary to that reverberating declaration. In a near daze, he did as he was told, slapped the clanking lid on the toilet tank, dried his arms, struggled into his coat, and hustled down the steps to his Trabant, which, thank the Lord, started immediately, like a miracle. He wound through back roads toward Rutno, and drove slowly through the village, a small place with one store. He thought it unwise to linger there conspicuously all day, so he drove some more, pulled off onto a lane in a forest, and waited until after dark, then returned to Rutno. When Zofia arrived, she ran back to the car, leaned through the window, and kissed him. "Follow me," she said. "Hurry."

He had been here ever since.

This summer cabin had belonged to her family, a "holiday house," she called it, for roaming the forest and picking mushrooms. Now that her father was dead, it was rarely used, and never in winter. There was a ceramic stove, though, for cooking, and a pyramid of damp firewood behind the house. She brought some food with her that night, and more the next.

He was, he realized, a fugitive of sorts. From what, though, he was not quite sure. His wife, certainly. From the law? Perhaps, but he was not without his defenses.

And, strange as it seemed, even to himself, he was happy. Trapped, for the time being, in this little house, walking about with a blanket over his shoulders, he felt released, liberated. He was witlessly in love, and she with him. It was one of their two topics: love and the other thing.

"Your nipples are unbelievable, Zofia. Like perfect raspberries."

She was propped against a pile of pillows. His head rested on her bare stomach, his hair coiled in her fingers.

She smiled, as though pleased at her surprising lack of modesty, even at the rightness of his words. Maybe they were perfect, if he thought so. Her smile widened.

"You are such a sweet man," she said. "How did I wait so long?"

"Why did I?" Farby asked.

"You were so busy. You work so hard. I thought you never noticed me, like I was a file cabinet."

"Yes, a file cabinet. I dreamed of opening all your drawers."

"Come here," she said, pulling him toward her and rolling over.

Then there were practical matters to discuss. Zofia knew, from the office and the town, that no one was actively looking for Farby, at least not yet. The machinery of the legal bureaucracy ground slowly and, she was pretty sure, no charges were filed and no warrants issued. She thought it possible that the records under review by the district controllers were indecipherable anyway. Kukiński, the wispy-voiced man from headquarters, was almost diffident, asking for records of procurement and purchasing. He had spoken to her with the utmost politeness, beginning every request with a timid "Please, if you wouldn't mind." The dreadful Twerpicz had steered him several times into a corner of the room, whispering suggestions or instructions, Zofia couldn't decide which. She retrieved the requested files, not many, really, and though she had filed them, she had only the vaguest idea of their contents. After another polite request, he asked to look through the file cabinets himself, and a stack large enough to fill one file drawer wound up going away with them. The quartet of men, including two she assumed to be policemen, did nothing to suggest that she herself was under investigation.

But she had an idea what they were looking for. Certain invoices, she knew, were not, strictly speaking, exactly accurate. There was the matter of the snowplow apparatus, for example. Paid for as new. The actual item was used. Rather considerably, as certain maintenance bills might attest, should anyone think to look for them. She was not sure they had. All of it could be explained, she thought. Sort of.

"To meet the payroll," Farby said to her.

And the payroll? Well, there was always something. The monthly emergency. The grade school roof buckling under snow last year. He remembered that.

"And your mother's roof," she reminded him. Replaced with town labor, perhaps town supplies. She was old and poor. Then there was the load of asphalt, spread and tamped onto his own driveway.

"It's Jabłoński," she said. "You know that, don't you?"

"But what's he doing it for?"

"Saving himself."

Farby wondered. Then he told her about the distillery. Of course, she had heard none of this before. She was shocked, but she could see the dynamic clearly, and she felt Jabłoński had used Farby as a pawn. Jabłoński was simply a bully. She wanted to smother Zbyszek in her arms again.

"So, you see, I know something, too," Farby said. He felt comforted by this. He wanted her to feel his reassurance.

Zofia was about to feed Farby a slice of cold sausage. Her hand stopped halfway to its target. Farby's eyes were closed and his mouth open.

"But hasn't Jabłoński thought of that, too?"

His eyes opened, his mouth closed. He couldn't think of an answer.

Andrzej the plumber once again brought Father Tadeusz the news. He didn't bring it, exactly, but rather possessed it to impart when their paths crossed, causing Father Tadeusz to wonder later if Andrzej had been assigned by Providence as the personal herald for an old and perhaps deliberately inattentive priest. Andrzej simply seemed to have materialized behind the rectory on the path that served as a shortcut between the town center and some of the older houses at the southern margin of the village. Father Tadeusz, arms loaded with altar linen, was on his way to the side door of the church. Andrzej tipped his cap and after a moment of pleasantries reported that he had worn himself out helping his cousin Paweł repair the corner of his house, which had nearly collapsed. Now he was going to Janek Smurc's house, where the same thing had happened, and, after that, if there was any light left in the day, he promised to help Kazimierz, who had started digging at his house and now couldn't wedge open the front door.

"Why?" Father Tadeusz asked.

"The foundation settled. Did at my cousin's too, but the door is on the other side, so at least he can get in and out. His wife is throwing things at him. She thinks he's gone crazy."

"Because he's repairing the house?"

"No, for digging out the foundation, looking for gold, coins, things like that."

"Gold? Why's he looking for gold?"

"Not just gold. Jewelry, maybe. Hidden valuables. In the old houses."

Father Tadeusz blinked. He was not following this.

"These other people you mentioned," he said, "they're looking for gold, too?"

"Of course."

"I don't understand, Andrzej. Why are these people—what did you say?—digging up their foundations? For treasure?"

"Gold, probably."

"Yes, yes. But *why?* Who said there was gold?" Father Tadeusz's voice rose in exasperation, and Andrzej flinched.

"Well, it's the old houses, Father. The old houses. You understand. Where the Jews lived. Before the war."

Andrzej edged away as the expression on Father Tadeusz's face shifted from impatience to wonder. He cocked his head, as though listening for a distant noise.

"I must go, Father."

"You say there are other people doing this, Andrzej? Looking for gold?"

"Yes, Father."

"Many people?"

"A few, Father."

Father Tadeusz searched out Paweł Stępien's house and several others that day and the next, encountering attitudes ranging from frank determination to mild embarrassment. Pawel Stepien had "gone away to get drunk," said Magda, his wife, who was as furious as Andrzej reported.

"The bedroom wall almost fell down, Father," she said. "The pictures crashed off the wall. My figurines fell down and broke. I told Paweł this is madness. My father and mother moved into this house after the war, and I was born in this house, right in that room there. It isn't Paweł's house to go digging up. There's no gold buried here."

"I'm sorry, Pani Stępien," Father Tadeusz said. "Can you tell me, who said there was gold here?"

"It's just something he heard in the bar. It's an old story. We always heard things like this when I was a little girl. It's just surfaced again. I don't know why."

"Where was it supposed to be, this gold?"

"People said it was buried in the walls. Places like that. Hidden between the foundation stones."

"But why?"

"The Jews. You know. They hid their things. Their valuables."

"Because of the . . ." Father Tadeusz stammered, not sure of the correct word. "Because of the war?"

"They say they were misers. You know, they didn't believe in banks. Well, who could blame them? But they hid things from the Germans, too, when, uh, when the war came. Here, I mean." Father Tadeusz was aware of Pani Stępien's discomfort. She continually glanced away from him, and her blunt hands folded the hem of the apron she had removed when he arrived.

"Has anyone found anything?" he asked.

"Now? No. I don't think so. When I was young, though, there were stories. I don't know. It was a long time ago. I was little. But I have lived in this house all my life, with all my family, and if there were gold or jewelry hidden in this house someone would have come across it before now. But my husband, Father, God forgive him, he spends too much time in the bar, and he thinks he can get something for nothing, and it doesn't matter what I say to him."

She sobbed softly. They were standing in the clutter of the kitchen. Dirty dishes were still on the table. A yellow cat dozed in the corner. Father Tadeusz wanted to comfort her, but he needed to find out more. "It's a trial, I know," he said.

"I can't do anything with him," she said.

"Do you know who lived here before your father got the house?"

"I didn't know them, Father. It was before I was born."

"Did you ever hear who it was?"

"Their name was Bernsztajn. That's all I know. He repaired watches and clocks."

"Do you know what happened to them?"

She looked up at him sharply, as though surprised at the question, and he saw the damp glistening in creases below her eyes.

"No, Father." She paused. "Like all of them, I suppose."

Like all of them.

There was no history here, no archive, no memorial.

He went to the town library, but it was not meant as a repository of village history. Housed on the second floor of the building where the volunteer fire truck was kept, the books here were the property of the town's "cultural center," and amounted to a few shelves of novels, technical manuals, and textbooks. There was Hemingway and *The Grapes of Wrath* (two copies), and studies on the diseases of poultry and the processes of bovine digestion. In a remote corner a student could examine the critical refinements on Marx and Lenin as propounded by Polish politburos (from 1958 onward) and the National Academy of Science. When he asked the young woman in charge if the library possessed a history of Jadowia, she stared at him blankly. She said all they had was on the shelves. She had never seen such a book. "We're just for entertainment," she said.

He left the cultural center, skirted the church, and headed across his familiar path into the forest, the route of his daily walk. How little he knew! How little he had bothered to find out! How complacent he had been, how comfortable—was that the word?—in his disappointment! He had sought to muffle himself against his surroundings, to serve out his time, to resist any involvement beyond his priestly offices. He had stopped searching in other eyes for pain or need, an empathy that had come naturally to him when he was a young priest. This village had been his home for nearly three years now, and what did he know of it? What did he know of its time in the war? Had he been, as he suspected of most of the population, tired of living so close to it? He wandered deep into the stillness of the woods, the pines overspreading the gray sky above his head.

He knew only what everyone knew, or less. That most of the villages here, and scattered to the east and south, were filled with Jews before the war. They owned houses and shops. They ran the small hotels along the routes to Zamość and Białystok and on to Vilnius and Kiev and Lvov. And then they disappeared into the trains. And the trains operated on a track that was still there, the main line that stretched from Warsaw to Białystok, a roadbed straight as a wire that sliced five miles north of Jadowia. The trains then passed again and again along the line, but they didn't go to Białystok. They stopped, actually, at Treblinka, done up to look like an ordinary country village. It was thirty miles, almost exactly, from that faked station and collection of false fronts to the point at which Father Tadeusz abruptly halted on his walk along the path, looking up, as he might have done at the croak of a raven.

He would have to ask the old ones, the ones who had been here and remembered. He would have to find the history for himself.

He went, that evening, to see Mrs. Skubyszewska.

She settled into her rocker, a crocheted shawl draped around her shoulders. As she talked, her veined hands plucked at the folds of a dark print dress as she remembered some detail she hadn't summoned to mind for years. She would rise and thread her way through the crowded dark furniture to search for an old photo, or a book, in the desk or the glass-fronted bookcase. Then she would return to the rocker and arrange herself again, her hair wispy and white against the leather headrest. Her husband, Łukasz, now and then called out from his overstuffed chair syllables Father Tadeusz could not decipher.

"Yes, darling, Father has his tea," she said once. "He asked if I had gotten you tea."

"Yes," he said. "Thank you."

She had a face rarely seen in the country, Father Tadeusz thought, a fine-boned, delicate face, the face of a vanished aristocracy. An educated face, a cultured face, a tracery of lines around her eyes, her mouth. The eyes themselves were clear, bright and blue, like the blue on Dutch tile.

Oh, there was so much to remember, she said. She could not tell it in any particular order. She apologized for that more than once. And Łukasz broke into a spasm of coughing, death-defying, it seemed to Father Tadeusz, in its length and loudness. She rose to help him through it, pressing a handkerchief into his hand, fastening a button on his sweater.

"Ninety," she said, resuming her place.

"Pardon?"

"Ninety. Łukasz is ninety." She was eighty-seven. They had been sweethearts in school together. She found old photographs in a wooden stationery box, the kind that had not been made for years and, from a wall in the hallway, a framed photograph of the teachers in Jadowia school, taken sometime in the thirties, she said. "Łukasz was principal then," she said. She pointed him out, a tall man with a barrel chest and a full head of dark hair.

The village was bigger in those days. More important than now.

And Jewish? Yes, you could call it that, she said. Her thin voice wavered on, and Father Tadeusz sat back, listening. The Jews were in the town mostly. Not many were farmers. It wasn't their work. The Poles were the farmers, poor mostly, and they worked the land and the forests in the countryside around the village, and traded in the town, bought hardware and shoes when they could afford them, and clothes and bread.

The Jews purchased grain and eggs and vegetables—produce—from the farmers. And from their own traders they bought goods from the city. They baked bread and repaired shoes. They sold needles and buttons, candy, tea. They gave credit. They lent money. Oh, no, they were not rich. Of course, some said they were, but if it was true you couldn't see it. They had children, many, many children, and some of them were ragged and outgrew their clothes. And some of the adults were ragged, too. It was an economic depression, all over the world, you know, not just here.

And there were outbreaks of sickness, too, rheumatic fever, and there was tuberculosis, and she could remember the anguish in the faces of the mothers, and the tag-along children of the itinerant tinkers, their noses running and their eyes lively and huge, their pale cheeks, their earlocks. No, no, they were not rich. They were poor as everyone, just different poor. They sold, the Poles plowed. Scarce profit in either, with depression, all over the world.

The Jews could all read, or most could. They educated their children. Not so the peasants, not so much. That was a difference. There was a separateness. Catholic and Jew. Tiller and trader. Well, Father, she said, you must know; you're Polish. The old class system—nobility, aristocracy, burghers, Jews, and peasants at the bottom. There was a difference, of course. Resentments, maybe. Suspicions and superstition. But it was the thirties. And chaos coming, don't you recall, Germany a frenzy. Well, she guessed there was hope, or call it delusion, for some, that it would all turn out, but frankly a fool could see it coming.

Was it Klejn, or Klemztejn? She couldn't remember. Anyway, people called him Moishe the Baker. She remembered October of that year. Yes, '39, of course, the guns all night, the cannon fire, and everyone terrified, hiding in cellars and under beds, pitch black all night except for the flashes in the sky, first in the west and then in the east, and all lights off except the lanterns at Moishe's, which was just across the street from where they lived then. She was alone—her husband had volunteered and was, at that moment, in retreat eastward across Silesia with several entire Polish divisions—but she dared to look through the windows and even step out into the night. The shells whistled overhead, sailing beyond the town on the way to the forest. She saw Moishe's light, and Moishe's shadow, back and forth across the opaque glass. And in the morning, in the stillness and the sunlight of the hottest autumn in twenty years, on Moishe's shelf, free for the taking, there was bread for everyone. When someone asked him how or why he had baked bread all night he said he did it to keep from losing his mind with fear.

Then the Germans came, here, and to every village around, and after a while Moishe and his family, along with every other Jew and his family, were confined to a few houses surrounded by a wire fence ten feet high, and Jews from smaller villages around were marched in and confined. Only the children got out, somehow, to buy food or beg for it. And then, a year or so later, 1941 it was, the Jews were moved to the town square, right down by the bus stop. Where the bus stop is now, she said, that was one side of it, and put in another pen, fenced all around, and more were marched in to join them. And then, one day, they were marched out, all of them, down the road toward the railway line. She knew a man, a Polish farmer, dead now, long dead, who was one of the Poles the Germans ordered to follow the column with his wagon and load the bodies of the ones the Germans shot on the way to the trains, and his wagon finished the trip, he told people, loaded like a hay wagon so that he and the boys who worked with him looped rope over the load to keep it from toppling.

She didn't see this, she only heard it, but she could believe it easily enough, because she did hear the gunshots, starting at the edge of town and in the distance as the column progressed. She saw what happened next, in the mud square, where not even a blade of grass was left even though it was only September, because, she supposed, they were hungry and ate the grass that they didn't trample. When it was empty, and the gunshots receded down the road, and the Germans with them, the wire gate of the pen stood open and unguarded. Poles filed quietly in then. Some used sticks, or their bare hands, some even employed hoes and shovels, and they dug in the ground, scavening for buried things, for coins, gold, silver. They were sure it was there. They'd seen money offered through the wire at night, shown in the palm held back from the fence, in exchange for half a loaf of bread, an apple, a turnip. A necklace for a son's life, a pearl for a potato. She saw them, watched as they entered the flung-back wire gate and scattered evenly across the packed mud, hunched and hushed as squirrels, digging with their sticks and implements for muddy coins, for small bundles bound in rags.

Everyone was poor, she said. You must realize. Everyone was desperate.

"And people found . . . these things?"

"I don't know," she said. "I couldn't watch, and I never asked."

Mrs. Skubyszewska knew, too, the meaning of the splintered door-jambs, and if there were others who understood it as well, it was she who had voiced it first. There were people older than she in the village, but she had the advantage not only of age, but of alertness and a clear memory. She told it to her neighbor, and to the baker across the street (the fourth successor to the space once occupied by Moishe), and to the young doctor at the clinic where she went for Łukasz's medicine. Sitting in the evening in her parlor—it was late for her to be up she told Father Tadeusz, who didn't at first know what she was talking about, so slow was his reception of local news.

"There were four houses where it happened. Smorenda's. Kowalczyk's. The Sylski house just near here, two doors down from the baker's. And Jasnowicz, old Mrs. Jasnowicz, near the clinic. You see?"

Father Tadeusz shook his head.

"Old houses. Jewish houses."

"Ah."

"The mezuzahs."

"The what?"

Mrs. Skubyszewska rose to tend her husband. He had fallen asleep in his chair. She tucked a wool wrap higher over his lap.

"Mezuzahs," she said. "In niches in the doorways. The Jewish houses had them. They held miniature scriptures. From the holy books. The Torah, yes? Or the Bible? Verses from the Bible in little niches in the door frames. Every Jewish house had them."

"They're still there?"

"Covered up, mostly. Or replaced. People changed the houses, fixed things. Put in new doors sometimes. But some just covered them up. It meant nothing to them, you see, these customs, these artifacts. And they didn't want to look at them, be reminded. They nailed over them."

"Reminded?"

"That there were ones who were . . . who are gone. Or that they were ever here. In these houses where *they* now live. Who wants to remember that, every time they go through the door? It was better to cover them, to not see. Tell me, Father, do you see any reminders?"

"No."

"There was a cemetery somewhere. West of the village. It's grown over now, I expect. But no, there is nothing. So. You understand now?"

"It is only these four houses?"

"All I've heard, and seen, so far. I went and looked, except for Smorenda's. I couldn't walk so far. But it was described to me."

"But that's not all the houses. There are other . . ." He hesitated at the word and realized, in that instant, that he had absorbed long ago the pattern not just of this place, but of the country. He resisted forming the word. "Other *Jewish* houses?" he said.

"Oh yes. A dozen. Twenty. Maybe more."

"So there could be more of these . . . these incidents?"

Her rocking halted for a moment. Father Tadeusz became aware, for the first time, of a clock ticking somewhere in the room, like time itself hidden amid the crowded furniture, the framed pictures and mementos.

"I think someone is remembering," she said.

"Was there any . . ." he hesitated again. "Anyone who was, uh, left?"

"Not that I know of."

"Then who?"

Her white head rested against the back of the chair. "I don't know, Father."

CHAPTER NINE

LESZEK

The quiet turmoil in the village reminded me of a dairy barn when a strange dog has wandered in. Unease was in the air. Whispered rumors flew: reports of money missing from the town offices, predictions of imminent arrests. Naczelnik Farby's whereabouts, and his connection with the investigation, figured in the speculation, but were not its central curiosity, for in truth no one took Farby seriously. In everyone's mind he was first and foremost an accessory. More sensational was the fear, which spread like an outbreak of flu, that certain houses in the village were about to be claimed—or reclaimed—by families of those who had owned them before the war. The Jews. No direct evidence fueled this apprehension, only the odd vandalism on certain doorways in the village. This deduction was attributed to Pani Skubyszewska, and no one disputed it. And yet no one had been visited by strangers from out of town, or by lawyers representing parties from Israel or America. No one had sighted strange automobiles cruising slowly along the village lanes as though searching out familiar landmarks. But people watched closely, alert for any sign.

On market days the gossip circulated and recirculated, embellished and embroidered as it traveled from the feed salesman to the butcher's, the baker's, to the bar and the bus stop.

"I hear they're coming back to Hungary," Janowski, the baker, told Powierza and me.

"Who is?" asked Powierza.

"The Jews," Janowski said.

Powierza was biting into a doughnut and seemed not to hear him.

"They are coming to Prague in flocks, too," Janowski went on. "They are looking up old records. They want their property back."

Powierza licked sugar from his fingers. "No one's coming here, Janowski," he said.

"And why not?"

"Why would they come back here? Everyone who is here wants to leave."

"I don't want to leave," Janowski said. "Where would I go?"

"You asked at the town offices, didn't you? What did they tell you?"

"Nothing. They have no records. There is nothing. All they do there is sip tea. And worry about this young priest."

"So why are you worried? No one can take your bakery."

"Who can promise that, Staszek? Can you? What if someone shows up and takes me to court?"

"Has anyone come?" Powierza asked. "Have you had any strange visitors?"

"No one arriving through the front door. But someone dug into the foundation of my storehouse. Someone has been making revelations in the old houses. What are we to think of that?"

Powierza told me a couple of evenings later that he thought of it all as "craziness," by which he meant it was an attempt to divert attention from the matter most important to him. He had become convinced that the authorities were somehow connected with Tomek's death, or, at the least, were trying to distract us from their own difficulties.

"They want everyone to look the other way," he said. "Father Jerzy has got them on the run." The unmistakeable note of admiration in his voice surprised me.

"You said Father Jerzy was 'all politics,'" I said. "I thought you didn't like him."

"He's not so bad. He's young, but he has the right idea about these people."

I was taken aback. As long as I'd known him, Powierza had played the role of traditional Polish contrarian. His previous barks of cynicism about Father Jerzy had been in that familiar mode. What had brought this change?

"You've been talking to him?"

There was a brief silence, as if he didn't want to answer me. We were sitting in his kitchen. The television murmured in the other room, where his wife sat with her sewing on her lap. Powierza leaned his elbows on the table, cradling a bottle of beer in his huge hands.

"Yeah. I saw him. He's going to get to the bottom of things, Leszek."

"How? What's he going to do?"

His eyes brightened, and I could feel the return of his former energy, the old and familiar Powierza, his voice alternately quiet and conspiratorial, then loud, punctuated by thumps of his hand on the table. Answering me now, his voice was nearly a whisper.

"They're looking at everything, everything they bought and sold."

"They?"

"The village. Farby. The road repair unit. You know. Korczak. And Tarnowski at the village shops. Where they bought coal, how much they paid for it. Gasoline sold on the side, diesel fuel. It's a lot of money, over time. A lot of money."

"Who got it?"

Powierza shrugged. "Who knows?" He shifted in his chair, a thumbnail digging at the bottle's label. I thought of beetle-browed Korczak, the chief of the village works department, known to every-one in town as dim-witted but pleasant, packing his road crews with cousins and the half-wit sons of favored citizens, employed by personal appeal—sweetened by the gift of a hen or a side of bacon. Korczak lived with his wife at the edge of town in a ramshackle house nearly dwarfed by the town dump-truck parked proudly beside it. The other man he mentioned, Tarnowski, ran the shops owned by the township, half a dozen of them within a five-mile radius of Jadowia. In my memory, he had worn the same pale green shirt and shiny suit for years. He had six children, two of them crip-pled and retarded. He seemed a pitiful target for all this effort.

"Father Jerzy's people have all the records," Powierza said. "But they're probably doctored anyway. They're going to go for the people involved, he says. He thinks they'll talk."

"Like who? You mean Korczak?"

"He didn't say. Korczak for sure, I guess. Farby, whoever."

"Jabłoński?"

"I don't know. Maybe."

"He must know everything in this town."

"You know he used to run a secret slaughterhouse? Yeah, he did. Years ago. When meat was rationed, everything controlled. Your father and I, we couldn't move a pig across the road then. It was all black market. That's how they're going to get Skalski."

"Skalski?" I was visibly startled.

"Karol Skalski, the vet. He organized the whole thing."

I'm not sure what Powierza said after that, although it was clear he had no details. My mind was running off on its own. Did Powierza know what he was talking about? For that matter, did Father Jerzy know what he was talking about? Meat rationing had ended a few years ago. It had lingered well after martial law was suspended, but still far enough in the past that no one thought of it anymore. Circumstantially, it made sense; Karol would be well placed to organize it, to know how to do it. But so what? It was all in the past.

I left Powierza's kitchen feeling confusion and dismay. Did Jola know about this? I halted by the sagging gate between Powierza's barnyard and my own. The kitchen window cast a yellow glow, and the light from my grandfather's room upstairs flickered behind the poplar's tossing bare branches. A cold wind sliced in from the north with a moan like a train in the distance. A weight of depression filled my chest, a foreboding, for the things Powierza had said and not said, for the forces let loose. And I sensed, by instinct even before I thought it through, that if what he said about Karol Skalski were true, it made my chances with Jola more difficult, not easier. I could sense it in her sympathy for him the last time we met; if he were in trouble—of the sort Powierza mentioned—she would stand by him.

Why should these past offenses, real or imagined, matter now?

All of this "investigation," if that was what it was, seemed pointless and irrelevant to me. I thought of Farby, with his placid pumpkin face: he would be gone soon enough anyway, swept away in elections this autumn. Korczak? Likewise. Or Tarnowski? I'd seen him only that morning, peddling his wobbly bicycle to work, his nose dribbling and knuckles red on the handlebars, an absurd lime-green stocking cap pulled over his ears. Did he know he was about to be caught up in this and possibly prosecuted? Was this what the "revolution" was all about? I found it hard to believe.

I was staring at the sky when I heard a clatter of metal from the direction of the barns. Wondering if a cow had escaped from the barn, I walked back to see and found Grandpa in the covered shed that connected the two barns, rummaging behind a pile of old lumber. There was no light in the shed, but I could hardly mistake his form, the slope of his shoulders in his old coat and the flat cap on his head.

"What are you doing, Grandpa?"

He answered with a muttered curse, and I realized I had startled him.

"You okay?" I said.

"Of course."

"I didn't know you were out." Usually he was in bed early, soon after supper.

"Went for a walk," he said, emerging from the corner of the shed. The cross-cut saw and the single-blade ax that usually hung on the shed wall lay against the pile of lumber, and he picked them up and replaced them on their pegs. Ordinarily, I would have gone in and left him alone, but I felt like talking with him, or, rather, hearing his gruffness dissolve, the way it would sometimes, into a free-form soliloquy. He was more talkative in the daytime, mostly in the morning and when he could pause in bright sunlight between some chore or another, when he would rest on a wagon wheel or sit on a milk can and ramble on.

"You coming in?"

"Yep." He went to the bench along the shed wall and I heard the sound of nails dropping into a tin can. We walked toward the house.

"What have you been doing?" I asked.

"Fence," he said.

"At night?" I didn't ask which fence. I was already irritating him enough.

"Wanted to get out of the house," he said. "You been to Powierza's?" He was changing the subject. His fence was his fence. Period. He was cranky, but I didn't mind. I liked Grandpa, which was something different from love. People don't necessarily like the people they are supposed to love. Anyway, Powierza was on my mind.

"I saw him," I said. "He's okay, I guess."

We entered the house, stripped off our coats, and went to the kitchen, which was still warm from supper.

"He's going to be a politician now, huh?" he asked.

I had only begun to suspect that myself.

"How did you figure that?"

He shrugged. I poured tea from the kettle on the stove. He stirred three spoons of sugar into the tea and wrapped his hands around the cup, his enlarged thumb held aloft. "Might as well," he said. "He was never much of a farmer." In Grandpa's book, you couldn't be a decent farmer—or maybe anything else—and work in a barn lot that looked like a junkyard.

"I want to ask you about something," I said.

"What?"

"Why is all this stuff going on in town? Not the politics. The Jewish stuff. Why is everyone so worried?"

"Because they're idle and lazy and they'd rather spend their time gossiping and worrying than doing useful work." He sipped his tea. "They ought to worry, if there was any good reason for it."

"But there is no reason?"

"No. If the Jews were really going to return, which they aren't, then they damn well ought to worry. But no Jew is going to come back here."

I could understand this notion. What was there to come back to, beyond a few old buildings?

"It was a misery for them," he went on. "Do you think you'd come back?"

"I guess not."

"No. You wouldn't. I can tell you."

"So why are people doing all this digging in their houses? What are they looking for? Is it true there's gold or something?"

"Of course not. The Jews had no gold. These people are ignorant and hysterical. They think it's like a lottery, a big hidden prize. People who live here now have no idea of what life was like then. They don't remember, or they came from somewhere else, or they believe the swill the government handed out for years."

He meant official propaganda against the Jews, which had recurred in waves in the past.

"They made demons out of the Jews, for their own reasons. Poles like to believe in demons and fairy tales. Demons are best. It makes them feel better. Gives them an excuse."

"For what?"

"For complaining. For surviving and not earning enough of the world's sympathy. For not being appreciated as victims. They feel like they got cheated out of it. The Poles are still here. The Jews aren't. Tell me, what do you think Poland is known for in the world?"

I tried to think what he meant.

"Copernicus?" he teased. "Lech Wałęsa?"

"The pope," I said.

"Ach." He made a face. "Okay, the pope. And what else?"

I said nothing.

"Auschwitz, that's what. Auschwitz, Treblinka, Sobibor. The concentration camps. Six million Jews died, and people think they all died in Poland."

"That's not Poland's fault."

"No, but there are things people don't want to remember."

"What things?"

"I don't know. It's complicated. Many things."

"What things?"

"Moving into their houses. Burning down their temples. Stealing the stones off their graves and using them to build houses, barns."

"They did that?"

"Yes. They did that."

"You mean after the war?"

"After, during. Who knows? There's more than a few barns in this part of Poland built on tombstone foundations." He stood up and pushed the chair back under the table. "I'm tired, Leszek."

"Why did they do that?"

"It was a horrible time. You've heard about it, over and over. People couldn't find food. There wasn't even a brick. People had to get by however they could. I thought your grandmother and your father might starve to death. I thought we all might." He stopped by the kitchen door, but didn't glance back at me. "Good night, son."

His footsteps creaked on the stairs. The door to his room opened and closed. He was right, I had heard it before. Grandpa was serving with the army at the outbreak of the war, retreated with units that broke up in disarray as they fell back eastward through Pomerania and Masuria. He found temporary refuge, finally, between the German and Russian armies in the forests that extended in broad reaches across Eastern Poland. For years, bands of partisan guerrillas, including one he led, fought throughout the area, harassing the Germans, the Russians, and, by the end, each other. They lived off the land and used their knowledge of the terrain and the forests to hit and run and hide. Much of their activity was ineffectual, but it was not surrender. For some months, he had been encamped with his men in the forests only a few miles from this house, where his wife and son—my grandmother and father—clung on throughout the war.

This narrative I recalled from many tellings, heard mostly as a child over the remains of Sunday dinners when my father and Grandpa would push back from the table to light their cigarettes. Some thread of memory would be tugged—a name, a place—and I would listen, again, as the thread wove a tapestry whose whole I never quite saw. It was as though they spoke to me, told it all for my benefit, and yet they really spoke above and beyond me, for themselves, for each other, arguing sometimes over a date, a place, a sequence of events, matters irrelevant to me but central to them, to their ordering of things, to their remembering. These stories held me rapt, my eyes darting from face to face as they corrected, amplified, prodded. Grandpa talked the most because, I suppose, he had seen the most. My grandmother was never talkative, never a story-teller, and yet it was she who supplied corrections and settled disputed chronologies, as though her memory were the accepted reference. My father was six years old in 1940, a fact that seems to have been planted in my brain from these conversations, because, even now, to calculate his age, I begin by subtracting six from 1940. His stories had the stark simplicity of shadows cast upon a wall, but he also knew Grandpa's as well as his own. My mother, five years younger than father and from a town forty miles away, could contribute only her own family's secondhand experiences. Together, she and I were listeners.

Though I heard the stories often, I remembered them as fragments. Once, I heard, my grandfather came at night to the house with half a slaughtered forest piglet, and my grandmother confronted him with a butcher knife in one hand and a candle trembling in the other, until she recognized the face she had not seen in more than a year. Or Grandma watching from the window the day that the much-feared Commandant Haupt himself stood smoking his cigarettes by the fender of his staff car at our front gate while his soldiers ransacked our barns and departed finally with four chickens and a goose. Or Grandpa's story of falling asleep in a Masurian haystack and waking up to find a German platoon camped in a corner of the field, forcing him to burrow to the center of the haystack, where he stayed for two days until the Germans departed.

Why did so much of this history seem disconnected to me? Why had I never asked? I thought of Powierza, scheming at his kitchen table, flailing around to solve the puzzle of his son's death. He was a man who did things, who acted. So, too, had been my grandfather. I climbed the stairs to his room and tapped on the door. He was in bed, reading from an old newspaper.

"Tell me about the Jews," I said.

He folded the paper and set it on the table by the bed. "What's to tell? They suffered, they died."

"How they lived."

He reached for the light. "Another time. When it's not so late."

"What were they like?"

He found the switch. The light went out.

"Normal people, Leszek," he said. "Men, women and children. They were not something mysterious."

When I rose in the morning, he was already gone, out with his horse and wagon. I made up my mind to try to talk with him before the day was out.

But then two events intervened. The first was a town meeting. The second was a summons for a conversation with Roman Jabłoński.

The town meeting was the regularly scheduled monthly session of the village council, and it normally would not have attracted enough observers to fill a pew in the church. But hints of scandal had assured a major turnout. The mood of anticipation was heightened by the rumors flying around town. Among them was speculation that Father Jerzy himself would assume command over village affairs, and another suggested Twerpicz, as the young priest's approved choice, installed as his tribune. Another prediction was that the council, as a countermove against the Citizens' Committee activists, would call an executive session and ban public observers from the meeting. The grim-faced Wanda Gromek, a fixture of town politics for two decades, would chair the meeting in Farby's absence, as the senior representative on the council. The gossip said she had been making the rounds of other council members throughout the week. Presumably she was building a defense for the incumbents against guilt-by-association with Farby. As for Farby himself, rumors circulated, then were dismissed, that he had turned himself in, or was somehow in custody, and would arrive at the meeting to spread blame like an infection among the town officials.

I had not attended a town meeting since I was force-marched to one by my high school class, but clearly this was not an occasion to miss. Distinctly present in Jadowia's atmosphere of conflicting gossip and confusion was an odor of vengeance, anger, and ambition that amounted to a kind of low-grade anarchy. This was perhaps most vividly expressed by the frequent mention of an urgent need for "order." Naturally, there was no consensus, at least that I could detect, on what "order" should look like, or by whose hand it should be imposed. Although I had never paid much attention to politics, it didn't require deep political acumen—in this country of natural-born subversives—to predict that whoever was on top now would not be for long.

A crowd of sixty or seventy gathered an hour early in front of the meeting hall, the same building that housed the town fire-truck and the library on the second floor. Jan Moskal, the coffin maker who was the chief of the volunteer firemen, seized the opportunity to slide apart the firehouse doors and drive the truck out, which stood idling and blowing a cloud of diesel exhaust, until Lech Matusak, standing with a group that had strolled over from the bar, yelled at him to kill the engine. Then Moskal got out and polished its fenders with a soft rag.

"Keep it shined, Moskal," Matusak called to him. "Wanda will need to pawn it soon."

Moskal frowned and vigorously polished, supervised by a clutch of small boys.

"It's probably already mortgaged," Janowski said to me. "Probably to the Party. Or Jabłoński." We were leaning against Krupik's police car at the edge of the road, waiting with everyone else. Krupik was not in sight. I looked around for Powierza, but he wasn't there either. The air was still, and cigarette smoke hovered over the group. A few soft flakes of snow began to fall.

Stefan Wilk, who owned the sausage shop, sidled up to us. His shop was next to Janowski's bakery. They were known to have squabbled with each other for years, the way neighbors will, but the baker, who had been in a state of high agitation since discovering the damage to his storehouse foundation, seemed happy to see Wilk, as though their arguments through the years had made Wilk a potential witness in his behalf. Janowski carried a fat envelope, loose papers poking out of its open end. He was preparing his case against a mystery plaintiff, like a general planning a defense against an army he couldn't see.

"Tax records," he said, holding up the envelope. "Twenty-five years of taxes. All here." He slapped the envelope. "Electricity bills. Coal receipts. Everything."

"That's good, Józef," Wilk said. "You won't have to worry."

"Well, I would certainly think not, I must say," Janowski said. "With all I have here, I'm ready for any conspiracy."

"Did you see the scrawling on the wall of the bus kiosk?" Wilk said. "It said, 'Jews to the gas.' "

"No!"

"Yes."

"Who did that?" I asked.

"Who knows," Wilk said.

"Take your pick," Janowski said.

"Kids," Wilk said.

"I wouldn't be so sure," Janowski said. It crossed my mind, momentarily, that he might have done it himself. Or at least didn't disagree with it. If Janowski felt concern—not to say panic—he wanted company. "They're back in Prague," he said. "As I told you before, Leszek. And Budapest, too. Yes, indeed. I've read of it. Warsaw, too. And now here."

"How do you know?" I asked.

He looked at me as though I were a slow-witted child.

"What exactly happened, Józef?" I tried again. "I mean to you. Was there a mezuzah?"

"There was no mezuzah. What happened to me was the same as with others. It was the foundation of the storehouse. Dug up. Disrupted."

"Just the storehouse?" I said. "Why not the main building, the bakery?"

"The bakery has a brick foundation. With mortar. The storehouse has a stone foundation. I don't know why. But there is a connection. Everyone says it. A connection to the Jews." He lowered his voice, "There is, what would you say, a fifth column. An agent. I know it."

Wilk rolled his eyes, but said nothing.

"I want to look at your storehouse," I said. "Do you mind?"

He glanced up the street as Pani Gromek approached. "The storehouse? Be my guest."

Gromek marched past the knots of waiting people, and if there had been any doubt that village officialdom were under siege, it evaporated in the moment of her arrival. The swell of voices ebbed and all eyes followed her to the door. She carried a worn plastic briefcase and went in the door without a word. In her wake followed Kazimierz Paszek, the council secretary, smiling and nodding to no one in particular, as if to deny any connection with the figure who entered before him. The door closed behind them, and then, in quick succession the other council members arrived: Samborski, Trela, Matlak, Struszek, and Bartkowski. Bartkowski, who had managed a state poultry farm into bankruptcy five years earlier— one would have thought that impossible, but he accomplished it— left the door ajar. The crowd then trailed the council members into the building. I moved with them, near the rear, along with Wilk and Janowski. Before I got to the door, I saw people peering up the street, and turned myself to see Father Jerzy advancing in a small phalanx that included Twerpicz and several others. Just behind and towering over them was Powierza.

"It's Father Jerzy!"

"Pan Twerpicz!"

"Bless you, Father."

"Make them confess!"

There were shouts of laughter and approval as the crowd parted. Hands reached out to grasp the priest's arm, to shake his hand, or to pat Twerpicz on the back. There was a small but enthusiastic burst of applause. The priest nodded modestly. Twerpicz, jostled by well-wishers, seemed worried about losing sight of Father Jerzy's cassock. Powierza smiled and kept stride with the priest's entourage.

The room was as cold as a meat locker, even with the crowd. Two long tables waited in front, with rows of benches facing them. Gromek stood behind the table, still in her coat and withdrawing pieces of paper from her case. "Can we get some lights on in here?" she said. Paszek jumped up and walked back along the aisle. "Lights?" he shouted.

"Can you pay for them?" someone shouted in reply, accompanied by loud guffaws. But the lights came on.

Pani Gromek gaveled the meeting to order, and instructed Paszek to read the roll. More benches were dragged in from outside, causing Gromek to demand quiet at the back of the room. The group with Father Jerzy sat on the side, Twerpicz now and then whispering to the priest. The rest of the audience watched them expectantly.

"We will proceed," Pani Gromek said, "with the discussion of the plan for the new Jadowia Commercial Park, which, as the council of course remembers, was discussed in the previous meeting. Pan Matlak, I believe you had some comments regarding the access to the proposed location?"

"Comrade Chairman," Matlak said. "Thank you. Yes, some question about its boundaries, actually."

"Madame Chairman." Twerpicz was on his feet. Wanda Gromek did not look up from the papers in front of her. "Madame Chairman!"

Matlak halted and blew his nose. Gromek lifted narrowed eyes over the rims of her glasses. "The floor," she said, "is occupied at present, Comrade Twerpicz."

"*Mister* Twerpicz, if you please, Pani Gromek. I demand to hear the report on the financial condition of this township."

"This is not on the agenda for this meeting, uh, *Mister* Twerpicz, as the agenda clearly states. Please do not interrupt."

Twerpicz stayed on his feet. "I believe this matter should be placed on the agenda with immediate effect, in the light of recent events in this village."

"You have not been elected to this council just yet, Mr. Twerpicz, and it is not your matter to decide." A soft titter of derision rippled from the benches. Then someone called out, "Tell us who's stealing from us."

Twerpicz ducked down to confer momentarily with Father Jerzy. "We demand to hear a financial statement," he said.

"In due course," Gromek said, "all matters will be discussed . . ."

"Where's Farby?" a shout echoed from a corner of the room.

" . . . In the meantime," Gromek continued, rapping her gavel and lifting her voice. "We will not succumb to anarchy here! Now, Matlak, please proceed."

Matlak resumed, but no one, even at the council table, seemed to be listening. I saw that the older parish priest, Father Tadeusz, was standing by himself in a back corner, and I wondered why he was not with the group around the younger priest. Powierza had taken his seat with Father Jerzy's people, a mountain in their midst, his arms folded across his chest and staring straight ahead. A low buzz of conversation persisted around the room while Matlak recited the dimensions of the "commercial park," which, in fact, was nothing more than a new location for the weekly market that was growing steadily larger. I wondered if it would continue to grow when the Russians no longer showed up to peddle screwdrivers and underwear. Two seats down from me, Janowski was pulling sheets of paper from his fat envelope, his knees locked together and his hands fluttering. When Matlak paused, he leaped to his feet.

"Madame Chairman," he said, his voice cracking, "I want to know what is happening with the Jews."

There was a sharp silence at first, and then yelps of "Yes, hear, hear," from the audience.

"What is going on?" Janowski said. "I mean, what is being done?"

"You refer, I presume, to the, ah, the events," Gromek said.

"Yes. What's being done? I demand to know," Janowski said. His hand was trembling and some of his papers slipped to the floor. I felt a pang of sympathy for his nervousness, even if I found it hard to understand his alarm. I liked Janowski, who, as far as I knew, was an honest and hardworking man.

"I believe Mr. Bartkowski may have something on this," Mrs. Gromek said.

Twerpicz shot to his feet.

"Madame Chairman," he shouted, "is this subject on the agenda? I insist on an answer to our demands for a full financial accounting."

"We are on another matter now. Mr. Bartkowski?"

"Yes," Bartkowski said. "Measures are being taken." An expectant silence followed, but Bartkowski was evidently finished.

"*What* measures?" Janowski asked, his voice breaking again.

"Perhaps Officer Krupik . . ." Bartkowski said, searching the sides of the room. Krupik, as though emerging from protective cover, rose slowly from the far end of one of the benches.

"The office of police," he said, "that is, myself, has been conducting a systematic investigation into these unfortunate phenomena, which are, of course, a matter of concern, and we are being most thorough and complete." Then he halted, though he remained standing.

"Well, what?" someone called. "What have you found?"

"We are, that is, I am, in the intermediate stages of a full analysis of the reports and data to hand at this point in time. As you may or may not be aware, the property of the police residence was, significantly I believe, the first of these, uh, assaults, and I can assure you special precautions have been taken and will be taken as regards the security of the police residence. Should it fall under further assault."

A few snorts and guffaws responded to this, and Janowski stood up again and called out, "But what is going on?"

"I am working on the theory," Krupik said, "that there are disruptive forces at work." He spoke slowly, as if mustering great reserves of patience. "Perhaps the efforts of a . . . a fifth column."

"Fifth column of what?"

"I believe we will have the answer in due course," Krupik said. "We are exploring all avenues and conducting a full analysis of the situation." He sat down.

"Comrade Chairman, if we may continue with the commercial park discussion?" asked Strużek, a hopeless toady employed by Gromek's brother in a brick factory in the next town. "The matter of revenue generation from this new facility has been given considerable study by myself with a view to correcting the deficiencies of the former system, and I wish to present the council with detailed projections . . ."

The room again stirred with audible inattention. I saw Father Tadeusz leave his solitary position in the corner of the room. He stepped to the door and went out, closing it quietly behind him. On one of the rear benches, a bottle drifted from hand to hand and was tucked into a tattered denim jacket. The men with the bottle wiped their lips and whispered among themselves. Andrzej the plumber slipped into the room and sidled along the wall. Father Jerzy's group was in huddled conference, the priest's head at the center of the consultations. Gromek watched it all though hooded eyes.

I got up to leave. There was something I wanted to do, and it seemed to me that the standoff between Father Jerzy's group and Pani Gromek would outlast this meeting. As I reached the door, Andrzej stopped me.

"I was looking for you, Leszek," he said. "I'm supposed to give you this. Okay?" I accepted the envelope he pressed into my hand, and, as I did, a commotion, then applause, rang out in the room.

Father Jerzy himself was now on his feet. Strużek had ceased talking.

"We believe this has gone on long enough, Madame Chairman," the priest said. "We are present here, representatives of the Citizens' Committee, to request in a civilized manner a full report on the financial state of the village administration."

"You're out of order, Father," Pani Gromek said.

"And, may I add, we are prepared to call for the immediate intervention of higher authorities if this report on your maladministration and corruption is not forthcoming at the earliest possible date. If it is not, the Citizens' Committee, under the guidance of Mr. Twerpicz, will issue its own report."

"Your authority, Father, does not extend to this particular body. As for the higher authority you refer to, perhaps it exists in the building where your schemes are planned . . ." Cheers and catcalls erupted from the crowd, the way it might if a pair of brawlers had squared off behind the barroom. Gromek slammed her gavel. "Perhaps you need assistance in finding your way back to your church where your subversion and disruption must, however unfortunately, be tolerated." She was shouting by now, her face flushed. The gavel banged down again. "This meeting is adjourned."

The building emptied swiftly, and amid a good deal of laughter. The audience would have preferred if the fight had gone on longer, but at least it was a fight and it promised more rounds ahead. Gromek and the council vanished, perhaps out some rear door. Father Jerzy and Twerpicz left within a circle of admiration and curiosity, and the rest of the crowd dispersed back to the bar and into the village. I did not see Powierza, though I assumed he departed with Father Jerzy's crowd. I looked for Janowski, too, but he had gone on. I walked over to the bakery and saw him in its lighted interior, behind his counter, as the evening darkness settled.

I went through the alley to the back of the building. The storehouse was wooden, with a padlocked door and a dark stone foundation. I walked around three sides before I found the spot. A crude patchwork of brick had been used to replace the missing stones, marking a gash about three feet long and roughly the thickness of two rows of brick. The original foundation had been laid with care and skill, employing stones of varying shape, some round and about the size of a football, some flatter and rectangular. These seemed to me the kind of stones cleared from fields or hauled from stream beds—who knew how long ago. But I was looking for another kind, and, on my hands and knees, I found them. They were laid at irregular intervals, but all at a certain level, fitted into the wall about eighteen inches up from the ground, at the same level as the brick patchwork. The edges were rough, but obviously worked by mallet and chisel, and they extended in a broken band along the foundation wall.

I needed a lever, a stick or crowbar, to wedge one of the stones loose, which would just be possible since no mortar held them, only their own weight and layers of damp moss. Fortunately every backyard in the village contains its heap of discarded objects, and near the back fence I found a firm stick of wood and a bent piece of angle iron, and I took them to the rear of the storehouse, out of sight from the bakery's back window. I picked a stone that looked as though it could be loosened without toppling the row of stones above it, and pried carefully at its edges. After several minutes, digging with the stick, the piece of iron and my fingers, the stone began to move. By fractions of an inch, I shifted one side, then another, coaxing it gradually outward. After a few more minutes it protruded an inch. I kept at it. Crows were squawking in the bare-limbed tree behind me, flapping in to roost for the night. After another inch of progress, the stone slid more freely, so that I could wiggle it outward, back and forth, with my hands. I paused when I had wedged it out six inches, not wanting to remove it for fear the wall above it might collapse. The upper side of the stone was smooth. On the underside, though, I could feel the surface etched by a regular pattern, deep as a fingertip. Words written into stone. I sprawled on my back, squinting at the stone's underside, and fished into my pockets for some matches, for now it was too dark to see. The match cupped in both hands, I peered at the surface above me.

I couldn't read what I saw there. I might even have been looking at it upside down. But I was sure it was Hebrew.

With my feet I pushed the stone back into the wall. It went in much easier than it had come out. Making another circuit of the building, I located about a dozen or fifteen stones of the same size and shape. They were almost certainly what Grandpa had described: cemetery stones used as foundation blocks.

I left through the alley and entered the street, wondering if all the other reported incidents amounted to the same thing—old cemetery stones pulled from their foundations. If Krupik knew, he had not mentioned it directly, and I had heard no one else speak of gravestones in the foundations. If the other incidents were the same, who was doing this? And why? And why now? What connection was there to the ripped door facings, the exposed mezuzahs?

As I crossed the street by the bus stop, I saw Andrzej go into the bar and I remembered the envelope he handed me. In the hubbub at the end of the meeting I had shoved the folded envelope into my shirt pocket and forgotten it. Under the streetlight I opened it. Inside was a short typewritten note:

Dear Leszek Maleszewski:
   There is a matter of mutual interest I wish to discuss with you. If it meets with your convenience, I would be pleased if you could pay a call at my office around 6 P.M. this evening.
                                                    Roman Jabłoński

It was nearly six o'clock now. Apprehensively, I stared at the note. What did Jabłoński want? I saw a splintered bench at the edge of the square and sat down on it. He would confront me, I thought, about my inquiries in Warsaw. Well, so what? I had done nothing wrong. There was nothing Jabłoński could do to me. I sat for some minutes. Across the square, drinkers tumbled into the street, the lights inside the bar blinked out, and Pani Agnieszka followed, locking the front door after her. Perhaps I should ignore Jabłoński's summons, or at least consult with Powierza first. After all, this was no police order. I could go or not go, as I pleased. Perhaps, though, I would learn something useful. I saw Andrzej heading down the south road to his house. The drinkers one by one disappeared into the darkness, and I was the only person left on the square. To hell with it. I would go.

Lights burned in the Farmers' Co-op, although no cars waited in the driveway. I rapped on the door, heard nothing, then pushed it open and called out.

"Hello," came an answer from down the hallway. Jabłoński stepped out of an office, wearing a gray cardigan sweater and staring at me over the rims of his glasses.

"Leszek," he said. He spoke warmly, as though he had known me a long time. "Come in. Come in." I went down the hallway to his office. "Please, sit down."

I don't think I had seen Jabłoński at close range for years, possibly not since I was a schoolboy, in the brief time that my father had served on the town council, and there would certainly be no reason for me to have made any particular impression on him. As nearly as my own memory served, he seemed not to have changed, for he was still a slight man with thinning, colorless hair, pale skin, and pale blue eyes behind glasses with transparent rims. On his desk were a full ashtray (which he now emptied), some papers and file folders, and a small plastic tray with two glasses and a bottle of vodka. His office was tidy, ordered, a room where no clutter was tolerated.

"A drink, Leszek?"

"No, thank you."

"I will, if you don't mind. Sure you won't join me?"

"No, but please go ahead."

"Your health." He drank and placed the glass on the desk. "Good," he said. "You're well?"

"Yes, thank you."

"And your family?"

"Yes, thanks."

"Glad to hear it. Now, Leszek, I'm a direct man, so I will get to the point. I know you are interested in the matter of the death of your neighbor, young Mr. Powierza. You made certain inquiries in Warsaw, I believe."

"Yes, I—"

"Never mind. I know about it, of course. I don't know if you intended to embarrass me in some way—no, no need to say anything, anything at all. I would suggest that you might just as easily have approached me directly and saved yourself some trouble."

"Embarrassing you was not the point, Mr. Jabłoński. It was—"

"Never mind. As I say, I know about it. The point is, Leszek . . . or perhaps I should call you Mr. Maleszewski, you are a grown man now. The point is, Mr. Maleszewski, I want this business stopped. Now. And I am prepared to make it stop. It's not the Powierza matter I refer to, at least in itself. I know nothing about that. He did some trivial work for me, as I told his father. The truth is, Tomek was a limited young man, although of course I did not say that to his father. But, as I say, it is not this which perturbs me. It's rather the general atmosphere, this climate of hostility that seems to have descended upon us, this open season for libel and slander. It can lead to no good end. As I say, I intend for it to stop. And I count on you for assistance. I count on you, may I say, for your good judgment."

I was flabbergasted by the entire speech, but especially its conclusion. I did not know whether I was angry or simply amazed.

"How do you think that would happen?" I said. "What do you mean, my assistance?"

"You are an intelligent young man. I simply don't think you want to see this go further, this air of accusation, this unnecessary sifting of ashes. You are perhaps too young to remember the era of the show trials, which was a less than noble feature of our Socialist history. I sometimes wonder if we are headed that way again. Under a different guise, of course. In any case, I intend to enlist your aid in the assurance that it does not happen here."

"Pardon me, Mr. Jabłoński, but I am not following this at all. In the first place, I don't know how I would help you. Or why I should want to."

He poured another shot of vodka for himself and studied me closely.

"You resemble your father quite strongly," he said.

I didn't answer.

"Taller, of course. But the same bones. Similar manner of speaking. I knew Mariusz quite well, did you know that?"

"He was on the town council for a while."

"Yes, of course. But I knew him quite well, apart from that. Quite well. He worked for me, actually, I should say. Or we worked together, is perhaps a better way to put it. Harnessed to the common goal." He smiled. "You might say."

"He served four years," I said.

"The council, yes. Symbolic service, really. He actually contributed far more. Did you know that?"

"He refused to stand again."

"I suppose he might have put it that way. But, as I say, the council was mostly a symbolic—a public—contribution."

"There was some other . . . contribution?"

"Considerable, indeed. Your father worked for the Party, is what I'm saying, Leszek. Ah, there I go again. Lapsing into informality. The memory of your father, I suppose. I was fond of him. Those were difficult days, the late sixties, early seventies. The nation needed vigilant partners, vigilant citizens. I understood that. So did your father. Even in a small place like this, we were all called on for our—how would you say it?—yes, for our eyes, our ears. There was economic crime, and there was subversion and unrest, and, although we did our best, I would submit that the proof our vigilance was less than perfect is the mess we inherit today. Alas. But we tried. Your father contributed, yes. To the best of his abilities."

I had the sensation that my fingers were freezing, as though I were sitting in some dank cave. My ears rang.

"How contributed?"

"He spied, is the way people would say it now. In the current, relativist climate. This *unforgiving* climate. He informed on his neighbors."

"Bullshit!"

"No, Mr. Maleszewski, not bullshit. Good, useful information, is how I would characterize it. Helpful." He tapped his desk with his fingertips and said the word again. "Helpful. Patriotic even. But it wouldn't be called that today, would it? Anyway, your skepticism is natural. Anticipated, I should say. Here, let me show you something."

He unfolded the file at his elbow and slid a piece of paper across the desk.

The print danced before my eyes: a typewritten report on a form labeled as subdistrict so-and-so of the Ministry of the Interior, office of supervisor of such-and-such, numbers and boxes, filled in with dates, more numbers, a gibberish of bureaucratic coding. Out of the typing below, a name leaped up at me. "Powierza, Stanislaw," the words rising, as through water. "Subject peasant farmer Powierza . . . unauthorized cutting of wood for sale . . . trees cut and concealed on above date . . ." And below this the typed name, Mariusz Maleszewski, and then his signature. Yes. His signature. Compact, cramped.

I wadded the piece of paper and threw it onto Jabłoński's desk. "This is garbage," I said.

"Ah-ah." He picked up the ball of paper. "Be calm now." He smoothed it and slid it back to me. "Go on. Take it, study it at your leisure. It's photocopied anyway. And, as I'm sure you will comprehend when you've settled down, there is more where this came from. Quite a lot more."

"It's all shit," I said. "I don't believe any of it."

"If you don't now, I assure you, you will. I could put others in the mail for you. Spare you these visits."

"Hang them from the lampposts if you want," I said. "Nobody cares." I felt a choking in my throat. "Nobody will swallow it."

"They do care, and they will believe. As I think you know. People will believe anything, but they believe the worst easiest of all. I'll give you some time to think about this. Your reaction is normal, entirely. But you are a mature man, for your young years. You are hardworking, I'm given to understand. Serious. Sober, unlike most of the population gracing our picturesque little hamlet. You have— yes, indeed—a future. Perhaps you didn't realize. People think of you as a potential leader here. Perhaps a bit like your father. Not in all respects, of course."

"You don't know anything about my father."

"Oh, I knew him all right. Respected him, to a point. Let me just say that he had a potential, but ultimately not quite the steel, the resolve, one might have hoped for."

I wanted to throttle him. I tried to stand, but my feet felt disconnected.

"Just one more moment. I have a last thing to say. Don't talk, just listen, and then leave. Call off Powierza. How, you are going to ask? Just do it. Appeal to him. Tell him what I told you, if you wish. Tell him what you will. He has been your neighbor all his life, and he has been a friend to your family all his life. He has helped you and your family more than once. Wait! One moment, please. There are other files, other people. This misery will not love company. Stop this, and keep it stopped. Use your head."

I managed, finally, to get to my feet. My head was pounding. My throat was dry. I could not find my voice.

Jabłoński stood, too.

"Yes," he said. "Use your head. Try to think in terms of consequences. And, oh yes. Try to use more prudence than you display in your romantic interests. An attractive woman, the veterinarian's wife. But still . . ."

"You disgust me, Jabłoński."

"Life is difficult sometimes, Mr. Maleszewski," he said. "We have to persevere, and think clearly. Good night to you."

I made it to the door and as far as fifty yards down the road before I doubled over in the darkness and retched up bile from an empty stomach.

Chapter Ten

Father Tadeusz left the meeting, walked quickly through the village, past the coffin maker's and the turnoff to the veterinarian's clinic, and followed the west road out of town, flanked by open fields. Far ahead a bank of forest rose at a fork in the road like the prow of a great dark ship. The countryside was nearly empty. A truck roared past on the way to town and a farmer with a horse and wagon clopped past him, the horse's nostrils blowing plumes of vapor in the damp air. Mud was hardening in the cold. A light snow commenced as he reached the edge of the woods, more than a mile from the last house in the village. The grass gave stiffly under his foot as he left the road.

It was his second trip here in as many days. He had found it the day before, at the end of his walk through the forest that wrapped itself around the town, a course that crossed only two main roads, so that when he happened upon the place it gave him a surprise, as though he had expected some warning, some mark or announcement of terrain or topography. He had been distracted, in fact, by a pair of ravens, croaking back and forth as he strode through the forest. He had been peering up through the trees and saw them for an instant, black wings knifing through a wedge of darkening sky. And then he saw where he was, amid older and taller pines, at a verge of hummocky ground, devoid of forest undergrowth and dotted with dark forms, suspended in a quiet so deep that his breath caught, then came to him through his open mouth, as though the air were rationed.

It was already late then, the winter dark falling quickly, and he stayed only a short time. That night, he lay awake a long time.

Now he stepped into the woods, tracing as nearly as he could remember the route of his departure the day before. He picked his way around brambles and fallen branches, moving steadily and making no noise other than the soft rustle of wet and frosted leaves beneath his feet. The pale seawater light of the pine grove slid into view. He halted. A faint wind-sigh sounded in the high branches of the pines along with a creaking of limbs, like the sound of a ship's rigging. Without knowing why, Father Tadeusz had the sensation he was not alone. He stepped over a fallen log, skirted a dry thicket of brambles, and emerged at the earthen berm that lay around the old cemetery like a low collapsed wall.

He saw the dog first, staring at him, its ears cocked. A dark Alsatian. It might have growled, but perhaps that was imagination. It was another second before he saw the man, or rather his black-coated back, for he was squatting, or kneeling, facing the opposite direction and busy somehow with his hands. But as Father Tadeusz stood still he heard—distinctly this time—the murmurous warning from the throat of the Alsatian, which still did not stir, but looked straight at him. The man at the dog's shoulder, still on his knees, straightened and turned. His face was shadowed, with thick brows and dark hair protruding under a seaman's black knit cap. Slowly, he got to his feet.

A few seconds earlier, Father Tadeusz might have pivoted and stolen away, had he been able to do so undetected, for there was something in the scene before him that suggested a privacy better left undisturbed. There was no choice now but to step forward, and as his foot sought the spongy ground, he loosened the scarf around his neck, so that his priest's collar was visible.

"Hello," he said.

"Hello." The voice was deep, hoarse. The man advanced a step, then stopped. The dog moved at his side. After a few steps, Father Tadeusz halted as well. He thrust his hands in his pockets and consciously glanced away from the man before him, his gaze surveying the hummocked earth, the dark stones and finally toward the sky and the over-arching boughs of pine. The impression he hoped to strike was that of a casual walker, a hiker on a woodland path, however preposterous that might be, especially since there was no path here.

The man watched Father Tadeusz guardedly, his hands hanging at his sides and caked with mud.

"Interesting," the priest said, shifting his gaze again.

"Excuse me?"

"This place. It's, uh, it's very quiet here. Peaceful."

The man did not answer, and remained motionless.

"I'm Father Tadeusz. From the church. In Jadowia."

"Yes."

"I didn't know about this place until recently," he said. "Then I wanted to see it."

"You've been here before?" the man asked evenly.

"Only yesterday. I wanted to see it again."

"Only yesterday?" he said. His tone skeptical. It seemed an opening to Father Tadeusz, like a lantern's flicker in the night.

"Yes. The first time. And you?" The man relaxed enough to pick at the mud on his fingers.

"What about me?"

"You come here often?" He studied the man's hands. "You're . . ."

"Making order."

"I see."

"Vandals come here," the man said. He shifted slightly, as if to show what he had been shielding with his body, but only part way, as if he thought better of it. Father Tadeusz stepped toward him, cautiously, as the man looked uneasily toward the ground and a slab of curved stone beside him.

"People disturbing things," he said. He backed away a step. "This is a place of the dead. It should be . . ."

"Honored."

"Left alone," he said. It sounded like a correction. The priest was struck by the lines etched on the man's face, like a drawing done in black ink on yellowed parchment. The unruly brows, the spiky curling hair, the creases about the eyes combined in a portrait not merely of hardness, but a kind of ferocity, a sketch of a prisoner wrongly accused.

He swung about abruptly, clicked his tongue at the dog.

"Just a minute," Father Tadeusz called. "Who are you?"

"No one. I'm from nearby, that's all."

"What's your name?"

"Czarnek."

"I'm Father Tadeusz."

"Yes, you said."

"Oh, yes. Sorry."

"Good-bye."

"Wait. Where is it you live?"

"The distillery," he said. "Just nearby." He pointed the direction with his chin. "I must go."

He walked on without a glance back, the dog trotting ahead of him, and disappeared into the trees.

The horse and wagon were waiting in the concealment of woods a quarter of a mile behind him, and Leszek's grandfather watched the cemetery from a depression in the forest floor. He could not hear what the two men were saying, but he recognized them. The priest, he realized, was the man he had passed on the road. He identified Czarnek from the dog, the big Alsatian. That explained the footprints, the dog's prints in the frost and mud, along with the heavy boots.

The old man was out of sight, he knew, a hundred yards away, maybe more, and the wind was in his face so the dog had not scented him. From this distance, they would see nothing. This was his domain. He knew how to move here, and how to be still, and never snap a twig with a step, a skill not forgotten.

He recognized the depression he was in as a foxhole. Not his, nor those of his men. Blaski's, he reckoned. Polish Worker's Party, the poor Stalinist fools. The Communists shot him after the war, the very people he thought he was fighting for. Tossed him in a pit and scattered lime on his corpse.

His gaze followed the old defense line, holes banked to the northwest and tracing a slight crescent. People no longer knew what these depressions represented, even though they were pitted all through the forests. Blaski's men would have been here for days, he figured. You could shovel in the earth here and likely find old mess gear. Broken knives, shell casings. Bones maybe. Unmarked graves behind him. He tried to recall the deployments, then, insofar as he knew them at the time. Christ only knew. Could have been Blaski, could have been anybody. Germans maybe. No, in Poland, Germans didn't dig in. They *moved* in. Stayed. Murdered. Then ran, of course. Careless in the end. Demoralized. You couldn't kill like that and keep sane.

He studied the old line of defense, the curving flank to the left. It had been a good position, actually. He had dug positions like this one, he and his men. It was a winter like this one, too, a winter of rain and mud. His code name, Raven, like a radio signal. Raven to Fox, Eagle to Raven. Accepted orders from Eagle and never met him, never knew his real name. Killed, he heard. But you never knew. Home Army, the Peasant Battalions, the People's Guard (Blaski's bunch). Socialists, nationalists, anarchists, monarchists even, right wing and left. Fighters shuttled back and forth, unit to unit. Rotten discipline. Spied on each other. Contested for food, local loyalties, intelligence. He remembered leading a raid once to steal a radio from a unit of the People's Guard. Blaski's outfit. Tied them up and commandeered the radio. Didn't hurt them. They were all fighting for Poland, one way or another. Fighting *over* Poland, was the truth of it, by the end. Everyone wanted control, to decipher the coded commands from headquarters, then improvise. Modify. Issue orders. Out-maneuver a rival. It was easy, now, to forget the danger in it, forget how quickly you could be cut to ribbons, lined up against a wall or in front of the hole you had just dug for yourself. His men had derailed a German supply train once, just outside the freight yards at Siedlce, then got caught by two truck loads of Wehrmacht troopers rounding a bend in the road just as they were sprinting across, careless, giddy with success, sure they had made it to safety. The Germans chased them into a quarry— Raven's sense of direction having failed him. Górski was dead by then, God bless him, Górski who would never have let him misread a map. He had intended to lead his escape toward the cover of a creek that ran into the Liwiec River, but Górski wasn't there and Raven did misread his map and they were boxed in. Somehow he clawed his way up a rock face, his fingers raw and bleeding on the flint, while half his men were caught below. Their ankles were roped to the trucks, eight of them still more or less alive, and then dragged five miles to the center of Siedlce and displayed as a warning for those who would sabotage the pénal colony of Poland. Or a lasting punishment to a leader who would misread a map.

It was the beginning of a bad time, with worse yet to come. Already he had the memory of Górski's head in his lap. Outside Siedlce that day, he had seen Paweł, his lieutenant, slant left and then look back in surprise as Raven darted right. Pawel started to shout a warning, but didn't. He followed his leader. And returned to Siedlce at the end of a rope. There would be more snap judgments, wrong turns, nasty surprises.

After Siedlce they haunted the forests of Jadowia a long time. Almost home. Until the night in the field at the edge of the forest, with the flashlight beams, the shouts, the dogs barking.

Alsatians, of course. Mouths dripping.

The boy's face had been wild, his huge eyes gleaming, rolling, like a pony's in a burning barn, his skin pale as the moon, his head shorn, his grip like a talons.

His name was Chaim. How could he remember that? Nowadays he forgot in the afternoon things that people told him in the morning. Was he supposed to butcher that calf for Dąbrowski this week, or was it the next? What was the name of that priest? Why did he sometimes seem to be deaf to voices, but hear every breath of wind in the forest? Because he heard what he wanted. The deafness of old age was an acquired skill. Was memory the same, a practiced art? He forgot what he was told yesterday, but not what happened forty years ago. And deaf to voices sometimes, but never to the forest.

It whispered now, needles singing in the air. He had been sitting a long time. He got up, discounting the sound of the bones popping in his stiffened knees, and stared into the sea-light of the clearing in the distance.

It was empty now, he knew, the men gone. Raven walked in, across the soft, mossy ground, and saw that the last stone he had taken had been replaced.

Very well, he thought. Only one more and it's done.

He chose another, one he could carry more easily. He was tired. He pulled it loose and hoisted it up, lacing his fingers beneath it, and carried it back through the forest toward his wagon.

After several days, Farby's wife, full of disgust for her husband and loathing for her neighbors, who liked nothing better than seeing someone brought low, phoned her sister in Gdynia to warn her she was coming. Then she packed her clothes, found a large box for the television set, and cleaned out the small amount of money from the bank account in Węgrów. Returning from Węgrów and doubly irritated by the slowness and lateness of the bus, she marched into the town offices (where her husband had always discouraged her visits) and slapped both hands flat on the service counter with such force that she caused Pani Teresa, who was dusting a desktop, to overturn the teetering "in" basket. Zofia looked up from her own desk with a start.

"Well," Mrs. Farby said, "I'm leaving this place. If anyone sees the little shit, I have gone to my sister's." Then she stamped out. The next day, struggling with her suitcases and the rope-bound box with the television set, she was seen boarding the bus for Warsaw.

Farby seemed relieved when Zofia informed him that night of his wife's departure. Zofia seemed less sure.

"It's all right, Zofia," he said. "It was her television set anyway."

"It's not that, Zbyszek. I'm afraid you will miss her. Will you miss her?"

"No, sweetheart," he said, reaching across their little crumb-sprinkled table to caress her smooth, plump hand. "She couldn't even make a decent poppy seed cake. Besides, I have you."

Her face lightened, but the cloud of worry did not lift altogether. She was trying to think ahead, to devise a plan. More than ten days had passed since Zbyszek had arrived here at the summer cabin. The store of coal and firewood behind the little house had dwindled and Zbyszek looked ragged, although he seemed placid enough psychologically. Actually, that worried her the most.

"You need a haircut," she said, almost absently, as though she were talking to herself.

He smiled and shrugged.

"Bring some scissors tomorrow," he said. "You can cut it for me."

"I think we need to do something, Zbyszek, darling. I think it's getting time."

She had already described for him the town meeting, emphasizing its anarchic and inquisitorial tone, its unnerving lust for justice, for—yes—a trial. She could feel the town's mood, and sensed herself as a nearly notable personage, a kind of celebrity, as she circulated on her errands, stopping at the bakery where Janowski seemed especially eager to spring to her assistance, or at the grocery, where other women retreated a step as though in meditation over the blood sausage, surreptitiously assessing her while she bought her cheese and milk. In fact, she realized, no one quite knew whether she was to be regarded, as a permanent employee of the beclouded town office, as heroine, victim, or villainess. People treated her politely, but asked her nothing. She found the ambiguity over her own persona interesting, even exciting, and, almost unconsciously, found herself attending more carefully to her appearance, applying a touch more blue to her eyelids or choosing a pretty scarf to complement her sweater. She wore nicer underwear now, too, having traveled all the way to Węgrów to find it, but of course that applied to her greater secret, Farby himself, which she was confident remained secure. As a precaution, she had even started buying the extra food supplies for him outside of Jadowia, on the way to the cabin, where she arrived, invariably, with a rapidly beating heart.

She had never done anything remotely like this before, never a love affair worthy of the term. She was entranced by its excitement, but also protective of it and therefore practical. Steps had to be taken. The future had to be considered. So she was devising a plan.

"I think we should see the priest," she said.

Farby's jaw stopped laboring at the morsel of sausage in his mouth. He had an immediate vision of sacraments, confession. He swallowed with difficulty. He hadn't been to church for fifteen years, at least.

"Perhaps we should wait until things settle down, sweetheart," he said.

"No, I think now is the time," she said. Then she saw the alarm on his face and realized his misunderstanding. "No, dear, not for us. I mean, yes, for us, but not for, well, for *that*."

"Oh."

"Father Jerzy, I mean. I think it would be useful now. I think it could help us. Look, Zbyszek, you can't stay here forever like this. We have to do something. And I think he might need us. Or at least he needs you."

"You mean he needs to have me arrested."

"I mean he needs information."

"He's got information."

"What's he got? A bunch of papers. Bookkeeping. I've seen that bookkeeping. Who could possibly understand it? What he has is mainly gossip and supposition. Guesswork. Plus, the atmosphere is on his side. The whole country is going through this, so he thinks why not here? Why not him? He gets the people all excited. It's like a show."

"Somebody sold me out. Jabłoński, probably."

"Maybe. But you can fight back. Just as you said. Remember?"

"Maybe so. But I'm not sure about the priest. He wants to put me on trial and put that little shit Twerpicz in charge."

"Twerpicz thinks so. But Twerpicz doesn't help him now. He's just a front."

"He's an opportunist. He couldn't hold a job before this."

"They're all opportunists. But the priest is the one to think about now, and what he needs now is information. Something solid. He has to keep it going."

"And you think we should give it to him?"

"I think I should go see him," she said. "I think we can bargain."

"For what?"

Zofia stood and glided around the table to his chair.

"What do you want?" she asked, her voice low.

With one hand she smoothed his scraggly hair. Poor thing, she thought, he needs a bath. With her free hand, she loosened the buttons on her sweater, watching as his eyes followed her fingers. The sweater fell open. Her breasts pushed proudly upward, like rising, unbaked loaves from the glory of a new, lacy black bra.

"What do you want, Zbyszek?" she whispered. "Tell me what you want most." He lifted his head toward her, lips parted. "Tell me, and it's yours."

"Pass the butter," he said, and she giggled in delight.

*   *   *

Jola did not hear the horse and wagon arrive in the driveway of the clinic. She had been upstairs in the apartment, slicing carrots and celery root for a soup. The baby was asleep, Anna was playing with her dolls in the bedroom, and Karol was out. It was a cold, overcast day, and she was hoping that fresh snow would cover the mud and the colorless field that stretched away to the forest that lay beyond her kitchen window. Then she heard a fist bang on the door that led from the clinic to the apartment stairs, and went to answer it.

An old man, with a rumpled coat and the blurred, dissipated face of a drunken peasant, stood apologetically at the door, hat in hand. She thought she should recognize him, but then so many of them looked alike.

"Please pardon me, Pani," he said, stepping backward as he spoke.

"Yes?"

"Pardon me, I'm sure, but I've come . . ." He backed into the steel examination table, braced himself with one hand, then withdrew it quickly, as if it burned him. "I've come . . ."

"My husband is out now," she said.

"Yes, I know."

"Can I help you?"

"He's asking for you," the man said. "I mean, I thought I should come for you. He's . . . your husband is at my house. I'm Piwek, Pani. My apologies. He's at my place. He's, uh, that is, your husband doesn't seem well."

"You mean he's been drinking? Yes?"

"Well, yes, this is true, he has." Piwek lowered his eyes to his spattered boots. The sole of one was pulled loose from his toe. "He has had some drinking, yes. But it's . . . He's not well, Pani. He calls for you. I thought I should come. To take you to him."

"You want me to come? Is that it?"

"Yes, Pani." Piwek twisted the cap he held in his thick hands, his head slightly bowed, an image of an old-time serf visiting the master's house. She stared at him, trying to comprehend the situation. She could imagine, with no effort whatever, Karol having drunk himself insensible, but however much he soaked up during the day, out and about, he had always managed to make it home under his own power.

"Is he hurt, Pan Piwek?"

"Pardon?"

"Jesus. Has he injured himself? Has he wrecked the car?"

"No, ma'am, the car is at my house."

"Then, he's all right?"

"No, ma'am. He is ill, perhaps. He is calling for you. He won't move. From the barn. He's asking for you, you see. So I thought I should come."

"You came in your wagon?" She could see the horse, a chestnut with a yellow mane, out the clinic window, steam rising from its flanks. "Why didn't you bring him with the car?"

"I can't drive, ma'am. Besides, he won't move."

She felt she was spinning in circles. What was she to do? She could not leave the children, and she could hardly haul them along with her. Why should she do anything? If Karol was lying drunk in a manure pile somewhere, he should stay there until he sobered up enough to find his way home. She would not leave the children to go riding off in an open wagon to play nursemaid to a drunken husband. She had seen that sort of thing enough in her life.

"Pan Piwek, I cannot come with you. I have my children here. Do you understand?"

"Yes, ma'am."

"Go back. Give him some coffee. Get him sober and tell him to come home. There is nothing I can do."

She walked to the door and held it open. "Thank you. I'm sorry you came all this way."

Piwek went unsteadily to his wagon, his foot missing the iron step on the first try. His weathered hands fumbled with the reins.

"Wait, Pan Piwek. Wait."

Without knowing quite why—perhaps it was something about Piwek's heavy and fumbling hands, and the trouble he had taken to ride through the cold weather—she abruptly changed her mind. "Just wait here," she said. Inside, she wrote a note to her mother, saying, without explanation, that she needed her to come and stay with the children, and that she was to ride back to the clinic with

Piwek. Outside, she painstakingly recited the directions to her mother's house. "Bring her here," she told him, "and then I will go with you."

Piwek seemed relieved and set off, urging his horse to a brisk trot. Within fifteen minutes they were back, and Jola helped her mother down from the wagon.

"Where are you going?" she asked. "Is something wrong?"

"I don't know, Momma. It's Karol."

"Well, what is it?"

"I don't know. Don't worry. I'll be back as soon as I can."

She climbed onto the wagon seat. It was cushioned by a worn blanket. Piwek's coat smelled sharply of sweat and wood smoke. She grabbed onto the seat as the wagon lurched forward, then tucked her hands inside her coat. Piwek did not speak to her as they rode along. He seemed too shy, or too exhausted by his painful explanations earlier. She could not think of anything to say herself. She pulled her collar around her chin, feeling her breath warm her neck, and stared down at the road's margin sliding by in a blur. She tried not to imagine the scene that awaited her, except to think that, somehow, in some way, the forces in her life were reaching a critical point, propelling her in a direction she could not predict. She could not even be sure, now, why she was making this trip, why she should care enough to bother. Perhaps, she thought, she wanted to see how terrible things had become. "Let's see the worst," she said, speaking aloud into her coat collar. Her muffled voice surprised her, but Piwek showed no sign of having heard. He yawped at his horse, "Yo, get on, hup." His stubbled jaw worked as though he were chewing leather.

They skirted the village, passed the barren fields to the west, headed north through flanking woods, bouncing over a frozen, rutted road, and entered the gate at a small yellow house, yellow coal smoke curling from its chimney, set about with unpainted ramshackle barns and sheds. Karol's car, mud-covered but intact, waited in the barnlot. A short-legged cur yapped and charged repeatedly against its chain. Jola climbed out of the wagon.

"Where is he?" she said.

"This way, ma'am."

Bowlegged in his rubber boots, Piwek led the way to the largest barn, swung open the door for Jola, then stepped in behind her. The barn was dim, with one bare bulb dangling from the rafters and cracks of light latticed through splintered boards. She did not see Karol.

"Pan Doctor!" Piwek called. "Your wife has come." He walked on toward a partition at the far end. Four cows, tethered to the walls, stirred in the muck of their stalls. Jola followed.

Karol was sitting on a bale of hay, his head in his hands. He did not look up.

"Pan Doctor."

"Karol?" Jola said. He didn't move. She touched his shoulder. His hair was matted, wet from cold sweat. "Karol." He lifted his head, and Jola was jarred by the sight of his face. His eyes were reddened, the skin beneath them circled and darkened, his complexion an alarming jaundiced pallor.

"Love," he said.

"Karol, what's wrong with you?" She knelt beside him.

His lips tried to form words, but no sound came. Piwck stood behind them, watching intently.

"Pan Piwek," Jola said. "Please leave me alone with him."

"Yes, ma'am. He is ill, perhaps?"

"Yes, I think. Thank you. Please excuse us now." Piwek stood rooted to the spot. "Please!" she said, her voice sharp.

"Yes, ma'am." He shuffled away. She watched until the door of the barn closed, then she faced her husband.

"Karol?"

He stared at the floor. In their years together, she had never seen him like this. She had seen him fall down drunk, stumble on stairways, bang into door frames, stagger over an obstacle as slight as a carpet, had listened to him rambling and incoherent, heard him retching fearfully in the bathroom. She had endured his sarcasm, his verbal abuse, his threats, the deep bitterness he inflicted on objects animate and inanimate, on the very air he breathed. And, although he might have been out of control, contemptible, revolting, even pitiable, Karol was never without some portion of himself that suggested strength in reserve, a will, a potency. She sensed now the failure of this strength, as though it had been bled from him, and this realization plumbed some spot deep within her. She extended her hand to his shoulder, which gave way like sand beneath her touch. He leaned slowly sideways and rolled off the bale of hay. Struggling, she held his head to face her.

"Karol. Sit up. Talk to me."

The sunken eyes opened. He reeked of alcohol, and yet did not seem quite drunk, at least not the way she knew him drunk. She grabbed his jacket with both hands and hoisted him enough to rest his back against the hay. She glanced around the barn, saw a tin cup hanging on the wall and filled it with water from the trough. "Here," she said. "Drink, Karol, drink."

She held the cup to his lips. He drank. She wiped his face with the cold water. He shuddered, blinked, and gradually revived.

"Jola."

"Karol. Come on. Pull yourself together. Let's go home. Come." She tugged his arm, but he made no effort to rise.

"Jola, wait. Let me sit. Just sit with me. Let me think."

"What is it?"

He groaned.

"Tell me at home," she said, and pulled at him. This time he struggled up, grasping a post to steady himself. "Come to the car," she said. "I'll drive."

She maneuvered him to the barn door, then to the car. Piwek emerged from the house to help her. She thanked him, then settled behind the wheel. She backed the car around and drove out of the barnlot. Karol reclined in the seat for a while, his eyes closed, his mouth working as though chewing, his tongue laboring to restore feeling to his face.

"Jola?"

"Yes." She saw his eyes were open, staring straight down the road.

"We have trouble."

"I know we have trouble," she said. "We have nothing but trouble. It can't go on. It can't." His head rested against the door post, the wind from the open window plastering his oily hair against his face. "You're killing yourself, Karol. You're killing both of us."

"Jola. I am sorry. I know what you say. I am so sorry."

His eyes fixed on her face. They were watery, yellowed. She could see, now, he was sick, of course. His liver was giving up the battle. Whose liver wouldn't?

"I know, I know. I'm sorry. I mean it. I don't know how to tell you." His voice had lowered to a gravely whisper. "I can be better. I can promise you this. I'm so sorry. I've been crazy. A fool. Please believe me. I love you. I love the children. But there's something else, Jola. Something else."

They were back at the clinic now, steering into the driveway.

"Something else?" She braked the car and switched off the engine. "What something else? What is it?"

"Things you don't know about," Karol said. "Jabłoński. Things I did for him. With him."

"What things?"

"Things to make money. Various things. Now there is an investigation. There is trouble, Jola. There is going to be trouble."

There was a sudden rapping on the car window. It was her mother, her coat on, worry on her face. She pulled open the car door.

"Is everything all right?"

"Yes, Mother. Come. I'll take you home. Karol, go inside while I take Mother home."

She got out and helped Karol from the car. He was steadier now, and she walked him part way to the clinic door. "Go in. I'll be right back. Go."

She volunteered nothing to her mother on the short drive to town, and her mother, having lived much of her life facing down the sour, whiskered face of drunkenness, offered silence as though it were advice, the only kind she knew. There was the church, of course, the Blessed Mother, but she knew better than to mention this. Her only comment, as Jola drew up to the house, was, "He seems to be getting worse, doesn't he?"

"Yes."

"God help him," she said, and shut the car door behind her.

When Jola returned to the clinic, she was surprised to find Karol in bed, his clothes folded on a chair, the covers tucked to his chin. He was asleep, and for a few minutes, she sat with him, watching the slack and ravaged face on the pillow. Then she doused the lamp and left him to rest.

When the note arrived at his door, in a small and neatly typed envelope wedged above the door knob, Father Jerzy regarded the enclosed invitation for a visit with Jabłoński as a suit for peace from a distant opponent. Now, he decided, the forces of darkness were clearly on the retreat, appealing for a settlement, ready for negotiation.

Father Jerzy saw his position as dominant, and the timing of the appeal propitious. He considered calling in his "advisory commission," as he had encouraged the group to call itself. The usage had met with universal approval. Twerpicz quickly adopted the style of referring to it by its initials, "the A.C.," relishing the fashion for abbreviations in the national press, envisioning the day when these initials, too, would be instantly recognizable to journalists and television panelists across the country. A movement swelling up from the grass roots to national significance. Who knew what could happen? The Advisory Commission operated under the officially collective impression that it was a leaderless body, and that all decisions were arrived at by consensus without so much as a show of hands around the room. Such foolishness was actually suggested once. Naturally, Father Jerzy noted ruefully to himself, it was Twerpicz who proposed with the notion. He observed, also, that the increasingly impressive farmer, Powierza, had not been the author of so witless a suggestion. You did not run an operation like this on the basis of a democratic vote. Yea verily. Not in Poland. Not with Slavs anywhere. Maybe in Norway it worked. In any case, however delicious the idea of sharing—no, announcing—this news to the A.C., Father Jerzy preferred the course of executive action. Besides, there wasn't time, strictly speaking. The note from Jabłoński suggested he "drop by" in the early evening, and it was already late afternoon, too late to round everyone up.

Outwardly, he was calm, and set about tidying his desk, picking up dirty socks and underwear from his bedroom floor. That done, he paced back and forth, basking in the internal heat produced by the chain of events he had set in motion. This could not be ignored, this strategic and organizational skill, this deft orchestration, this awakening of the slumbering consciousness of a benumbed village in a benighted countryside. Notice would be taken, of course, but Father Jerzy resolved to be modest. Modest, yes, but of course determined. Quiet and calm, yet undeflected. Soft-spoken—he needed work on that, he admitted—yet forceful. The bishops would see this, could not avoid it, much as some of them might like to, not out of disagreement, of course, but, one had to face it, the church was a marketplace like any other, a competitive arena. Gladiators in cassocks? No. Salesmen? Not quite that, either. More like designers in a big corporation, advancing their ideas up the line to the marketing people. It was all about strategy—yes—the way forward! He would be with the dynamic wing. The implacable tide was with him.

He had not foreseen Pani Zofia's visit, much less her startling and useful information. Out of the blue! Well, he decided, a good commander makes his own luck. Jabłoński and Farby were selling off alcohol from the distillery to bootleggers, and had been for years, so far back that Farby wasn't even sure when it started. Except that, since chaos reigned in Moscow and borders were flung open, the buyers were now vodka-starved Russians and the money involved tripled overnight, then tripled again, and truck drivers from Georgia and Ukraine were filling up fake gas tanks with the stuff or loading it in false-bottom barrels labeled as sulfuric acid or copper sulfate or axle grease. The rest, she explained, was easy: a phony manifest, blurred handwriting on flimsy paper, the smack of a rubber stamp, and all was in order. The truck traffic to the distillery, or the quarry nearby, was, she said, a regular detour on the road between Warsaw and Tarnopol, the major limitation being the distillery's capacity. Other details seemed hazy in Father Jerzy's (or Zofia's or perhaps even Farby's) understanding, matters concerning state inspectors, or the lack of them, and their missing or falsified reports. Simple bribery, most likely, although Farby, Zofia maintained, claimed to be ignorant of the details.

Whatever the case, as Father Jerzy thought about it he decided that Farby was not interested in drowning all hands on board, but on grabbing a piece of the wreckage substantial enough to float himself to safety. Father Jerzy liked this immediately. He had seen enough television imported from America—he couldn't resist it—to understand the concept of the "stoolie" (a great word, he decided), the plea bargain, immunity in exchange for information. All of this from the opiate glow of *Kojak, Barnaby Jones* and *Dallas!* It took a great nation, he believed, to project such innovations so painlessly. In any case, Father Jerzy seized the idea from Zofia's lips with such speed, virtually in mid-sentence, that she sat blinking at him in silence, first in consternation and then with a smile of pleasure. Caught in the spirit of agreement, even euphoria, Zofia then volunteered the chip she had held in reserve.

"Tomek Powierza was involved," she said.

"Who?"

"The Powierza boy. The one who was murdered."

"What? Are you sure?"

"He was there the night he was killed."

"Farby saw him there?"

"Yes. But that's all. He doesn't know what happened." She explained that whatever befell young Powierza had to have occurred after he left. Nor, she insisted, did Farby have any certain idea of Powierza's exact role in the enterprise, except that perhaps he served as a "finder" for the Russians, a salesman, in effect. As for the three Russians, a rough-looking lot, he had never seen them before. Nor was he asserting Jabłoński had any connection with the killing.

"It's just that we are—that is, Zbyszek is—uh, being made the scapegoat. That isn't right, is it? You see that, don't you, Father?"

"I believe I do."

"Anything that's wrong in the town office, the way things were done, you see, he just inherited all this, and now people—certain forces, I'm not saying you personally—well, they're blaming him, and that's not right."

"I understand what you're saying, Pani Zofia," Father Jerzy said. He reached out to pat the back of her hand.

"He has to protect himself," she said, snuffling slightly as her eyes dampened.

"And assist in this, uh, difficult transition."

"And consider the future," she said. A tear gained the broad plane of her cheek.

"Perhaps a small business somewhere," the priest said. "With a clean slate."

"The south, we were thinking."

It was well past Jabłoński's suggested meeting time, and, more importantly, well past dark, when Father Jerzy set out for the Farmers' Co-op office. Unlike Father Tadeusz, whom Father Jerzy considered the recluse of the rectory, he was familiar with the village's byways after dark, and he did not want to encounter any acquaintances or observers on his mission. By now the bar would be closed, evening meals consumed, television sets flickering in the windows like blue hearth fires, the good parishioners nodding off in their chairs, unaware that a major force in their town's history was striding past them, light-footed as freedom's commando. He should remember this night, he thought. He should be keeping notes, recording his feelings. A diary, perhaps, would be of great interest someday, the whole feeling of it recorded—the brooding, hairy-trunked poplars, the dogs howling in the distance, his footsteps— Was there someone following him? He halted, listened, heard nothing. He went on. The lighted window at the Co op was just ahead, a dim bulb burning above the door. He crossed the yard and stepped into the cone of light.

"Good evening, Father."

The voice leaped out of the darkness to his left, and Father Jerzy visibly started, a muffled yelp rising involuntarily from his throat. His hand, about to reach for the door, jerked upward defensively. Then he saw Jabłoński, who seemed to materialize, as though from separate shades of darkness, out of the shadows.

"Jesus and Mary," the priest said.

"Sorry, Father. I didn't mean to startle you."

"Goodness."

"I'm sorry," Jabłoński said. "I was just coming back from the garage. I thought perhaps you weren't coming." Jabłoński opened the door, but paused to wave at someone in the road. Indistinctly Father Jerzy saw the figure of a man, waving back as he walked. Someone *was* following him. Was it coincidence?

"Please," Jabłoński said. "Come in."

"Who was that?" the priest said as he stepped inside.

Jabłoński closed the door behind him. "Oh, that was the plumber. Pan Andrzej. Lives just nearby."

"He works for you?"

"Andrzej?" Jabłoński chuckled. "Andrzej works for himself, which is to say for everyone. The town's only plumber. He's our last monopoly. Except for the church, of course."

Father Jerzy entered the office. He had expected something more substantial, something more in keeping with Jabłoński's reputation. Nothing that caught the eye suggested authority or power. The desk was old, battered, its cheap wood scarred, its edges blacked by cigarette burns. No sign of nostalgia for state authority or Party primacy decorated the warped paneling on the walls. Shelves behind the desk contained boxed binders of records and stacks of paper. In front of the desk stood two wooden chairs and behind it a larger cushioned one, tilting to one side, foam padding crumbling through its frayed upholstery. As Jabłoński settled into it, Father Jerzy noted a hole the size of a large coin in the sleeve of Jabłoński's shapeless gray sweater. He dressed like a weary school teacher, Father Jerzy thought. And yet, for all his colorlessness, Jabłoński projected a keen cutting edge. Was it the barb about the church's monopoly? Father Jerzy felt the need to urge his confidence higher, to summon a reminder of the strength of his position. The leverage was his; he was the cleansing force, the wind of change. He ventured a smile.

"We meet at last," he said, seating himself, at Jabłoński's gesture, in one of the creaking, straight-backed chairs. From behind the clear-rimmed spectacles, Jabłoński's eyes had a distinct glint.

"Yes," Jabłoński said. "I've looked forward to it. Actually, I expected a visit from you some time ago." He smiled thinly. "But everything in good time. Of course you are new here, and there has been much to learn."

"I consider my relative newness here an advantage, actually."

"Oh, certainly," Jabłoński said quickly. "A fresh eye, unclouded by—what shall I say?—by history, complications."

"I see nothing very complicated."

"No?" Jabłoński unfolded his hands, palms up. "Well, you are a quick study, I'm sure."

"What I see is a village that is only beginning to learn how to shake off its lethargy, to catch a glimpse of the future. It's as though the people are crawling out from under a blanket, with no idea what's been done to them for the last forty years."

"And you are lifting the blanket for them," Jabłoński said, suppressing a laugh, "preparatory to remaking the bed." He swiveled the chair sideways, reached to the shelf below him, and retrieved a fresh bottle of vodka, as though plucking a hooked fish from a bucket. "Will you join me?"

"No thank you."

"You don't mind? May I offer you tea?"

"No, thank you."

Jabłoński poured, hoisted his glass in Father Jerzy's direction, and drank. "You were saying, Father?"

"Shall we get to the point, Pan Jabłoński?"

"By all means."

"Excellent. The point is, you are finished here. You and your kind. The Citizens' Committee will insist on a complete evaluation of the records of the town offices. This will include the period in which you were the naczelnik, running the town's business, as well as records of the Party, which operated under your direction, and of the Farmers' Co-op, which was once—whatever it maybe now—a public enterprise. We will uncover all activities, irregularities, and I mean of the distant past, the recent past and ongoing schemes. The truth will be revealed to the people for what it is, and then they will understand the exact nature and, most importantly, the cause of the blight that has befallen them."

"I miss church but get the sermon anyway," said Jabłoński, smiling mildly. "And you think the people regard this 'blight' as a great mystery? Something requiring ecclesiastical explanation, like immaculate conception?"

"It is not a matter of mystery, Pan Jabłoński. You and your kind have made sleepwalkers out of the people. They are numb, dulled. It's not that they don't know, they simply stopped seeing so long ago that they have forgotten how to use their eyes. They must be taught there is no longer any need to live with your fear. If I play some small role in this, well, I see it simply as my contribution."

"You are too modest, Father," Jabłoński said, pouring another inch of vodka into his glass.

"My duty only," the priest replied. "It is the role of the church to look to the welfare of the people."

"Ah, yes," Jabłoński said, "perhaps we will get to that."

"Perhaps, if that subject interests you suddenly, but there are practical matters to discuss that perhaps I should inform you of." Father Jerzy paused, looking at Jabłoński as he sipped and set down his glass.

"Please," Jabłoński said.

"We have evidence, in bookkeeping accounts, supported by interviews, that points clearly to a system of graft wherein profits or surpluses in village-operated enterprises were hidden or siphoned off. Kickbacks were made to village officials, sometimes in the form of favors, gifts, vacation trips, certain considerations, what the Americans call 'sweetheart deals.' Officials had their houses repaired, free coal delivered, supplies of meat provided, holiday dachas built in remote areas. A whole system of exchanged favors, involving contracts for purchase of flour, concrete, building blocks, road contracts—who knows what else. No doubt money was paid. I tell you this not because you are ignorant of these things—on the contrary—but to let you know we are not." He sucked in a breath. "Not ignorant of them." Father Jerzy sat back, feeling winded.

Jabłoński looked back at him with an expression of mild wonder, as though he were watching a rare species of moth, one with black wings and a face like a harvest moon.

"Interesting," Jabłoński said. He seemed to wait. "Is that all, or do you have notes to recite on the operation of Newton's Third Law?"

"I beg your pardon?"

"There's more?"

"As a matter of fact, yes. Concerning the scheme with the distillery. Oh, yes. This, too, is known. A racket of long-standing, illicit alcohol sales to Soviet smugglers and criminal lowlifes. As usual, a case of state complicity in the poisoning and moral degradation of society. Not to mention, as I'm sure I don't have to remind you, a case of murder."

Still, no ripple of agitation crossed the pool of Jabłoński's calm. His pale, high forehead, above the colorless glasses, betrayed no sheen of tension, not a bead of apprehension. Meanwhile, Father Jerzy could feel his own sweat, like particles of ice, sliding down the sides of his rib cage. He had talked too much and by now spent his ammunition. He had expected, by now, a target in tatters, an appeal for reason, mercy, bargaining, heavily leveraged cooperation. But Jabłoński was as calm as the air, as impervious as gas. Father Jerzy's own mouth felt like cotton. His eyes followed Jabłoński's hand to the vodka bottle, and watched it pour.

"Perhaps you would join me now, Father?" The priest didn't answer, and Jabłoński filled a second glass and slid it across the desk. "There," he said, as though offering a glass of milk to a child.

Father Jerzy sipped from the glass and felt his breath catch on the fumes. He tried, but could not suppress his cough.

"Relax, Father," Jabłoński said. "You're a young man and the world is too much with you. I'm reminded that I used to share a glass now and then with old Father Marek, may he rest in peace. A good man, a practical man. Of course, you wouldn't have known him, but he was much beloved here. You've heard him spoken of, no doubt?"

"Yes, the parish house was built while he was here."

"Indeed, and a handsome edifice it is, too. A tireless man, he was. Though never tiresome. He was blessed with patience. And a sense of reality. A quality strangely lacking these days, don't you think? A sense of reality? By the way, pardon my curiosity, but I wonder, how are your relations with Father Tadeusz?"

"He is my colleague. Our relations are cordial, of course."

"Just cordial? I would have thought he might be an example for you." Jabłoński watched the young priest's face betray a flicker of irritation, a faint tightening of the mouth.

"How is that?" Father Jerzy asked.

"He has a . . . what shall I say? . . . a 'priestly' quality. Quiet. Calming. An attribute, I would say, in a priest. But not quite your sort of vocation, is that it?"

"I think it's safe to say," Father Jerzy said lightly, "that you're not dealing with Father Tadeusz here, if that's what you hoped."

"I see," Jabłoński said. He smiled. "Just so. But there are other considerations, aren't there?"

"Other considerations?"

"The church, I mean."

"What about it?"

"Your place in it. Your own future." Jabłoński spoke quickly now. "I mean, you have ambitions, obviously. Places to go. This, too, is an admirable quality in a man. Although curious, perhaps, in a priest. Nevertheless. You wouldn't want your work here to impede your progress so early, to become a millstone for you to drag."

Father Jerzy started to speak, but Jabłoński, begging pardon with a gesture of his hand, went on.

"Excuse me, I'm digressing. I was speaking of old Father Marek, of that admirable sense of reality he had. I miss that, you see. I think there was a clearer understanding of what was required to partici-pate in a calm social enterprise. I must tell you, my young and inex-perienced friend, the challenges were enormous, but the spirit of cooperation evoked was often inspiring—not always, of course, but often. Such things you now describe as 'graft,' I gather. I enjoy these colorful terms that creep into us from America. However, simple management is the term I would use."

"You call it management?"

"Administration, perhaps, creatively applied and under pressure. I won't clutter your mind with all the complexities. You're already trying to grasp too much in too short a time. But think of it, if you can. You would have been a youngster then, perhaps even unaware of your budding vocation. But consider: you want flour, or coal, or concrete. I think you made reference to such items. Or building blocks, for a new school—or your house? A snowplow? A fire engine? How do you think these essentials are provided? The open market? Or simply by contacting suppliers in Hamburg, say? Or Rotterdam? Please, sir, for a boxcar load of Polish złotys—equal in value to a similar volume of fresh manure—will you be so kind as to send us one of your new fire trucks? No fire trucks? Then how about a container of flour? And, by the way, some of your nice Dutch tile for the fireplaces in the monsignor's new rectory? Not to mention a flatcar of red brick for the same purpose."

Father Jerzy started to speak again, the eyebrows on his broad forehead poised for a question or protest in advance of his lips. But again Jabłoński held up his hand.

"You see, Father, it's a question of improvisation. It's hardly your fault you don't understand immediately. You've been swaddled in the seminary. A child, may I say. Please, I mean no insult. What you've been exposed to is twenty years of catechism in the evils of a supposedly atheist system. But I would make the argument, not entirely parenthetically, if I may digress a moment, that the system your brethren and your catechists in the seminary bemoaned for so long was, in fact, your greatest ally. How thrilling for everyone, your radical priests with their sermons for the Fatherland! Better than television. Now I see newspaper photographs of priests praying over the opening of partisan election campaign headquarters, sprinkling holy water on new garbage trucks and ambulances. Dabbling everywhere, in other words. Haranguing the people over abortion. Complaining about materialism and greed after preaching for years on the merits of individual initiative and free enterprise. And what is the result?"

Jabłoński poured once more into Father Jerzy's glass, and then his own.

"Pan Jabłoński, your jaded evaluation hardly—"

"Just a moment, Father. I let you speak without interruption. Allow me another minute. As I was saying, what is the result? Well, it has hardly gone unnoticed, especially by the hierarchy, has it? The people are falling away. Church attendance is in sharp decline. Yes, they publish these facts in the newspapers. They do surveys. The 'faithful' are put off. There are other diversions now. They are bored with you, Father. And still you cannot shut up. You want to crow. You want to be heard. Mostly, you want to take credit. You want to hear applause from a grateful nation. Tell me I'm wrong. Tell me, Father Jerzy, that you don't see yourself, here in Jadowia, as the cowboy riding in with the silver bullet."

It required a few seconds for Father Jerzy to reply.

"There are many complexities," he said finally. "It is a time of searching. There are certain dislocations. But the people know who is right. The people know who won, who will prevail."

"The people, yes. Stalin spoke of them often. Now they watch what you do, as you invoke their name at every opportunity. There must be as many priests walking the hallways of the parliament these days as there are in the primate's palace. You think you've won, as if it were a boxing match or a football game. Or a marching army. But you don't realize what happened, Father. You didn't win. The game was forfeited. It may feel the same to you, given your weakness for self-congratulation, your eagerness to reverse the roles. But let me tell you, my friend, you simply happened along at the scene of a disaster, a train wreck, let's say, brought about by incompetence and weakness and gullibility. By failure of character, the delusion of compromise. We lost to our own deal-makers, worn out, naturally enough, by their own wheedling. If you want to call that winning . . . well, let's just say that delusion, like the flu, is an impartial infection. So now, Father—please, I'm almost finished—now your side will have its chance. Based on what I've seen so far, here and among our neighbors, I would give you less time than we had. And then we'll watch, as the latter-day fascists strike up their march, shielded, as usual, behind some respectable banner, some urgent public goal. But have a go at it. As I say, we will watch with interest. And we will go quietly."

Suddenly Jabłoński rocked forward in the swivel chair, a move of practiced and almost serpentine swiftness. Both elbows were planted on the desk, his head low, his gray eyes cold and staring above the rims of his glasses.

"We will go quietly, my young friend, and we will go undisturbed. Do you understand me? Unmolested."

"Immune from any responsibility?" Father Jerzy answered. "Absolved of answering for any crime?"

"Absolved of the struggle, Father. Undisturbed. Unmolested. I shouldn't, by now, have to warn you."

"Warn me of what?"

"Your responsibilities, shall we say. To your stewardship of the parish. To its good name and reputation."

"You mean Father Marek?"

"Yes. Father Marek Stołowski, that good man. Eighteen, twenty years in this village. How many here, would you guess, he must have baptized and buried? The builder of the largest parish house between here and Warsaw." Jabłoński slowly reclined in his chair. "Those fine fireplaces, the marble in the foyer. The mirrors in the dining room! I was present at the dedication myself. The monsignor was very proud. Glowing. He considered it his monument. I myself considered it a monument to cooperation. How else could such a fine thing come to be built? A monument, as I said, to calm social cooperation."

"*His* cooperation? Is that what you imply?"

"Mutual, you may infer. But, from your point of view, yes. His cooperation."

"But he is dead, Pan Jabłoński. That doesn't enter into it now."

"Doesn't it?" Jabłoński said. "The church may be dying, too, Father, but you don't want to be the one to shove its local franchise over the precipice. Or to damage your own position with guilt by association. Or as the bearer of bad news. Do you think you would gain a great deal with your superiors by dredging up dishonor for the dead? Do you think the bishops will enjoy your handiwork? Or the village parishioners? Your own credibility would sink beyond detection. Memories are long here, Father, I assure you. The monsignor died only two years ago. On the payroll, in a manner of speaking, to the end."

"Why should I believe you?"

"Because of the future, Father," Jabłoński said. "Because you will realize your future is not in the past."

Jabłoński swiveled to the bookcase and swiveled back, tossing a fat yellow envelope on the desk.

"Take it," he said. "Photocopies. There is one matter I'll call your attention to. A certain veteran school teacher used the church mimeograph machine to reproduce religious tracts salted with sly political homilies which he surreptitiously handed out, on a regular basis, to the youth of the school chorus, which he led. He did this, unwisely, on school grounds. Of course, it could not continue. He was an older man, a bachelor, and unfortunately after his dismissal resorted to drink and subsequently took his own life. It was distressing, of course, and there was much sympathy for him."

"And Father Marek informed you? About the teacher?"

"Well, I'm sure he had warned against such activities and certainly he acted with a heavy heart. If I'm not mistaken, he officiated at the funeral. A nice touch, that. But please, read for yourself. I would be careful, though, to keep it under lock and key."

Jabłoński felt pleased with himself. It was a good day's work. But tiring. He smiled, thinking of Father Jerzy's defiance, so easily marshaled. So deftly guided toward its collision. Ah, youth, its careless energy!

Silently, alone, he raised his glass to the memory of old Marcin: ancient, yellow-faced, hollow-eyed Marcin, the skin tight across the hairless cranium—gnarled, it looked, by years of the human chess game.

We'll see, he said to himself. He might have admired this.

Yes, he was tired, ready for sleep. It would be a relief, really, to let it go at last, do something else, earn a living, relax a little, watch someone else wear themselves out trying to run the country.

CHAPTER ELEVEN

LESZEK

Politics, to me, had always been a distant noise. My opinion of the system was as dismal as everyone's. When the old order crumbled at the top, I held out hope that it would be possible to have a "normal" life as a farmer. In that, I realize, I was merely parroting what everyone said: We would now have a "normal" life. Perhaps, as I try to think about it more exactingly, our notion of what was normal was extremely vague. For myself, I imagined adding to the land we owned. The prospect of Kowalski's field, as a first step, was as real to me as a fistful of earth, as soon as I could muster the money or the credit to buy it. Somehow, too, I would acquire better machinery. I had visions of a large greenhouse where I could grow produce that was marketable the year round, for I saw as much profit in that as in meat or dairy farming, and it would mean a productive use of the long, slow winter months. I was impatient, but I would be steady. I would be cautious and diversify as I could. My concern with politics was limited to the hope that, at least, the new system would make it possible to plan and invest and expand. The idea of security, some comfort, a thing well done—all that seemed possible.

How those conditions were to be brought about did not concern me much, not in the actual mechanics. I would listen to the politicians, I would vote. Those who got the votes would do their jobs and I would do mine. I did not expect their work or my own to advance in an unbroken upward line. I was a farmer, and I would farm. Few enough had been able to accomplish this—not, in fact, since science and machinery had replaced superstition and tradition and horse-drawn plows. But a few centuries ago grain from this part of the world (or not far away) fed half of Europe and earned fortunes for Dutch shippers and banking houses. It was still the same land, and it was land I knew. I would make no fortune, but the idea of security, of a thing done well—all that now seemed possible.

My father could entertain no such ambition and never spoke of it—in the same way, I suppose, he never spoke of owning a Mercedes-Benz. For him, farm work proceeded day to day, year to year, for something of his own father's exactitude had been ingrained in him. Now and then he bought a piece of second- or third-hand equipment, or he spoke of acquiring better land (Kowalski's foremost in his mind), but his perspective was short-range and foreclosed.

I thought I always saw in him a deep quiet and sadness—or did I imagine his portrait differently now, shaded more darkly by Jabłoński's information? I had felt this melancholy before, and always attributed it to the death of my sister, which seemed the defining event of my youth—that sense of quiet that never fully lifted from the house. I do not know how other families deal with such an blow. I had always thought that if ours had been larger we would have absorbed it more readily, gone on in the hubbub of other children, birthdays, name days, school, first communions, all the small events, emergencies, and celebrations of a large noisy family. As it was, we remained hushed, shut down in introspection. But maybe the cause was something I could never have fathomed.

It is perhaps a distortion of memory, but I recall my father laughing more when I was small, in the years before the baby died. I remember his present to me of a toy truck, made of heavy cast iron, that I played with, crawling under furniture to push it on the floor.

I remembered, too, building Marysia's crib with him. He seemed, in his calm way, to know how to do everything. We worked in the barn, two or three hours every day for weeks, drilling holes for the dowel rods that formed its sides, my father showing me how to use the brace and bit. I watched him cut with the coping saw along the traced pencil lines to shape the scrollwork of the head-board. Over the weeks that its components took shape, I walked beside him to town to buy materials, bringing with us a piece of the oak to test the color of the stain, then purchasing sandpaper (from Nardów, the coffin maker) and returning home to sand the wood and round the edges. He sat on a box to guide me as finally I was allowed to apply the stain. The crib was a surprise for mother, and she was not permitted to see it until we finished. She was pregnant then, her belly large and so firm to the touch that it would give me a tinge of fright when she let me feel the baby kicking. Her face glowed. When the crib was done, the wood gleaming and silken to the touch, we carried it into the house. We asked her to sit on the couch in the living room, her eyes closed, while we set it before her. When she saw it, she laughed and cried at the same time. My father leaned against the doorway, smiling, a curl of wood dangling from the sleeve of his sweater, praising my hard work.

What secrets was he keeping from us then? Or was it later? My fingers trembled as I fingered the soiled papers I had carried away from Jabłoński's office. The stillness of the house seemed magnified by this pile of secrets. The papers gave off a poisoned air, like radiation. I sat cross-legged on my bed and arranged the sheets in front of me, under the light. They appeared to be copies of smudged carbons, of differing sizes and shapes, in no particular order. The dates ranged over nearly fifteen years, the years of my childhood and youth. What Jabłoński had chosen to show me were evidently samples. Did the last papers mark the end of his service? No termination suggested itself, only the plodding phrases, information seemingly plucked from an ongoing stream of watching, as stages from a work in progress. The notes on Powierza were like the others: brief but implicit in their suggestion of sustained observation. "Subject peasant farmer Powierza, Stanisław, of the Lipki Road felled eight scotch pine trees, approx. 40 feet length. Trees located NE quadrant forest bordering Piwki Creek and Wrona Road. Peasant farmer felled trees with ax and crosscut over period 1–10 November. Trimmed logs stored in hollow adjacent property on Lipki Road period 12–16 November, using horse and chains."

At the bottom, in a small box, was the tight ball of his initials. I had seen his signature many times.

His signature marked each of the other pages as well. There were names on those pages, some I recognized and some not. A two-line notation recorded that Pani Wanda Gromek received at her home a male traveler whose car bore a license plate from Poznań. Another identified a storekeeper, now retired, receiving packages from England, hand-delivered by a bus driver on the Warsaw-Węgrów route. Another detailed the weight of a shipment of rye flour to Janowski's bakery, led by the remark, "as per request of Section 6."

My eye fell then on another name I had missed at first. Wojciech Kowalski. It did not register immediately, but then I remembered that old man Kowalski had a son named Wojciech, one of his grown children, presumably the son who, in spite of his father's stubborn hopes, would have nothing to do with the family farm. Wojciech Kowalski, the report said, "has been approached, will cooperate," and gave a date. It was eight years ago.

Eight years ago? Wojciech Kowalski visited home and was "approached?" Approached for what? Would cooperate in what? Could my father have been a part of this? I shuffled through the papers, trying to fight the heave of my stomach and quaking as if I were sitting naked in cold rain. I studied the signatures, lifting each close to my eye, then thrusting them away at arm's length, hoping to detect a forger's flaw. But I could not. These marks, even this terseness were his. I realized, with a despairing shame, that the pile Jabłoński had pressed on me was genuine.

The room around me shivered through tears at the weakness these documents represented. My father. My strong father, one step in front of me, full pails of milk gliding unspilled from each square, calloused fist, his shoulders like oaken beams, his footprints laid down in thawing earth with a deep and even weight, a force of stone. My own foot, in his print, left no mark. He could lift a calf without a sound. A pen fit in his muscled hand like a straw, overpowered, squeezed down to that knot of motion that formed his signature, his mark.

How far did it travel, that constricted scrawl? The combination of letters and numbers coded in the boxes of the forms—Section 6, Department 2, Section 11—seemed to diagram no place where I could imagine him. I pictured a maze of dim hallways whose closed doors sealed off rooms hazed with cigarette smoke and desks sticky with spilled tea and indifference. Did the originals of these papers find their way to such places, grimy government offices in Węgrów or Siedlce or even Warsaw? To some gigantic repository for potential prosecutions? Was the information to be used against those on whom it was collected, or on those who collected it? Possibly it didn't matter, for nothing was wasted in this enterprise. Stuff they called information was all piled up somewhere, invisible but potent. Here in the countryside, we could barely imagine it, as though we were insulated by forests. And insulated, too, by the presumption that everyone knew everyone else, or thought they did.

Outside, I heard our rooster crow, though it was still dark; another day advancing. Dealing with this in daylight seemed impossible. To whom could I confess? It would have to be Powierza, of course. Who else was there? And this, too, brought me up short, for I had no one, really, but him. Tomek, had he been alive, might—one day—have been close enough. So many others were gone, off to the city, to factories, or abroad with the diaspora of busboys and moonlighters. At some point, I would talk to my mother about it, but not now, for I was sure, although I could not say why, that she did not know about it. Someday, but not now. Grandpa, too, perhaps, although the thought of what it might do to him stopped me. He had spent his life barking contempt for the Communists and all their works. They were a curse upon the earth, and most particularly his country. He vilified Hitler less for his invasion of Poland than for double-crossing Stalin, which denied the Western Allies a chance to destroy not only the Nazis but the loathsome Bolsheviks as well.

It was inconceivable to me that Grandpa could have known about my father's activities. There were rough spots in their relationship, periods punctuated by mutual withdrawal, by arguments over fields and stock, by disputes over the timing of planting and mowing, and the friction was enough at times to extend a silence between them to three days. Maybe all parents living into old age with their children are equipped with a gauge that measures the gap between what should be and what is. But their disputes never threatened a deeper sense of mutual respect and regard. At some ill-defined point, the decisive weight simply shifted from the older to the younger, with a gradual smoothing of the edges between them, to a point close to gentleness. "Your father says . . ." Grandpa would tell me when, between the two of us, we set about some task according to my father's instructions. True, by then my father was ill, but Grandpa's deference did not seem to be borne of sympathy or pity, rather an unspoken acknowledgment that he had accepted a secondary position and with it the privilege of no longer having to decide. Now more than ever, Grandpa was inclined to go his own way. Nothing about him, or my memory of him with my father, suggested the bitterness or fury that would have signified a breach in political agreement. No, Grandpa could not have known.

The rooster crowed again. The first gray light touched the sky. I turned off the light. At the end of this long, grim night, I made one resolution: I did not know what to do, or how, but I would not join Jabłoński's little choir of silence, his conspiracy, whatever it was. I would try to resist without spreading damage and pain like pus from some putrid infection, but I promised myself that I would not acquiesce. I would fight him, somehow.

But before that, before I could consider anything else, I had to see Jola. I rolled over on top of the scattered papers, my insides raw, and tried, for an hour or so, to sleep.

We met at the cabin. I had to wait an hour for her, and I had begun to think she might not come after all. My call to her, from the post office, was hurried, and I was insistent enough to forestall her resistance. Always, I was careful to call when I was sure Karol was away from the house, usually only when I had seen him or his car in town. I let that precaution go this morning. The phone rang, she said, as he was pulling out of the driveway.

"I have to see you right away."

"It's not good this morning."

"Right away. Please. It's important."

She appeared amid the trees, finally, her face paler than usual, her eyes faintly circled. She was obviously tired, her mood fragile. When I kissed her, the slight deflection of her face and the coolness of her lips transmitted a change as palpable as the weather, as when a cloud passes over the sun. I started to lead her to the cabin door. She withdrew her hand.

"No," she said. "Let's stay out here." A rough log bench stood beside the cabin door. She sat down.

"Have you heard anything?" I asked her.

"Heard what?"

"About us."

Her eyes were sharp, quizzical. She folded her arms tight to her stomach. "No, I haven't," she said, her voice edged with annoyance. "But it wouldn't surprise me if I did. Making a mess of my life is what I do. I suppose the world knows it." She leaned across her folded arms, her head down, and I crouched in front of her. I lifted her chin, expecting to see tears. But there was only fatigue. And something new, some resolve I had not seen before. I put both my hands on her cheeks, but she drew back, her head bumping against the cabin wall's weathered planks. "What?" she asked. "What is it? What have you heard?"

"Jabłoński knows," I said. "About us."

She said nothing at first, but color rose slowly to her face. "How do you know that?" she asked evenly.

"He told me."

She stood up and stepped past me, facing the forest. "It figures, the little bastard," she said. "When did you see Jabłoński?"

"Last night."

She stood motionless, her arms folded.

"If he knows," I went on, "someone else does, too. Has Karol said anything?"

"Jesus."

"Has he said anything to you?"

"No, nothing directly. I don't know. He has troubles, Leszek. Maybe he knows. I suppose he does. Oh, Christ, it doesn't matter."

I was about to say that it didn't matter to me, either, that I was ready to take her and the children and withstand whatever storms followed. But although I could not see her face, I knew that was not what she meant. I gathered her to me, but her arms remained limp at her sides. For a few moments we didn't speak, and I closed my eyes and hoped for that scent of summer and grass and dust, but it was not there, only bitterness and distraction. She pulled away.

"What happened? What did Jabłoński say?"

I told her all of it, the meeting with Jabłoński, the folder full of papers, his smirking revelation at the end of the meeting about "the veterinarian's wife." She listened in silence, now and then closing her eyes in tired disgust. I told her about my father's signature on the petty reports, the names of his unsuspecting neighbors and victims, Powierza, Janowski, Pani Gromek, Kowalski. "God knows who else," I said. "I think that's only part of it. My father's other life."

"Kowalski?" she said.

"Yes, Kowalski, Powierza, Gromek . . ."

"But Kowalski was one of them?" she asked.

"Yes."

"Maybe that's why he won't sell you the field," she said. "He refused to sell it to your father. Now he refuses you. Don't you see?"

"Why?"

"Because he knows, probably. Knows your father did something to him."

"Knows what? You couldn't even tell what it was about. It said nothing."

"It doesn't matter," she said. "It's something. Something *they* know. Something Kowalski knows. Some compromise, some stupid offense, something for them to use. It doesn't matter what it was."

Up to a few hours ago, my attitude was that none of it mattered. It was all irrelevant. Now I felt ashamed of my acquiescence, of my gullibility.

Jola returned to the bench and sat knotted within herself, bent over her folded arms, staring into the trees.

"It's worse since the changes," she said. "Worse than ever. Karol said it would be this way. He's right. It's just as rotten. Only now we have the privilege of smelling it. I want to be done with it, Leszek. I want it out of my nose. I want to get away from here."

"Away to where? This is where we live."

"It's where *you* live."

"And not you?"

"I told you. I want out, Leszek. We're leaving. Karol and the children and I. We're going."

"What are you saying?"

"I've said it. I can't stand this place anymore."

"Jola, please. You don't have to do this." I knew, in that instant, that I might as well have been talking to a mountain or shouting in futile protest as I fell off a cliff, but I went on. "We made plans. We can have a life together."

"No, Leszek. *You* made plans. *You* have a life here. I had no business doing this. Meeting you this way, hiding out, sneaking away into the forest. I'm not surprised Jabłoński knows. I'm surprised the whole town doesn't know."

"But what happened? Why now?"

"It's not just now. I've been trying to tell you, but you don't want to hear it. You don't want to face it. Sometimes I think you don't want to live in the real world. You can't ignore things around you, as if they don't exist. This town, your family, my family."

"But you said . . ."

"I know. Just say I was confused. I got caught up in it, too. I wanted to believe in it, dreaming, thinking it was all going to come true. It was like some story, like a book we were reading. Both of us. I'm sorry."

"It wasn't a story to me," I said. She spun away. "Jola."

"I'm sorry," she said. "I do love you, if you have to know that. That's not the problem." She faced me again, wiping fiercely at her eyes with balled tissue. "I have to go now," she said.

I reached out to grasp her shoulders, but she slipped from my hands, effortlessly, like smoke.

"Just let me go," she whispered. "It's better."

She stepped around me and walked away through the forest, and I didn't move or look after her until I could no longer hear her footsteps in the leaves.

The sun had vanished now behind low clouds, dark with winter. A sharp cold wind whined through the forest. The cabin door in front of me was still locked, for I had not opened it before she arrived. I removed the old smooth key from my pocket. The worn lock chunked open in my hand like a living thing, so easily that I wondered, momentarily, if it had been securely locked. Probably we had been followed here, I thought. Probably the lock had been picked, the interior inspected, the covers on the bed folded back by Jabłoński or whomever he found to do such work for him.

But the inside seemed undisturbed, the small bed unmussed, the frayed red blanket as smooth as we had left it. I lay down on the bed in the stillness, stared at the roof's dim carpentry. I thought of her legs lifting over me, her lips tracing patterns on my chest, my stomach, the feel of her skin on mine, the light touch of her fingers, the floating shiver of sensation within a cottony, hollowed-out place, this place, from which the world and the walls of the shed receded. I thought of the yellow field in August, the gentle slope of the golden hillside where we rested side by side, concealed in the humming grass, staring into the sky. Her hand on my leg. Her sly smile. I thought it all belonged to me, the sky, the field, her.

I felt a fool. Not made a fool. Was a fool.

I rolled onto my side. And slept.

When I awoke, it was nearly dark. I left the cabin, picked my way out of the forest, and walked the rough cobbled road back to town. The cracked bell sounded from the church; it was five o'clock now and fully dark. Dim yellowed lights shone from windows. Fluorescent tubes threw a sickly pallor from the windows of the shops. I shambled along the street as though estranged from the place, or as though I were seeing it for the first time, the broken fences, the piles of junk stacked beside every house, the silly trash receptacles painted to resemble penguins, chipped and rusted and overflowing with litter. I regarded the deserted streets, the low houses, the smeared shop windows, the heavy darkness of the church, with a sensation of bleakness I had never felt before. I needed to go home, to help with the milking and feeding, but I halted on the eastern side of the square, sat once more on the broken bench in the shadows, and simply stared at the place. Across the square, the bar was closing. The familiar gaggle of men tumbled from the door, swayed like stalks in the wind while they lighted cigarettes off a single match, and Jadwiga bent to lock the door behind her. One by one, they staggered off. I sat, watching scraps of trash blown by the wind. I felt unable to move, paralyzed by this grimness. After a while I heard voices and saw a group of high school boys congregating around the old concrete bus kiosk at the far edge of the square. Their voices and laughter rose and fell on the wind. They gathered close around the kiosk wall. One of them let out a whoop, then there was laughter, and another shout blown apart by the wind. They walked noisily away, past the bar and into the darkness. I got up then and walked straight across the square to the kiosk. In the faint light from the street lamp, wet spay-paint glistened, trickled down the concrete in black rivulets. The words said, "Jews to the gas."

I found a scrap of newspaper and wiped furiously at the paint, but I only smeared the wet drippings. The words remained, soaked into porous concrete.

I hurried home then, nearly at a run. Mother had started the milking. She asked sharply where I had been. I apologized and said nothing more. Grandpa was not there. He had gone out in the afternoon, Mother said, and had not yet returned.

"The men are all out minding their own business, I suppose," she said. She left the barn. I finished up, impatient with the work, and yet in no hurry to enter the house. When I did go in, my bowl of soup was waiting on the stove and my mother had gone to bed.

My own lights were out when I heard Grandpa downstairs, then his footsteps slow and weary on the stairs. What was he doing? Mending another fence in the darkness? Chopping wood when there was plenty already? Would the time come when I would have to go out in the middle of the night to try to find him?

His door closed and the house was silent. Three people in this house, breathing the darkness, alone. Across town, over the darkened rooftops and leafless trees and trash blown square, would Jola be lying awake, too? And feeling what? Relief?

I woke in the night with the shards of a dream in my head, dream-logic splintered like a pane of glass crushed underfoot. Two images: a childhood toy and my father. The toy was the cast-iron truck, the plaything I pushed along the floor for hours as a child. My father had taken it, over my protests, and instructed me to wait. But when I searched him out, he was in the barn, where he had been trying to convert the toy into a real truck. The expression on his face was consternation and alarm, for the thing had somehow been made larger, though not near to the size of a real truck. Its parts, fenders, bumpers, doors, were scattered in disarray, and he was unable to proceed. He held his hands out before him; they seemed withered, incompetent, and faintly trembled. The former toy refused to become a real truck, a useful object, and now it could not be coaxed back to its original form. It was not a toy; it was not the real thing. It was a confusion, a cartoon, a useless, broken mess, and he could only stare at it in silence and horror.

CHAPTER TWELVE

The question of Farby's whereabouts had not much concerned
Jabłoński at first. Minions were minions and behaved like minions,
that was a working principle. You couldn't control everything.
Couldn't run everything. All that mindless paperwork. Put a good
unambitious fellow in place and he would function like a gear forever, low-maintenance material in a sealed machine. Just a squirt of
grease now and then. Farby, where was Farby?

You couldn't control everything . . . The phrase popped back into
his mind. The odd unforeseen circumstance. Lust. Or worse, love.
He wasn't sure how he knew this, didn't remember what caused him
to notice it. Nothing he saw, really. Their body types, maybe. Perfect match. He had just made a crack one day at Farby's expense,
and there it was: he blushed. A shot in the dark, and back came this
silent yelp from the heart, Farby's soft, slow, fat-padded heart. Tits,
of course, would be his weakness.

Jabłoński had asked Krupik, the cop, what he knew, but he
might as well have asked a tree. Put an idiot in a police car and that's
what you got: an idiot in a car. Krupik spent his first month on the
job polishing it. Not exactly the ideal situation, but suitable candi-
dates for the job were not easy to come by. You didn't want a local
and you didn't want someone flighty. You wanted a placid dolt from
out of town. That's what he got, except that Krupik was exception-
ally thick. A redundancy he could have done without.

Not an ideal situation.

It was time to flush Farby out. Zofia was the key, he was sure. No cipher, that one. Jabłoński wondered what she saw in Farby. Bits of dried egg around his mouth. A man of appetites, he supposed.

He summoned Andrzej, who deposited his clanking leather bag of tools on the second chair in the office and watched in silence while Jabłoński ruffled through the papers in front of him. He glanced up over his glasses.

"I'm supposed to be at the school," Andrzej said.

"The boiler again?"

"Yes."

"Time to replace it."

Andrzej shrugged. "They were supposed to do it last summer."

"And the summer before that."

Andrzej offerred a little palms up gesture.

"Yes," Jabłoński said. "Well, it's not my job anymore."

"No."

"Where's Farby?"

"Who knows?" Andrzej replied.

"Someone does."

"Warsaw?"

Jabłoński thought about this. No, cities intimidated Farby. He'd be lost there, even more than usual. "I don't think so," he said. "Hard to find a decent kielbasa there."

Andrzej made no reply.

"I need to speak with him," Jabłoński said. "I need to find him."

Andrzej squirmed in his chair and said nothing.

"Pani Zofia," Jabłoński said. "You suppose she might know?"

"You could ask her."

The tone of the quick reply caught Jabłoński by surprise. He was not used to flippancy from Andrzej. He scrutinized the plumber's face for some sign of sarcasm or naïveté (on the limited chance he might have meant it), but the angular features, under the pushed-back cap, were composed and blank.

"I don't think so, Andrzej," Jabłoński said, his own sarcasm unambiguous. He picked up the papers on his desk and tapped their edges straight, a gesture meant to approximate the rap of a judge's gavel. Let's move along here. "Why don't you see," he said with slow authority, "what you can find out?"

"You want *me* to ask her?"

Jabłoński leaned forward, his face now showing open concern. He spoke gently, with a tone of sincerity.

"What's wrong, Andrzej?"

"Nothing." He withdrew a single cigarette from his shirt pocket and lit it.

"Come now, Andrzej," Jabłoński said, his voice soothing. "What's bothering you?"

Andrzej's eyes shifted to the grimy window, reflecting the sunless light beyond.

"Why is this still happening?" he asked. "I thought this would be over now."

Jabłoński eased back in his chair, to the accompaniment of its squeaking springs.

" '*A luta continua,*' "Jabłoński said.

Andrzej regarded him uncomprehendingly, squinting through the smoke coiling from the cigarette between his lips.

"Che Guevara, I think. Or maybe it was Castro. 'The struggle continues.' But I always thought it sounded better in Portuguese."

Father Tadeusz tried making inquiries as discreetly as he could, but he realized that in a place as small as Jadowia no inquiry could be reliably counted on as discreet. He went first to the aged Mrs. Skubyszewska, but his unannounced visit seemed to surprise and confuse her. She was not having a good day. Her husband was confined to bed with a cold, but he called out to her repeatedly from his sickbed. The house was stuffy and smelled of medicine. In any case, she said she had no memory of a pupil named Czarnek—not that her memory should be taken as reliable, she hastened to add. There were too many students, too many years. Father Tadeusz asked her about the distillery, but she had no knowledge of it beyond the fact that it was "very, very old." He heard a long, wracking cough from the direction of the bedroom. "I didn't know it was still operating," she said.

"Mama!" her husband called out.

"Excuse me, Father." She stood to answer the summons, and Father Tadeusz got up to take his leave.

"I'm sorry to intrude, Pani Skubyszewska. I shouldn't have

dropped in by surprise, but I simply wanted to make use of your memory again."

"Mama!"

"He has a terrible cold," she said. "He's not well at all."

"One more thing, if I may. Do you remember, Pani, was there once a Jewish cemetery in town? Not the old one. Was there another one, here, in the village?"

Again the long terrible cough echoed from the bedroom, and Mrs. Skubyszewska flickered at the sound, her hand holding the front door open. "What? Oh, yes, the cemetery. Yes, yes, there was."

"Where was it?"

"It was near the clinic, I think. Yes, somewhere near there."

"Mama!"

"Thank you, ma'am. I hope Mr. Skubyszewski is better soon."

"God willing."

"God willing."

He proceded farther out the same street to the clinic, a two-story building painted a stained yellow. Muddy cars were parked beside it, along with two horse-drawn wagons. On the side of the clinic nearest the town's center were an old barn and three dilapidated sheds belonging to the house next door. On the far side was an unfinished concrete-block foundation. Father Tadeusz remembered that it was the stalled construction of a proposed nursery school— he believed that was the story—for which the money had run out. A pile of concrete blocks waited beside the low foundation wall, weeds grown up around them. The area around had been leveled off with a grader or tractor. A row of gnarled old poplar trees flanked the lot left and right. A wire fence stretched across the far end and beyond that was an empty field.

He walked back to the rectory. It was probably a mistake to rely on Mrs. Skubyszewska's memory, he thought. But then what memory was to be relied on? He went once more to the town library, on the chance that old maps of the village were available among the curious collection of Party theory and romance novels. The vacant-eyed girl in charge didn't think so, but invited him to look. It was a brief and fruitless search.

He bought a bun from Janowski, the baker, when he saw his shop was empty, and ventured a question to him. "Do you know the man who works at the old distillery?" he asked. "His name is Czarnek, I think."

"Czarnek," Janowski said, declining Father Tadeusz's offered coin. "Yes, he runs the distillery."

"Yes, that's him."

"What about him?"

"I just wondered if you knew him."

"He comes in sometimes. Why?"

"He's been here a long time?"

"Oh yes. Always, I guess. Never says much. He has a dog. Big, black dog. Always with him. Why do you ask, Father? Anything wrong?"

"No, nothing. I just met him, spoke to him. That's all."

"He's not a talker, that one," Janowski said. "Wonder he spoke at all, even to you, Father. Can't say as I've ever seen him in church. What did he have to say?"

"Oh, just pleasantries," Father Tadeusz said, waving his hand dismissively. He thanked Janowski for the bun and left.

That was the pattern of his further halting queries, not that there were many of them. He brought up Czarnek's name to Barski, the druggist, and, naturally enough, with Andrzej, the plumber, and each time elicited responses similar to Janowski's. These rebounding questions, he decided, grew out of the atmosphere created by Father Jerzy and his group. Father Tadeusz had no part of this, and yet had not distinctly separated himself from their affairs. An air of anticipation and suspicion prevailed, and so people wanted to know why he wanted to know. These were not questions Father Tadeusz wanted to answer, so he stopped inquiring. Besides, he had to admit, he was not good at this business of drawing people out, at easy conversation with a disguised purpose. It was, he said to himself, his failing as a priest, his inability to connect with people in a way that prompted them to reach back, open up, reveal themselves or relieve their pain. Why had he been denied a life of research amid bins of books and musty papers, when that was all that seemed to suit him, a life of contemplation in historical theology, safe from living questions put by living people, for which he had no answer?

He did decide, however, to ask one more question at the town office, for surely there they would know. One small kernel of identity he had not learned—indeed, had forgotten to ask—was Czarnek's first name. This he would need, at least. A woman rose from her desk when he came in. She smiled at him with an air of familiarity.

"You're . . ." He feigned a struggle to remember her name.

"Zofia Flak," she said. He caught the scent of perfume as she approached the counter.

"Yes, Pani Zofia. Could you help me with a small question?"

"Gladly, Father, if I can." She held a pen at the ready, as if preparing to jot down notes. "What is it?"

"Mr. Czarnek, who works at the distillery? Could you tell me his first name?"

"Of course. I suppose Father Jerzy wants to know." She glanced away at a woman mopping the hallway floor and leaned closer to him so that he felt the warmth of her breath. "It's Krzysztof."

"Really?"

"Yes. Krzysztof."

"Thank you, Pani."

"Not at all."

He started to leave and then hesitated.

"There is one other thing."

"Yes."

"Do you have in this office any old town maps?"

"Maps of Jadowia?" She laughed. "Surely you're not lost."

"No. I mean old maps, a plan of the layout of the town, churches, buildings, things like that. An old one."

"How old?"

"Before the war."

"Oh, no. There's nothing here from before the war. It was all taken away, or destroyed." She looked at him quizzically, clearly speculating on the motive of the request. "Nothing like that here, I'm afraid. Perhaps in the district archives at Siedlce. Maybe there."

He thanked her again and left her standing at the counter, still watching him as he closed the front door.

*   *   *

He was surprised how easy it was. He drove to Siedlce the next day and at the Voivod offices was soon directed to the basement level. At the end of the corridor he found a thin old man reading a newspaper at a desk. He wore a janitor's smock, and behind him were ranks of shelves and records receding into dim light. The old man came to the counter and listened first to Father Tadeusz's request and then departed without a word and disappeared for five minutes into the maze of shelves. Father Tadeusz regretted not being able to roam through this forest of paper himself, but the old man offered no sign of invitation to this preserve of uncertain history, so he waited, his hands clasped on the counter.

The sound of the old man's shuffling feet on the waxed concrete floor preceded his return. He carried a narrow cardboard file holder containing thin loose-bound files, each one secured with dusty ribbon ties.

"Jadowia, you said?"

"Yes."

"Should be in here." He thumbed though the box. "Here." He withdrew one, tugged at the ribbon and opened it. Inside was a piece of heavy paper, folded in quarters.

"What is the date?" Father Tadeusz asked. "Does it say?"

The old man removed spectacles from his shirt pocket and bent over the map. "1929."

"Good," said Father Tadeusz.

"You may use the table if you wish," the old man said.

Father Tadeusz spread the map on a table behind him and sat down. It was an official map, blue lines on thick draftsman's paper, hand-drawn with a T-square and straight edge, with a surveyor's clear freehand lettering. He was surprised by the extent of the village as it was depicted here, and he realized he had never seen a current map of Jadowia. For a moment it all seemed unfamiliar. Then he picked out the central intersection of the north-south roads and next to it, clearly marked with a cross, the church.

To the north of the church, then, was the square. To the northeast of the square, the town offices. His finger traced the road east from the square to the main cemetery. It was there on the map, where it should be. His finger ran back along the road to the square, then to the church, then straight along that road to the south, and there it was: square across the front, bounded irregularly at the west end, and distinctly labeled "Cemetery for the Jews," signified by a Star of David.

Father Tadeusz gazed at it for some minutes, recalling, in his mind's eye, the surrounding buildings. There was no mark indicating the clinic, although some structure was shown. The map showed the location of buildings, but only a few were labeled as to purpose, and these appeared to be public structures. What he needed to pinpoint the cemetery's location was a reference point that still existed.

He searched the whole map once more, his hand guiding his eye as he sought other landmarks. He started again with the square, following his hand to the top border, then left and right, stopping sometimes to close his eyes and visualize the streets as he remembered them. On the street west from the central square he saw the mark of a building labeled with another Star of David. He looked below for a key further explaining the symbols, but there was none.

He stood up. The old man was back at his newspaper.

"Sir," he said, "could you help me, please?"

The old man stood wordlessly, took off his glasses, and came around the counter.

"Are you familiar with these maps?"

The old man stood there, peering down. "What is it?"

"This," said Father Tadeusz. He placed his finger at the Star of David. "What is this?"

The old man unfolded his glasses and put them on. He bent over the map.

"Church for the Jews," he said. "What do they call it . . .?"

"Synagogue?"

"Yes. Synagogue."

"Could you help me with something else?"

The old man gazed at him, waiting.

"I want to find out exactly where this is," Father Tadeusz said. "Can you tell me exactly how far from the church?"

The old man glanced down at the map, then went back to his desk and found a ruler. "Now what was it?"

Father Tadeusz pointed out the cemetery, the synagogue, and the church. The old man measured, then placed his ruler against the scale.

"Three hundred fifty meters to the synagogue," he said. He measured again. "Four hundred twenty-five from the church to the cemetery. Approximate."

Father Tadeusz wrote down the figures in a small notebook.

"Is that all?" the old man said.

"Yes. Thank you. Thank you very much."

The old man nodded and delicately refolded his spectacles. He stood by while Father Tadeusz carefully refolded the map and placed it inside its cardboard cover.

"Are they coming back, Father?"

"Pardon?"

"The Jews. They're coming back? Trying to get their property again? Is that it?"

"No, I don't think so."

"Well, I hear that, Father. They're going to come back. You know why?"

"No." Father Tadeusz handed him the folder.

"Just what you'd expect. They want their money."

Father Tadeusz went to the basement of the rectory the next afternoon and spent six hours there before he realized he had skipped his lunch. He stopped himself by a determined act of will, leaving a welter of boxes and record books behind him, and climbed the stairs, uncharacteristically, two at a time. Jadwiga had departed for the day, but she had left his soup in a covered bowl on the table, along with bread and a small pitcher of milk. He sat down and ate rapidly, not minding the coldness of the soup or the bread's dryness. This, too, was unusual, for he was normally punctual about his meals and long ago indicated this to the old housekeeper, who quickly adjusted to his habits. The food calmed his racing mind, enough so that he leaned back, both arms extended to rest on the table, and reflected that, indeed, his regular routines, established over the last two years as imperceptible to him as the movement of the slow hand of a clock, had altered sharply. He stayed up later, got up earlier, and rushed though duties that he had always performed methodically. His walks, once a daily late-afternoon feature of his life in Jadowia, were now erratic in their schedule and their course. He was now out and about more than he had ever been since arriving here, and more observant and, yes, he thought, more wakeful. At the end of the day, when he extinguished the lamp in his room, his eyes closed, gratefully weary, yet regretful of the need for sleep and eager for the next day. His dreams were vivid and, in some way he could not explain, gratifying.

He had taken up smoking again, twenty-one years after giving it up. The urge arrived out of nowhere, catching him by surprise one evening after dinner. The next day, passing a shop in the street, he went inside and bought two packs. Now he enjoyed a cigarette after his meals and again late at night, and although he had quit all those years before because it seemed a profligate's luxury and an abasement to his health, neither consideration troubled him much now. Tobacco smoke curling around his nostrils, the rasp of it on his throat, felt like liberation, a denial withdrawn. He even ventured so far as to think he had earned it, although just why—beyond having lived to his "mature" years—he could not say. He flicked the ashes onto the saucer of his empty teacup and reminded himself again to instruct Jadwiga to place an ashtray beside his plate. He carried the dishes to the kitchen, doused his cigarette in the sink, and descended to the musty storeroom in the basement.

It had taken him some time to find it. More recent church records, going back five to ten years, were kept in the small office upstairs, and he had walked through virtually all of the building's sixteen rooms before he thought to check in the basement. What he needed were the records of baptisms, confirmations, and funerals, and he found them in a closed room across the hallway from the boiler, its door yielding with an extended groan. The place seemed as though it had been undisturbed for years, perhaps since the rectory was built, and he felt a thin current of excitement at the sight of those banked shelves, the stacks of boxes, the piles of old song books, missals, bulletins, their yellowed labels written with a ghostly, elegant penmanship, in India ink applied with square-nibbed pens. The enclosed air, scented with paper yielding to decay molecule by molecule, filled his chest like pure oxygen, and for some minutes he simply stood in the room, absorbing it, as if he had stepped into a long-sought trove of ancient volumes, the frustrated scholar granted access at last. The pages of the old hymnals, falling forward beneath his thumb, gave back a liquid sound, like water over stones, and threw up a fine dust that tingled in his nose. Methodically, then, he set about finding the order in the room, saying silently to himself, "I am in no hurry."

He commenced with funerals because he wanted to get the feel of the books and because he wanted to be deliberate, to circle in from the edge. He started with the volume dated 1935–1937, and stood for a while with the book propped open against the shelf, but when that grew tiring, he went out to the hallway and retrieved an old wooden chair and dragged it back to the storeroom and sat under the ceiling light, turning the thick leaves of the book on his lap.

A brief form listed each funeral, the name of the deceased, the year of birth and the date of death, the nearest survivor or, in some cases, several survivors. The handwriting changed sometimes from entry to entry. He was struck by the skill of the penmanship, its uniformity and small stately flourishes. It was a vanishing skill, he thought, good penmanship. The record keepers were not identified, but he presumed they were the priests officiating at the funeral masses.

Nothing in the entries suggested the prominence or position of the deceased. The book, like the process it recorded, rendered all equal. The name Czarnek was not among them.

He went on. The book encompassing the war years began with 1938. He had heard it said that in time of war all but soldiers put off their dying, as if death by natural causes assumed a lower priority. People were too busy surviving to die. Testament to the adage, the book was thinner than all the others. It did not represent the full population, of course, this being a record of those receiving the last rituals of the church. No Czarnek lay inscribed here, either.

Nor through the rest of the forties, although the books fattened once more, as though making up for lost time, gathering a postwar harvest. The calligrapher here seemed hurried, appropriately nerve-racked. In the nearly exhausted book of the exhausted fifties he found the name: Danuta Czarnek. Date of birth: 1893. Date of decease: March 7, 1959. Next of kin: Krzysztof Czarnek.

He searched for older books, the ledgers of christenings and confirmations, but they started in 1911 and he went through yellowed pages rapidly, scanning now, without finding the name again. In any case, Czarnek was mostly likely a married name. He set the book aside, feeling slightly dizzy, and stiffly climbed the stairs for his late lunch.

He returned to the storeroom and its smell of old ink and paper and dried bindings, and moved toward the center of his search. He tried to picture Czarnek. It was a guess, but judging by the lines about his eyes, the thickness of his body, Czarnek must have been about fifty years old. He opened the ledger of christenings and worked forward from 1935, through the pages listing the anointed infants, their parents and godparents.

It did not take him so long, now that he had grown accustomed to the books and had passed through his initial mood of hushed care and deliberation. He went through to the early fifties. There was no Krzysztof Czarnek, nor Danuta listed as mother, nor any Czarnek at all.

The confirmation lists went even faster. Czarnek was not there, either.

None of this meant anything certain. The family could have come from somewhere else, from anywhere in Poland. It was the war, after all, with all its dislocations. And yet he had a feeling this was not true, a sense that he had found, or not found, just what he had expected.

He heard footsteps on the floor above him, the rattle of the hallway door. It was late now, and dark, he knew, although there were no windows in the storeroom to verify that fact. A voice called his name. It was Father Jerzy.

Father Tadeusz did not answer for a moment, but his eyes surveyed the old ledger books and registers lying open on the floor. The call came again.

"Here," he answered, and stepped into the hallway. The footfalls above hesitated.

"Here, Father," he said.

Father Jerzy appeared in the light at the top of the stairs, hesitating. "Is that you, Father Tadeusz?"

"Yes. I'm here." He started to climb the stairs, but Father Jerzy came down and marched perfunctorily past, taking in the storeroom with its confusion of open books, and then stared back at Father Tadeusz, eyes narrow as knife slits in a lump of cheese.

"What are you doing, Father, if I may ask?" he said.

Father Tadeusz wiped the dust from his hands and reentered the storeroom. "I didn't know all these old records were down here," he said. "I was looking through them. They go back quite far."

"Financial records, I suppose?" Father Jerzy asked.

"Mostly christenings and funerals, I think," he answered. He smiled at Father Jerzy, hoping to relax the young priest's stern expression. "The old commerce of birth and death."

"I see. Well, Father, I came to talk to you about something more immediate."

"Yes?"

"Yes. You've been making inquiries about one Mr. Czarnek, the man who operates the distillery. Correct? In any case, your inquiries have come to my attention. I would like to know your interest in this matter."

Father Tadeusz could feel his face reddening. For a moment he bit his tongue to keep from speaking back sharply. He was, after all, the senior priest in this parish. He had not endeavored to rein in Father Jerzy in his enthusiasms, whatever his own misgivings. Now Father Jerzy, evidently, was monitoring his activities. He took a deep breath to calm himself.

"Matter?" he said. "I don't know about any 'matter.' I simply asked his name. I met him briefly and he aroused my curiosity. Why should that trouble you?"

"It troubles the Advisory Commission if your curiosity impedes our inquiries. We would appreciate it if you coordinate your activities with our own. If you wish to join our efforts, to work with us, or in behalf of reforming this place, then I'm certain your contribution would be more than welcomed."

Father Jerzy picked up one of the ledger books from a pile on the floor, glanced at the label on its binding, and let it drop with a thump.

"Why does my question about Mr. Czarnek trouble you?" Father Tadeusz asked.

"I'm sure you know."

"No, I don't."

Father Jerzy grimaced, a sign of ill-contained impatience. "The distillery," he said, "as many people have long realized, is the center of a racket to sell alcohol illegally. To bootleggers. To smugglers from Russia. For the profit of various officials. And with the assistance, needless to say, of the man who ran the distillery. You shouldn't seem surprised. The commission has been looking into this actively."

"You've become a commission now?"

"It takes cooperation and coordination to expose and punish this corruption. It is deep and extensive." He paused and moved along the shelves, his eyes passing over the tall, dark-bound books. "You say you've not been examining the financial records here?"

"I'm not aware there are any."

"Perhaps," Father Jerzy said. "We'll need an inventory. Perhaps they have been removed, if my suspicions are correct."

"What suspicions, Father?"

"Doctored records, perhaps."

"Of the church?"

"Unfortunately."

"Father, this has gone on long enough," Father Tadeusz said. "What are you talking about now?"

"This place!" Father Jerzy said, sweeping his arm backhanded over his head. "This building!"

A moment of uncomfortable silence passed. Finally Father Tadeusz said, mildly as he could, "Go on."

"I hope, Father Tadeusz, that the financial records, such as they are, have not been removed or tampered with in any way." He stared at Father Tadeusz as though he expected a blurted confession.

"Merciful God," Father Tadeusz muttered. "Will you please, Father, get to the point?"

"The point is that this parish house was built with the coin of betrayal, Father. Yes. With Father Marek Stołowski's helpful cooperation with the Communist officials of this village and this district. He was a puppet of the Party, Father."

"I find that hard to believe."

"Do you? Tell me, Father, how do you think it was possible that Father Marek managed to have built for himself the largest parish house in a hundred miles at a time when the church couldn't obtain a building permit for a woodshed? Why do you think it got built?"

"The question hadn't entered my head, Father."

"It got built because of collusion. A record of connivance, of cooperation with atheists. He, kindly old Father Marek, the great friend of the Party chairman, helped keep religious instruction out of the schools. Saw to it that those who defied Party dictates were hounded out of their jobs—persecuted, disgraced even to suicide. Condoned abortions in the village clinic. That's why the parish house was built, the church kept in good repair. An empty monument to Jabłoński and all his people."

With some initial difficulty, Father Tadeusz suppressed the urge to argue loudly, to denounce Father Jerzy's declarations as childish and preposterous. But he held his tongue. His face was blank.

"I know all about this, Father," Father Jerzy went on, his voice lowered now. "My source is excellent. The information was aimed at blackmail, at buying further cooperation. But it will not work with me."

"Yes, I see. What are you going to do?"

"We are gathering our evidence. As I'm sure you know. And when we are finished, we will lay it all out—all of it. In public. We will send the guilty to jail. Everyone in the town office. Everyone who worked with them. The road department. The village counselors, the distiller, the town veterinarian, and we will see this village disinfected and run according to democratic and Christian values. There will be accountability and morality. The church will cleanse and redeem itself. This may shock some, but in the end we will be hailed for this model course of action."

"Model?" A curious word, Father Tadeusz thought.

"Yes, I do see it rather as a paradigm. A pattern for dealing with these issues across the country. People will see what's been done here. The church will see the renewal our efforts have brought. It will be noticed and understood." He paused, thrust his hands in his pockets. "Probably journalists will be coming here soon," he said.

Father Tadeusz hadn't thought of that, but yes, it seemed to follow.

"And after the renewal, Father," he said, "will there be anyone left? After you've sent so many people to jail?"

"Perhaps I over-emphasized the idea of punishment. I'm not interested in seeing people suffer. That isn't the point, is it? I'm interested in the truth. I don't care what sentence a court imposes, or if it imposes one at all. But at least there's some truth in a court. Wouldn't you agree?"

"I wouldn't guarantee it."

"Then where do you look for it?"

"I'm not sure I would, Father, not in the way you mean." Father Tadeusz studied his hands, at the fine gray dust from the old books rubbed into his fingertips. "There is the truth of Jesus," he said, hesitantly. "He taught forgiveness."

"Yes, Father. He also drove the money-changers from the temple. But this isn't a religious discussion."

"Perhaps not. But we're religious men."

"We're men with a religious vocation living in the real world. We have duties. One of them is to truth."

"Or truthful memory," Father Tadeusz said.

"Memory?"

"That's what it is, isn't it? A remembered version of truth? Aren't you forcing everyone to remember the wrongs done to them? Or by them? I wonder if that's healthy, or right."

"I would call it a good lesson, then, if you want to put it that way. An ounce of memory for a pound of prevention. So it doesn't happen again."

"Aren't you stopping short? Is it sufficient, once you've started, to draw the line somewhere and call it finished?"

"Where would you draw it?"

"That's what I'm asking you. What about the Jews?"

"What about them?"

"Eighty percent of the people in this village before the war were Jews. Did you know that?"

"So what?"

"So they are gone. There's not a mark in the village to remember them, discounting, of course, the hateful slogans scrawled here and there."

"That's old stuff, Father."

"Is it?"

"Yes, it is. Poles are sick of being held responsible in some way for what happened to the Jews. It was not our fault. Enough."

"Enough so that we comply in the obliteration of their memory?"

"I cannot account or answer for things that happened before I was born. It's enough to find the truth about what's been going on here for the last ten years."

"I'm not sure the truth is something you command, Father. You can't herd it about, like a flock of sheep." He felt, suddenly, deeply depressed, for if he believed anything about history, or scholarship, or "facts" as they sifted through layers of time, it was what he just said. "Truth has its own mind, its own way."

"Very profound, Father. Also convenient. So you do nothing, is that it? An old excuse for the status quo. Well, I'm too busy for that. I'm sorry if a more activist approach disturbs you. There's a plan to carry out."

"Yes, the paradigm," Father Tadeusz said. "And you, you intend to adapt this model to other places? Larger communities, perhaps?"

"Wherever my skills can be of service, Father." He shrugged. "I will go where I am sent."

"Yes, I know you will," Father Tadeusz said. "Successfully, too, I'm certain." As he stood up to leave, he caught Father Jerzy's wondering, almost quizzical expression, and with it the first glimmer of self-doubt he had seen in the young priest. What he yearned for most, Father Tadeusz saw in that glance, was approval. "I mean it, Father. I'm sure you will be a success. Wherever you go."

"Thank you." Father Jerzy beamed.

"It's late for me, Father. I'm going up to bed. I'll leave all this for you. The door is always open, as far as I know. So if you want to come back . . ."

He started for the door, but another question occurred to him. "And Father Marek?" he asked.

"Let the chips fall," Father Jerzy said.

"I see."

They said good night. Father Tadeusz climbed the stairs. He left the light on in the downstairs hallway for Father Jerzy to find his way out. Then he went up to his room and knelt to say his prayers. He prayed for a long time, and it was longer still before he slept.

Father Tadeusz did not delude himself that he might qualify for special favors from any level of church hierarchy above him. The years before had convinced him. He had let his wishes be known, in the matter of assignment, and gained nothing for the effort. Bishop Krolewski had listened wordlessly to his appeals, his smooth skin taut over the chiseled cheeks and brow, his white hair closely and impeccably trimmed, his pale blue eyes intelligent and sympathetic. In the end he was unyielding—smiling, gentle, but decided. The word was sent down later: It would be as it was ordered. The bishop wanted it this way. It would be best.

He had gone quietly the last time, his old arguments worn out, no sap left for it. He did venture a single phone call, but the bishop's secretary, an efficient screener of appeals from below, inquired of his needs. His voice, in practiced understudy of his superior, glided along the wire on the finest of oils. "May I say what matter you wish to discuss?"

"My assignment," Father Tadeusz had said.

"He is busy today and tomorrow and then will be traveling to Toruń for a retreat. But I will see your message is passed on." No doubt it was. But no return call came, and Father Tadeusz made no further attempt to deflect the will of church administration. He had packed his bags for Jadowia and went quietly. And quietly remained. Or so it must have appeared to his superiors.

As Providence would have it, the previously efficient assistant was absent or replaced, for the call was put through after a mere thirty seconds on hold. The bishop's voice was silken, as remembered. Father Tadeusz was conscious of trying not to hurry or to adopt the tone of a supplicant in requesting a meeting; this, he told himself, was business. His concern was irrelevant, for the meeting was granted quickly, without question. "Two-thirty tomorrow afternoon is good for me," the bishop said, "if that gives you time to drive here. Good. I look forward to seeing you, Father."

Seniority, Father Tadeusz thought. It must count for something.

*　　　*　　　*

Powierza wondered why he had not drowned all these kittens last spring. Got away from him, he supposed. Now the barns were crawling with cats, all of them watching him with the same wary, sidelong glances, yellow eyes in identical striped faces, scrawny creatures that slid like shadows in the corner of his eye, making him think he was seeing things. They were nearly wild, with claws like fishhooks and teeth like carpet tacks. Well, at least no mouse survived long here.

He muttered to himself. The farm was slipping. The milk shed was filthy. Good it was winter; in summer you wouldn't be able to stand inside it for the flies. Door falling off. Tractor with one of its chewed-up old tires flat. On its last legs anyway. He had painted it last year, thinking he could sell it with new paint. Paint never sold anything. Never sold a tractor. He liked doing it, though, the red paint from the spray can spreading an even coat over rust and grease. It gleamed until the paint dried and the grease bled through. He should have cleaned it better first.

He thought of painting Tomek's room. Mentioned it to Hania, but she said nothing, like she didn't care what he did. Actually, now that he thought about it more, she looked at him like she blamed him, blamed him for not painting it before, when Tomek was alive. As if to say that if he had thought of it before Tomek would still *be* alive. She had switched her brain off, Hania. Sat with her knitting and stared through the television set. Or out the window. She didn't say much, didn't talk about him. She wrote letters to the girls. Knitted lumpy little sweaters for her grandsons.

He'd paint the room anyway. Next week, maybe. He didn't know why. Maybe for when the girls visited.

There was not much in there. A big picture of an American motorcycle hung on the wall, dried tape curling. Bed. Shelves. A dresser full of his clothes. He brought it up with Hania, but she didn't do anything. Finally he did it himself. Found a box, folded the clothes into it. When the box was full he didn't know what to do with it, so he left it, on the floor by the foot of the bed. Now he had carried it to the barn. There seemed no place for it here, either. He forgot it and went searching for the lug wrench for the tractor.

*   *   *

It was there in the barn that Andrzej found Powierza, one arm draped over the tire for support, his boot pushing on the wrench to loosen the lug. It released with tight little honks, like ducks quacking.

"You want to sell it?" Andrzej asked. He slipped his bag of tools from his shoulder.

"You want to buy it?" Powierza replied, fitting the wrench on the next lug nut.

"Nice paint," Andrzej said. "I'll ask around."

"How do you know I want to sell it?"

"You don't?"

Powierza pressed down on the wrench with his foot. "Right price, I'll sell it. Ask around."

"Okay," Andrzej said. "I can do that."

"I wouldn't go to any trouble," Powierza said. The damn thing was nearly fifteen years old. No one wanted anything that old anymore.

"No trouble. Glad to do it."

The nut spun free and the wrench clunked onto the dirt floor. Powierza nudged back his cap and stared at Andrzej. "Why would you do that?" he asked.

"Just being helpful."

Powierza picked up the wrench. "You got a job out this way today, Andrzej?"

"No. I wanted to talk to you about something."

"Not tractors?"

"No." Andrzej pulled up an old wooden crate and sat down, then opened his tool satchel and withdrew a bottle of vodka. He opened it and passed it to Powierza.

"You remember I mentioned the quarry to you before?"

"Yes."

"You should go to the quarry tomorrow night, Mr. Powierza," Andrzej said. He accepted the bottle back from Powierza, wiped the top on his sleeve, and drank.

"Why?"

"Some trucks are coming."

"What trucks?"

"Different trucks," said Andrzej. "Interesting for you, I think."

Powierza found another crate and sat down facing Andrzej, the satchel and the bottle resting between them on the ground. Powierza folded his arms across his chest. The plumber removed his cap, raked a hand through his oily hair, and leaned forward, his elbows on his knees.

"Trucks," Powierza said.

"Yes."

"I went to the quarry to see," Powierza said. "I didn't find much. Some tracks, maybe. Old ones."

"Eleven-thirty tomorrow night," Andrzej said. "Jabłoński is meeting a truck from Radom, outside Węgrów. I know because he wanted to get gas for his car. He asked me to get it and I said, Chairman, where can I get gas? And he was impatient, the phone was ringing and his secretary was saying it was Radom on the line, and he said to me, I don't give a fuck where you get it, I've got to meet a truck from Radom tomorrow night and I need enough gas to get me to Węgrów and back and I haven't got time to hunt for it, goddamn it, so just do it."

Andrzej swigged from the bottle, then went on.

"He seldom goes anywhere," he said. "Never has gas when he does. Someone always has to get it for him. So I took a can to the Road Department and got ten liters."

"So how do you know there will be trucks at the quarry?"

"Because that's where they go."

"What for?"

Andrzej offered a weak smile. "Some business, Mr. Powierza. Who can say? One of the trucks is a Sovietov transport. Russian."

"Russian? How do you know this?"

"That's what I heard. The trucks before were Russian, I think. Late in the night."

"Why?" Powierza held the open bottle before his lips. "Why do they come to the quarry?"

"For the distillery, before. It is nearby. But this is not for the distillery."

"How do you know?"

"I don't. But the truck from Radom is a Polish truck. The Russian trucks were transports. Coming from Germany, usually."

"How do you know all this stuff, Andrzej?" Powierza watched him cautiously. Andrzej made a small noise in his throat, like an abbreviated whimper from a dog.

"I stay awake nights," he said. "I keep my eyes open."

Powierza mopped his lips and replaced the bottle between. He studied Andrzej's face. It was faintly lined, creased about the eyes, and yet placid, unworried. It was not a face that was carefree at this moment, but it could be, easily enough, perhaps with a few more drinks. Ease, not worry, was the natural state of this face, Powierza thought. A face of accommodation.

"I still don't know, Andrzej, why you are telling me all this."

"Because," Andrzej said. He shifted uncomfortably on his seat.

"Because why?"

"Because I am a useful man, you see. I make myself useful. I know how to do it. I was useful to Jabłoński. In small ways. But, you understand, he is finished. Even he knows this. He speaks of it sometimes when he has a few vodkas in him. He pays me in vodka. Anyway, I know this too. He is finished, this is sure. He is bitter. A little crazy, too, talking of Cuba. But you are a smart man, Mr. Powierza. Staszek, may I call you? Yes? You have a future. People respect you. I know this. They talk of you for mayor. I can help, be of service. Do work for you. I have to have a future, as everyone else. I can see which way the wind blows. So. Here I am. Of service. You see? You can understand, can't you?"

He raised the bottle.

"What happened to my son, Andrzej?"

"I don't know."

"Andrzej . . ."

"Really, Staszek. I do not know."

"Was it Jabłoński? Did he have something to do with it?"

"No. Jabłoński is many things, perhaps. But not that. My opinion."

"Then who?"

"The Russians, maybe. They are criminals and they don't care."

"What Russians?"

"Who knows?"

Andrzej saw Powierza's face redden. "Really, Staszek, who knows? It is a country full of thugs and Mafia gangs. Now they all come here and do their business. Who knows what it is or where they go? They come like locusts. They care for nothing."

"And Jabłoński? You think he cares?"

Andrzej shrugged. "He would be afraid of the trouble. It isn't his way. He likes to stay behind the curtain, where no one sees. He is sometimes nasty, but I don't think he kills."

Powierza said nothing for a moment. A cat crept along the edge of his vision. He didn't disagree about Jabłoński, really. He had lived here too long. Jabłoński had lived here too long. Jabłoński's business was knowing, not killing. The question was what he knew.

"Tomorrow night?" Powierza asked.

"Yes," Andrzej said. "I think so."

"You come with me."

Andrzej glanced up at Powierza with a quick wince of surprise.

"You come with me," Powierza repeated.

Andrzej considered this a moment, his face back to its placid deadpan blankness. "All right," he agreed.

Powierza's heavy hands dangled between his knees. "Good," he said.

"Mr. Powierza?" Andrzej said.

"Yes?"

"This is an important matter. For Jabłoński, I mean."

"Why?"

"Because he is going to be there himself. I think, usually, he would not do this."

Powierza considered the picture, the Chairman out so late at night, needing a drink, in his sputtering little Fiat.

"I mean, Staszek, you should be careful. What do you plan to do?"

"I don't know," Powierza said finally. "Go see what happens." He rubbed his head with both hands, as if waking from sleep. "Do you have a flashlight, Andrzej?"

"What plumber doesn't have a flashlight?"

"A strong one?"

"No, a small one only."

"Then we'll borrow Maleszewski's."

"Maleszewski?"

"My neighbor," Powierza said. "Leszek."

CHAPTER THIRTEEN

The kitchen windows were rimmed with morning frost. Grandpa stood looking out, his jacket and cap and boots already on. He dipped the last of his bread crust into milky tea, his usual breakfast.

"Bobiński wants a calf," he said.

"Today?"

"Yes."

Bobiński was a trader from Węgrów who now and then bought a butchered calf from us and other farmers. It was rumored that his customer for the veal was the Italian Embassy in Warsaw, but he was careful never to reveal the identity of his customers, fearing he might be cut out of the deal. He drove a hard bargain, but Grandpa had been selling to him for years and always got a good price. Usually Grandpa would butcher in the morning, and Bobiński would come the next day to pick up the quartered carcass. Grandpa went about this work intently—he was a skillful butcher—and sometimes I would help or sit nearby and watch. It was a good time to talk with him.

We did the milking and feeding first. It was February, the day dark and overcast, the horizon across the fields to the west murky with mist. From the forest on the slight rise of land behind our barns a flock of crows squabbled. As I hauled the last pitchfork of hay from the loft to the cow shed, I could hear Grandpa sharpening his knives in the archway between the equipment shed and the barn.

The calf was nearly four months old now—one of the two I had

Jola's husband look at when they were barely two weeks old. I
untied it from the stall where it stood by its mother and led it across
the lot. It was a pretty thing, a male, its black-and-white hair still
soft and curly, its nose gray and wet and healthy. Grandpa took the
rope lead with one hand and with the other struck it a short sharp
blow on the top of its head with the blunt end of his ax. The calf
sank to its knees and fell on its side, and Grandpa cut its throat with
one of his knives. The blood poured steaming onto the ground, and
Grandpa lifted the calf by its hind legs so that the blood ran down-
hill, away from his work place.

I never much liked slaughtering calves. It was not that I was
squeamish. You don't grow up on a farm without seeing animals
butchered. The slaughtering of pigs was commonplace, of course.
We never kept steers for beef cattle. The heifers we bred and then
kept for milk cows. The bullocks we killed and sold to Bobiński—
two or three a year in recent times—and I was always a little regretful when one of our cows gave birth to a male. Still, it was a profit in
cash, and cash is what I needed to buy Kowalski's field. Or so I once
thought. I looked at the ground as the blood puddled and thickened.

"What's the matter, son?" Grandpa said. "You don't look like
yourself lately. What's on your mind?"

A gust of wind whirled through the archway, sprinkling bits of
straw and dust onto the congealing blood. Grandpa moved away
and pushed the end of a rope through a pulley hanging from the
beam of the shed. His back was toward me and I could see the
patches on the seat of his pants when his denim jacket billowed
with the stretch of his arms. He jerked the rope to free a tangle.
From the shadows of the shed he retrieved a bucket and two big
enamel pans, dropped them, and looked at me questioningly.

"It's Poppa," I said.

"What about him, son?" he said.

"I've heard some things," I said.

He went back to the bench in the shed and returned with his
knives. He rested them on an upended block of firewood he used as
a stool, and stared at the calf lying on its side in the dust. From the
barn came the low bawl of the calf's mother.

"What things?"

266

I did not know what to say. More than anything I wanted a denial. I simply stared at his boots.

"I guess you can tell me when you're ready," he said. He rotated the calf by its forelegs and pulled it toward him, rolling it onto its back. He took the large knife from the stump and sliced through the skin and flesh of the neck. Then he picked up the ax, held it close to the blade, and cut through the neck bones with a soft chop. He placed the calf's head aside.

"A man hears lots of things these days," he said. With his old skinning knife, its blade worn thin by years of sharpening, he split the hide up the belly. "Most of what you hear is yokel nonsense." The knife blade traveled up one foreleg, circled the shank. "Told by yokels." Then the other foreleg. Again the soft chop of the ax blade, removing the hooves. "Gossip. People tell the same kind of stories they like to hear."

"Sometimes."

He peeled back the hide. A soft steam rose with it.

"What did you hear, Leszek?"

"I heard that Poppa worked for the Party. Did things for them."

"Is that so?" The point of the knife flicked between muscle and hide at the shoulder, the skin gathering over his wrist, draping onto the ground.

"For Jabłoński," I said.

"What things?"

"That he spied on people. Made reports. Watched people and informed on them. People told him things, and then he informed on them. All kinds of people. Even Powierza."

"Who told you this?"

"Jabłoński."

"You believe him?"

"He showed me papers, Grandpa. They had his signature all over them. I saw them. It was his signature. It wasn't hard to recognize."

"Jabłoński did this?"

"Yes."

"When?"

"A couple of days ago."

"Why?"

"Because he wants something. He wants me to call off Powierza."

"Because of Powierza's boy?"

"I don't know. Because of everything, he says. All the investigations. He said there's a witch-hunt going on, everyone is persecuting the Communists, and if it doesn't stop, people will pay."

I watched Grandpa's face as I spoke. He did not stop working, but a cold, hawklike ferocity hardened the planes of his face. The aquiline ridge of his nose, seen from the side, sharpened to a line of whiteness, the skin taut. He had removed the hide from the carcass. He laid the hide flat, folded the legs to the center and rolled it up tightly.

"Did you know?" I asked. "Did you know about any of this?"

He stood, picked up one end of the rope, and knotted it around the forelegs of the carcass. "Give me a hand," he said, and I rose and held the hoisted calf while he tied the line fast to a post. The skinned animal, pale and bluish, swayed at the rope's end. He steadied it with one hand.

"Grandpa?"

"Yes?"

"Will you answer me? Did you know? Did you know he was doing it?"

"What does anybody know, son?" He sorted the knives.

"Did Mother know?" I pressed.

"I wouldn't think so."

"Then *you* did. You knew, didn't you?"

He picked up his knife and sliced down the belly. The blue tangle of guts lurched forward, glistening and quivering like something alive, giving off a fresh steam in the cold air. He shoved the big enamel pan into position beneath the dangling hind legs. The muscles of his jaw worked as though he were biting through sinew, grinding down words he did not want to speak. This was his anger, but I could not be sure where it was aimed—me, my father, Jabłoński, or somewhere else. I sensed an explosion building, two fuses burning short, but having gone this far, I was not going to walk away.

"Did he tell you?" I asked.

"What was he supposed to tell me?"

"Good God, Grandpa, how do I know? Did he tell you he spied

on Powierza? Did he tell you he informed on him for cutting trees in the forest? Did he tell you he watched people for them? Kept an eye on Pani Gromek, for God's sake? Old man Kowalski's son? Kowalski hated Poppa. Is that why? Did he tell you that?"

He stood looking at me, bowlegged in his rubber boots, his knife clenched in a fist sticky with blood and viscera. We stood face to face. A fleck of animal matter adhered to the white stubble on his chin.

"I'm not interested in the details," he said. "I didn't ask."

"But you *did* know?"

He turned to the carcass and worked the knife through connective tissue. The guts dropped from their upper moorings and hung swaying above the pan.

"He worked for them, didn't he?" he said. "He sat on their council."

"You mean the town council?"

"Whatever they call it."

"But that was before. He did it for what—two years? Many people did that. And he quit."

"Yes."

"So what happened then? Why would he do this?"

"Do what?"

"Damn it!" I kicked in frustration at the pan at his feet, sending it skittering across the ground. As my foot lashed out, his knife sawed though the last knot of gristle and tendon, and the guts fell in a pile across his boots. He didn't move, just stared at the steaming mess across his toes as the silence swelled between us. Instantly, I was ashamed.

"Why don't you talk to me?" I said. "Who else do you expect me to talk to?"

Slowly, then, he moved. He retrieved the pan, while I stood frozen, rattled by my own outburst. Anger, when it happened in our house, receded to quiet and silence. He came back wordlessly and by great handfuls filled the pan. I bent to help him. "I'm sorry," I said.

"What I mean, Leszek," he said, "is what did he really do?"

A bit of offal quivered on his chin, betraying a tremor in his face. This old man, whose manner to me, and perhaps to most who knew him, was that of a man hard as scrap iron, seemed suddenly shaken. His creased eyes were reddened and weary.

"Did he harm anyone?" he went on. "Did it really matter?"

I could not find an answer.

"I don't know what he did. He didn't talk about it. Acted as if I didn't know. You father had many burdens. He saw a lot, saw too much. He saw things when he was half your age—less than half your age—that no one should have to see. He kept a lot to himself. He was strong, and he saw things his own way, making up his own mind. He was not my generation. When fathers talk, Leszek, sons hear foolishness. He wasn't like your generation, either. He had the worst of it. He came between us. Not my time, not yours. They always had the worst of it, his generation. You should understand that."

"Why? Why did they have it the worst?"

"Because they tried to believe, didn't they?" The hand with the swollen thumb lifted from his knee, and he rubbed at his cheek with the back of his fist. I reached up and removed the fleck of tissue from his chin. "They had it pounded into them. They wanted to believe, so they lent their hands." He stood up, his knees cracking like twigs under a mat of leaves. "Shoulders to the wheel, that's what they thought. They tried to make it work, took it all in, and got the worst of it. Your father wasn't like some of them. At least he didn't spend his whole life trying to look the other way. Not at the end. By the end he knew, thank God."

"But why would he do all this? Why would he make reports to Jabłoński, or the police or the Party or whoever it was? Why did he have to do that?"

"What did Jabłoński tell you?"

"I didn't ask him. I was too mad to ask him. Mostly, I didn't want to believe him."

"But you did believe him?"

"I told you. He showed me papers. Poppa's signature was on them, all of them."

"So the old chairman reveals his secrets."

"Yes."

"The convenient secrets," he said. "The useful ones. Do you see what bastards they are?"

"I knew that. I didn't know my father was one of them."

He halted in front of the carcass and took up his short-handled hatchet, and with short soft strokes cut through the bone and gristle of the chest. He pulled the ribs apart. Marrow oozed bright blood. In the open cavity, the lungs lay in their perfectly fitted folds; vein and vessel traced a map. The heart, at the center, held to its anchor.

"Would you rather have not known?" he asked.

I had wondered about that and didn't have an answer. "I want to know why, that's all."

"It's best to think they fooled him," he said. "Or because he wanted to believe. Because he thought it would be better. Wanting to believe is a powerful thing. That isn't so bad, by itself. Men want something to believe, Leszek. Men always do."

"Not women?" An image of Jola shot through me. Not a believer, Jola.

"Women have better sense," he said. "Lenin should have been a woman."

"But Poppa didn't talk about this stuff. He didn't argue for it."

"Because I was louder than he was, that's why. He did his time for them, he served a term with their council. I told him then his sentence was just beginning. But he didn't listen. Your father *would* argue, argue till he was hoarse. We argued in the fields, until neither one of us would talk anymore, wouldn't say another word. But didn't bring it home. At least *he* didn't. And then we stopped. Stopped arguing. Stopped a long time ago."

"Why?"

"Tired of it, that's why. Both of us tired of it. The whole damn country was worn out with it."

"I don't think he believed in it," I said. "I don't see how he could."

"Because that's the time you grew up in, Leszek. It's better to know that he believed. It's better that way."

"Is that supposed to make the stuff Jabłoński told me easier to swallow?"

"It's not so simple. You're a young man now, but you're still a child compared to what he went through, what everyone went through here. Now, don't take offense at that, it's just the way it was."

"I've been listening all my life to what people went through. Doesn't it ever stop? Can't we just get on with it?"

"You only hear what people tell you, but they don't talk about all of it. They don't talk about what they don't want to remember. Young people now think it was something in a book, and not even a very honest book. I've seen your school books. We walk all around history here, step right in it, and don't know it. Don't ask to know it, don't want to remember it."

"Now is now, Grandpa. I want to make a farm. I'm tired of hearing how hard it was. I don't want—"

"I know what you want. You want to get ahead, make a modern farm. But here you are, caught up in all this—" he waved his arm toward the village—"all this nonsense. And the reason you are is history, and half of it is lies and the other half is built on trying not to remember the worst of it. You know what else?"

"What?"

"It's automatic now, forgetting certain things. People don't even have to work at it anymore."

He severed the heart's arteries. Dark blood sprang weakly from the cut and trickled down his wrist. In the silence, the wind moaned through the gaps of the tin roof, like a note from a pipe organ. I knew the question I was meant to ask. He waited for it, but labored on with his knife.

"What do you remember that you don't talk about?"

"Things your father saw. All the Jews penned up like starving animals. The food he brought to us in the forest. Other things, things I'm glad he didn't see."

"What things?"

"Things I saw and did with other men. Men I haven't seen since. Things I haven't spoken of since. Things it would be a blessing to forget."

I waited and said nothing. He set the heart in the pan, removed the hatchet from the chopping block, laid it aside, and sat down. He picked up the liver from the tub and began talking while his fingers searched to find the gall bladder and cut it away.

"I remember the goddamned headaches," he said. "We lived every day with headaches, all of us. Just from the tension. I remember Górski walking in the forest in front of me holding his head with one hand, like it was going to fall off." He finished and dropped the liver into the pan with the heart. "When I get a headache like that now, I stop everything and go to bed. And the cold. Cold all the time, even that winter, when it wasn't a bad winter. And it made your stomach ache, like you were starving, even when you had food. We didn't know what we were doing most of the time."

"What were you doing?"

"Killing a few Germans. We thought we were doing more. We thought others were doing more. We did some things. The barracks at Siedlce. Mostly hit and run. Didn't know where our own men were. Didn't know where the Germans were. They moved around their patrols, looking for us. They got us pinned down, three, four times. More. We knew the forest, so we had a chance. We couldn't let them capture any of us."

"You've told me this before, Grandpa."

"I had to shoot Górski." He spoke sharply, as though rebuking me for my complaint against hearing old war stories again. "Did I tell you that?"

"No," I said. "You didn't tell me that."

"You want to hear it?" The irritation was still in his voice.

"Yes, Grandpa," I said, chagrined.

"We woke up in the morning and they were on us. Like that." He snapped his fingers. "We had a way out. But Górski got hit. First thing. Took two, three shots in the leg, high up. Nearly tore it off, bleeding like a pig. We couldn't take him. We couldn't let them torture him. I did it in a minute, Leszek. He wasn't looking. I shot him in the back of the head. We had agreed on it before. The Germans would have killed him by inches. He felt nothing. Didn't see it coming. It was the way. He would have done the same. We agreed on it. No talk. But I still feel the trigger under my finger. I feel it now. I see the hole it made in his cap. That's all. We got out, somehow. The rest of us. Not a scratch. Six, seven of us. Nothing. I don't know why."

"No one . . ."

"No one said anything. I said nothing. But I see it sometimes. His cap against the leaves. Green wool. I see it more now. It happened eight or ten miles from right here."

"You've not spoken of it before?"

"No."

"To Poppa?"

"No."

"Would you do it now? The same?"

"I'm not thirty years old anymore. I don't think of it like that. I just see it. I'm sorry. I'm sorry he had to die. But that's not it. I just see it. I have to remember it. I forgot it for years, and then it came back. Like a nightmare. I don't know why. Because I'm old, I guess. I didn't ask to remember it. Something made me remember it. Now I *want* to remember it."

"Why?"

"Because it's the truth. It's my life. It was one moment, but it was part of my life. Not *all* my life, but my life. No one else's. When I go, it goes with me. Sometimes I think it shouldn't. I don't mean me, I mean that moment, the hole in Górski's cap."

A pair of the barnyard cats nosed around the bloody pans. I shooed them away. Grandpa remained sitting, his big stained hands dangling between his knees. He cleared his throat, and spat into the straw behind him.

"Your father," he said.

"Yes."

"He used to bring us food sometimes. You knew that. Bread. Chunks of meat. You've heard those stories."

"Yes."

"You know where we were?"

"Yes, close by."

"Two, three kilometers from here. North. Between the north road and Piwko Creek. In the forest, back in the pines after the ash grove."

"Yes." I knew where he meant. I had been shown the place many times. The depressions of their foxholes were still visible, mounded on one side, toward the south, toward the straight-trunked ash trees and the open fields. Beyond the fields were more trees and then the village. It was hard to imagine the foxholes as an artifact of war; they were like man-sized nests, shallow, leaf-filled, banked against weather.

"We had a cache," he said, "where he could put the food." My father, age eight, with a bundle disguised as kindling wood, carried to a camouflaged hollow beneath a rotted tree.

". . . an old tree."

"Yes."

"We wouldn't see him most times. It was safer for him if we were gone. But sometimes I saw him. Only for a minute. To kiss him. Once or twice I watched him and didn't move. For safety. Just watched him do his job and leave. Eight years old and he was a soldier. He was careful. Quick. Wasted no time. Covered his work. Not a squirrel would see. He was a strong boy, shoulders like little blocks. He didn't call, didn't look around for us, didn't make a sound. Did his work and was gone."

He seemed to have gone back to that time. He clasped his swollen thumb, as though comforting or cradling it, a gesture I realized I'd never seen before. His moist eyes sought out the shadowed roof beams.

"Once he brought a boy with him," he said. "A little shaved-head. A little Jew boy."

All that came before this I had heard, over dinner plates or on the seats of wagons or with the thorns of wild raspberry canes tugging my trouser legs, the sponge of dry pine needles under my feet—or wherever he might have chosen to tell his old stories. But I had never heard this.

"Shaved."

"Who?" I asked.

"The boy. Shaved, he was. The boy Mariusz brought with him. I had not seen this before. Not yet. Mariusz took his cap off. He had huge eyes, black as coal, head like an egg."

"Why was he with Poppa?"

"How did he *find* your Poppa? I don't know. Hunting for food, probably, or begging. There wasn't time for details. By then, the Jews were all rounded up in the center of the village. They couldn't leave. But the little kids slipped out. Squeezed though the fences, traded for food, wherever they could get it, and brought it back inside. For their families. They were starving in there. So he snuck through the fence, probably. At night, maybe. I'm not sure. He was about the same age as Mariusz. The same size, anyway."

He spat again into the straw. His hand worried with the big thumb, massaging it gently. When he spoke, his voice was lower than before, so that I had to strain to hear him.

"He was very calm. A very calm little boy."

"Why did he come?" I asked.

"There was a plan. I don't know how it was done, but they bribed a guard. His father had done it somehow. Things like that were done sometimes. It happened. The Jews would pay money, or gold or something. And someone would look the other way. The boy crawled through the fence, made some approach, or maybe led someone to his father. I don't know. No way to know. He had money with him, though. He showed it to me, the money. Offered it."

"To you? For what?"

"Help. He wanted our help."

"Was it much money?"

"I don't know. A fistful of it."

"You didn't take it?"

"No. It was no use to us. Money wasn't what we needed."

"What did you do?"

"Told him to keep it."

"No, I mean what did you do? Did you help him?"

Grandpa glanced at me and then away, out across the barnyard, his eyes so fixed that I looked to see if someone had entered the gate. There was only Grandpa's horse, motionless on her tether, her head lowered.

"Did you agree to help?" His gaze held the distance while I waited to hear the right answer. "You didn't refuse, did you?"

"No. I did not refuse."

Some sign of relief must have shown on my face.

"Do you know," he added quickly, "how often I wish I had refused?" I said nothing. "These are the things you don't hear about, Leszek."

"Go on, Grandpa."

"It was to be the following night." He spoke quickly now, his voice low. "It was the boy, his father and mother, and three sisters. They had a plan. They needed to get past us and go north. I don't know where. Maybe they thought they had someone to take them in. A relative, maybe. Maybe they would try to find hiding places. Maybe they didn't know where they were going. They might pay a farmer to take in one or two of the girls and hide them. Pay someone else to take another. They didn't have much chance, probably. Not the parents, certainly. But they had no chance at all where they were. Everyone knew that. Already there were trainloads going by, nearly every day. Loaded with Jews. Nobody knew where then, but it was Treblinka they were going to. In the village the Jews were frantic. They were frantic in every village. They knew. So they were going to try. All they wanted was to get past us, pointed in the right direction. We could not take them, there was no way. They knew that. We could take them through the forest. Maybe draw them a map. That's all.

"In the dark, they would get their guard to turn his back. That would get them to the edge of town. Then the fields. We were supposed to watch for them. How they got to us was out of our control, but the boy knew the way. Mariusz was to have nothing to do with this, nothing at all. The boy knew the way. He would lead them. At the last, he would run ahead and give us warning."

He stopped for a moment, rubbing at his temples, and then went on.

"We were very close to town. There were German patrols, and they knew our units came and went, in and out. We never knew when there would be patrols, or why. I'm sure people informed on us. Sold information to them, or saw signs of us and told them just to curry favor. There were sympathizers, of course. Collaborators. Cowards who thought the Germans would be here forever. We could never be sure of anyone. We had to watch, always. Keep a guard on every moment, every night. Sometimes, if we heard them coming soon enough, we had places to hide. There were only a few of us, so we could move quickly if we had warning.

"You have to remember we had our own operations, too. Various actions to carry out. Sometimes they came without warning. There were couriers who carried messages from unit to unit. There was a larger group about eight miles east of us. Another about six miles west, north of Bowaszki. They were very active then, the Bowaszki group, and they had been under pressure. They had been in some fights in the days before, and they were moving back, and we were ordered to meet them. The orders to do this came on the next morning, the morning after I spoke to the boy, and we were supposed to move that night, and then link up with the Bowaszki group. We were to travel together and join a larger group, and then there was some action planned. We didn't know what this action was—we almost never did—but it was made clear to us by the courier that it was important, that it was crucial that we reach the rendezvous point with full strength and that we take pains to avoid any engagement or contact with German units."

"Who made these orders?" I asked.

He seemed annoyed at the interruption. His hands opened, palms up.

"A command," he said. "There was a command. It functioned badly sometimes because of communications. And because of infighting and argument. But it was all we had. We had to follow it. You understand?"

"Yes."

"We were not to move until well after dark. Górski wanted to go on, without waiting, as we agreed. But I said no. It was my decision. There were seven of us, counting the courier, who was to go with us. So we waited. Everyone was nervous. The men were always nervous when we were about to do something because they didn't know what it was, and it was always better to be moving at those times than sitting still. So after dark I kept everyone spread out, in a long line, so there was no talking, and we waited.

"It was a very dark night. No moon, no light, but a wind came up. Very strong, noisy in the trees. Sometime after dark, I heard trucks on the road from the village."

"Germans?"

"Yes, of course. No one else had trucks. I heard them on the road. And then nothing. The others would have heard them, too, and they were keeping an eye out. I was at the center of the line, watching the field. I could see no sign of them, the boy, the family. Nothing. I could see the outline of trees on the far edge of the field. Górski was with me and he had our light. It was a powerful light, with a strong beam. It was the only good piece of equipment we had, and we protected it well, but we didn't dare use it now. Finally, I thought I saw something in the field. Perhaps it was them, but I was not sure. And just then one of the men from our right flank came crashing through the forest. He said there was a German patrol, a large one, heading toward us. Forty, fifty men. And as he said this, I could hear them. Forty men in battle gear make a noise, even above the wind.

"And at the same time, the men from the left side came running. The two Nowak brothers, Paweł and Lech, and the others from that side after them, and they said another patrol was moving on us from their side. And the Germans on that side must have heard something, because all of a sudden I could hear them, too, hear shouts and voices.

"So we were caught, two German patrols moving toward us from opposite sides. They were both a hundred yards, fifty yards, on either side of us. The men were cocking their rifles and I was whispering at them not to fire, not to give us away, and then Górski said, 'Look!' and the little boy was there, in the ash grove. He was looking back to the field, waving his arms.

"I jumped up and snatched the boy and carried him back to us. He wriggled under my arm like a puppy, whimpering something, but I was not listening to that. The Germans were coming close. On each side we could hear them, hear them talk, hear the clank of equipment, coming toward us. Górski was hissing at me to move. The men were about to bolt, or start firing. Either one would kill us.

"And then I did it. I grabbed the light from Górski and somehow held the boy underneath me, under my knee, and I pointed the light toward the field and turned it on. And there they were. Five faces. Man, woman, children. White as pet rabbits, frozen. I shouted at them in German. 'Achtung! Alt!'

"Immediately, there were answering shouts on either side of us. Another light came on, pointed at the field. Then another, from the opposite side. There was more shouting. And then firing. And they went down. The mother fell. The children. Then the Germans moved, came out of the woods on either side of us, and out toward them. When I looked last, the father was standing alone. Then there was more shooting."

He stopped a moment. He drew in a long breath, then another. I felt cold to the bone.

"I didn't see any more. We retreated straight back, into the forest, quickly and quietly, and after a hundred yards ran as fast as we could until we were a mile away. They never saw us. Or if they saw us, they forgot about us." He stopped speaking and his eyes were fixed, as before, toward the dark beams above us. For a long moment there was silence between us.

"The boy?" I asked finally.

"You know, I could have fought them, Leszek. I could have killed some of them. We might have gotten out of it, some of us. But I would have failed my mission. Captain Maleszewski would have missed his rendezvous. It would be said that Raven couldn't be counted on. The men, of course, thought my action was brilliant, as if I planned it. 'Raven did it again,' they said." He picked up the hatchet, slowly rotating its worn wooden handle in his hands.

"Do you know what my main objective was? Not surviving, even, just the fixation in my head that I would be where I was supposed to be with the men under my command. Pride. I thought it mattered, but it didn't matter. There turned out to be no operation. Just argument. Some complication. I can't remember. Just waiting, argument, messages back and forth, off and on, it was all the same. We marched, we hid, we waited, we went somewhere else, and then somewhere else again, and my 'success' meant nothing because everything was confusion. Then the Russians came . . ." His voice trailed off.

"What happened to the boy, Grandpa?"

"That night I had him carried to safety. I had no choice."

"What do you mean, safety? How?"

"It took all night." He tossed the hatchet aside.

"What did you do with him?"

"Had him taken to someone."

"Who?"

"A woman."

Silence seized him again.

"Who was she?"

"An old woman. No. Not so old then. Older than me, she was. I knew she would take him."

"Tell me."

"He was taken there and left. I thought they'd be killed along the way. But they arrived safely. It was a long night. And I got the men moved out before dawn. And we got where we were going, on time. For nothing. I remember we killed a hare and ate it on the way. Raw. I remember the blood on Górski's face. Not when we ate it." His voice had grown distant, almost sleepy, dreamlike. "Later. In the lantern. I saw the blood on his cheeks, when he was sleeping, exhausted from running all night, and I remembered, looking at his face, that we ate the hare, raw, on the run. And when I looked I saw it under my fingernails, that blood."

"Grandpa, where did you take the boy? Who was the woman? Was she near here?"

"Not so far. She is dead many years now. For the boy, I tried not to know."

He shook his head sharply, as though rousing himself from sleep. He stood and picked up his knife from the block.

"Your father knew this. He saw the bodies of the boy's family dragged feet first behind a horse and wagon, past the houses, around the compound where the Jews were watching through the wire. The horse and wagon belonged to Powierza's father. The Germans made him do it. They made sure everyone saw it was this man and his wife and his daughters, people everyone knew because he had a shop on the street. People bought provisions from him. His wife made change and tied string on their packages. Your father saw all that. He told me later he disobeyed me. He went with them as far as the trees at the edge of town and he hid there. He heard the shots. But I never told him what happened, Leszek. I never told him anything else about it. What he saw was bad enough."

He put out his hand to the stripped blue carcass.

"I kept a secret from him, and he kept one from you," he said. "We fixed our faces so they didn't show."

He stopped talking. He was through now, and back to work. He would say no more, I knew. I sat for a long time, looking away toward the shadowed, jumbled corner of the shed and heard the slick wet whisper of the knife as though it came to me from a long distance.

"Get a clean bucket from the milk shed," he said after a while. "And bring a pail of water."

*   *   *

There is escape in routine, and for a while I used it as if I had gone on a voyage. I set about my own chores, pitching manure, repairing the loft ladder, mixing barrels of mash for the hogs, changing the oil in the tractor and replacing the fan belt, splitting firewood, scrubbing down the milk shed. But the images that kept coming back were the white faces in the field, a boy's shaved head, beams of light strobing through trees. These pictures battled with other images: Jabłoński's cool, gray countenance, strangely unaged and unperturbed; the sheets of old papers spread out on my bed; and Jola's pale, frowning lips, as though from a dream, telling me over and over, it was a fantasy, an escape from reality.

Farm work is reality, but as the ax sank into wood and the wrench slipped on the grease-caked nuts in the tractor's engine, solid objects under my grip gave no hold against the overwhelming sense of being surrounded by memories, misinterpretations, and illusions weeded and tended as carefully as a kitchen garden. Not least by me.

When I thought of Jola, my ignorance and arrogance were like a scald. I had discounted her life before I entered it, denied the force of her own conscience and the memory she would have to carry with her. I could say to myself—and I had tried—that her memories before me were bad, and best forgotten, and that together we would create new ones to supplant the old, good ones to cover the bad. But all around me, memories recurred; like stones in a path, they pushed up. Memory had a future as well as a past.

I wondered if I could remember that, or if I could overcome it.

I went, then, to see Powierza. He was way ahead of me, as usual, but by now I was not surprised.

Chapter Fourteen

"We'll import chocolate from Switzerland."

"Belgium. I bought some Belgian chocolate in Warsaw once. It was better than Wedel's."

"Wedel's," Farby sighed. "I love Wedel's. I want to take you there and spoon hot chocolate into your mouth."

"We could make it, you know," Zofia said.

"Hot chocolate? Did you bring chocolate?"

"No. I mean in our shop. We could make our own, with the candy. Think how it would smell. The aroma of it would bring people in right off the street. All those tourists. Summer and winter."

"Gift boxes in different sizes."

"Skiers in the winter, hikers in the summer."

"German tourists. Italians, too. They come to Zakopane. They like the mountains."

"They like chocolate, too. Did you ever have Perugia chocolate?"

"What's that?"

"Italian chocolate. I had some once. It's not as good as Swiss or Belgian, but it's good. It had pistachio nuts in it."

"I prefer almonds. Or hazelnuts."

"If it's good, plain is best."

"Of course. Just let it melt in your mouth."

They were silent a moment. Her foot rubbed his ankle under the sheets.

"Fillings are good, though," she said.

"What kind do you like best?"

"Cream, of course."

Farby shifted on the pillows, his left hand seeking its way to the warmth between her upper arm and chest wall. Her hand, under the covers, gave him a delicate squeeze, stole over his stomach to his chest. Farby made a noise in his throat, like a cat purring.

"We'll have to fix it up a lot," she said. "It should have nice curtains and little café tables, just three or four, for people to sit." She sat up from the pillows, her breasts swinging free from the covers. Farby resisted the urge to reach over and cup them with both hands. "It will take a lot of work, Zbyszek. My uncle hasn't done anything with it for years. Just magazines and souvenirs. It's so dreary and drab."

"He probably doesn't even see it. You said he was nearly blind, didn't you?"

"He's old and tired."

"Are you sure he won't sell it to someone else? Some German businessman?"

"He won't. He hates Germans. Even their money. Besides, he promised me. We'll pay him rent until we make enough to buy it. It's all right. He doesn't need much. Oh, Zbyszek, wait till you see it. It's in a perfect location. And we'll have the mountains all around us."

She sank back on the pillow and pulled the cover to her chin, her eyes distant, as if the lamplight were casting pictures of southern Polish peaks on the cabin wall.

"How much longer?"

"I don't know. Not long, I hope." She frowned. "Jabłoński's started to look for you, I think."

"He was bound to, sooner or later."

"Yes."

"Has anything happened? What makes you say that?"

She shrugged. "I just feel it, that's all." She hesitated. "I see Andrzej around a lot."

"Following you?"

"No. I just see him around. It makes me think he's watching." She paused, and Farby watched her profile as her pretty small teeth bit at her lower lip. "You know," she said, "he wouldn't have to follow me, would he, to make a connection?"

"No."

They lay for a long time without speaking. The lamp flickered on the table by the bed. Outside, the wind picked up and they heard the rasp of fine sleet against the window. Farby settled lower into the warm bed.

"Did you know that oil for the very finest chocolate comes from the blubber of baby seals?" he said.

"No."

"It's true," he said. "The harp seal."

"Where's it come from?"

"Russia. Norway. Places like that. I read it in *National Geographic.*"

"We'll have to have it," she said. "We'll make only the best." She rolled onto her side and nestled close to him. Her hand trailed down his chest.

"And the very best butter."

"We'll get it."

"We'll need big copper pots."

"We'll get them, too."

"Cocoa from Africa."

"Of course."

"And the cream filling?"

"Ummm. What about the cream filling?"

"You'll learn how to make it?"

Her lips brushed against his cheek, nuzzled his ear. She bit softly. "Yes," she said. "I'm working on it."

Father Tadeusz set out early. As always on the rare occasions he was forced to use a car, he drove slowly and cautiously, wiping at the windshield with the back of his hand and leaning forward toward the wheel as if a second's lost vigilance would send the old black Fiat careening into a ditch or a bridge railing.

The morning was wet, and passing cars threw up a muddy spray that the wipers then spread across the windshield in muddy streaks. Villages slid toward him through the murk, receded in the mist of his tires. Driving through one village, he overtook a horse and wagon, the farmer's faded denim jacket stained with the slow rain. The old man's face, as Father Tadeusz steered around him, displayed an expression of stony hostility, and Father Tadeusz imagined his steady slow anger, his frustration that he was too old now to ever have a car or a tractor, that he would never manage it, that he would go on doing things the way he always had. Never mind revolutions, talk of prosperity, politicians urging sacrifice to ensure a better future. It had all been sacrifice, always and ever, and all he had for it was this old horse and battered wagon.

He arrived in Lublin early, two hours ahead of his meeting with the bishop. He remained undecided what to do, what to say. He had prayed over the question, then, had lain awake in his bed staring into the dark. And still he did not know the answer, did not know if Father Jerzy was right or wrong, or if his own instincts were trustworthy. At the beginning, he had been sure enough that no good end could result from Father Jerzy's crusade, if that's what it was, to "expose" the past. His accusation of Father Marek, long dead, had been the last straw, had driven him to seek his appointment with the bishop. But, having made it, he was assailed by doubt. His doubt hovered not so much over his own feelings—Father Jerzy, he was sure, was wrong—but over the rightness of his intervention, if that's what it turned out to be. If forces in life have their own God-willed course, was it not best to let those forces, created, after all, in God's own wisdom, have their way?

He sat for a while in the cathedral, a dimness that glittered with old gold and flickering candles and air that smelled of wax and cold marble, the vaulted space surrounding him with faint echoes of creaking wood and unseen footsteps. Was it not right, as Father Jerzy asserted, that sin be punished, that guilt be exposed? Was his objection that Father Jerzy's obvious ambitions were unseemly, or was he resentful of the young priest's energy and his engagement with the town? Had not Father Jerzy, to a degree which he had not acknowledged before, awakened him as well to his surroundings? Had he not learned something important from Father Jerzy, or because of Father Jerzy?

He prayed. He said the rosary. There was no answer. Only the questions, over and over.

He found himself in the park next to the church. The rain had stopped. A soft haze hung in the branches of the trees. He sat on a bench, and after a while became aware of an old couple on a bench nearby. They seemed to have materialized out of the mist, although they must have been sitting there, he thought, as he walked past them.

The woman sat facing away from the man, whose head was bowed in a posture that suggested penitence, although, on closer study, Father Tadeusz saw he was just staring absently at the ground. They both had white hair and were wearing clothes of gray, or tending toward gray; even her maroon scarf provided no relief. Their faces were pale, hers particularly worn. His was the soft face of a man who has spent a lifetime indoors, behind desks.

The country was so full of these people now, Father Tadeusz thought. For them it was all over. The man had used up his ambition, which amounted to little more than self-protection, in a lost cause. He imagined that the woman never believed in it, this temporizing creed they lived with, yet never spoke, just stood in the lines, accepted her cheerless portion from her husband's slow career of being careful in the presence of authority—grateful for their allotment of three or four weeks every summer in a lake cottage that smelled of the previous occupants, and wherein they left their own smells for the next family of state employees.

Her children now believed in nothing—not the old system or the new, not church or God—nothing except escape and earning money. Their daughter a housemaid in Germany, their son a traveling trader in baby clothes, wrist watches and Bison Vodka, exported in clanking canvas duffel bags.

Now, Father Tadeusz said to himself, the man is unwell. He could see it: he awakens in the night and paces in his slippers in a darkened apartment until he tires and falls asleep sitting up in his chair. She finds him there sometimes at dawn, so pale that for an alarmed moment she thinks he is dead. She knows, when he does go, she will find him like this, gray as the winter light through the window. They are both ill, she knows, and she does not care. Father Tadeusz looked away, through the bare tree limbs, toward the hiss of traffic.

There was a noise on the park path, bright laughter like a burst of color. Two young mothers rounded the corner, both pushing baby carriages, one talking, telling a story, the other laughing, her cheeks flushed. They strolled by, oblivious to Father Tadeusz or to the old couple on the bench. They sat down at the far end of the pathway, rocking their carriages back and forth. Father Tadeusz glanced at his watch. It was time.

The diocesan offices were a block away, and when he got there, he sat for only a minute in the bishop's outer office before the door opened. The bishop smiled warmly as he glided forward.

"Come in, Father," he said, "I'm so glad to see you."

Jola sorted ruthlessly among their possessions, methodically, with a clear head and no hesitation. Packing, she thought, was something she was born to do. Clothes divided into boxes stood around the apartment's rooms. The old suitcases, those she had carried to Warsaw and then back again, were open on the bed, filling with the immediate essentials. Karol had gone to the city to see to the details. Her daughter was at her mother's, out of the way, the baby asleep. She had told her parents nothing yet. She would tell them at the last the moment, no sooner.

There would be no time for scenes.

Her parents could pick up the rest of their things later.

She felt, for the first time in months, alive, alert, resolved. She felt, at last, as though she had some control over her future, even though she was uncertain what it would be. She had been packing and sorting before daylight, room by room, drawer by drawer, discarding summer clothes and children's sandals, unworn dresses and shoes, and felt, with every armload packed into the boxes that would stay behind, a new lightness that was like relief, a new energy in her arms and legs, like an athlete's toned for a race.

It was movement, above all, that was both the craving and the relief. It was the notion of *going*, never mind where, that gave her strength and focus. The imagined confusion of airline terminals, of train stations crowded with the random motion of all those people arriving, departing, waiting, the travelers disoriented or impatient amid their children and stacks of baggage, the destinations announced magisterially, like a word of God, over unseen loudspeakers—all this quickened her now, dampened her lip with perspiration. Hamburg it would be, perhaps, or maybe Denmark or Sweden. This had been the bargain with Karol from the beginning until it had gotten lost somehow, bogged down, mired in his drinking, in the day-to-day life. One thing, then another. Karol's refusal to take any action toward finding a job elsewhere—it should not be impossible, he was a trained veterinarian, after all—irritated, frightened, and finally depressed her. This was not the bargain. The bargain was to leave, to escape this town, her parents, these flat wet fields, the gloomy fog-hazed forests. She saw this clearly now, as though she had forgotten it all for a long time, as though a wind had swept away the mist from her view.

Maybe she would always want a future she could not quite see. She was not like Leszek. Perhaps she was a nomad at heart. She was not like Karol, either, exactly, but there was something about him that exerted a pull on her. It was partly physical, perhaps, but wrapped within that was some force-field of sensed danger. Perhaps she would always go though life in danger, or looking for it, or skirting its edge. Leszek might have been that in the beginning, but not in a future she could see. Karol *was* danger. She could see it in him from the beginning, maybe without understanding it. Something about the way he drank was symptomatic of it. He had that edge. She had come to him seeking an escape from her parents, and to them from the squalor of the sojourn in Warsaw. But she felt that enticing force in Karol, too, something beyond refuge and certainly beyond comfort, something veiled. She acted not always because she could see the consequences of her actions, but more out of an instinct of what she needed, as though nature compelled it.

She hurried now. Mercilessly she weeded out, sorted the baggage for light traveling, pared-down living. Here, amid the discarded toys, folded blankets, the warped old shoes, she trimmed down her life, and not just hers, but her husband's, her children's. She wondered, as she stood clutching her daughter's old rag doll and stuffed it in a box to be left behind, if she were not instilling in her daughter her own sense of rootlessness.

No, she thought, she'll react against me, and when the moment arrives to decide her life she will choose the opposite course from her mother and spend her days in one place with one man. She would know, Jola thought, exactly what was best for her.

She buried the doll under a load of blankets and went on with her packing.

*   *   *

Czarnek opened the cabinet with the old books. He had taken most of them from the fire. Plucked from ashes. Books didn't burn well. A few survived. Their edges were charred, but brushed clean long ago. A script he could not read. Four of them. What books would be found in the ruins of a synagogue fire? He had stolen in at first light. Ghostly smoke curling up from timbers, ashes, bent nails. He fixed the shape of it in his mind, the blackened frame of the foundation walls. Who had set it? The Germans or the townspeople. The Germans seemed to have gone, busy somewhere else. Occupied on another front. He did not know when they had disappeared. The day before? Last night? He could not dare ask. Anyone might know him. Most of the wire still stood in the square. He saw the corner of it. A part torn down, scavenged, abandoned. It was irrelevant now. The town was still. If anyone saw him he would just go on, picking, sorting, like any beggar. It had already been picked over, he would tell. Beams pulled to the side. Footprints. Looking for what? Now he knew. Gold. They hunted for gold. They were mad, addled with their superstitions, their legends, their jealousy, their endless envy. Gold! People sold pots and pans, worked all hours, dressed their children in rags, patched boots for a living, restitched old clothes, saved bent nails in old jars, fed their families on cabbage soup, and people thought they had gold to hide! Then they burned the temple to look for it, or watched hungrily while it was done, then sifted ashes for molten lumps, carrying away hunks of brass in their blackened hands and dragging off unburned timber for firewood.

He remembered the warmth under his feet, feeling it through the soles of his shoes. He wanted to lay down in the soft ash, between the fallen posts, and go to sleep. He wanted to pour the ashes over his head, like an old man mourning, but he did not.

He had slipped away though the darkness and returned to the house in daylight. Danusia fell to weeping when she saw him, terrified he had been gathered up and taken away, and she smothered him in her arms and scolded and cried and made him promise he would never do this again, never steal off and run away and put himself at the mercy of people who would have no mercy. Who could betray him or sell him like a piece of information, or kidnap him or fling him onto the back of a truck. He was hers now and she was his, and they would always have to understand it this way. She was his mother, or his guardian if he preferred or even his aunt, the sister of his mother, dead from the war (if they wanted to push it), dead like her own husband, and now they belonged to each other and to no one else. Did he understand? They would have each other and protect each other and as long as everyone around understood that, and as long they as protected this idea and lived this idea, he would be safe. And she would have someone, a son; and he would have someone, a mother, to feed him and wash him, to give him clothes and school, a roof over his head and a bed to sleep in, soup when he was sick, a boy's chores to do. Could he see that?

She had wrenched his blackened hands free of the charred books, which lay spilled on the mud path to the door where she had flown out to meet him. His hands hung at his sides but they lifted then, uncertainly, hesitantly, to touch her heaving sides in all he could then muster of a child's embrace. She gathered up the books for him, but kept them hidden.

Do you decide anything at the age of ten? Was it a decision, or a slumber, a weariness, a longing for sleep, for dreams, or a surrender?

She was so unlike *her,* so much thicker, bigger. Her smell was different. Gone. He cried out for her in his sleep sometimes.

"Yes, yes. I know," she said.

"Mama."

"Yes, yes. It's all right."

"Mama."

"Yes."

The leaves of the trees folded over the little house, the covers folded in their layers over his bed, season folded in upon season, year upon year. They survived. They went on in that way, he variously her son, her nephew, a distinction never very important in a country so thick with death, with orphans, with love transferred, with love pulled up from the wet ditch and the ruin. Whatever she was or he was to anyone else, she was, at home, Mama, from then on, as if he knew, knew it all without speaking of it and understood his new name and the absence forever of the locks that curled once before his ears.

He had a new name and a new birthday, too, when one was needed, required by school or the blank space on some official form and he would not or could not remember it. Without hesitation she gave the date of the night of his arrival at her house; and so he was given as the date of his birth the date of his own family's death, so that his own false and yet real life began on the day his family blood ceased to exist. Lives laid down, a life picked up; it was an exchange he could never describe in words that fit the sounds in his head.

That date approached now, like footsteps with a rattle of gunfire behind them.

He fell to his task with the brass and copper and thick coils of solder and chunks of plumber's lead, the hammer and the portable gas torch in the distillery's open room, at night, a bare light above his head, the condensation tower still, the flame from the torch sharpened to a blue point, the copper and solder softening and melting, falling in a bright spattering chatter to the layers of newspaper spread below his makeshift workbench. The hammer laid its rounded print on the soft joints. The heat and smoke from melting lead steeped his face as he bent to the work, shaping tube and shank and cup, following the design in his memory. He learned to work the metal as he went, adding on chunks of old brass plumbing joints from the assortment collected over time in a wooden box. It was stuff scavenged here and there, the old spare pipes and petcocks and fittings chosen from a bin in the distillery's grimy storage room, objects flung aside over sixty, eighty, maybe more years of makeshift plumbing and repair, metal now softened and twisted and hammered and joined together into a shape never imagined through all the hydraulic improvisations carried out in this place over the whole of that time.

It took four days—or nights—working until well past midnight, and each time the work and its traces were cleaned up and put away from the sight of daytime workers and visitors. Finished, he hoisted the creation—it was heavy now—and bore it to his house next door and placed it in the space cleared on the floor of the cabinet with the old books. Then he closed and locked the door, the way he always did.

CHAPTER FIFTEEN

LESZEK

Late at night, in my room, I restored the papers from Jabłoński's file to their place beneath my mattress, where I imagined I could feel them under me and heard their muted crackle as I turned, and kept turning. I could not sleep.

As I tossed about, I remembered something that had happened at primary school when I was ten or twelve years old. A girl named Teresa Majek was a classmate of mine. One market day, her father, with a roundhouse swing of his fist, hit her mother in the face. This happened on the street in the center of town, in full view of scores of people. Mrs. Majek had fallen to her knees in the muddy street, her face and clothes drenched in the blood that gushed from her nose. My mother saw it, and was one of the women who went to help Pani Majek while the men dragged her stumbling husband away.

Of course, everyone at school knew about the incident the next day, even though we hadn't seen it. Some kids talked about it behind her back, some watched her curiously and said nothing. But inevitably someone threw out a taunt about her father "the boxing champion." Teresa was a pudgy, ungainly girl, a smaller version of her mother, with few friends that I knew of, and she walked past her tormentors, her face pale with mortification. Amid the laughter, no one came to walk beside her, to say it was all right, to give her comfort. She didn't come back to school for days after that.

Her family was still here, her parents together yet, her father still swilling vodka on market day.

I didn't know where Teresa Majek was, but she must have left town years ago. I wondered how I would have felt, at that age, if my father had done something horrible that everyone knew about—if he had been arrested for robbing a bank, or if he had regularly beaten up my mother. I wondered if shame would have been easier to deal with then. Did you get past it, or just leave town?

Kids are cruel, but no worse than adults, really. They're just more blunt, more open, less circumspect with the opinions they carry on to adulthood. Could more be expected of the people in this village if Jabłoński let word out that my father had been an informer? I suppose what he did might once have been more accepted. Or at least less shocking. Times had changed. Surely, back then, he would have had company, no doubt among some of his neighbors. Still, it would be the talk of the town, a feast of smug viciousness.

I was almost certain that Grandpa was right when he said that my mother knew nothing about my father's covert activities. If she had known, it would have been, somehow, apparent, for she wore her emotions and her worries openly. She had many friends, she enjoyed their company and their gossip, their trips to the market or to church, and she held a certain status among them as a lively presence, an organizer of small charities or outings to pick blueberries or shopping trips to Węgrów where they traveled by bus to buy skeins of yarn or buttons for the sweaters they all endlessly knitted. I imagined the effect Jabłoński's revelations could have on her life. These women would not scorn her, but they would feel sorry for her and talk about her and speculate among themselves over just how much Alicja might have known, or helped out, wittingly or not, with her husband's "business." Poor Alicja, I could hear them say: that poor dead baby and then him dying of cancer that way. It was the guilt that did it, they would claim, making him sick with his secrets, gnawing away at him like a punishment, like God's will. Poor Alicja. Of course she must have suspected something.

My own insides writhed at these thoughts, for I knew them to be as true as the childhood cruelty to Teresa Majek. It would be as terrible for my mother. I could see her walking the road alone from the village to the farm, past the houses of her friends, not looking for a friendly face in the window, not stopping to talk, marching on with her face rigid in that mask of weariness and determination I remembered from years ago. The thought of seeing it again, of having it return for an indefinite stay, was crushing.

For me, it would be easier. Whatever my father did was his business, not mine, and I could weather the repercussions with this knowledge as shelter. He was dead, and I had my own life. Perhaps I would go to Kowalski, tell him I knew why he refused to sell to my father. I would, in essence, confess for him. Kowalski wanted an acknowledgment of the wrong done to him or his son, whatever it was. Surely, I thought, he was due this.

Mother, however, was a different consideration. By marriage, she was implicated, regardless of her innocence. My choice—and it had taken days to realize consciously what I must have felt instinctively from the beginning—was to keep it all from her, to keep it all secret.

So, there were bargains to be struck.

Jabłoński had made his demand clear. I was to persuade Powierza to back off from any investigation or potential prosecution of town officials, including, most particularly, Jabłoński himself. The penalty for my failure to do so would be publication of my father's activities. The longer I considered this the more vain and curious Jabłoński's threat seemed. Not that I doubted his willingness to besmirch my father's reputation—or anyone else's—but that it was such a flimsy lever for influencing Powierza. If I knew Powierza at all, he would laugh at the idea, or it would anger him. Either way, I could not imagine he would be deflected. Surely, I thought, Jabłoński should know Powierza well enough to recognize his stubbornness. Powierza was never inclined toward obedience or reverence for authority. To my mind, he was close to fearless.

I did suspect that Jabłoński was right about one thing: that Powierza, not Father Jerzy, had emerged as the dominant force among the reformers. Father Jerzy had ignited it all, when he was newly arrived, full of himself and eager to make a mark. But it was Powierza, a man of the village with no political past and no obvious ambition, who had become the repository of judgment and trust, the moral center. And he bore a wound—the smashed skull of his son—and the sympathy it carried. The tragedy gave him a kind of authority. I saw the way people approached him on the streets of the village. They were respectful, speaking quietly, even confidentially, their hands reaching tentatively to touch his sleeve, as though to make him pause long enough to listen to one more observation, one more piece of advice. Powierza had the moral force to deflate Father Jerzy's investigations, whatever they were. All he had to say was "enough is enough." He could point out that new elections would be coming soon, in a few months in fact. He could argue that a little patience would save everyone a lot of bother. And people would listen.

Midnight. Beyond midnight. Dogs barked in the distance, calling, answering. Where had sleep gone?

The barn's rough wood was ash gray in the morning light. Skim ice lay veined on the trough, breaking like fine glass. The breath of cows bloomed in the barn's dimness, close with the smells of milk, the reek of damp stalls, the sound of flop on straw, the squeals of pigs hysterical for breakfast as Grandpa clattered with the buckets into their shed. Hay dust drifted down from the loft like snow on a windless day.

"Snow?" I asked.

"Tonight," he said. He stacked the buckets, slung slop off his hand. "By evening." His amendment. He walked to his horse's stall, two carrots poking from his jacket pocket.

I ferried the milk cans to the road for the morning pickup. A family of jays screeched from the poplars across the road. Crows flew in a line above the field beyond. The country spread open and still, birch trunks etched in sharp lines against distant pines. As I stood looking at them, I understood how Grandpa knew there would be snow by nightfall: the fog had lifted. He seemed to understand these things without thinking about them; knowing, on a summer night, that rain was approaching because there was no dew on the grass; reading rings around the moon, wide rings, close rings, no ring; the way a head of barley crumbled in his fist.

He was leaving as I loped back up the driveway. He slapped the reins gently across Star's back and started up the road, off about his business. It was time I set about mine. I went to see Powierza.

"Come in," he said. "I was going to look for you in a few minutes anyway." He held a folded slice of bread in one hand. His old suspenders dangled from his waist. He was wearing a long-sleeved undershirt pushed up at the sleeves. A slice of sausage remained on his breakfast plate. He stood over it, dipped his bread into a cup of coffee, and jammed it into his mouth.

"You were coming to find me?"

"Yes. Coffee?"

"Sure."

He found a cup and poured the coffee, but there was only a trickle left in the pot. "Damn," he said.

"That's okay," I said, looking at him expectantly, waiting for him to tell me why he was about to go look for me, but not really sure I wanted to hear. I had to tell him, and it was going to be hard enough without distractions. But I sat watching as he moved about the kitchen, and saw nothing forbidding in his expression. He seemed hurried, nothing more.

"I want to borrow your old flashlight," he said.

"What old flashlight?"

"The spotlight, with the big battery. Remember? You used to have one."

"Yes," I said. "Sure, if I can find it."

"And you, too," he laughed.

"Me?"

"You want to help me do something?"

"What?"

"An adventure maybe. Tonight."

"What is it?"

"A little rendezvous," he said, his eyes glittering. "We'll do some spying. Everyone else spies around here. We might do some of our own. What do you say?"

His reference to spying seemed, in my frame of mind, to have an accusatory edge. Had Jabłoński seen him? Had he told him already? "Who's spying?" I asked.

He faced the sink and flung the dregs from his cup.

"Christ only knows," he said. "Everyone but me and you, I suppose." He winked, picked up his shirt from the back of the chair, and wrenched his arms though the sleeves.

"It's tonight," he said. "That's why we need a good light. Will you go with me?"

"Only if you tell me what you're talking about."

"Okay," he said and sat down at the table, folding his heavy hands in front of me. "It's Jabłoński."

I swallowed hard, but said nothing.

"He's up to something. Something I heard about. I don't know what it is. Smuggling, maybe. All I know is that it involves some trucks. They're supposed to meet tonight at the old gravel pit west of town. You know where I mean. Out near the old distillery."

"What trucks?" I asked.

"That's all I know. But Jabłoński is supposed to be there. Now, tell me, what the hell is Jabłoński doing out meeting trucks at midnight in a gravel quarry? He's usually too drunk to move by that time of night, I would have thought."

"You tell me."

"I don't know, but I think it might be interesting to see, don't you?"

I had not expected this. I tried to think how I should proceed. Should I interrupt now with my confession? I could see that Jabłoński was not high on his list of mercies this morning.

"Well?" he said. "Don't just sit there, Leszek. What do you think?"

"I don't know," I said. "I mean, what do you care what he's doing? It's probably just some business of his."

"Yeah, but what kind of business goes on at midnight in a place where no one can see it? If it's just business, why not do it in daylight, right there at the Farmers' Co-op? Why midnight in the middle of nowhere?"

I started to say "So what?" but I was already sounding too contrary, so I held back.

"How did you find out about this?" I asked.

"From Andrzej, the plumber. Seems he's been doing little errands for Jabłoński for years."

I remembered it was Andrzej who delivered Jabłoński's summons to talk with him. What else did Andrzej do? Spy on Jola? Me? My mind was veering down too many tracks at once. "He came to you?"

"Yeah," Powierza laughed. "He said he likes to be helpful. 'I'm a helpful person,' he told me. Says he'll try to help me sell my tractor. Strange."

"Sell your tractor?" I said. "Why?"

"Fucking thing's fifteen years old. Been trying to sell it for two years. So I can buy a new one."

I remembered when he got the tractor. People dropped by his house just to see it. They circled around it and didn't say much, their hands caressing the paint and the huge treads on the tires. It made me think: No one managed to buy a tractor then. It was nearly impossible.

He helped plow fields for us. My father rode with him.

"So then he tells me," Powierza said. "About the trucks. Said I might like to know. A Polish truck from Radom and a Russian truck, and that Jabłoński had to meet them at the quarry."

"But he didn't say what for?"

"Said he didn't know. No idea what was on the trucks."

"You believe him?"

"Believe what?"

"That he doesn't know?"

"I don't care. I believe him about the trucks. That part's simple enough. I'm going to make him come with us."

"Andrzej? Why?"

Powierza shrugged. "Why not? Sort of a test, I thought. If we're going to stay up past midnight for nothing, he might as well come along. If he was lying about it, I figured he'd back out and change his story."

"So he agreed? He's coming?"

"Yes."

I hesitated, looking him straight in the eyes. He seemed no more keyed up or perturbed than if he were about to feed his hogs. Was now the time to tell him? I wondered. Would it change everything?

"Staszek," I began, "have you spoken with Jabłoński?"

He shook his head. "Not since I talked to him about Tomek. I haven't even seen him."

"I have."

He seemed not to have heard me. He was staring toward the frost-rimmed window, into the gray light.

"Four months," he said.

"What?"

"Four months tomorrow."

Tomek, he meant.

"I saw Jabłoński, Staszek," I said. "I talked to him."

"Yes?" He glanced around the kitchen, as if bringing himself by degrees back to the conversation. "Jabłoński? You spoke with him?"

"Yes. He asked me to come see him."

"What about?"

I had a thought, which shamed me as quickly as it struck me, that I might impute my father's crimes to Powierza by announcing that it was Powierza that Jabłoński had implicated. And I might have done it—there was something about that tractor that triggered the thought—had I seen a way out of it, a way to go ahead that would lead me to an end of all this, that would stop this cycle of accusation, revelation, and buried shame. Might it work? Of course not. I simply wanted to will myself beyond this, to sail past the frosted window, past the black hedges and silvered ditches to that hillside field, to see the toes of my boots parting the winter grass that I knew now would never be mine. I cannot say what expression was on my face, but it may have been an idiot's empty stare.

"Are you all right?" Powierza's hand reached out to my sleeve. "You look like you need some sleep, boy. I'll make some more coffee." He stood up and reached for the pot. "What about Jabłoński?"

"Did you know it was my father who put you in jail?"

"What are you talking about?" He pivoted to look at me. His face, backlighted against the window, was like an eclipse.

So I pressed on, recounting everything Jabłoński told me. Throughout the recitation Powierza listened without speaking, betraying no sign of agitation or indignation, as if someone were telling him the plot of a television show, or a story about acquaintances in some distant village. After a while he went on making the coffee and returned to sit at the table.

I did not stop until I got to the hook, the blackmail—my blackmail—and my tongue thickened with it. However much I wanted to go on, I halted. I needed a breath.

"So we know what he wants." Powierza spoke for me.

"Yes," I said.

"Silence for silence."

"That's right," I admitted, feeling the shame of it.

"Well, we can bargain, too," he said.

"How?"

"Play the same game with them."

"What's that?"

"Like buying and selling." He rose and poured the fresh coffee. "It's like the system they always say they hate, like capitalism. Buy low, sell high. You see?"

"No."

"They buy at one price, the price they set. And they sell at another. And if you don't like it, too bad, go somewhere else. Except there is no where else. It's their monopoly."

"You sound like Grandpa."

"Exactly. He was always right."

"But they aren't as stupid as he says."

"Yes, they are. That's why they like a monopoly. When you have a monopoly over everything, you don't have to think. You can be stupid about everything. You can even put Farby in charge of the ministry of finance."

I laughed.

"Yes," he went on. "Make him prime minister! It's okay. You don't need a clean suit to lay a wreath on the Unknown Soldier. We've had worse."

I couldn't stop laughing, partly at the image of Farby, hapless and befuddled, guiding the nation's affairs with a bacon sandwich in one hand. But it was also a laughter of release and relief; and gratitude to Powierza, this irrepressible, ungrudging mountain of a man I had the good fortune to have as a neighbor. I realized it had been days and days since I had found anything in the world to laugh about.

"Except there is one thing," Powierza said. "You have to be smart enough to keep the monopoly."

"But they're not. They lost it, didn't they?"

"They lost the power, but not the instinct. Self-preservation. It's a different thing, you see. They lost power because they went broke. This is where they are stupid. They never knew how to run a business. Not even a farm. Never mind a country. Then Moscow went broke. They never thought this could happen. But the instinct is still there. It's like a fox in a trap. He'll chew his leg off if he has to."

"And be crippled."

"Yeah," Powierza said, "and be grateful to have three good legs."

"You say we can bargain with Jabłoński? Isn't it Jabłoński who's bargaining with us? Or with me?"

"Maybe we can give him his own leg to chew on. Let's see what happens. Let's watch him tonight."

I said nothing for some moments, uncertain what any scramble around the gravel quarry would accomplish.

"Did you know about my father, Staszek?"

"Let's not talk about that now. We have things to do."

"I want to talk about it. You knew, didn't you?"

Powierza didn't answer.

"When I told you, just now, you weren't—"

"I knew he got me arrested."

"How?"

"He told me."

"When?"

"Before he died."

"What else did he tell you?" I asked. "Did he tell you the rest?"

"He told me about me. He also asked me not to speak about it. Especially not to you. That's all. I've kept my word. I'll go on keeping it. There's nothing more to say."

"What do I do, Staszek? What do I say?"

"Forget it for a while, Leszek. You think too much, you know that? It must be like an old closet in your head. More junk in there than there is in my barn. There's nothing to do right now. Come on. Let's find that flashlight." He stood up, yanked his coat from the hook by the door.

I had not seen the flashlight Powierza wanted for some time. It was a red rectangular box, with a handle and lamp attached, its paint chipped, the chrome rim dented. Powierza followed me while I searched drawers and closets in the house, then out to the barns where I finally found it in a box beneath a workbench, buried beneath a tangle of rags and rusted pipe. Naturally, it didn't work. The battery, an old heavy dry cell with a paper cover, was dead.

"We'll get another one," Powierza said.

"Where?" I asked. "Not in Jadowia."

"Węgrów then. Let's go."

"Why do we need it?" I said. My skepticism had not diminished.

"Because, Leszek," Powierza said with elaborate patience, as though he were talking to a child, "it's dark at night. Come on."

We reached the square as the bus for Węgrów revved up to leave. We ran to catch it. The trip required twenty minutes, and since the bus was fairly crowded, we spoke little. The bulk of his shoulder squeezed me toward the window. I watched the stippled fields roll by, the bands of forest stretched out behind them, and beside the road the ramshackle barns and the clots of yellow coal smoke that drifted over farmhouse roofs in the windless air. Down a crossroad a horse slowly pulled a wagon and a huddled driver.

"How's your grandfather?" Powierza asked. The horse and wagon reminded him, as it did me. The old man, with his memories and solitary errands, seemed more withdrawn since our long conversation.

"He's all right," I said.

"Goes his own way these days, doesn't he?"

"He prefers his own company."

"I pass him in his wagon sometimes," Powierza said. "Never seems to see me."

"He doesn't see so well anymore."

"He sees okay," he said. "I saw him the other day at the edge of my north field. I was coming out of the woods and I saw him with his wagon. Unloading something. Brush, I think. Four hundred yards away, and when he saw me he walked all the way over to speak to me." Powierza laughed. "Told me it was going to be a dry winter."

"He's usually right," I said.

"He said he was cutting fence posts."

"He mentioned that."

"You don't have any fences there, do you?"

"No, not there. Maybe he's planning to sell them." I pictured him, bowlegged in his boots, muttering to himself behind his shield of solitude. "It's winter. It gives him something to do, cutting fence posts."

The bus wheezed into Węgrów and we stepped off at the square. Węgrów was the biggest market town in thirty miles, several times larger than Jadowia, and almost congested in contrast with our own empty streets. Powierza wove through the shoppers, aiming for the nearest hardware store. It seemed to have gone over to a trade in soap powder and plastic kitchen utensils. We left without even asking about batteries. Powierza led the way down a congested street that curved down behind the square. In that short expanse of cobbled pavement, we might have been on one of the teeming old streets in the armpit of Praga, across the river from Warsaw. This was the country, though, and the people here wore clothes that were rougher and more garish than in the city. Their faces were not as pallid as in the city, but ruddy, fed on potatoes, salt pork, and cabbage, their glance not as quick-darting or nerve-stretched as city people. Their voices were louder, blunter.

All around them, cramped storefronts sported new cardboard signs in bright oranges and greens against black backgrounds, and tinny music blared from every other door to meet and mingle in an unintelligible pulsing voice in the middle of the street. Former farm boys sold music cassettes from stand-up trays beside parked cars. Their mothers, aunts, or older sisters peddled machine-knitted stocking caps in the same luminous colors as the signs on the stores. They sorted though plastic-lined boxes labeled "Manufactured in Bangladesh" and held up mittens or gloves or a stack of American-style baseball caps. Busy, distracted, watchful, murmurous, they fingered the goods with one hand and with the other clutched wads of money in their coat pockets.

The traffic slowed us down, but it was also interest, the attraction and allure of *things,* objects to pick up, hold, buy. This spray of color, this wonderland of stuff that was almost-but-not-quite trash, things that you didn't need but might use, things you might buy and take home and offer as a present, a toy, a novelty, a small bright newness. Powierza stopped, fingered a pile of pastel knit gloves, and chose a pair for his wife, borrowing bills from me to pay for them. He folded them into his pocket and walked on, pausing in front of a store window offering pornographic videotapes from Germany and Holland, along with a display of electric can openers and kitchen mixers. Powierza ducked inside, received a curt response to his inquiry about a battery for the flashlight, then lingered to look at the illustrations on the video-cassettes, ripe thighs tantalizingly imprisoned behind locked glass doors. He grinned slyly. I grabbed his sleeve and steered him toward the street. "Better stick to gloves, Staszek," I told him.

We wound on through the gauntlet of peddlers and stores to the end of the street where the crowds thinned and older buildings stood like dark worn cliffs set back from the gaudy wrack of a shore. Here were the gargoyle faces of men standing in doorways, drunkenness working at them like magnified gravity, tugging flesh earthward, slowing words and motion. An old woman, gray as bone, veered wide around them, tugging her tiny frightened dog. The drab shops in this quarter remained unchanged, marooned among the plain little stores selling cabbage, beets, celery root, and dusty potatoes, the root vegetables of the Slavic winter. Powierza dodged in a plumber's shop and stepped around sinks and toilet bowls sitting on the floor like monuments in a cemetery. He showed the proprietor the battery. "Do you know where we can find one like this?"

The man dropped a coil of copper tubing and clasped the battery in a grimy hand. He studied it and handed it back. "The electric shop."

"Where is it?"

"Down the street." He pointed with his chin. "Then right."

We continued down the crumbling street, the foot traffic reduced now to the careful tread of the elderly, took the first right and encountered a street faced by dull brick facades: government buildings, solid to the sidewalk, unrelieved by commerce. Retracing our steps, we spotted a narrow passageway. A few steps into its twilighted reek of freshly emptied garbage bins, a small sign indicated the way across a cold stone courtyard. Steps led down to a half-basement, a lighted window, and the pliant rattle of a worn door latch.

A man with pouched eyes and gray hair glanced up from behind a narrow counter. On the bench in front of him an array of small objects—dismantled motors, wiring, worn delicate tools—seemed frozen like miniature players in the warm pool of his work light. His hands, interrupted, replaced tool and object soundlessly on the worn surface before him. The room had a strange dim quiet accentuated by the sound of classical music from a hidden radio. He squinted past his circle of light to the rising moon of Powierza's face.

"I'm looking for a battery," Powierza said. "Do you have one like this?"

The man rose from his chair with deliberate care, as though the silence were a curtain he was reluctant to part. Powierza handed him the battery and held up the old flashlight. "It's for this."

"Ummm." He took the battery to his bench and studied it under the light. "Perhaps," he said. He retreated into the darkness of his shop, vanished amid rows of shelves into another room. A pale light spilled from its doorway. Powierza stood at the center, cradling the empty flashlight in his hands. The music from the unseen radio, I noticed, was religious—a mass, in fact. The walls were not quite bare: a picture of the Virgin, faded in a dusty frame; the pope, mitered, with monstrance, taped up from the pages of a magazine or calendar. Below it, on the bench, a small stand-up picture frame with a black-and-white photograph of an elderly woman. Powierza waited, humming to himself.

There seemed to be nothing for sale here, no goods on display. Objects rested on the shelves, things vaguely electrical, but electricity had always been a mystery to me, a sort of alchemy. I had touched a hot wire in the milk shed when I was a child and never since could I determine which wire was harmless and which could kill you or fling you across a room.

"What does he do here?" I asked Powierza.

"He fixes things," Powierza said. "See there. A clock, a fan. Some radio parts. Old-fashioned radios. I don't know." He lowered his voice. "Probably junk, mostly."

I thought of the noisy passage we had just negotiated, where the new plastic radios, TV sets, and tape players broadcast a racket like fistfuls of dried paper ripping in front of a microphone. These appliances were all printed circuitry now, stamped out on green plastic shingles that looked like diagrams of miniature cities. I had seen them for sale in the flea markets of Warsaw, peddled by kids wearing

Russian army field jackets and caps that proclaimed "No Fear." In this cloistered place, a quieter music prevailed—and then seemed to swell—and then I noticed that the old man had emerged soundlessly from the back room and stood facing the shelf along the wall, his hand poised before the radio I had heard but not spied. Powierza started to say something, but the man lifted his hand, palm out toward us. "Just a moment," he said. A voice rose out of the radio and the man stood, motionless, his eyes half closed. No one spoke. The voice from the radio soared, floated like a swallow catching the wind, dipped, fluttered, fell. His hand readjusted the knob.

"Mozart," he said.

"Pardon?" said Powierza.

He moved toward us. "Mozart." The name came with an exhalation, a sigh. I saw one leg lagging as he walked, a faint disguised limp. He held the square lump of a battery in his left hand.

"You have it?" Powierza asked.

"Let's see," he said. He fitted the battery into the box of the lamp and as he did the sleeve of his left arm caught on some snag of the counter and slipped the sleeve upward, revealing on his forearm a row of tattooed numbers. I had never seen this before. He did not seem to notice, nor did Powierza, who was peering at the lamp's bulb. The sleeve slid down into place, covering the tattoo.

"Now let's try it," the old man said. He found the switch, but no light came.

"Maybe the bulb," Powierza said.

"Corrosion," the man said, and he opened the case and withdrew the battery. He sat down with it at the bench. Was it only Jews who were tattooed with numbers in the concentration camps? I scanned the room again, the pictures of the Virgin and the pope, the small, tidy plainness of his workshop, and the man itself. His head bent to the lamp. His hair sparse and cloud-white. Poles went to the ovens, too, of course; were lined up and tumbled into their self-dug graves. But I had not heard they were tattooed. If this man was Jewish, why the religious pictures? I tried to sense his life from the clues in this place. I imagined him alone, living in one or two compact rooms somewhere nearby, with a ring to cook on, a covered chair surrounded by books, a radio, and, maybe, a phonograph to play his records, his Mozart.

"How long have you been here?" I asked. He was intent with his work and did not seem to hear me. "Sir," I said, more loudly, "how long have you been here, in this shop?"

"Many years," he said, without glancing up. "A long time."

"Since the war?" I said.

"Since after the war." His hands skimmed the tools with a small, precise grace, an economy of effort. He dismantled the box, rubbed the terminals with a wire brush, and put the thing back together. He stood up. "Now," he said. The bulb came on.

"A little corrosion," he said. "Better to keep in a dry place."

"How much do we owe you?" Powierza asked. He gave the price. I dug for my money and slowly counted it out. I wanted to ask him about the tattoo, about the war, about his life, but I couldn't think of a tactful way to do it, and Powierza was leaning toward the door, impatient to leave. I pushed the money across the counter. We said good-bye and walked out. We made it through the courtyard to the street before I stopped.

"Staszek," I said. "Wait for me a moment."

"What for?"

"Just a moment. Wait here." I hurried back through the alley to the shop. The man looked up startled, as I swung open the door.

"Sir, excuse me. I want to ask you something."

"Yes?"

"I saw, on your arm, the tattoo."

"Yes?"

"I'm sorry if I'm being . . . impolite. But I wanted to know were you in a concentration camp."

He hesitated. "Why do you want to know that?"

"I've never seen anyone who . . ."

"Who had numbers on his arm?"

"Yes."

"I see," he said. He searched my face for a reason to go on. "Yes." he said, finally. "Auschwitz."

"Are you . . .?"

"A survivor, yes."

"I mean, are you . . .?"

"Living. I am living." He smiled wanly. "For the present."

"I mean Jewish. Are you Jewish?"

"I was born a Jew."

"And now?" I nodded to the pictures on the wall. "Are you Catholic now?"

"I am an old man now. And I am in Poland." He paused a moment. "You see?"

I said nothing.

"Perhaps you don't." His fingertips played over the electric motor on the bench in front of him. "There are no Jews in Poland. Or not enough to count. You know that, don't you, young man?"

"Yes sir," I said. I felt chided.

"I believe in God."

"Yes."

"But I am not a congregation of one. I am a Jew who believes in God, if you want to say that. It is no consequence how I worship, is it? To you, I mean? or anyone?"

"No sir, I just . . ."

"I believe in God. I believe in music. Perhaps they are the same. I worship with Poles. I worship because I am alive."

"But you could have left, couldn't you?"

"You mean to Israel? You think I shouldn't be here?"

"No, sir, please. I didn't mean that. I mean, you changed, you had to change, your religion?"

"Did I?" His pouched eyes regarded me closely. "We all breathe the air that's in front of our faces." He stood up and switched off the lamp above his workbench. In the light that remained, from an overhead tube, he seemed ghostly, pallid.

"It's a long story," he said. "But, really, it is not so interesting."

"I'm sorry to have bothered you."

He reached for the switch on his radio. It clicked off into silence. I could see the pale flesh of his forearm, but not the numbers. "No bother," he said. "Good-bye."

Powierza had wandered down the street some distance.

"What were you doing?" he asked.

"I wanted to give him some more money," I said. "He seemed like he could use it."

Powierza looked at me like I'd gone soft in the head, but he said nothing until we reached the end of the street. Then he said, "He's a Jew, you know."

"How do you know that?" I asked.

"I saw his tattoo," he said. "And he overcharged us."

I said nothing. He picked up the pace beside me. "Come on," he said. "Let's get a coffee."

At a small hotel off the square a *kawiarnia* sold cakes and coffee and shots of vodka. It was a big, crowded room with heavy dingy curtains draping the front door against the cold, filled with cigarette smoke, its windows steamed over. We had sat there only a moment when I saw a face I recognized but which required a few seconds to register. It was Bielski, the man from the Rapid Trading office in Warsaw. And then, in the next second, I realized that the man with him, sitting with his back almost squarely toward us, was Roman Jabłoński. I slid my chair sideways so that Powierza blocked his view of me, and pulled my collar over my chin.

"Staszek," I said. "Don't look around. It's Jabłoński."

"Where?"

"At the far end of the room. He's talking to the man I saw in Warsaw."

"What man?"

"His name's Bielski. He's from the trading company, remember? It was one of the phone numbers Tomek had, one of the numbers we called."

"The one who threw you out of his office?"

"Yes."

"What are they doing?"

"Talking." I edged a look over Powierza's shoulder. "Drinking vodka, I think."

"Where's the waitress?" Powierza said. "I could use a vodka myself."

Bielski and Jabłoński were leaning close over their small table, both with their coats on. A waitress brought two more glasses of vodka. A cloud of smoke billowed over Jabłoński's head. Bielski listened while Jabłoński spoke, his head nodding emphatically like a chicken pecking. The waitress came to our table.

"Vodka, please," Powierza said.

"Coffee," I said.

She cleaned a tableful of dirty cups.

"They're leaving," I said. They stood. Bielski counted money onto the table while Jabłoński stabbed out his cigarette and buttoned his coat. He did not look in our direction. I watched, head bowed, as they parted the door curtain and went out. Powierza was on his feet, just as the waitress arrived with her tray. He tossed back the vodka. "Pay her, Leszek." I paid and caught up with Powierza on the sidewalk. Bielski and Jabłoński were fifty yards ahead of us, Bielski towering over Jabłoński, gesturing with gloved hands. Then they halted, facing each other on the broken sidewalk. Bielski's gloved hand now rattled a set of keys. He was standing next to a dark Mercedes, probably the same one I'd seen on the street in Praga. Powierza and I stopped, mutely facing an empty store window, until Bielski was inside the car and Jabłoński was hurrying on down the street. Bielski drove quickly past us and rounded the next corner. Jabłoński kept walking.

"Let's see where he goes," Powierza said.

We followed, staying well behind him.

He crossed the street, making for his muddy little Fiat, parked half on the curb on a nearly deserted block. He opened the door, removed a stick from the back seat, and went around to poke the starter in the rear engine of this ridiculous car. Jabłoński got in, slammed the door, and drove past us, his face a blur behind the grimy window.

We returned to the square to catch the bus home. It was late, the queue gathered around us, the darkness settled rapidly. The street peddlers packed up boxes, nylon duffel bags, folding tables. The bus arrived and we stood squeezed in the center aisle for the ride back to Jadowia. When we walked past the Farmers' Co-op on the way home, the lights were on in Jabłoński's office and his car was parked at his flat across the street. We parted at Powierza's gate; both of us had work to do.

"Come about eleven," Powierza said.

"Maybe we should watch him," I said. "Jabłoński, I mean."

"No," he said. "It doesn't matter. We can't follow him on foot. We'll go to the quarry. Andrzej will meet us here."

I had forgotten about Andrzej. Powierza held onto the flashlight.

He tried it now. In the full dark, it cut a bright narrow beam to the trees across the road.

I trudged on to the chores, feeling weary and ineffectual. In a detective story, the sleuth would have braced Jabłoński against the side of his car and forced him to talk. But this was no detective story and I didn't see Powierza, much less myself, slamming anyone up against his car. Instead, I was in a cold barn, squatting in manure up to my ankles, wiping down the udders of a Holstein cow.

It had been a strange day, and I was only halfway through it. I had met the only Jew I had ever seen in my life, so far as I knew, and had no idea what to say to him or what to make of what he said to me, even though I came from a village where hundreds of Jews once lived. Powierza said he overcharged us. That was nonsense, but it was the normal nonsense. "We all breathe the air that's in front of our faces," the old man said.

Maybe that simple sentence served as an explanation. All we knew was nonsense and myth. And rationalization. We craved some reason to understand why they were no longer here, and it required, for most, a cause that was even bigger, deeper, and older than Hitler, some reason for why, when they *were* here, they were such a force, such a presence, in tiny places like this. (They buried gold—gold!—in the walls of their houses.) We needed some way to comprehend why we bought *from* then and sold *to* them, why they could read and Poles couldn't, why they could do business and Poles tilled the fields. Maybe in the cities, where there were no fields, it was different. Maybe they had a different way to explain why Catholic Poles were Poles (and not just Catholics), while Jewish Poles were always just Jews. The Poles and the Not-Poles. Now it was the Poles and the Not-Here, the Poles and the Vanished.

Or nearly. What we had now were ideas of hidden gold, and old stones laid in foundation walls. Memory buried and put to practical use.

I ate supper, wolfing down three bowls of heavy stew and thick slices of bread. My mother sat watching me, happy to see the stew disappearing. "You've got your appetite back," she said. Grandpa ate little and read a newspaper two days old. Mother piled up the dishes and retreated to the living room to watch an imported Australian television series that had become a national mania. Grandpa went to bed and I climbed the stairs to my own room and stretched out on the bed with my clothes on and fell asleep immediately. When I woke the house was silent. It was past ten o'clock. I got up, slipped on two sweaters, two pairs of socks, and crept down the steps. Then I put on my boots and coat and a wool stocking cap tugged down tight over my ears. I stepped outside. The snow had started while I was sleeping. It was an inch deep and still falling, fine-grained.

Andrzej was sitting at Powierza's kitchen table when I entered. He stood up, quickly, offering his hand. I shook it. He seemed as thin as wire, his clothes worn and threadbare. I could smell the vodka on his breath, but he was clear-eyed, alert as a squirrel. "Pan Leszek," he chirped. "How are you?"

"It's a cold night," I said.

Powierza entered from the living room, wrestling a thick woolly sweater over his stomach. "We should go," he said.

"Wait a minute," I said. "Shouldn't we know what we're doing?"

Powierza stood for a moment, leaning against the stove's white tiles. The fire in it had nearly gone out, and he bent for a scoopful of coal from the bucket on the floor and jammed it into the firebox. He shut the firebox door with a kick of his boot.

"I don't know what we're going to do, Leszek. Let's just go see what happens."

"Andrzej," I said, "what is supposed to happen with these trucks?"

"Powierza told you, didn't he?"

"Yes, I told him," Powierza said.

"Do you know any more now?" I asked.

He shrugged. "No."

"Have you seen Jabłoński?"

"No," he said. "He was gone most of the day, I think. His car was not home when I came by on the way here."

"We don't have to do anything," Powierza said. "We'll just go there and watch, see what happens. That's all. Let's just go." He grabbed his coat. "Are you coming?"

"I've got this far," I said.

"Good."

The snow was accumulating in the frozen ruts of the road. The wind, steady out of the north, drove the snow on a slant. We walked down the road without talking. The houses, as we approached the village, were dark. The night lights of the grocery and the baker's were smeared through the snow's blur. We skirted the village's northern edge, taking familiar paths until we intersected the road running north and then continued along the edge of a forest-bordered field. The wind ran unbroken across the field, causing my eyes to water. Powierza had kept his light off so far, but he flicked it on and off now, picking out the faint path and the looming pines. We walked on for several hundred yards to the field's end, crossed though a thicket, thorns crackling against our pant legs, then threaded our way through a band of trees and frozen leaf fall to a narrow dirt road. Powierza veered left and led us, after a minute, to a twin-rutted forest road. He hesitated, consulting with Andrzej consulted while I stared up at the overarching limbs and listened to the wind moaning through the pines. I wasn't sure precisely where we were. After a minute of debate we plunged through the forest to the next crossing. It occurred to me that we could not be far from the place where Tomek's body had been found. The roads here were cross-hatched in an uneven grid pattern, tracks that were laid out decades ago by foresters and used now mostly by farmers with horses and wagons shortcutting their way to their fields or town. We made another left and after about a hundred yards, Andrzej, halting behind Powierza, pointed to the right, through the woods, and said, "Here."

Powierza flicked on the light. There was no discernible path. Through the trees, the terrain sloped downward then appeared to rise. Again Powierza led the way, moving slowly through the undergrowth. Branches slapped against my face and frozen twigs snapped under our feet. The trees thinned out as we climbed the slope and found ourselves in high dried grass on the lip of an indistinct clearing.

It was the quarry. The open sky above it was rimmed by the faint outlines of forest on three sides, with a road and the entrance to the quarry at the opposite end from us. The quarry's surface was as barren as the moon, pocked and uneven. Except for the swirling snow, no movement was visible, no truck nor any other vehicle. Powierza motioned for us to fall in behind him, and we circled to the left along the rim of the quarry until we reached its south side and paused behind a stand of thick brush. "Here," Powierza said. "We'll watch from here. We can see the road."

The sleet stung our faces. Against the dry leaves and frozen grass the grainy snow sounded like the rise and fall of whispered conversation. Andrzej braced his back against the wind and raised the collar of his jacket. I unwound my scarf and held it out to him.

"No, it's all right."

"Go ahead. Take it." He was visibly shivering.

"Thank you," he said finally. He wrapped it around his neck. Powierza paced a few feet away along the bank and sat down, his hands in his pockets and the flashlight resting on the ground between his boots. "What time is it?" he asked.

"Eleven-thirty," I said.

Andrzej fished a cigarette from his pocket and lit it. "Smoke?"

I shook my head.

He looked at me through the quick burst of the match flame. "So," he said, "I guess we'll be getting a new vet."

"Pardon?"

"I guess we'll be having a new vet come." He gave a long, wracking cough. "Since Skalski's left town."

"Karol Skalski? What do you mean, left town?"

"Left town. Gone. Packed up his family."

"His family?"

He took a drag from the cigarette, the glow reflecting a wet, slitted eye.

"Thought you might be interested."

I swallowed, unable, for a moment, to speak.

"The kids?" I asked, finally.

"And the wife."

I turned away, giving my face to the stinging wind. At my back I heard him say, "Sorry." I whirled around, saw him staring at me intently, gauging my reaction, and I knew then that Andrzej knew, that it was Andrzej who was Jabłoński's eyes and ears, his messenger, his spy. He had followed us, watched us, reported to Jabłoński. I stepped close to him and grabbed the lapels of his jacket. A button popped off. My face was two inches from his. "When, Andrzej? When did she leave?"

"This afternoon."

"Where did she go?"

"Warsaw."

"Where in Warsaw?"

"I don't know. To meet her husband. They're leaving the country."

"How do you know what they're doing?"

"That's what I heard."

"You know everything, don't you, Andrzej? You make everything your business." I wanted to strangle him.

"I know you were friends with her," he said quietly. "I thought you would want to know." He lifted his cigarette to his lips in a slow, cautious movement, and clutched my wrist firmly. "You were friends, weren't you?"

"Quiet!" Powierza hissed. In the distance I could hear the sound of a truck engine. Andrzej stepped backward and I loosened my grip.

"When are they leaving, Andrzej?"

He stared at me, the cigarette dangling on his lip. "Tomorrow, maybe," he said.

"Jesus, will you be quiet," Powierza said.

The slope that curved behind us blocked the view of the road. Then the amber running lights of a truck cab flickered through the trees. The headlights flashed on, then off, and it wheeled into the approach to the quarry, lumbering over the uneven ground until it was well inside, then stopped, its engine idling. There was no movement for some few minutes, the driver or any passengers unseen within the cab's darkness. A door slammed and a broken silhouette of a lone figure moved around the truck. The door slammed again and the engine was cut off. The amber lights on the roof of the cab stayed on, snow swirling in a yellow halo around them.

Powierza had squatted on his haunches in the brush and pulled me down beside him. He leaned across to Andrzej. "Do you know who it is?"

"No," said Andrzej, "but Polish, I think, the truck."

"How do you know?"

"Russian truck is bigger," Andrzej said. "Wait. Listen."

It was a car, the sewing machine rattle of a little Fiat. It poked up the road, with only its parking lights on, into the quarry and braked.

"Jabłoński." Andrzej and Powierza spoke at the same time. The engine stopped and the parking lights went off. A tinny door shut, and I saw, indistinctly, someone move toward the truck. Then two doors successively slammed and a figure edged along the passenger side and converged with two others at the rear of the truck. The big doors were opened and a flashlight, shifted from hand to hand, shone into the interior. Then the three men stood in the glow from the running lights on the rear of the box, evidently waiting for the next arrival.

"Is it Jabłoński?" I asked.

"It's Jabłoński," said Andrzej.

Several more minutes passed. At the rear of the truck three men paced around. Jabłoński—I took Andrzej's word for it—walked over to his car, retrieved something, then returned. It was now a few minutes past midnight. Then a truck engine in the distance, louder, larger, slower: a diesel, crawling in low gear. A car preceded it into view, the unmistakable boxy shape of a Mercedes. The truck behind it was a large international transport, a high white blunt-nosed cab and a trailer that seemed as long as a city block. The Mercedes led the truck into the driveway, then angled to the right and stopped. The other men began directing the transport parallel to the smaller truck. The Mercedes doors opened and four men emerged.

Slowly I stood up, for we seemed secure from our vantage point on the quarry's darkened rim. The two groups of men below us merged as the air brakes of the big truck gasped and spat through the wind. Voices reached us, indistinct, like scraps of blown paper. The driver from the newly arrived truck climbed down from his cab and joined the others. There was a brief huddle, and evidently orders were given, for the group then split up. The doors of the big trailer were heaved open. Some of the men climbed aboard and began unloading what looked like wooden crates, heavy enough so that two or three men were needed to lift them.

Powierza clambered to his feet. "Can you hear anything?" he asked. I shook my head. "Do you recognize any of them?"

"Is that Jabłoński?" I said. Three men stood off to one side while the others worked. Jabłoński, a small-brimmed hat perched on his head, was dwarfed by the other two, who wore long leather overcoats that glistened in the light.

"I mean the others," Powierza said. "Is that the guy he was talking to this afternoon?"

"I think so. I think that's his car, the Mercedes."

"We've got to get down there. We can't see shit from up here." He peered down the quarry wall. "Let's work our way down." The slope was littered with sparse dried brush growing out of loose rock, not especially steep, but the footing was unsure. "If we get down there we can watch from behind that pile of gravel," Powierza said. He ventured forward a couple of steps and glanced back over my shoulder. "Andrzej, you stay here."

"All right, let's go," I said.

Cautiously, we maintained our footing and grasped at weeds and bushes for support. Below us the unloading proceeded, the crates now emerging from the back of both trucks and stacked in pyramids on the ground. We were about halfway down when Powierza's foot kicked loose a large stone. It rolled through the dried brush with a bright crackling noise that continued as the rock tumbled all the way to the bottom. Powierza had fallen on his side and lay there motionless while I crouched behind him, my eyes fixed on Jabłoński—I could see him clearly now—and his two companions supervising the work on the trucks. One of them, I thought, started at the noise, but evidently dismissed it. The last thirty yards of the slope was a scree of old rock and gravel with no cover at all. A few steps beyond that would give us the protection of the gravel mound. For some minutes we waited at the edge of this exposure, imagining the noise the loose rock would make.

"Let me go first," I said. I shouldered past Powierza and crawled down feet first on my hands and heels, dragging my behind in a half-sitting position. When I reached the shelter of the gravel mound I saw Powierza following me in the same crablike manner, his form hugely visible from where I waited. I heard the soft scatter of tumbling rock and hoped that the men in front of us were looking in another direction. Powierza caught up with me finally, breathing heavily. I crept up the side of the mound and peered over the top.

The unloading seemed to have been finished. There were several stacks of crates on the ground now and some of the men leaned against them, smoking, while Jabłoński and the two others moved amid the piles, shining a flashlight on stenciled labels. Two men stood on the tailgates of both trucks, waiting for instructions.

Powierza crawled up beside me. His flashlight clanked softly on the rock.

"What are they doing?"

I said nothing. He could see as well as I could. We were still thirty to forty yards away from them, and whatever they were saying was still inaudible. One of the men with Jabłoński went to inspect the transport's trailer, then into the box of the smaller truck. Then one of the men on the tailgate offered him a hand and hoisted him up. He disappeared inside, the beam of a flashlight piercing the opening like summer lightning. He reappeared on the tailgate, barked an order, and the men on the ground began picking up long wooden boxes and loading them aboard the smaller truck. The man with the flashlight watched for a few minutes, then jumped to the ground. Something about him seemed familiar to me, but I could not tell why. It was not his face, which I could not see clearly, but something about the set of his shoulders or the way he walked. He joined Jabłoński, and the two of them, shoulder to shoulder, walked away from the trucks.

"Leszek," Powierza said, "we've got to find out what's in those boxes." His fingers clutched my arm. "They've got to be guns."

"Probably."

The crates were the right size, but they could contain many things, legal or illegal. "Leszek, we have to find out."

"Why?" I said in exasperation, wondering what difference it made to me, or even to him. "How?" I said. It was a more acceptable question.

He squeezed my arm harder. "Why, because they killed my son, he was with them, he knew them. How, I don't know. Maybe I'll just walk out there and take my chances." He lurched to his knees and for a moment I thought he might charge over the gravel pile. I grabbed his sleeve. "Wait," I said.

I could see now that Bielski had joined Jabłoński and the other man, the one I could not quite place. Powierza squirmed on the gravel beside me. The snow thickened as the crates were reloaded. The men who had loaded the long, thin, coffinlike boxes from the transport were now hoisting them aboard the smaller truck. Jabłoński and the two men parted, Jabłoński toward his car, and Bielski and the other one toward the trucks. They spoke for a moment and then Bielski ran to catch up with Jabłoński. The two of them climbed into Jabłoński's car and left.

The loading was done with care, and slowly, with the sound of the heavy crates being shuffled around inside the truck. Several large piles still remained to go aboard. I had an idea. I'd have to hustle, and Powierza would have to be strong enough to lift one of the long crates. I was sure he could if only I could provide a distraction. Hastily I explained the plan to Powierza. I would take the spotlight, circle the quarry, and shine the light on the trucks from the opposite side. If they looked in that direction, or advanced toward me, Powierza might be able to snatch one of the crates, and we could hope that they were not keeping close count of their cargo.

"What if they don't come toward you?" Powierza said.

"I'll walk toward them. They will. Just watch for the light."

I grabbed the flashlight and scrambled up the slope to Andrzej crouching in the brush. "Stay here," I told him, and kept going, back the way we had come, along the quarry's rim. I stumbled over the uneven ground, raking my face across dried raspberry canes. It took several minutes to reach the opposite side of the quarry. The descent to the bottom was easier here. Behind me the tops of the pines sounded steadily in the wind. The lights of the trucks were a filmy blur in the distance. I could not make out the mound of gravel where I had left Powierza, but I stayed high enough on the bank so that I judged he could see the light as I steadied it against my chest and switched it on.

The beam was powerful and compact, and I could just detect its reflection against the side of the truck. For a minute, maybe two, I could see no response from the trucks. I could not, in fact, see any movement at all. Nor could I hear anything with the wind blowing at my back. Still I stood with the light pointing toward them, waiting for something to move, a light to point back, a shout in my direction. There was nothing I could see.

Picking my steps carefully and keeping the light pointed toward the trucks, I descended the slope and walked slowly toward the trucks. I was still about a hundred yards away when I saw that the men had in fact moved, in two groups, at either end of the larger truck. They were all looking right at me. I stopped.

"Stand where you are, sir." The voice came from my left and a little behind me and a split second later the beam of a powerful flashlight shined directly into my eyes.

"Put out your light and drop it. Do it now." I was trying to place that voice and had just done it when I heard a rustle behind me and then a blinding orange detonation of pain at the back of my head and my knees buckled and I saw nothing.

What I saw next was a blur above me, a face reflecting some indirect light, darkness beyond that and sparse snow swirling in the cold night air. I felt something soft behind my head. A hand. Then a voice in Russian, a response from someone, and footsteps fading across the ground. My skull radiated a pain, hot and liquid, a deep splitting throb. I closed my eyes. I was on the ground, I thought. Where?

"Pan Leszek." The voice again. The hand lifted my head slightly. "Pan Leszek."

I opened my eyes and the blurred face whirled. My stomach heaved and I could taste bile in my throat. The voice again:

"Pan. Leszek, what in hell are you doing here, huh? You should be on your farm, no? Minding your own business, milking your cows. Come, wake up."

My eyes seemed to cross, for there were two wavering half-faces over me, darkly stubbled, each breathing a faint tang of vodka, each mouth jeweled with the glitter of a single gold tooth.

"Here." He lifted my head. A flask appeared under my nose. "Come. You'll remember this, Pan Leszek. Drink. That's it."

The vodka burned in my throat. I sputtered and choked.

"That's better."

He shifted around somehow and I realized I had been lying partially across his extended leg. He lifted me by my collar with one hand and adjusted a folded coat beneath my head. It was Valentin.

I had seen him last through the haze of vodka in the dim hotel room in Warsaw. Perhaps it was the vodka that brought it instantly back. Valentin, speaking in the riddles of his commerce, helping to lead me down the steps to my room. "Valentin?"

"Yes, it's me." He looked at me over the silver flask, a dented touch of elegance, then swigged from it himself. His body blocked my view, but I presumed the trucks were still there. Focus was returning through the pounding of my head. Where was Powierza? Had they caught him? I tried to sit up. Valentin's hand restrained me. "Relax," he said. In the waist of his pants I saw the handle of a pistol.

"Help me up," I said, trying again. His hand stayed on my chest, gently enough but resistant.

"Rest a moment, Pan Leszek. You've had a blow. Here. Another sip. It's cold out here."

My head felt split. I wondered if I was bleeding. I felt at the back of my head, but found no blood. My stocking cap was gone.

"You got hit. I'm sorry. Now tell me, Leszek, what are you doing out here so late?" He looked down at me, his head cocked slightly. The flashlight laying on the ground rolled away. When he picked it up I could see his face more clearly. He waited for an answer.

"Let me sit up," I said.

"Don't be in a hurry," he said. "I guess you were out running your fox traps, huh? You do that, don't you? Trap foxes in the woods? You must get a good price for winter fox pelts, no? I've seen them in Praga. It's good fur, the Polish fox. Not good as Russian, but good."

I said nothing. Gingerly I sat up. He let me.

"So," he said, "I am right, of course? Your fox traps are okay? The hunting good?"

"Yes," I said.

"Good," he said. "I thought so. My colleagues will be interested. Relieved. Here." He handed me the flask. "You feel better, you go back in the woods, look after the rest of your traps. And go home, go to bed. Okay?"

I drank, willingly, the heat in my throat welcome now. My head throbbed. I felt again for the lump on the crown of my head.

"What are you doing here, Valentin?" I could see the men darting around the trucks. One of them climbed into the cab of the transport.

"Business, Leszek. Not interesting for you. You are trapping foxes, remember? I tell them that, it's okay. It's a lucky chance, I meet my old drinking companion here." He slapped my leg and laughed. "My old drinking companion." He laughed again. "I wondered if you would wake up the next day."

"I woke up," I said. "I have my headache now."

"Sorry," he said. "You'll feel better. I tell you, we were lucky. It could have been worse."

"You hit me?"

"An associate. I had the light in your face. But I didn't recognize you at first."

"Yuri?" I asked.

"You remember Yuri? No, not Yuri. Yuri might have shot you. By accident, of course. Yuri's here, but he's busy. We have to get our work done and keep moving, Leszek. Maybe there are others trapping foxes in the woods, eh? Are there other trappers about, Leszek?"

"No."

"Good. I hope that's right." His hand hitched at his belt, brushed the pistol's handle. Perhaps it was unconscious, perhaps not. "I hope that's right, because I'm going out of Poland tonight. Over the border with the little truck. A stop in Ukraine, and then home. And then you know what, Leszek?"

"No."

"Brooklyn! I go to Brooklyn."

"In America?"

"Brooklyn, New York, America. My new address."

"You can go to Brooklyn?"

"Why not? There are many Russians in Brooklyn. Many Poles, too, I think. We get along better with no border between us. No old history. I make a new business there. I think I make a restaurant."

"You're going to stay there?"

"Why not? I do this business, I make my money, now I go invest for myself. Is easier, I think." He laughed. "Is the U.S.A. dream, huh?"

"The American dream."

"Yes, American dream to leave Russian nightmare. Maybe, when I am old and rich, I come back. For a visit. Go pee on Lenin's tomb. Another?" He offered the flask, giving it a shake. "Ah, finished." He held it over his opened mouth, then stuck it in his pocket.

"I must go, Leszek. Come. Can you stand?"

He clasped both my hands and hoisted me to my feet. I was wobbly but upright.

"Okay?"

"Okay." He looked me over, as though preparing to catch me if I fell.

"Now," he said, bending to pick up his coat, the one I'd been resting on. He put it on and gathered up his flashlight and then mine. He laid it in my hand. "Now," he said again, "you go that way." He grasped my shoulders and spun me to face the slope of the quarry and the woods beyond. "You go back there. You go check your fox traps and you keep going. All right, Leszek? Agreed?" He tapped the handle of the gun. "You know I have this?" He sounded apologetic.

"Yes, agreed."

"Good. Now go."

"Valentin?"

"Yes?"

"My friend, Tomek, the one who was killed. The one I told you about in Warsaw. What happened to him, Valentin?"

He said nothing for a moment. I wanted to see his face, but he kept his hands on my shoulders.

"Money," he said. "What else? I only hear this, Leszek. They were Georgians. You don't play with Georgians, huh? Stalin was a Georgian."

I turned slowly and he dropped his hands. He gazed at me steadily.

"Your friend should have known this," he said, "but he was young. He made some demand, so . . ." He shrugged. "They don't care, the Georgians. But this is just what I hear, Leszek. Just talk. Anyway, they are gone now. Maybe they are dead, too, from fighting with Ghamzaghordia. Or the Chechens. The weekly civil war. Forget them and remember your friend. Okay, Leszek? Come to Brooklyn."

He seized my shoulders again, pulled me to him, gave me a Russian bear hug, and then, just as quickly, spun me round.

"Now go," he said, pushing against my back. "We are out of time. Go!"

I started walking. "Good-bye, Valentin."

"I see you in Brooklyn," he said.

I regained the slope and started climbing without looking back. I heard the engines of both trucks start up. When I reached the top, I looked back and saw Valentin in the distance, running toward the trucks. He paused briefly at the transport and the Mercedes, then climbed aboard the smaller truck. The car preceded the caravan slowly onto the road. From my vantage point I could follow their lights out to the main road, the one that, with a left turn, led back to Jadowia. The wind had quieted now and, by listening carefully, I could hear that the trucks made a right at the junction, on the road that would join the main highway and would then, if they headed east, carry them on to the border. Of course, the highway ran west toward Warsaw as well, but perhaps, as Valentin claimed, the quickest way to Brooklyn New York America was not through Warsaw, but east.

Warsaw was where I had to go.

I switched on the flashlight and focused it on the quarry's far edge. I saw nothing in response, but I was too far away. I stumbled on and finally heard Powierza calling me. He and Andrzej were on the quarry floor. I could see them now in the light's cone. As I approached, my foot caught on a root and I rolled half the length of the embankment, the flashlight skittering wildly in front of me. Powierza pulled me out of the gravel.

"I got it!" he said. "They didn't see me. They didn't miss it." He slapped me on the back. "I got it!"

My legs were trembling. I sat down. He bent over me.

"What happened to you?" he asked.

I took the first bus I could to Warsaw. I had gone home only long enough to change clothes, hurrying in and out of the house well before light, encountering only Grandpa. I told him I would be gone all day and offered no further explanation. He asked for none, just grunted and went out to the barn.

The bus was late, then maddeningly slow. At the outskirts of the city, where crowds were waiting at bus stops, passengers filed on as though they were embarking on a trip to the gallows, crowding the aisle and shoving sullenly against each other. On the streets, the city traffic thickened, halted, inched forward, halted again. Peddlers sold newspapers, threading their way through the traffic. The bus sat through two red lights at a huge intersection, and I had visions of planes roaring skyward, of trains receding from platforms, of Jola fleeing out of reach before me. My head still pounded, the lump on my head painful to touch. I felt hungry, sour-breathed, and jumpy. The bus, with all the crowd packed aboard it, was overheated and airless. I stood up, immediately lost my seat, and decided to get off at the next stop and wave down a taxi.

It took ten minutes to find one empty among the dozens that shot by. When one finally skidded to a stop on brakes that locked in the sand at the curb, I asked for the Central rail station, then sat for another twenty minutes as the driver fought through the traffic.

At the station I rushed inside, half expecting to find Jola waiting for me, with the children and her packed bag, her worried face breaking into relief as I ran toward her. What I saw first was an encampment of Gypsy women begging on the floor, their skirts and dirty children spread around them. Around the perimeter of the station, I wove through the crowds pressing toward the gates of trains whose numbers had been called. I tripped over suitcases and children, but I did not find her. I stood on the seat of a bench and scanned the waiting room until a policeman ordered me to get down. After another circuit of the huge hall I remembered there was a lower level, and then bolted down the stairs, through more Gypsy women and children, and fruitlessly searched the dim platforms below.

I went back upstairs, looking around me as I walked, so that I repeatedly ran into people who shoved back and barked "Excuse me" sarcastically as I rushed on. I had no time for apologies, though. I decided to try the airport. It was another long and expensive taxi ride away.

I was familiar with the train station, but the airport was foreign to me. There were, in fact, two terminals now, the flights divided between the old and the new one. I went to the new terminal first, through one of its many entrances, and fell upon a world glazed in chrome and pink metal and glass, a place far too orderly for all the customary confusion of Poland. Still I had no idea of where to go, no notion of where she might be going, where her husband might be taking her. There were flights to London, Helsinki, Budapest, Bucharest (not likely), Milan, Brussels, Frankfurt, Copenhagen. The list of destinations fluttered like bats on a gigantic board. Slowly I walked past the ticket counters, the lines of passengers and suitcases. I saw families, men and women with their children, and I stared hard at each one as though I might fathom in their arrangements, their management of children and baggage, where she might be going, and how. I made two circles of the terminal, walked back outside to inspect new arrivals approaching in taxis and buses. I went back inside, approached the ticket counter where the Lufthansa agents were processing passengers for Frankfurt. I stood for a moment watching the travelers press their tickets forward, heaving their bags onto the scale, while the waiting passengers eyed me suspiciously as though I were about to crowd the line. I did not fit among these travelers, with their suits and topcoats and briefcases.

"Sir?" I said to the agent, a Pole, self-important and proud of his crisp uniform, who tapped a computer keyboard with one hand and clutched a handful of baggage tags with the other. His eyes did not waver from his screen, and I realized it was useless anyway. What would I ask him? "Please, sir, where is Jola Skalska?" I left the terminal and hurried across a mud-covered open space strewn with construction debris to the old terminal.

It seemed nearly haunted by its emptiness, its few waiting travelers. I took only a minute to check it.

I went outside and inhaled the cold Warsaw air, tinged with the smell of jet fuel and the tang of distant coal smoke. Departing jets tore at the air and rattled the windows behind me. I thought of canvassing the hotels—but what hotels? Surely not expensive ones, and the cut-rate places I could remember were spread all over the city. For some minutes I paced back and forth on the sidewalk, trying to figure out what to do. Finally I decided to go back to the train station.

Surely, I thought, Karol would not have the money for plane tickets. They would cost a fortune. No, of course, they would go by train, wherever they might be going. My own money was nearly gone, pressed into the hands of the merciless taxi drivers. I boarded the bus. I didn't have a choice, really, but it dawned on me, at last, that if I found them, it would be a matter of luck, not timing, and that speed would not help me.

It took more than an hour to get back.

The Gypsies, now, had been corralled by the police, four or five officers standing uneasily over the women and children, who had been forced to sit on the floor, awaiting further orders. The women, laughing and hooting, mocked the police. I simply stood there, a long minute or two, trying to muster some calm, saying to myself, "God, let her be here."

I walked slowly to the center of the terminal. And then I saw them.

They sat, a tableau of exile, like refugees, amid a circle of baggage, with Karol's large head rising over all. Jola, her head and shoulders facing away from me, was just visible behind Karol's bulk. As though responding to some inaudible signal, he looked up, across the distance of dirty marble and heaped baggage, past the dizzy movement of people between us, and fixed his eyes on mine. For a moment, neither of us moved. Then, without a word to Jola or a look behind him, he stood up and walked my way, slowly, steadily, his eyes not leaving mine. His expression was calm, deliberate, and, in a way I'd never quite seen in him before, determined. His face was not angry or aggressive. It was sad, and yet firm.

"Leszek," he said simply.

"Karol."

"You came to see Jola?"

"Yes."

"I'd prefer if you didn't."

I said nothing. I peered beyond him to the bench he'd vacated. Jola was fussing with the boy's clothes, intent, and not watching us. She had not seen me.

"I'd prefer if you didn't," he repeated. "But I won't stop you. If you must."

"Yes." I started to step around him.

"Listen to me first."

"All right."

"I knew about you. I found out." He looked at me, his eyes tired but not glittery the way I saw him always, half drunk. He reached in his pocket and retrieved a cigarette. His fingers, fumbling with a book of matches, trembled with the effort. He was holding himself together, by an act of sheer will. People hurried around us. A woman struggled to put a coat on her little boy, giving him a furious jerk by the arm. "You didn't think I would let it happen, did you?"

"That's Jola's choice, isn't it?"

"Yes. It's her decision. And she's decided. We're leaving. We're leaving Jadowia. We're leaving Poland."

"You're forcing her?"

"It's not your business. But no, I'm not forcing her." He blew out a stream of smoke. "You're like a thief, you know that? You're like a house burglar. You got into my house and you tried to steal my life. Not just my wife. My life. You had no regard for her family, her children, not even her."

"We are not trying to hurt anyone, Karol. Not you, not the children."

"What do you know about it? What do you know about hurting? Did you think you could go on with your secret, your little adventure, and no one would know? Did you think you could keep yourselves buried in the leaves, hidden out there in the woods? No consequences, no damage? One day you just walk out of the forest and down the road, arm in arm, and everything's okay, everyone's happy, and the whole village lines up to applaud and smile and throw bouquets to you?"

He dropped his cigarette on the floor and ground it out with his toe. Now his eyes were flooded, whether with anger or pain I could not tell.

"What kind of dream world do you live in?" he asked. "Do you know anything about real life?"

I could not find an answer. If real life was pain, I could feel it now. Karol's shoulders hunched, his face contorted. For a second, I could sense muscles knotting and expected his fist to fly at my face. Instead, tears welled from his reddened eyes. Over his shoulder, I saw that Jola had turned now, looking for her husband, and she sat motionless, a child's coat in her hand, her eyes on mine. I tried to find in her expression some trace of pleasure or welcome, or even fear, some quickening sense that she was about to stand and come to me—to return to my house, to go with me forever. What I recognized was weariness. In an instant, I saw I was a bother, a distraction. Not a heartache, just a complication, a last-minute irritation. I should have left, right then, but I did not. I stepped around Karol, brushing past his shoulder. Jola stood.

"Why did you come?" she asked. Her voice was steeled, polite, as though she were talking to a stranger. A curl of black hair clung damply to her forehead. She seemed not to have slept. Lines creased the corners of her eyes and the question held me through the length of an echoing loudspeaker announcement.

"I wanted to take you back," I said.

She looked away. The baby was lodged on the bench next to Agnieszka, the daughter I had plucked out of the street all those months before. The boy had started to cry. She lifted him up and rocked him on her hip, and the crying hushed.

"No, Leszek," she said. "No. Don't you understand the word? Go home now. Go live your life."

"But why, Jola? Why are you doing this?"

"We've got to get away from this place," she said. "No, I mean *I've* got to get away. If I had met you years ago, if I didn't have all this . . ." Her daughter was worrying at the hem of her jacket. ". . . if I didn't have Karol. But I do. I just can't shed my skin again, run from one thing to the next."

"But you *are* running. You're running now."

"Not in that way. I'm a traveler, Leszek. I've got to get out of here. I can't stand that shitty little village anymore, the fog, the mud, those lumpy faces, the gossip. I don't want to live on a farm, Leszek. Maybe I'm running, but I'm running with my family."

"Why is Karol going? Why does he want to leave?"

"You don't know?"

"No."

"You. You and me."

"That's all."

"That's all. Isn't that enough? I thought it was. I thought it was a compliment." Agnieszka was tugging again at her coat, and Jola squeezed the child's hand. "I'm sorry, Leszek. I'm sorry you came here. I'm sorry it all happened, I'm sorry you feel so bad. It's better this way, believe me."

The loudspeaker boomed another incomprehensible announcement, the destination of Berlin the only discernible word in the echoing din. Trains now ran to places once forbidden; now we were free to flee for whole new sets of reasons. And free, now, to come back, although I knew she would not.

"So it was all a . . ." The word stuck in my throat, but I spat it out. "A lie?"

"All what?"

"All we talked about. The future, the plans."

"A mistake, maybe. It doesn't matter what it was. Call it what you want." She shifted the baby to her other arm. "Go home now, Leszek. Please, go home."

She stepped away down the bench, her pale neck exposed as she leaned down to listen to her daughter. I turned and saw Karol a few yards behind me, his back to us, his hands bunched in the pockets of his jacket. I walked past him without speaking and kept going out the doors, past the throng of Gypsies and into the boulevard, and kept on walking through the crowded, jostling streets until I wore myself out with the people and the noise and the dirt. Then I found the bus and rode home through the silent countryside.

CHAPTER SIXTEEN

The monsignor, Father Jerzy noted with an envious curiosity, was startlingly young for his rank. Father Jerzy suppressed the urge to inquire how long he'd been out of seminary. The monsignor's handsome face, his perfectly trimmed hair, and the bladelike fit of his clothes cut off the possibility of too much informality. He was efficient; he had not come for a social chat. Father Jerzy sensed that at once.

"I'm from the diocese," the monsignor said. "Please sit down."

The reversal of protocol also rang alarmingly. This stranger spoke as if the office were his, as if, indeed, the church were his own parish and Father Jerzy were the visitor.

"I gather you've been waiting for me," Father Jerzy said.

The monsignor consulted his watch. "About an hour," he said.

"I'm sorry. I was rather occupied at a meeting."

"Yes. I understand you've been quite . . . busy . . . here."

"Indeed." Father Jerzy ventured a modest smile and was about to offer a morsel of explanation, something tantalizing by way of introducing the complexities, but the monsignor went on.

"I'm afraid the church has other plans for you," he said.

"Other plans?"

"Another assignment, that is."

Father Jerzy felt a rush of excitement. Already his reputation was becoming known, as he had known it would be. His talents were urgently in demand. The church was even now laying out its master plan for him. There was so much more to be done. He suppressed a smile, although he felt warmth and pride bursting within him. He picked up a pencil from the desk and held it in both fists, as though for an anchor, as he leaned forward.

"That's excellent, Father," he said. "Of course, I'll need a little time to get this situation in hand before moving on to the next one, but it shouldn't take too much longer, I don't think."

"I'm afraid the bishop has a change of pace in mind for you," the monsignor said, his thin lips meeting in a straight line. "He wishes a quicker transition to your new duties—in keeping, of course, with your energies." Here the monsignor managed a quick, chilly smile. He opened a slim black leather portfolio and withdrew a sheet of paper. He studied it a moment. "A chaplaincy," he said. "St. Joseph's. It's an orphanage. In Zabrze, near Katowice. Do you know it?"

"An orphanage?" Father Jerzy's face blanched.

"Do you know it, Father?" the monsignor repeated.

With difficulty, Father Jerzy found his voice again. "No," he said. "An orphanage?"

"The bishop believes you can be of very good use there, and the orphanage of good use to you. He asked me to make that point."

Father Jerzy sank back slowly in his chair, his face pale and motionless. As though rising unbidden from the recess where connections of cause and effect reside, he saw, too late, the trap into which he had blundered: old Father Marek. "Jabłoński," he muttered. He was speaking, really, to himself.

"Pardon?"

"Nothing."

"The decision was the bishop's, as I said," the monsignor answered evenly as he closed the leather portfolio.

"Why?"

"I believe I stated that as well," the monsignor said. "I should think that sufficient, but were I to hazard speculation it would be that the bishop is thinking of the good of the church and your future in it."

"I see," said Father Jerzy. "When . . . ?"

"He suggests you report tomorrow." The monsignor looked again at his watch. "Although it's possibly too late to make bus connections today, since the morning is nearly gone."

"Yes." Father Jerzy spoke in a barely audible voice. "I have to pack."

"Of course. But priests always travel light. You may want to have your books or other things sent after you."

"Of course."

"After your arrival, you're entitled to a month's leave. If you wish it, that is. The bishop suggests you might want to consider a retreat for your leave time. It's sometimes helpful for young priests after their first assignment. He mentioned Jasna Góra."

"Yes, of course."

"Good, they'll be expecting you at St. Joseph's tomorrow night," the monsignor said. He handed the neatly typed sheet of paper to Father Jerzy and stood up. "I have your bus tickets here." He placed them on the desk, flicking their edges audibly, like a card player. He offered his hand to shake. "Safe journey, Father," he said.

Father Tadeusz had gone out for a long walk that morning and so had no idea of the conversation that had transpired in the rectory office in his absence. In fact, Father Tadeusz had been given no indication by the bishop as to what action, if any, would be taken by the diocese. But then, last night, came the telephone call from the bishop's auxiliary, Monsignor Orłowski. It was a brief courtesy.

Father Tadeusz sat down on an old stump. In truth, he wanted no action. He wanted only the forest's stillness, the flicker of birds in the brush, the intricate pattern of the leaves matted beneath the trees. He raked at the leaves with a dry stick and dislodged an acorn, its shell split by damp and the pale shoot of its tap root probing its way into the earth. Gently he positioned the acorn in the loam and covered it again with leaves.

The bishop had been an astringent presence. He had listened, head tilted slightly, slender fingers tapping at his temple. The light from the high windows near which they sat accentuated the stately bones of his face. Teacups rattled discreetly on a low table between them as the bishop poured. His manner, Father Tadeusz thought, was that of a judge hearing a squalid case. When Father Tadeusz approached the accusations concerning the late Father Marek, the rhythmic tapping of the fingers paused, then halted altogether. He then asked a few questions, mostly regarding the reaction of the parishioners to Father Jerzy's activities. He did indicate that the church had already been "alerted" to the general situation, though by what means he did not make clear. This familiarity surprised Father Tadeusz. The church seemed to possess an intelligence-gathering system as efficient at the state with which it had coexisted. A necessity, he supposed; the church was a government of sorts itself. The bishop's hands folded tidily in his lap, as though they were instruments of decision themselves, employed and put away. He thanked Father Tadeusz for his lengthy drive, for his work in Jadowia, and inquired after his health and the local climate.

"The same as here, I suppose," Father Tadeusz said. "Damp."

"Yes," said the bishop. "I suppose." He smiled and rose from his wing chair. "It seems to agree with you, though. You look well."

Father Tadeusz departed feeling something less than well. He would have appreciated some assurance from the bishop that he had done the right thing by coming, but he stopped short of a question that pleaded so abjectly. Clearly, from the point of view of the church, he had. His own feelings were decidedly more mixed. Father Jerzy was wrong, about that he was sure. What troubled Father Tadeusz was his own inability—perhaps it was unwillingness—to deflect the young priest from a crusade of revenge and self-glorification. Father Jerzy angered him, but at least a part of the anger, Father Tadeusz suspected, was envy for Father Jerzy's energy, his engagement. The envy shamed him. He had tried to wash his hands of the matter and now felt stained by the effort.

He did not see Father Jerzy that evening, but when he finished mass early the next morning and opened the door to the office of the rectory, he was taken aback by the sight of a pile of baggage—a suitcase and two nylon duffel bags—stacked in the vestibule. Father Jerzy waited by the desk as though he had been watching as Father Tadeusz approached along the walkway from the church.

"Good morning, Father Tadeusz," he said. "You had a nice walk yesterday?"

"Yes, thank you." He glanced at the baggage. "A visitor?"

"No. It's mine. I'm leaving. I've been reassigned, as I expect you know."

"Now?"

"Yes. 'Reassigned' is what they called it. 'Removed' would be more accurate. To survive here I should have followed your example and spent more time observing squirrels in the woods."

Father Tadeusz felt the sinking sensation of failure as anger welled in his throat. He had prayed about this only minutes before, asking God for a sense of charity and patience toward Father Jerzy. The prayer had brought him no closer, yet, to deliverance.

"Where are you going?" Father Tadeusz asked, the only words he could muster immediately.

"An orphanage. I'll be a chaplain, guiding the spiritual development of teenaged boys. Maybe they'll let me instruct the soccer team so I can learn the art of losing gracefully." He buttoned his coat.

"I'm sure you'll do well," Father Tadeusz said.

"I won't ask what your part in this was," Father Jerzy said. Father Tadeusz stated to speak, but the younger priest hurried on. "It doesn't matter. I just want you to remember something."

"Yes?"

"It was no joke what they did, Father. The Communists, I mean."

"No."

"Vigilance, Father. Vigilance, or they will be back. That's what I was about here." He shook his head. "Your liberal values are like chicken soup to them. You know that, don't you?"

Father Tadeusz stared at the floor. "We're priests, Father Jerzy. Not policemen and prosecutors."

"They'll take your willingness to forget, and they'll turn it to advantage. Some may think you have a generous heart. They think you have a soft head. To beat them, you have to be as hard as they are. You have to hunt them down, put them away. Anything else is *foolish weakness!*" The last words were shouted. Father Jerzy's face was crimson with anger. Father Tadeusz did not speak. In the silence that closed around them, Father Jerzy seemed, slowly, to deflate. Out the window, Father Tadeusz could see people passing on the street, a bustle. Easter approaching.

"My bus," Father Jerzy said quietly. He stepped around Father Tadeusz and lifted his bags. Father Tadeusz held the door for him. "Thank you," Jerzy said, and left without looking back.

*   *   *

Father Tadeusz threaded his way through the frosted crosses and ranked marble headstones, as crowded and close as the buildings in an old city, the faded plastic flowers amid the graves as varied as clothes on a crowd in the street. The place was empty, though, raked by wind and the calls of crows in the trees. Not knowing where to begin, he tried to devise a system in order to be thorough. The dates on the stones stretched back far, decade upon decade, family upon family, the plots of the once-prominent marked by heavy iron fencing around massive stones, old graves from a day of manor houses and tenant farmers, lord and peasant called alike to this final uneven distribution of earthly holdings. He walked first up the central path to the end where a brick wall, cracked by settling earth, bordered the cemetery from the soggy field beyond. He turned right, walked to a corner, and then began his search, back to front, path by path, rank by rank. The paths did not, in fact, run straight, but swayed in and out, like the lines of a fingerprint. Now and then he found himself on a path he had traversed in the opposite direction only minutes before, surprised by the sight of his own footprints approaching in the frosted mud, or by the reappearance of a name cut so emphatically in stone that it had left a shadow in his mind.

He happened across the grave of Tomek Powierza. A spray of weather-bleached plastic flowers rocked in the wind next to a pot of shriveled gladioli. He had almost forgotten having been here months before, praying at this spot, the stonescape blocked by the grieving faces around him. He crossed the broader central path and circled toward the opposite side. He was about halfway to the bordering wall when he found it, a gray granite stone with a simple black metal plate attached. "Danuta M. Czarnek, August 1, 1891—March 7, 1959." Atop the stone's rounded crown was a pebble, plucked from the ground and deliberately balanced there. Father Tadeusz quickly scanned the cemetery to reconfirm his impression: no other stone bore such an adornment.

He had not expected a husband's grave here, having found no funeral record in the registry books. But a smaller stone, pale and mineral-stained, tilted forward amid dried grass. When he crouched to inspect it, he read the words "Czarnek, Infant Daughter Malgorzata, August 7—September 15, 1938. Blessed are the children."

Father Tadeusz left the cemetery then and walked briskly back to the rectory, went straight to the basement storeroom and located the funeral records, opened the registry for 1938, and leafed through September's pages. He found the entry dated September 17. "Infant daughter, Malgorzata, aged six weeks." Under the next of kin were listed the parents, Danuta M. and Czesław Czarnek.

That's why he had not seen a Czarnek child born when he had searched through the baptismal records. The child must have been given its baptism and its last rites at the same time. Probably the baby had been born prematurely, or had been ill from birth, and only as the child's death was imminent—her condition must have been fragile from the first—did the parents tend to the religious observances. Now, also, he had the father's name, Czesław. The records, then, contained two gaps, two unanswered questions: What had happened to Czesław Czarnek, the husband and father? And why was there no record of the christening of Krzysztof Czarnek, listed as the son and sole surviving relative on Danuta's funeral entry?

He searched again through the christening records, but they revealed nothing more. Clearly, the boy could have been born somewhere else; perhaps his parents moved here after his birth. Or perhaps not.

He sat staring at the pages. All these were lives, these names and dates, parents who cradled their infants with love and wonder and the best of human intentions and hopes. And these children and parents and priests, with their thumbs in baptismal oils, had gone out of the church to a world waiting beyond that would expose them to further wonder and birdsong and sunlight, to cold and sickness and fright, to smoke and bombs, blood and death. To a thousand variations between bravery and cowardice or good and evil, the struggle for footing in a world that pulled ceaselessly toward its polar extremes. The strokes of pen and ink could tell nothing of the lives they were meant to represent. Somewhere in Tarnów his own christening was recorded, the names of his parents duly entered, his own origin marked—like a stake driven in the ground. Run a string from that stake to the stone awaiting him, and what would it show?

He shut the book softly, fastened the storeroom door, left the rectory, and set out for the distillery.

He had to ask directions for the last part of the walk, but, as he neared the grimy building with its old blackened smokestack, he realized he had seen it before, although from the forest's edge. A car, an old Skoda, was parked next to it. Two bicycles leaned against the wall next to the front door. The door itself was painted a bright, incongruous blue. The door was ajar, and, after a moment's hesitation, Father Tadeusz pushed it open and went in.

At first he saw no one, although he heard voices. The room itself was wide but only a few paces deep. A short stairway to his left led up to what appeared to be an office; a desk and telephone were visible though the open door. The ceiling in the outer room was two stories high, rust-stained and crossed by pipes draped with dead cobwebs that swayed in the air like tropical moss. An odor, vaguely medicinal yet organic and earthy, suffused the air, accompanied by sounds of fluids and the sputtering hiss of leaking pressure. In a glass case to his left, clear liquid bubbled from a small metal spout. Voices rose again from the veil of background sound, followed by the clank of quick footsteps on iron stairs, and Czarnek emerged from around the corner, a heavy screwdriver in one hand. He hurried past Father Tadeusz with no more than a glance and took the stairs to the office two at a time. Father Tadeusz followed him. When he entered the office, Czarnek was standing on a chair to reach an electrical junction box on the wall. He jammed the screwdriver into the box, crowded with old porcelain fuses, and a shower of sparks arched over his head and shoulders. Father Tadeusz stepped backward involuntarily.

"Whore!" Czarnek swore, climbed down off the chair, and dodged around Father Tadeusz without even a nod acknowledging his presence. Father Tadeusz was uncertain what to do. He ventured onto the stairway landing and again heard voices over the noise of machinery. One voice, he could hear now, was Czarnek's, barking orders. Answers, perhaps argument, stammered in response. He decided to wait where he was.

It was several minutes before Czarnek returned. He was still carrying the screwdriver. This time he nodded and motioned for Father Tadeusz to enter the office ahead of him. Czarnek tossed the screwdriver onto the papers on his desk.

"The wiring," he said. "From the time of the czars." He remained motionless behind the desk and made no indication that Father Tadeusz should take the chair across from him. "You have business with me?" he asked finally.

"Business? No, not business. I wanted to speak with you."

"Yes?"

Father Tadeusz indicated the chair. "May I?"

"I am busy at the moment."

"Yes, I can see. Perhaps I should come back."

"You're here. What is it you want to speak about?"

Father Tadeusz remained standing, watching Czarnek's suspicious dark eyes. Clearly he had not chosen a good time. "Really," he said, "I could come back."

Czarnek's severe expression eased. He glanced toward the door, then looked back to Father Tadeusz, who stood with his cap in his hand, his fringe of white hair ruffled like mussed feathers.

"We've been having some mechanical problems today," he said. "The electricity." The tang of electrical smoke was still in the air. "We're almost finished for the day. If you give me a few minutes, my workers will be leaving."

"I'll wait."

Czarnek grunted and left the room. Father Tadeusz sat down and waited. He tried to place the odor in the air, and then realized it was like the smell of a sliced loaf of fresh bread. Yeast, of course; this was a distillery. The floor seemed sticky, even here, in the office. There were battered metal closets and wooden file cabinets. It was cluttered and dusty. Yellowed papers and forms lay askew in a wire basket on the desk. Various tools, pipe wrenches, mallets, boxes of grimy bolts and pipe joints, plastic containers, dark stoppered bottles with stained labels were scattered on shelves behind the desk, along with thick books that looked like reference manuals. A calender hung on the wall and a clump of keys as large as a grapefruit dangled from a nail. There was no other adornment, no touch of personal occupancy except for the coffee cup on Czarnek's desk. He stared at the calendar again and saw that the date of March 7 was circled faintly in pencil.

He heard voices in the large room behind him, a fit of coughing and laughter, then the door's bang and the rattle of bicycles. The footsteps on the stairs behind him were Czarnek's. Like a quick preceding shadow, the dog came before him and settled, with a silence that seemed feline, on the floor beside the desk. The dog faced Father Tadeusz, its head up, its eyes almost studious. The light from the window highlighted its glistening coat. Czarnek circled the dog and sat down at the desk.

"Remarkable dog," Father Tadeusz said quietly.

"Yes?"

"Yes. You don't see many dogs like that around here, do you?"

"I don't know."

"Most people here have little dogs. Mixed breeds. Short-legged little things. Farmers here don't spend money on dogs. They keep them chained. Not many are real companions."

"Farmers don't give much thought to animals. An animal is an animal to a farmer." Czarnek stared at him. "Did you come here to talk about dogs?"

"No, I just like dogs. No, I came to find out something. I thought maybe you could help me, if you don't mind."

Czarnek's chair retreated a few inches, its rollers giving a squeak. He folded his arms across his chest.

"I'm just the manager here," he said. "If you want to see records, you'll have to inquire at the town offices. There is nothing here."

"Oh, no," said Father Tadeusz. "I'm not interested in that. I wanted to know something about the town."

"Why come to me?" Czarnek said. "If you want to know about the town, go ask the people who run it. I have nothing to tell you."

"I thought you might know things others don't."

"I told you, I'm an employee here," Czarnek said. He glanced quickly about the room as though he might detect someone listening in the shadows. "I make sure the place runs. If you want to know any more you should go to town."

"Excuse me, Mr. Czarnek," Father Tadeusz said. "I'm afraid I've misspoken myself. I don't care about the distillery. The town's business doesn't concern me. I'm interested in other things. Older things, things other people have forgotten." Czarnek watched him warily.

"What other things?"

"As I say, things people have forgotten. Or maybe I should say things that people don't want to remember. The cemetery, for example. The place I met you."

"What of it?"

"It interests me. Most people don't seem to know of its existence."

"As you say, they forget."

"But you don't."

Father Tadeusz sensed he was heading in the wrong direction. He did not mean this to be an inquisition. Czarnek, he knew, would not be a man to reveal himself easily. It was Father Tadeusz who would have to surrender something, to offer some exchange.

"Everyone here forgets too easily," he said. "All of us." He tapped his chest to include himself. "Now everyone is trying to remember the last forty years. Or the last twenty. But there's more. Isn't there?" He drew in a breath, hoping to see Czarnek do the same, or reveal some sign of relaxing. "Of course, I am not from here," Father Tadeusz went on. "I grew up in a city. Kraków. So this place is, well, strange to me, in its particularities. But then these—what would you say?—these phenomena are more or less the same everywhere. Did you come here from the city, when you were a child?"

"No, I did not."

"You were born in Jadowia?" There was a touch of skepticism in Father Tadeusz's voice.

"Yes."

"Then you remember."

"Remember what?"

"How things were. Who lived here. The people who occupied the houses. Before the war, I mean."

"That was long ago."

"Yes, you would have been a child. Perhaps too young to remember very much. You were born when? What year?"

"1933."

"Do you know, I think I saw your mother's grave. In the church cemetery. Danuta? Was that her name?"

"Why would you look for my mother's grave?" Czarnek said. "Why is that any interest of yours?"

"I was curious, that's all. I wonder, can you remember Małgorzata?"

"Who?"

"Your sister?"

Czarnek's face betrayed a hairline crack of uncertainty. "No," he said. "She died before I came."

"Before you were born, you mean?"

Czarnek hesitated. "Yes."

"But she died in 1938. I believe she lived only six weeks. You were very young. I suppose it's not something a person wants to remember."

"Why are you asking me these things?"

Father Tadeusz leaned forward, his elbows on his knees, fondling his cap in his hand. He wanted to explain how he once had an ambition to be a scholar of religious thought, pursuing linkages of time through clues embedded in obscure manuscripts, a way of illuminating belief by tracing the route used to arrive at it. He wanted to allay Czarnek's apprehensions.

"When I was young," he said, "I wanted to study religious history, to read and write about it, you see, as a scholar. I didn't do that. I became a parish priest. Perhaps I was unequipped. It's like a discipline, I suppose." He looked at Czarnek for a glimmer of sympathy, but saw suspicion and dwindling patience. "So," he went on, "I didn't do that. And I found myself here. And here I found there is another kind of history."

"I don't know what you're talking about, Father," Czarnek said. "And I don't know why you're talking about it to me. You want a scholar, you're in the wrong place. You're in the wrong town."

"Well, yes, I suppose." Father Tadeusz let himself be chastised. "But let me ask you about the cemetery. There is nothing about it in the town offices. I asked. No records exist from before the war. Did you know that? I believe there was another one once. That is, I found it on an old map, in the archives in Siedlce. It would have stood near where the clinic is now. I suppose it still does. The graves, I mean. The stones are gone."

Czarnek studied him for some time without speaking, his arms still folded tightly across his chest.

"Do you know why?"

Czarnek didn't answer.

"Or where?"

"Houses," Czarnek said. "Barns. Sheds for animals."

Another silence lengthened between them. Father Tadeusz looked at his hands.

"And the old one," he said. "The old cemetery?"

"What about it?"

"The stones remained? Undisturbed?"

Silence again.

"Mostly," Czarnek said. "It was forgotten. Or inconvenient." He paused. "Lately some have been taken. A few."

"They have? Why?"

"I don't know."

Father Tadeusz was puzzled. "Do you mean that the stones have been removed?"

"Some, yes."

"There's no explanation?"

Czarnek shrugged.

"Do you think someone is looking for something?"

"People will believe anything," Czarnek said. "And they find some things easier to believe than others, even fantastic things."

Yes, it was true, Father Tadeusz thought; the rumors of gold. The place was awash in the fantastic, the mythical. It was a form of entertainment. A conspiracy of ghosts was easier to accept than mud beneath the feet. He wanted, now, to pose his question to Czarnek, but, though he could frame it in his head, he could not bring it to his lips. Besides, he thought, didn't he know the answer? He tried another way.

"I think it's good," Father Tadeusz said, "that you keep watch over it, take care of it."

"How do you know what I do?"

Father Tadeusz sat blinking. He didn't, was the answer. He had seen Czarnek there once, and he seemed to be doing the work of a caretaker.

"I had an idea after I saw you. I thought, perhaps, since you seemed to be caring for it, something could be done to help you. Perhaps a restoration. A renovation."

"Stay away from it," Czarnek said quietly.

"Excuse me?"

"Leave it alone. Leave it in peace."

"I wasn't thinking of disturbing it," Father Tadeusz said, a little sharply. "I was suggesting a way to help you take care of—" He hesitated, then went on, as if helplessly, "Of your people."

"So now," Czarnek's response was quick, low as a cat's purr, "now we know what you've come looking for."

The tension in Czarnek's arms and shoulders—the cotton of his coveralls was pulled tight as skin—suggested not so much a physical danger as an internal pressure about to break. The bursting might leave furniture wrecked, Father Tadeusz thought, but the damage would be to Czarnek himself. *I should not have said these things,* Father Tadeusz thought.

Czarnek's arms uncoiled from his chest in slow motion. He stood, slowly. "Go ahead. Say it straight out. Ask me your question."

Czarnek was a stocky man, not tall, and yet he seemed, to Father Tadeusz, to rise above the desk hugely, like a cloud above a field. "Ask me your question," he demanded.

"No," Father Tadeusz said. "I'm sorry. I'm sorry I came and disturbed you. It's not what I meant." He had done enough. His coming had been a mistake, he could see that now. He rose and edged toward the door.

"Did you know, Father, that I prayed to your saints when I was a boy?" Czarnek said. "Do you think I prayed enough?"

"Excuse me?"

"Do you think they heard me, your saints?"

"I'm sure they did," Father Tadeusz said. He kept backing away, buttoning his coat. "They don't make demands of children."

"Oh, of course not." Czarnek laughed, a drawn-out, throaty growl. "Do you know who taught me? My Polish mother. Yes.

346

There it is. That doesn't surprise you, does it?" Czarnek's face loomed closer. Father Tadeusz felt the door against his back. "My *Polish* mother. She taught me how to talk to the saints. She made me learn. She said if we talked to them the saints would protect us. Protect *me*. Do you think she was right? Do you think I've been protected?"

Father Tadeusz smelled the sour sweat from Czarnek's clothes, saw the razor's line from the last time he shaved.

"I think we're all protected," Father Tadeusz said.

"Oh, yes. I'm sure my sisters, my little brother, would have lived if they talked to your saints. Do you think if they talked to the saints, they would be here to remember?"

"What happened, Czarnek? What happened to your family?"

"Shot," Czarnek said quietly. "If they talked to your Mary and Jesus, they would not have been dragged from their beds, kept half starved. They would go to church, kneel down, and see nothing. They would be like all the ones who kept solemn faces but could see all the reasons why these things were happening."

"Surely it was not like that."

"You wouldn't say so now, now that it's all over. Now there is no evidence you can see. No memory. You can be benevolent now. Everyone can say, oh, yes, it was a bad thing the Hitlerites did. A horror, oh yes, they were terrible times, and we *all* suffered, *Poland* suffered, the Christ of nations. They remember their poor grandmother foraging for food. Her feet wrapped in rags, that's what they say. They don't remember their uncle selling bread at five times the price to the Jews starving behind the wire, or taking their children to work in the fields and then claiming they risked their lives to protect the little Yid children."

"People *did* risk their lives to protect Jews."

"People sold them, too, for a chunk of bacon or a drink of schnapps with the *ober-führer*."

"It was war, Czarnek. Do you think people wanted that?"

"Want it?" Czarnek laughed. "Who could even dream it? But I think it was like a big storm that blows down the tree you wanted to uproot. The tree falls on your barn, and you don't like that, but then the storm is over, the barn is repaired, and the tree is gone. You do not miss the tree. You are happy to be rid of it. Let me ask you, do you see any sign that they are missed? Do you see even a sign that they were once here? Any indication of who built the houses along the streets? Do you hear any of the old ones, even, remember the *challah* from Klemsztejn, the baker? The quiet on the streets on Friday afternoons? Do you hear them remember that there was once a man in the village who knew how to repair shoes? Or sew a coat? Do you see any marker for them? Any stone left where their dead rest? Do you see any notches still in the doorways of the houses where they lived, where they put their mezuzahs?"

Czarnek's face had grown pale, the lines on his forehead etched as clearly as pen strokes on parchment.

"It was you, then?" Father Tadeusz asked gently. "I mean the doorways in town. It was for the mezuzahs?"

"Yes."

"And the foundation stones?" The priest's voice was gentle, without accusation. "For the same reason?"

"For the cemetery. To replace the ones taken. That's all."

"I see." And Father Tadeusz, indeed, thought he could see it: this powerful man, moving like a shadow through the darkness of the town, a crowbar in his fist.

"Tell me about your family, Czarnek. Tell me what happened to you."

"You don't need to know more."

"Perhaps it would help to tell it to someone, to talk."

"You would like to think so, wouldn't you? Perhaps you want to hear a confession. We could talk together to the saints. My Polish mother wanted me to talk to them with her, but I stopped. She kept them for herself."

"But she cared for you. She protected you, didn't she?"

"Yes. She was a poor woman. A widow. We were poor together. A little house, two cows. I hid with her. She taught me how to keep quiet. She taught me about the Elders of Zion. She taught me how the blood of Gentile children was mixed into the matzoh. So many things I didn't know! She told me it wasn't my fault the Jews killed Jesus. She told me no one could help how they were born, but *I must never let anyone know!* She told me that if we weren't careful, they could take me away. Even years later, it could happen. She taught me it could be very dangerous to ever stop hiding. I went through school and never showed my circumcised penis. She was right. All I had to do was listen. Listen to them talk in school, listen to the teachers, listen to them explain how the dirty little Jews brought it on themselves. They stayed to themselves, they died by themselves. Their own fault, Father. Little bloodsuckers."

The room fell silent except for the distant hydraulic flow that seemed to reach them from an underground river.

"Did she teach you to believe this?"

"I told you, she taught me to keep my ears open," Czarnek said. "She was a good woman. She took care of me. I was a gift to her, something good that came in the night. She held me when I was sick. She fed me, clothed me. She read to me. She cut my hair." His voice faltered. "She taught me to protect myself."

The silence settled again. Father Tadeusz felt a tightening in his throat.

"No one knows this?"

Czarnek took some time to answer. "Who knows? Someone, probably. Someone watches, don't they? They do that, they always have. They watch."

"Who?"

"It doesn't matter who. I don't care. They're coming for me anyway, so I don't care."

"Who is coming?"

"Never mind. It doesn't matter. They're too late."

"No, Czarnek. No one is coming for you."

"You don't know."

"I know that."

"You know nothing." Czarnek splayed his hand on the open door. "I want you to leave now," he said. "I have things to do."

"Just a moment, please," Father Tadeusz said. "Just one moment."

"What is it?"

"About the cemetery. Isn't there something—"

"What cemetery?"

"The old one. I had an idea . . ."

"No!" Czarnek thundered. "No, there is nothing. Stay away from it. Do you hear? Don't you have enough to occupy yourself? Just stay away!"

"Czarnek, please." Father Tadeusz inched backward on the landing. "Please."

"Get out," Czarnek said. "You got what you wanted. Now go." Czarnek strode down the stairs first, then spun around, and Father Tadeusz saw that Czarnek's eyes seemed to have shifted to another place, to a cold remoteness from which he could hold his solitary defense and stand off any further approach. Slowly, heavily, Father Tadeusz descended the stairs and crossed the room to the outer door. Czarnek opened it. Father Tadeusz stepped out.

"I would like to talk to you again," he said.

"No," Czarnek said. "I will be busy. Don't come back."

The door closed and the bolt behind it slammed home.

The horse and wagon toiled along the margin of the field. A fog hung low over the land. The trees on the far side, toward town, stood shrouded and distant. The countryside was silent. Except for the tableau of horse, wagon, and driver, nothing else stirred, only the mists sliding imperceptibly on the imperceptible motion of the air.

The wagon wheels parted the mud in furrows. Leszek's grandfather kept the horse plodding steadily, talking to her in a low mumble of syllables as steady and familiar as the creaking of harness leather. He knew she wanted to rest. "Hup, hup, hup." The big hooves found firmer ground and the wagon jerked free of the worst of the mud. "Hup, hup, good girl." The reins fell in a gentle encouraging slap across the wide chestnut rump.

At a faint break in the line of trees, the old man steered the horse left and urged her some twenty yards into the forest, until the interval between the trees narrowed and the forest thickened with younger saplings.

He went to the rear of the wagon and threw back a dirty gray tarpaulin, uncovering his tools: a one-man crosscut saw, a mallet, a hammer, a bag of large nails, a wooden-handled and much-honed knife, a coil of twine, an ax, a wedge, and a shovel. The tools lay bundled in a piece of sacking, which he gathered up with both fists and lifted over the wagon's side. With the tools shifting and rattling together he walked into the forest and continued along familiar landmarks through the trees. His footsteps in the leaves rustled damply.

He reached the place where the clearing in the trees formed a chamber, over-arched by the limbs of great ashes, the trunks of even gray bark rising like columns, and dropped his load of tools.

He retraced his steps to the wagon, removed Star's bundle of hay from beneath the wagon seat and tossed it on the ground in front of her. From the rear of the wagon he took out four notched posts of rough-cut pine, each six feet long, carried them back to the clearing, then tugged four longer poles from a concealing pile of cleared brush. These, too, had been notched, two neat cuts in each post. He dragged them to the top of the clearing, and with his foot raked away a covering of sticks and leaves to expose four prepared holes. Into the holes he stood the four poles. He retrieved his shovel, hauled gravel from a small pile cached nearby, and filled the postholes until each upright was firm and straight.

He fitted two diagonal braces, notch to notch, and drove two nails at each end. He halted after the first nails, peering into the distance and listening, as though he expected approaching footsteps to answer the hammer's echo. After a while he rested, sitting on the canvas where his tools lay, his back braced against the trunk of the ash. His shoulders ached. So, in fact, did his right hand, from arthritis. There was still much to do. He had left more work than he anticipated, but he would finish—this day.

This was the day.

Even the weather was the same.

He stood up, stretching his back, and went back to his task.

The prepared beams were fitted, but a few pieces still needed to be cut. He had located the wood he needed a short distance away in the forest. He felled the small trees with the crosscut, dragged them back, notched them with the hatchet and knife, then fitted them in place and nailed them fast.

He started on the roof, pruning the small rough pieces to length, using only ash limbs that he had stripped of bark. One by one he set the cut pieces in position and tied them with twine, each piece lashed to the other by the same skein, wrapped and rewrapped in figure eights, so that, as finished, the pieces seemed to have been stitched into place with heavy thread.

The structure now had a shape, but much more work remained. He began the back wall, employing straight green maple limbs for the vertical pieces. With the bark peeled away, the wood was the color of pale gold. It would weather eventually, but under the shelter it would hold its lightness a long time. Gradually, the light and shadows in the clearing shifted, but the thick overcast and the low fog cloaked the forest behind him. He did not stop and rest, but ate as he worked, chewing chunks of bread and pieces of kielbasa from his jacket pocket. The two sides of the structure were now in place, formed of narrow pine logs, nailed vertically to allow light, slanting sunlight, he imagined, to fall across the interior.

He arranged short pine logs to border the approach, two on each side. He backed away to look at it straight on—the open front, the wide, sloping roof, the pale backdrop, the barred sides.

He went then to the old depression, where, weeks before, his work had begun, and shoved the damp leaves away from the first of the stones. He had forgotten how heavy they were, how dense, as though they had accumulated a mass that transcended dimension and volume. The rough surface was damp and hard to grip. He struggled to the lip of the depression, gained his balance, and teetered awkwardly under the weight. At his finished structure, his knees popped with the strain as he let the stone slip through his fingers. With his shovel, he measured the base of the stone and prepared its place, then he settled the stone so that it stood firmly.

He returned to the depression and hauled out the second largest stone and, in the same way, set it in place. Then the three others, these smaller, the first one centered in front of the first two, and the two remaining flanking the third—a symmetrical arrangement, the three in front, the two larger behind.

On his hands and knees, he brushed away the loose earth and leaves, until the surface around the stones was uniform and even. With the shovel he smoothed the pathway.

He gathered up his tools then and carried them back to the wagon.

It was finished, but he wanted to see it whole now, its approach, its place in relation to what happened, in relation to his memory. He walked wearily now, and, in his fatigue, he could see it again like a dream. In the waning daylight, the forest closed in, ushering in his vision of that moonless night. It was a blend of what he could not see in the dark of midnight and what he knew was there, in his old guerrilla fighter's knowledge of the terrain. Just as they all knew, that night, the way behind them, through the passages in a forest that seemed to have no passage, no path. They had seen their way to the rear as though it had been lit as it was now, somewhere between night and a partisan fighter's subdued sense of day.

The old ridges of their holes were still there, eroded by fifty years of weather.

He stood looking out from the margin of the ash grove, through the pines—huge, thick old trees now, miraculously spared the logger's saw—and the aspect was still unchanged. A field, muddy, stubbled, furrowed, seeming to float under the slow-moving mist, the light drawn into the surrounding distant trees. Before his eyes, the light seemed replaced by dark, and the stillness to fill with the clank and clatter of men stumbling in the night. He wanted to feel this once more, to make another mark in his memory. He walked back to the clearing. They would have dragged them here; fetched the peasant with the wagon, the old horse, the rope. Rope around soiled ankles, children and parents, limbs lashed together.

Ahead of him it stood, his imagined plan taken form. Along the perspective through the trees, a natural path, the eye was led up this clear approach toward the wooden structure, its ashwood roof seeming to cast off its own glow, the line of its exaggerated eaves extending toward the ground, like draped wings or a cloak, the peak at the center suggesting also the attitude of hands clasped—a plea or prayer?—an accidental grace note of construction.

Beneath the shelter of the roof, the five stones waited, darkly gathered, two behind, three in front. The writing on each faced outward, though the Hebrew carved upon them and chipped by age and frost might have named old men as easily as children. But the shape and placement spoke enough to him and represented what he knew and could not forget. Faces in the field, pale faces, white palms, lifted, lifted in the light, his light; hands raised not to ward off the onslaught or to surrender, but hands lifted, palm out to say, *Here we are. We have come as you said. Give us the sign. We are ready.*

Powierza had hauled the crate home from the quarry in his wagon and didn't open it until he was in the barn. The lid came off easily with a crowbar. The contents were packed in layers, carefully labeled in Polish and clearly identified by factory of origin: Państwowe Zakłady Metalowe Radom, Polska. Grenade launchers, individual, shoulder-held, 60mm. There were twenty-four in the crate, laid in alternating order, stock to barrel. He selected one and held it to his shoulder. It felt lighter than it looked, its stock and grips made of molded army-green plastic.

Powierza, having managed to avoid military service in his youth, had little idea of weapons. In any case, the technology of war, he knew, had advanced since the days when he might have been a conscript. Nor was he conversant with the state regulations regarding the export of munitions. But he did know that laws had been passed—new laws—that forbade the export of weapons to certain countries, and that the "countries of the East" were among those proscribed from receiving them. This euphemism was not meant to indicate China, but anything on Poland's eastern border. It was a fair guess that these weapons, handed off from truck to truck in the dead of night, fell almost certainly in the category of contraband. He did not have to know the details of the law to operate on that presumption.

He was also reasonably sure that no one had detected the missing crate. The men at the quarry had been rattled by Leszek's appearance near their transfer point; they were cold, wet and in a hurry. They saw nothing.

Alone in his barn, Powierza contemplated his next move. It did not take him long.

He walked to the Farmers' Co-op. Jabłoński's secretary happened to be in the hallway as he entered the door, and she advanced toward him, a sheaf of papers in one hand and an empty coffee pot in the other, her elbows out as though to repel any sudden charge around her. Powierza's gait did not slacken. "The chairman in?" he asked, and brushed past her. For all her bulk, she had the resistance of a down pillow. Powierza pushed open the door. Jabłoński, behind the desk, was clutching the telephone to his ear. As Powierza loomed over his desk, Jabłoński said, "I'll call you back," and hung up.

"Mr. Chairman," Powierza said.

"Powierza," Jabłoński said. He nodded at the secretary, still standing in the doorway. She went out and closed the door. "What can I do for you?"

"It's what I can do for you," Powierza said.

"All right. I'm happy to have someone do for me. A nice change, I'd say. What is it you have in mind?"

"I'm going to let you stay out of jail."

"Really?"

"Maybe," Powierza said. "Unless you'd rather."

A slight smile came to Jabłoński's lips, but his expression betrayed no agitation. "Do you think that's your option? Or have the local crusaders made you an officer of the court?" He chuckled and shook his head in amusement. "Do I hear the charges now, or will they be revealed at the trial?" He laughed again. "Perhaps the old days come back again, with their efficient judiciary. They were always the best, weren't they? Tried and true."

Powierza had the feeling Jabłoński was talking to himself—or at least not to him.

"I have something to show you, Mr. Chairman," Powierza said. "Come." With his hand cupped, he beckoned to Jabłoński as though he were coaxing a puppy. For a moment Jabłoński didn't stir. Then the huge slab of a hand reached across the desk toward him. He shied back.

"Come," Powierza said. "Get your coat. We can take your car." He started to circle the desk, but Jabłoński, sensing that refusal was not a possibility, rose to follow Powierza out the door.

It took Jabłoński a while to get his car started. Powierza waited by the passenger door while Jabłoński poked with his stick inside the rear engine compartment. When the car sputtered to life, Powierza squeezed into the passenger seat. The springs sagged heavily under his weight. Behind the wheel, Jabłoński glanced at him uneasily.

Powierza filled the space like stacked bags of feed grain, his head jammed between his shoulders so he could see out.

"I hope we're not going far," Jabłoński said.

"My house," Powierza said. "Turn left."

Pressed so closely by this bunched physical presence, Jabłoński felt constrained to silence. His wits were accustomed to performance across the stage set of his desk; here he felt a suffocating pressure, as though the tin seams of the little car might split, ejecting him onto the road. He held his tongue. Powierza directed him through the gate of his house, along a muddy driveway and into the barnyard, where chickens scattered. Jabłoński was struck by the smells: manure, wet feathers, chicken shit—a huge animal toilet. He had always hated farms.

Powierza squeezed himself out of the car. "This way." He opened the barn door and held it for Jabłoński.

The open crate rested on a bed of straw, a half-dozen of the grenade launchers propped against its side. A bare light swung from cord above them. A pitchfork leaned on a post nearby, its worn tines gleaming in the light.

"Your men missed something last night, Mr. Chairman."

Jabłoński was seized by a fit of coughing. Powierza, slouched against a post, his hands in his jacket pockets, waited for Jabłoński to speak. Finally the chairman managed one word: "Yes."

"Yes, what?" Powierza said.

"You're right, they left something behind. Evidently." Jabłoński scanned the dark corners of the barn. Powierza turned a grain bucket bottom up, and motioned for Jabłoński to sit down.

"I gather you were present?" Jabłoński said. "I understand there was some, uh, interruption. I can attribute this to you, I suppose. And perhaps Farby. You're in touch with him, no doubt."

"Perhaps."

"Yes, well. It is not what it seems, Staszek."

"I'm Staszek now?"

"Mr. Powierza, if you wish. No, it's not what it seems."

"What is it?"

"As I say, not what it seems. But I'll confine myself to reality."

"This should be good," Powierza said.

"Reality, you see, has its own complications. Reality forces difficult strategies."

"Don't talk that gobbledygook to me."

"Look. There is a business enterprise at stake. People's livelihoods. Jobs. Certain activities have to be undertaken to ensure survival. Certain things we'd prefer not to do, but which become necessary under the strained circumstances of the national economy, or the callous incompetence of its architects."

"So, you're selling arms?"

"Oh, no. No, no. That's what it *seems,* perhaps. We are selling only transport. We were—let me make that past tense—we were selling, shall I say, arrangements. Yes. Arrangements. Transport. Only this. A certain expertise, you could say. Do you understand?"

"These are guns, Mr. Chairman. Rocket launchers, it says."

"Whatever. But they're not *my* guns, Mr. Powierza. Or our guns. To sell them, you have to own them. Or make them. We do neither. Now, if you have need of disposable diapers . . ."

"Do you unload your diapers in the middle of the night where nobody can see you? I think what you're doing is a crime. It's illegal."

"Only because there's a new definition of what's illegal."

"It's still law. You break it, you go to jail. It's pretty simple, Mr. Chairman. All I have to do, if I want to, is cart this crate off to Warsaw. I can carry it straight to the Parliament building if I want to. I wouldn't deliver it to Krupik. I think it's more than the local policeman can handle. It would be a big sensation."

The conditional phrases struck Jabłoński's mind like the slivers of daylight seeping through cracks in the barn wall. He pushed his glasses up the bridge of his nose. The tremor in his hand was slight, but he could not suppress it. He wanted a drink. "Do you, perhaps, have . . . ?"

Powierza anticipated him. A fresh bottle rested in the crotch of a roof brace above his head. Powierza smacked the bottom of the bottle, twisted the cap, and handed it to Jabłoński.

"Thank you," he said, and drank. He looked straight ahead at the crate and the weapons, then at Powierza, who leaned against the post.

"You have another idea?" Jabłoński asked.

"A bargain maybe."

"What do you want? Do you want money? I hope not, because there is none."

"No, I don't want money."

"Then what is it? What do you want?"

"Information first. And then some other things."

"In exchange for what?"

"In exchange for not using these to send you to prison."

He asked, first, for all Jabłoński knew about his son. Perhaps the story from Leszek's Russian was true, but he wanted to hear Jabłoński's version. To a point, the chairman was apologetic. As he spoke, Powierza simply watched him, with an expression on his face that was both pained and quizzical and yet that told Jabłoński he was understood, and, more than understood, believed. And why not? Tomek found customers for the distillery, Russians he encountered around the markets in Praga and Warsaw, spoke to over a few drinks, a few cigarettes. Arrangements were made, he brought them at the appointed time. But Jabłoński guessed that Tomek had been promised something directly by the customers—perhaps a sort of finder's fee. Or he demanded one, and they refused and . . . Who could say? They went off together after they finished at the distillery. Perhaps they simply robbed him. Yes, he had money, the hundred dollars paid to him by Farby. As Jabłoński had heard it from Krupik, there was no money on Tomek's body when he was found, so that was a definite possibility. These Russians—Georgians, actually, Farby had said—they were a brutal lot, Mafia gangsters, they didn't care. They could kill for a hundred dollars. Or an insult.

Powierza's face was a portrait of abysmal woe. Jabłoński never had children. He could hardly imagine the anguish of seeing one lost in one of the million ways a child could perish. He tried to feel for Powierza, but he could not see himself to blame, any more than he might had the boy died in some highway accident. It was tragic, yes; but it was, well, an accident. Powierza's powerful frame, in that moment, seemed almost to have withered beyond animation. Jabłoński rustled his foot in the straw, just to hear some sound in the barn's stillness. He drank and caressed the bottle in his hands.

That was it. There was nothing else to tell. Jabłoński wondered if he could be considered an accessory. But how could he be? He hadn't even been there.

It was some minutes before Powierza spoke. When he did, his voice was husky.

"You're leaving," he said. ·

"I beg your pardon," said Jabłoński.

"Leaving town. You're going to pack up and go. That's the second part of the bargain."

"What is this, some American cowboy movie? By whose authority?"

"By this authority," Powierza said, nudging the crate with the toe of his boot. One of the rocket launchers slid sideways and knocked the others to the straw, one after the other. "You have a choice, Mr. Chairman. You leave, leave behind the co-op, everything in it. Resign. Pack up your clothes, your belongings, your wife, and leave town. Go somewhere else. Away from here. Either that or I load these in a truck and drive to Warsaw and drop them on the carpet in front of the new attorney general."

"You wouldn't."

"You could try me, Jabłoński."

Jabłoński considered. He drank again from the bottle, lowered it, then drank again. Well, he thought, business was business, wasn't it? He was not without old friends in other places. He could always be useful. Required a certain ingratiation, but one thing he had was connections. Like men of the cloth that way; always a bed and a meal, so to speak.

Another cheering thought occurred to him.

"You're afraid of me, aren't you?" he said. "You're all afraid of me."

"That's the third thing, Mr. Chairman."

"What?"

"The files."

"What files?"

"The files. The bloody fucking files. You know what files."

Powierza's face had recovered its remarkable ripe-apple redness. Seeing it, Jabłoński was more at ease. Feelings of sympathy unnerved him. This was more familiar. He felt the vodka's brimstone inside him, the radiating warmth of renewal.

"You're protecting your son, is that it?" His thin smile of satisfaction returned. "Or his mother. Or yourself."

"All of us, Jabłoński. Everybody. I don't want to see the rot spread. I don't want to know."

"It was the only way," Jabłoński said. "You see that, don't you?" He lifted the bottle, but now in offer to his host. It was three-quarters gone. Powierza shook his head. Jabłoński went on. "You have to understand the realities, Staszek. I'll call you Staszek now, if you don't mind. Enough of formalities. I sense you are, in a way, a friend. You see, I appreciate intelligence. But you needn't speak of me like I'm some sort of evil wizard. You see, Staszek, I kept it running. Like a bus driver. That was my job. My only job."

"The files, Jabłoński."

"I made it work, you know. Not many could have. But I did. We had no trouble here. I got you food. No one got hurt. You're still here. You're fed well enough."

"You saved us from Communism, is that it?" Powierza said.

"Some weren't. You have no idea, Staszek. There's always a price. The price is cooperation. Without cooperation . . ." He pressed on, certain that Powierza understood him—even *believed*, for who could deny the force of such logic? Without cooperation, he argued, there was no order and no progress. Now there was no cooperation, and chaos was the result, everyone out for himself, pensioners standing in breadlines, foraging for scraps out of trash bins, prices doubling in a month. But it was nothing against the chaos to come, that was sure; the new president would become a dictator, the circle would close. Then everything would start over again. It would happen, truly. People would recall the Party more fondly, the banners would fly again.

"A higher intelligence—I mean a *better* intelligence—will carry the day next time. More common sense." Jabłoński smiled slyly. "The speeches will be shorter."

"We'll see," Powierza said. He picked up one of the weapons and laid it back in the crate. "But for now you go."

Jabłoński just stared at him. "All right," he said placidly.

"Except for one thing," Powierza said. "Your files."

"Ah, the files," Jabłoński said.

"Yes."

"Old Marcin's files." The withered face, the yellowed eyes, slid across Jabłoński's vision.

"Who?"

"The *Party's* files."

"Whatever."

Jabłoński didn't move or speak.

"We burn them, Mr. Chairman. Let's go find them. Together. You and me." He stepped from behind the crate. "Are you ready?"

Jabłoński didn't stir, except to peer up through glittery eyes at the wide face above him. Powierza's large hands reached down to the lapels of Jabłoński's coat and hauled the little man up until his feet barely touched the barn's dirt floor.

"Easy," Jabłoński said. "I can walk. I can always walk. He gave a soft belch. "I can walk through fire."

Pawel and Henryk showed up early that morning, just as Czarnek insisted. He had been pushing them hard for two days, producing at one and a half times the normal output. They had been sluggish and complaining, as usual, but they knew the limits of Czarnek's patience when a mood of efficiency and hurry—it was never quite haste—overtook him. As incentive, Czarnek had promised them three days off in a row, as soon as all eight fermentation tanks were full. This was not the usual pattern, filling all eight at once, and it would mean they faced a hard and noxious day of swabbing all the tanks at once when they returned to work, dragging around hoses and scrubbers through the stinging fumes of carbon dioxide, a day in boots, gloves, and gas masks. But it was a chore delayed, a day of complaining deferred.

Czarnek had conversed little with them, but despite his briskness, he was unusually mild with Pawel and Henryk as he labored along with them, intent on the tasks at hand and yet remote, distant, as though his mind were focused on a trip he was about to take.

"You going somewhere?" Pawel ventured to ask. It was the last day of the week. The priest had visited the afternoon before, but Pawel and

Henryk had not seen him. They had been resting for ten minutes and Czarnek had brought out three cans of Coca-Cola for refreshment, a gesture that was as much a novelty as the shiny, oddly flexible cylinders in their hands. Paweł glanced at Henryk, who was assessing the contents of the can as though testing for sour milk.

Czarnek didn't appear to hear the question.

"Are you going somewhere?"

"No," Czarnek said. "Where do you think I'd be going?"

They finished the work with rare dispatch, as if the week's hard push had conditioned them to reduce their usual wasted motion and slack attention. Paweł and Henryk managed to accomplish two or three tasks with the effort and time normally required for one. Instead of leaving their usual clutter behind them, they cleaned up, toting buckets, scrub brushes, and brooms to the storage bin in a single trip instead of three. At the end of the day they stood by the door, hats in hand, like a winning team waiting for congratulations. Czarnek passed by—he was still hurrying—and saw them watching him expectantly. He halted, a clipboard in one hand, a test beaker in the other. "Yes?"

"Tanks filled," Paweł said. "All eight, to the top."

"Cooker's scrubbed," said Henryk.

"Yes," said Czarnek, who knew all this already. "Good."

"In three days!" Paweł said. He shook his head at the feat. "Pretty good."

"Yes," said Czarnek. "Thanks."

"Okay?" said Paweł, still waiting.

"Okay," said Czarnek. "Yes. Very good. Good work. Thank you both."

Paweł and Henryk broke into smiles, seemed to relax, and shuffled toward the door.

"Tuesday, then. Right?"

"Yes."

"Everything all right?" Paweł looked at him with a questioning smile.

"Yes."

"Come on, Paweł," Henryk said, and shoved his companion out the door.

In the stillness left behind, amid the remote murmur of fluids and chemical exchange, Czarnek's pace slowed to another, more deliberate mode.

He washed his hands carefully, an elaborate soaping and rinsing in the cold water of the basin behind the office, then dried them on a clean square of frayed cloth pulled from a wooden cabinet. His hands had wrinkles now, that skin over the knuckles crinkling with the fingers held splayed, age where none used to be. How had it crept upon him so unnoticed? His hands were older now than his mother's had been. By twenty-seven years. He remembered her hand on the back of a chair, resting, relaxed, as she sat talking across the table: the scent of her skin while he stood as if hidden behind her chair, his head barely at her shoulder's level. The vein that rose out of her wrist met another to create the pattern of a diamond, then vanished again between her knuckles. The tiny diamond-shaped patterns of skin caught in the light—from a window? a lantern?—a softness he touched with a finger, then with his lips, while she sat and did not move, listening to his father talk across the table.

"Chaim!" his father's voice. Her hand withdrew, the conversation went on. The memory stayed, like a magnified photograph. Her hand, able but soft, the muscles of her forearms rippling as she kneaded—was it bread? Clothes she washed and wrung out? He saw the soap sluicing to the drain, the water running clear over the backs of her wrist, the tightening bands of her forearm.

Diapers, he supposed.

He could remember the smack of her hand on bread, the thump of dough on the table. Flour and water rolled flat and hurried to the oven. It was Passover.

He dealt with yeast now, work-whore that he was. Tubs of it, working at this moment, a thing alive and breathing to fill up the room, beyond this wall, with air just for him. Passover, by his calculation; sunset two hours and some away. He emerged into the still air, clucked to the dog, walked past his house to the woods, and followed the dog along the half-mile of rustling path to the cemetery.

He paused at its edge, watchful through the pale sea-green light, and saw no movement. Nothing was disturbed. The pine boughs remained in place over his stored materials, the kerosene, the lamps, the glass globes nestled in a paper-stuffed box, the copper and brass construction. He uncovered them.

He filled the lamps first, the kerosene spilling over his fingers with a light oily breath. The lamps were of tin and brass, some fashioned from old paint cans, but mostly of glass—green glass, milk glass, clear glass—each wicked and stoppered, and now, one by one, fueled to the top. He knelt amid them as he worked, and set them aside, making places for them on the ground. From the cardboard box, he fitted each with a globe or chimney of clear glass. He put the wadded papers back in the box.

He arranged the lamps then, taking them two at a time and resting them securely and firmly in the shadows of the old stones, spreading them around randomly.

He crossed back over the bordering berm of the cemetery and took up the brass and copper construction and attached it to the upright base. Careful of his balance, he carried the finished whole back into the cemetery and set it down. He threaded the coupling to the reservoir and tightened it with a wrench.

The light was fading, the air beneath the pines deepening to blue-black. With the last of the kerosene, he filled the reservoir, secured the cap and wiped it clean. He fitted the eight globes over the eight wicks on the brass-and-copper arms. They stood at a level with his shoulders.

Slowly, he backed up and inspected at what he had made. It was rough, even crude, with one arm slightly askew, a degree lower than the other, but it was solid, durable. The clear glass chimneys glittered faintly from the light left in the sky. He went back to it and tested the base. It was firm; it would not fall in wind.

For a few minutes he sat down with his dog and waited as the shadows deepened and merged. Then he stood, removed a candle from his pocket, lit it with a match, then circled the cemetery and lit each of the lanterns. When these were done, he lit each wick on the wide metal arms, working straight across, right to left. The flames flickered in the glass, faded a moment, then held steady.

From his pocket, he pulled a lump of gnarled metal the size of a fist, brass showing through knots and scars of melting. It was an object dug from rubble and kept wrapped in flannel cloth and hidden in bookcases and drawers of old clothing for all the years since, its identity a guess that became a certainty year by year as he willed it to be what he thought he remembered, a crown of the Torah, sifted from the ashes of the temple fire.

He had fitted it with a threaded stem, and this he inserted in its centered place between the two rows of flame, and twisted it tight.

He stepped back to look, but only a moment.

He clucked again to the dog. It sprang up, and together they headed back along their path, leaving the glade of quivering lights behind.

With his elbow, he broke one of the glass faces on the case where the alcohol ran like a never-ending spring. Into the dancing spout he dipped the edge of a tall water glass and watched it fill. Then he drank it back, so fast it seemed to pour from the glass down his throat. He walked around the dark, lofted room, the light from the overhead fixture casting multiple shadows on the floor. The draught hit his stomach like a slow-fused ball of fire, brought stinging tears to his eyes, a growl from the back of his throat. "Praise God, king of the universe, who creates the fruit of the vine." And then, in another voice, rough and high, a voice that could have been his father's speaking over candle flame, the old dishes, a crude kitchen table, *"Barukh atah Adonai eloheinu melech ha-olam hamotzi lechem min ha-artz."*

He stood stock still, staring in wonder into the twilighted recesses of corroded pipes and plumbing, not at them, but beyond them. A shudder passed through his body, and he spoke again in the old words. *"Shema Yisroel, Adonai eloheinu, Adonai Echad."*

He stared upward, his face wracked and lined in the bulb's light. Hear, O Israel. Hear my bedtime prayer. My fear of dark streets. My father's voice. See my mother's hands, my sisters' faces.

He went back to the fount and reached through the frame, saw his arm reflected in the wet blade of broken glass, and dipped the tumbler into the spout.

"Barukh atah Adonai . . . " He drank, pouring again into his open throat and gasping for air. He paced again, circling with his carousel of shadows. "May the Merciful grant us a day of Shabbat rest . . ."

What was it? "World to come. World without end. Fruit of the vine. Forever and forever. Now and at the hour of our . . ." He stopped, gave his head a shake. A shudder again passed through him. *"Shema."*

He tasted salt from his eyes. This was not wine, not unleavened bread, not life, not death. What mercy was this? Why them, why me? *Whose will, Adonai?* He heard noise, like an ocean, like music. He drank again from the clear spring, holding its frame for support. Finishing, he let the glass fall to shatter on the floor. He climbed the six steps to the office, found a candle from the cabinet, seized the old book waiting on his desk, and lurched from the office, holding hard onto the rail. "Come, Moishe." The dog followed, across the room, up more steps, down a short passageway to the heavy sealed door. When the door opened, releasing the room's clamor and tangy breath, the dog hung back. *"Idziemy, Moishe!"* He clasped the dog's collar and pulled him in. The candle dimmed when the door closed.

He located the pole propped against the wall and, his feet shuffling slowly on the passageway, opened the lids of the great fermentation vats. Each one added its unmuffled voice to the others until all eight together produced a sound like wind and water, like fire. He made his way back to the end of the room, near the entrance, to a bed of scattered straw, and slowly sat.

"Sit, Moishe." The dog lingered at the door, nose to the floor, scratching at the metal surface. "Come, come." Whimpering, the dog obeyed. He stroked it, murmuring, as the candle flame weakened. Czarnek stared into the darkness above him. "Easy now."

Straw and cold. Always the cold. "Lie down, Moishe." Lie down and rest. The candle . . . going now.

Easy, Moishe.

. . . going.

. . . gone.

"Shema."

He rolled onto his side, the old book with the charred pages beneath his head. *"Shema."* After a while the light seemed to rekindle, soft, glowing, and in it was his father's face, staring up, searching for something in the sky.

*   *   *

Andrzej saw them, just at dark, as he walked along the road between the Farmers' Co-op offices and the old Party building whose basement housed Jabłoński's flat. The flame caught his eye, naturally enough, when he passed the building and could see into the rutted and stubbled field beyond the garage, where a thin boil of smoke and waves of heat shimmered the evening air.

One of the two was Jabłoński, he could see that, but he had to look longer to identify the one with him, for he was squatting next to the fire, on his haunches, either warming himself or feeding it. When he stood, Andrzej recognized Powierza, for who else was that big, with such a round head? Standing behind a fortuitously thick portion of the scrub hedge beside the road, Andrzej remained a while to watch. He opened the satchel, slung as always on his shoulder, had a drink from his bottle, saw no movement on the road in either direction, and so stepped into the thicket for a better view.

Three large boxes or bundles waited next to the fire between the two men. Periodically, one or the other leaned down to add more fuel—paper—to the fire. Jabłoński rolled and tore it; Powierza slid it forward, into the striving orange light, a few sheets at a time. Sparks flew up, swirled and vanished. Points of light flickered off Jabłoński's glasses. Bits of blackened paper caught the heat, flew up like broken crow's wings, fell apart and vanished. Powierza poked at the flames with a stick and a festive profusion of sparks whirled skyward.

It was a quiet evening, and Andrzej found the fire powerfully inviting. Manly talk, a fire, a fresh bottle—what could be better? He was just about to step from the thicket and onto the field, but some portion of better judgment restrained him. He was stretched a bit thin between these two men just now. Jabłoński laid more paper on the fire; Powierza's hand reached out, extending his own bottle for Jabłoński to take. Andrzej watched a while longer, feeling envious, but then retreated back through the hedgerow and went on, reluctantly, down the road, looking once or twice over his shoulder at the receding glow.

Chapter Seventeen

LESZEK

I am telling this now from a longer perspective, not of distance, but of time.

I don't know who first saw the lights in the forest. Somehow that information seems to have gotten lost. Perhaps several saw them more or less simultaneously. Father Tadeusz, however, was among the first to receive the news, perhaps on the reasoning that lamps lighted in a cemetery fall automatically within the provenance of priests. He went to see. It was Saturday, just past dark, the eve of Easter.

I should say here that I've gotten to know Father Tadeusz over the months that have gone by—a calendar's worth and more—and I know from his description that he was powerfully affected by what he saw. He had walked to the cemetery with company, naturally, a clutch of villagers who had heard the news and trekked with him along the road from town and into the forest that enclosed the old graveyard. He could see the lights flickering through the trees before he left the road, the same strange illuminations that had attracted passersby. The low babble of the group, including some who had stumbled along from the just-closed bar, ceased when they reached the clearing.

Father Tadeusz recalled the moment as one of near paralysis, transfixed by the sight before him. The sensation he felt was that of standing at the threshold of a vaulted chamber where columns caught a shadowy light and rose toward the suggestion of vaulted ceilings and archways—a cathedral, he said, was the image that imposed itself helplessly on his mind. At the far end from where he stood, over a sprinkling of solitary lights, the arms of what he quickly recognized as a menorah glinted under its wavering flames, the metal gnarled and rough, and yet shimmering as if formed of molten gold. Two of the lights, he remembers, were out, but those gaps in the row of flames added to the power, somehow, for he instantly understood how the lights came to be, and with what effort and by whose hand. He knew this, at that time, but no more.

As I said, I know more of Father Tadeusz now than I did then. He is a moral person, of course, but he is not what I would think of as pious. He does not belabor religion, he does not really speak of it much at all. I don't have much experience with priests, certainly not in a close way, since the only one I knew from my childhood was old Father Marek, who went about blessing flowers and children and speaking in Bible verses. Father Tadeusz was not this sort of priest, and yet he was deeply and religiously moved by what he saw. The reaction of those people around him that day was considerably more animated and suspicious. There was Janowski, the baker, still wearing his apron under his coat; Kamiński, a truck driver, beery-eyed from the bar; and several others. Who had done this? they wanted to know. They knew what they were seeing—the old Jewish cemetery, of course. But why was *this* here? What did it *mean?* Was it, indeed, a sign that *they* were coming back? Was it done by relatives, returning as heirs to reclaim a supposed inheritance? Shouldn't something be done? Father Tadeusz did not answer any of these vaguely accusatory speculations, but left, walking back home well ahead of the straggling column.

I was in church the next day with my mother. We did not yet know of the cemetery, we had only overheard some fragment about lanterns or candles; it was unclear. And yet in church that morning there was a palpable current of anticipation, of importance, that I could feel myself, something that went beyond the usual Easter extravagance of white flowers, bowed white ribbons, the children's baskets brought for blessing, beyond the smell of church—that scent of leather and tallow, of damp stone space and human breath, the smoke that rose like an oily mist from the bank of red flickering candles below the statue of the Virgin. The old women sat scarved with backs bent under the chords of organ music, eyes glittering with the fear of God and his unpersuadable saints, rosaries coiled about their plump fists.

When it came time for Father Tadeusz to speak, he rose to the pulpit, then stood for a long time in silence.

He said he would talk to us about history and sorrow.

He paused, as though waiting for an objection.

It was not, he said, the usual subject for Easter.

Then he began. I cannot recall his words fully or exactly, but they held the church, for the brief time they lasted, in rapt attention. We are a country, he said, obsessed with its past. This is for good reason, he said, because for all time the nation has been pressed between two straining and opposing forces, the Germanic peoples on one side and the most powerful Slavs on the other—the one always ambitious and the other forever nagged by a sense of inferiority. Geography, he said—his tone was here like a teacher's—has kept us subject to their maneuvers and slights, their treaties, bargains, and betrayals, and too often their invading armies. Historians and professors have explained these forces to us, taught us, for example, how Poland—ten percent of Europe's land mass—could actually disappear from the map of Europe for one hundred years. They were good teachers, he said, and we understood this history, and we understand it today.

"But there is another history," he said. "And there is another ten percent." The pitch and volume of his voice rose.

"A tenth of our population, people who used to live and work and walk among us. You know who I mean.

"They are gone now, and this is history, too.

"But it is also a sorrow. And it is this history and this sorrow which we have a harder time acknowledging."

He looked out across the church. "Think!" he said. "Ten percent gone. Like that!" His hand flicked, silently, in the air.

"It was a horror, yes. But what did it mean, the vanishing of that *particular* ten percent of our population? Think of it, brothers and sisters, and wonder. It is as if these people were a vanished tribe, except they left no great ruins behind. Only a kind of cavity. A hollowness. Something not discussed, like a dishonesty."

I thought, for a second, of the church as a vessel heaving on a swell, for an audible, creaking strain sounded in the wooden joints of the old benches, a wind of in-drawn breath, a heave of dismay and discomfort. It was delivered, on this day of all days, by, of all people, the most light-spoken, the mildest, of priests. "For too many of us, what happened to those people was not a sorrow. It was a horror, but not a sorrow. Do you see that there is a difference? The horror was not traceable to us. We were not to blame for it, and so, in a way, we could accept it. The sorrow should be ours to accept, but we reject it, for we have our own problems, our own crosses to bear. What we are really saying is these ten percent were something else to us—*among* us but not *of* us. We say, Yes, three million of them died on our soil, but then another three million of *ours* died, too, in the same horror. And so we have not a likeness, but a distinction. Our own, and *them*. Ours are Poles. *They* are Jews. We mourn for our own, as we should and must. Widows grieve for husbands, mothers for their sons. We have our own grief to suffer, to occupy us, and so it equates with theirs. They are canceled out. Their loss is canceled out by our own loss, as we canceled out their footprints, boarded over the marks of their devotion (to a God that gave rise to our own), leaving their burned temple unmarked by even a single stone, while this very church was repaired with loving care. We left their graves untended, forgotten, while looking after those of 'our own.' We walk the streets they helped make, enter buildings where they once conducted their business, under roofs where their families once slept in peace, and in doing these things we the living are occupied with the things of the living and with the memories of our own departed dead. And preoccupied, too, these days—it is human enough—with thoughts of those who have trespassed against us. We perceive many of these trespassers, because now, in the present climate, it seems possible to act on our grievances for the more recent past. We reject sorrow and have instead a desire for retribution and a hunger for revenge we can satisfy with punishment, with revelation, with a thorough examination of those we believe are guilty. We want to watch them wither under this examination, to see them agonize themselves with lies and excuses, to see them admit what we already know."

Father Tadeusz bowed his head for a long moment, then gazed over the silent church.

"We have more pressing business, my good people. We have more urgent needs. We must remember what this day is about. It is about forgiveness and generosity, about past and present made whole." He folded the pieces of paper in front of him. Perhaps he had been reading; I hadn't realized that. "When mass is finished, I want those of you who can to walk with me somewhere. There is something I need to show you. There is something we all need to see."

And so after the mass, there was a simple and unceremonious procession out along the street and past the square and onto the west road out of the village. By unceremonious, I mean there was no raised cross or other religious paraphernalia, no monstrance, incense, candle or banner. Father Tadeusz led, followed by three altar boys, their shoulders still sheathed, like his, in white, with the rest of us following, some two hundred in all, I suppose, a loose column strung along the road. The day had begun sunny and warm, but in the hour we had been in church a sheet of clouds had rolled over the sky, threatening an early spring rain. The trees were budding. The first white blossoms were clinging to the plum trees; green shoots of rye were thrusting through the fields.

At the point where the road bends obliquely to the right, Father Tadeusz plunged into the woods. The crowd slowed and bunched at the parted brush, then flowed through behind him. He halted at the ridge that bordered the cemetery. With his arms outstretched, he directed us to spread ourselves out before him. Voices, to the extent they were heard at all, were muted. There was the sound of brush crackling and twigs snapping under foot.

"Brothers and sisters," Father Tadeusz said, "look upon this. These, too, were our brothers and sisters." He faced away from us for a moment, and then back. The faces he saw, and the expressions I saw around me, were absorbed and astonished, uneasy. "We have forgotten them. Now someone has wanted us to remember. We do not know who, but this is unimportant. What is important is that we do remember." He bowed his head. "Our Father . . . who art in heaven . . ."

The voices rose with his. Then he stood for a minute in silence looking through the blue-green light and the pale flickering flames. Many, now, had gone out, their glass chimneys charred, but the effect of those yet lighted, and of the rough metal candelabra, was to stillness, to hush. Father Tadeusz left then, weaving through the crowd, back through the woods to the road.

Some time has elapsed, but I recall this is the way it happened: Paweł and Henryk discovered Czarnek's body when they reported for work Tuesday morning.

Paweł had no key, but when they waited for two hours and there was no sign of Czarnek, and no answer when they pounded on the door of his cottage, they applied a crowbar to a window of the distillery and climbed in.

The carbon dioxide hit them with a stinging rush when they opened the door to the room with the fermentation tanks. Czarnek's body was sprawled on a mass of straw in a pool of vomit. His dog lay dead beside him.

It was Powierza who found Grandpa's shrine. Staszek didn't say how he happened upon it, although he has a field nearby, and perhaps he, like the rest of us, is subject to unexplained and solitary treks in the woods. But he seemed to know who put it there and he came to tell me about it as soon as he saw it. I accompanied him to look. A wax grave candle burned in front of the stones, and a stack of fresh ones waited in the shelter as replacements, indicating an intention to keep the flame burning.

"Yes," said Grandpa when I ask him if he had made the thing.

"For . . . them?" I asked.

"Yes," he said. "You know." And that's all he would say about it.

I returned later, alone, and studied it for a long time. Someone coming across it might take it, at first glance, as another of the hundreds of *kapliczki* that dot the country's roadsides. There was no blue-robed Virgin here, no crucifix. But it was a thing of curious and arresting beauty. As I crouched in the wooded silence and ran my fingers over the rough Hebrew lettering on the stones and looked up at the careful lashing of the roof beams, at its intricate design and precise construction, I realized the pain and the plea for forgiveness it represented, and I thought of him here, assembling these pieces, his bowlegs and his stubbled iron jaw. I gave the corner post a shake. It was as solid as a house, as unyielding as fifty years of grief, and built to last.

It was soon after that that Father Tadeusz paid his call. He wanted to see Grandpa. Someone—it had to have been Powierza—had told him. He asked for "the older Mr. Maleszewski" and they spoke together for a long time. They conversed in the shelter between the two barns, Father Tadeusz sitting on the chopping stump. After a time they departed together in the wagon.

It was the first of many visits.

The news of Czarnek's death spread only a day or two before Powierza discovered Grandpa's memorial. The death caused a sensation, of course, and many versions circulated of what might have happened. Stories of foul play, of a drunken binge, of poisoning, all quickly flew about and then gradually settled, like a wreath of leaves on a spent wind.

No one made the connection between Grandpa's construction and Czarnek. And there was no general understanding of who had spread the lanterns in the old Jewish cemetery. It was Father Tadeusz, of course, who told us the story. Although he said he had no direct evidence that it had been Czarnek who lighted the cemetery, he didn't think it could have been anyone else. He thought, when he heard of Grandpa's "observance" (as he called it) in a forest on the opposite side of town, that its creator might explain the lights in the cemetery. Of course, Grandpa did that, in a way unexpected by both. Grandpa had not gone to church that Easter day—he hadn't been in years—and until he met Father Tadeusz and rode in the wagon with him to the old cemetery, he had not seen the lights, the lanterns, the beautiful copper and brass menorah. Father Tadeusz himself had seen to it that the lamps were replenished with kerosene, and they were burning when he took Grandpa to see them. It was Father Tadeusz who suggested to Grandpa that Czarnek's impulse to light the cemetery, to make *his* "observance," might have been stimulated by, ironically, Grandpa's removal of the old stones to fashion his own memorial.

Father Tadeusz had made an intuitive leap here, for Grandpa had been silent to that point on the origin of the stones he had used. When confronted (with a statement of seeming fact, of certain knowledge), Grandpa seemed defensive, shamefaced, and embarrassed, or so Father Tadeusz perceived it. The stones, he told Father Tadeusz, appeared to follow no order, tossed face-down from their original resting places, perhaps even vandalized many years ago. He meant no disrespect; he intended them for a good purpose. "They were going to waste," Grandpa said. Father Tadeusz assured him this was probably true and that what he had done had not been wrong, necessarily; it had brought about, Father Tadeusz said, a good effect. "People needed to see, to remember," he said.

Grandpa, however, extracted a promise from Father Tadeusz to say nothing of his identity as the fabricator of the memorial in the forest near Powierza's field. Yes, he said, he meant in a way for it to be seen, perhaps, but he meant it mostly to mark something that had happened to innocent people, and to him, something that he had brought about because of bad judgment and his soldier's mentality at the time, but he didn't want to become known in the village as "a lover of Jews."

The phrase struck Father Tadeusz as infelicitous, but he had no trouble comprehending the impulse behind it. How could he mistake it? The effect of Czarnek's lights in the old cemetery, and his own remarkable sermon, had released no outpouring of sorrow for the Jews. Father Tadeusz had not really expected that. And what, in any case, would such a sorrow produce? All he wanted to do was point out to people the reminders that there was once "another people" among us, and that their memory should be honored. Over the week that followed Easter, more people—people who had not been in church on Sunday—walked or drove out to the cemetery to observe it for themselves, having heard it discussed on street corners or the market. Word spread to the curious in other villages, a few of whom also came. By the end of the week, a newspaper from Warsaw also arrived, and its staff produced a small article and a picture that ran a few days later.

The newspaper people spoke to Father Tadeusz, who simply told them the "observance"—this was the accepted term by now—had been produced by "an element" of the village (a usefully vague term of the old system, something straight from meetings of the Central Committee), which had no interest in accepting "credit," but wished to remain anonymous.

Although it was only six paragraphs long, the article in *Życie Warszawy*, with its accompanying photograph, gave a sort of validation, or benediction, to the phenomenon, a positive note that calmed the unease. A copy of the clipping, fanatically defaced and addressed to "The Rabbi of Jadowia," did find its way to the rectory mailbox. Father Tadeusz was surprised, he said, there were not more like it. But in general, his message was accepted. Janowski, the baker, so worried about the lightning strike of a claim against the building his business occupied, stopped staring in alarm out the window every time a strange car drove by. He put away his sheaf of deeds and tax records and went to Father Tadeusz to suggest creating a fund for the the old cemetery's maintenance. He contributed the equivalent of a hundred dollars to the effort. And so it was done, quietly and without a fuss and without, as it happened, much more money, since all the subsequent contributions, Father Tadeusz confided, never added up to more than Janowski's original donation.

Investigative wheels turn slowly in the countryside, perhaps especially in a case like Czarnek's where no family existed to press for answers. The body was taken to the medical examiner's laboratory in Węgrów, where it was kept in the morgue for two weeks. The reason for death was listed as "probable suicide." The means of death was determined to be "asphyxiation by carbon dioxide gas." The body was released to the custody of Father Tadeusz, who saw to its burial in the old cemetery. To this, the reaction of the village was at first wonder and, then, a nod of recognition, an acknowledgment of Czarnek's taciturn, solitary strangeness. Everyone always knew he was strange; now they knew why. Father Tadeusz told me he thought Czarnek had chosen to die by gas not simply because he had the opportunity. "That's what happened to most of his people, you know. Treblinka."

Yes, I knew.

The months pass, and he is forgotten now. The distillery, in fact, has been shut down, for the first time in 120 years (barring war, of course). No one, until the news was announced, even realized how long it had operated. When it made its first alcohol, Catherine the Second was Empress of Russia and would have exacted a tax over its production, since she claimed suzerainty over the portion of Poland where it stood. Poland itself, as Father Tadeusz reminded us, existed at that time only as annexed territories of Russia, Germany, and Austria. Perhaps a Jew ran it even then. It is possible: they had education, after all. In any event, its contribution to the nation's vodka supply will not be missed, except perhaps in certain low quarters on the outskirts of Moscow, which are probably preoccupied with other hardships anyway. Paweł and Henryk, the only two employees, already on the town payroll, were simply shifted to the township road department, and can been seen frequently enough during clement weather, propped on their shovels with their new workmates. The idle distillery, its sooted smokestack cold, awaits some plan, or demolition, and will probably go on waiting for years. Weeds have grown over the porch of Czarnek's old cottage.

Father Tadeusz left the caretaking of the cemetery in the charge of Grandpa, or "Mr. Maleszewski, the Home Army veteran," the formality he uses to third parties, even, sometimes, to me. Accepting the duty, Grandpa saw to it that the undergrowth was kept down. He built a dark rail fence around the cemetery on the old berm and cleared a wagon path from the road to the pine grove. He and Father Tadeusz discussed putting up a small sign, but have not gotten around to it. The place was to be tended, Father Tadeusz said, but not "improved."

The maintenance has become my task now that Grandpa is sick, his lungs filling up and the arthritis curling his hands, and more days go by when he doesn't leave the barnlot or sometimes not even his bed. I don't mind doing it for him. For a farmer with less land than he would like there is always the odd spare morning or afternoon, and when I am there I usually have the peace of the place to myself. Two or three times, though, I have met teachers from the school there shepherding a class of students, and they are appropriately hushed and a little awed, as though they have glimpsed a secret that lived among them. None of them knows that the only new-comer here is Czarnek.

The one solitary figure I encounter there is Father Tadeusz, who comes, sometimes, on his walks, and I have found him, more than once, standing by Czarnek's grave. It is here that we have gotten to know one another. We talk as he follows me about, watching as I slice at the perimeter weeds with a scythe.

We were there one day when he told me he would be leaving Jadowia. It was retirement, he said, or semi-retirement, actually. He would be attached to a church library-museum in Kraków. "To dwell among books, at last," he said. He would have resisted the change, he said, but the truth was he felt tired. The young doctor at the clinic had suggested he see a specialist, and advised him to think of relocating to some place with better-equipped facilities. There was trouble with his colon, or perhaps it was a glandular thing; he wouldn't be more specific. He was fine, he said, but slowing down.

A younger priest would take his place. But not too young, he added. A well-seasoned pastor, a good man.

I said I would be sorry to see him leave.

He said he would be sorry, too, that his time here had been good for him.

Then he said something that surprised me. He said he had heard Jabłoński had relocated somewhere near Kraków. He said the idea of getting to know Jabłoński "a little better" interested him. Perhaps it was pure whimsy, he said, but he had this idea of the two of them, walking in parks and arguing. What, he asked, could be more inter-esting, more stimulating? Besides, he said, "I am a Pole; why would I not like to argue?" Perhaps it was possible now, he said; a relation-ship between old adversaries, real or symbolic, in their dotage. He said the life he had always hoped for as a priest, a life among the shelves of libraries, was, however fanciful, a life spent with the boxed and bound arguments of scholars. How many angels? How many leaves cover the graves of the ancestors? How many papers in the files of the Party's record vaults? And what did it matter? Yes, he said, Jabłoński would know; he could always tell you. And Jabłoński had a certain history in his head, Father Tadeusz said, a history of the town, of Jadowia. He might not be strictly reliable as to the facts, of course, but he would always have opinions. He would never run out of them.

The thought of it, far-fetched as it seemed, brought from him a soft laugh, and he walked beside me more lightly, his face lifted to the silver sky shining through the branches of the trees.

Father Tadeusz was right about Jabłoński's relocation, according to reports heard by Powierza. He joined old associates in business, buying cheap and selling dear. It was what they always did, really. Like cockroaches in an old house, they cling to the joints of the national plumbing, and endure.

Farby and Zofia Flak have gone on, too, and made a success in a modest way, thanks particularly to Zofia's head for business and Farby's willingness to stay away from the account books and the cash box. His affection for her is total and devoted. The sweet shop they opened in Zakopane is bright and cheerful. He stirs the pots and pours out the sheets of candy with the absorbed delight of a child making mud pies. All of this is secondhand gossip, sifted, I suppose, from Zofia's letters to friends, but the picture seems right to me, and I plan to take a trip there someday, if I can find a reliable hired man, just to see for myself, and to sample the candy and visit the mountains.

I observe my neighbors more closely now, not in suspicion, but with a certain wonder and curiosity that is new and with, I think, an appreciation of the connective tissue that runs, sometimes with minor inflammations, between us.

Powierza has become the *naczelnik* now—although that term, a relic of the past, is no longer used. Call him mayor. He is a good one, I think, elected by a wide margin over the abject Twerpicz, deprived of both rudder and crew in the absence of Father Jerzy. Powierza has streamlined the town's business—not hard to do, in fact—and his natural boom and energy have found their natural and effective outlet. Small projects abound. The roads are in better shape now, and the street lamps are all working. A new marketplace is under construction. The weedy lot where the synagogue once stood has been cleared and cleaned; a stone and plaque are planned for the spot, but have not yet appeared.

Powierza still broods over the murder of his son, sitting over a glass at his kitchen table and, when a little drunk, speaking of Tomek in the present tense as though he were still alive. Once, spurred by some report confided to him by Krupik, he journeyed to Ukraine to speak to some arrested Georgian smugglers. He returned weary and unenlightened and yet, at the same time, finished with it.

He held onto Jabłoński's rocket launchers a long time, but he couldn't stand seeing them in his barn any longer, so he brought them to me to keep. No one else, besides Andrzej, knew of their existence. They are in my barn loft still, concealed under hay, and my pitchfork finds them again as another spring approaches. I think sometimes I will bury them in the woods, and perhaps in the next century, as the next army marches over Poland, they will dig their foxholes and uncover them. Or I think I will load them in the wagon behind the tractor and pull them to some remote road and simply dump them in a ditch.

We seldom speak of my father anymore. Or if we do, it is not in that way, the Jabłoński way.

But Powierza did tell me one thing that I think about often. There were records of town business stored in the town hall, remarkably complete, given the chaos of the place, and mostly irrelevant. Powierza, with the help of a new secretary, rummaged through some of them. They stretched back for decades. Among them he found the period in which my father served on the town council. And it so happened that it was in this period that Czarnek was appointed to the distillery post. It was not clear from the record what he was doing before that, but Powierza found that out, too: he was trying to make a living out of odd jobs, four cows, and three acres of land. It was my father who nominated him for the job. More interesting, though, was that another nominee had been put forward, before that, by Roman Jabłoński, then the *naczelnik*. Under the circumstances of the time, acceptance of a *naczelnik's* personal nominee would have been a pro-forma matter. In other words, if the *naczelnik* wanted one Lech Kowalski to run the distillery, then Lech Kowalski would run the distillery. Period, end of story. But two meetings later, my father—Mariusz Maleszewski, comrade councilman—nominated Krzysztof Czarnek for the post, and, one meeting after that, Czarnek was confirmed, with no opposition. Jabłoński's nominee did not appear in the records again; withdrawn, rescinded, or stricken, he simply disappeared from view. Since the vote for Czarnek's appointment was unanimous, it meant Jabłoński's own vote was included for approval.

Was this the seed of the deal? There is nothing explicit. The records were not *that* complete, but Powierza saw it, and so could I. Does a bargain leave fingerprints? Did my father win a secure job for Czarnek at the price of certain favors for Jabłoński? Of course I don't know that. Powierza, pointedly, asked Jabłoński no questions and was volunteered no answers—just the usual high-flown preachments. And perhaps it is true that I don't want to know more. I am happy to be satisfied with this and with the acceptance of an idea that there is much we cannot know and will never be told. Could my father have sympathized with the aims of the Party? As Grandpa said, it is possible. Did he believe it represented a "better way?" Yes, that is possible, too. Against everything he'd seen, maybe it was.

I don't talk about this with anyone. It is only for myself. None of Jabłoński's information ever came out.

I did go to Kowalski, however, to explain, or confess, for my father. It turned out—of course—that he knew, as I would have understood had I known then what I do now. The tact and discretion of some people, people who have the right to possess none at all, is a constant affirmative surprise. I told Kowalski I was sorry. I told him I didn't know when I spoke to him. Although I avoided the question of the field, he brought it up. He was going to sell it, he said, to a German businessman who had made inquiries and agreed to pay a premium price, far more than Kowalski ever dreamed (or that I had hope of borrowing), an offer he accepted without hesitation on the shake of a hand.

So the yellow field belongs to someone else now, and it has become a sight to see: rows of glass houses—green houses—that are as opaque as quartz by day but that glow at night like spaceships, like ice lit from within. In the first nights they were illuminated, people walked out from the village and stood by the road to gaze at them as if, in fact, an apparition had landed in our midst. Even now, you can see travelers, or visitors from neighboring towns (more people seem to have cars now) brake on the road below the rise and look with a kind of pride at the German's new enterprise. He is said to be pleased. He selected the field for its orientation, banked against the southern light, and found the workmanship for the construction of high quality and the local labor costs a bargain. So the greenhouses glow now in the night, and on evenings when clouds descend low over the land I can see their yellowish reflection in the air, as though the night sky were throwing back to me my remembered dream of an autumn harvest.

In the meantime, I have my eye on another field. It is not so well situated, and the drainage at one end is less than perfect. But I can work around it, gradually contour it into shape. Its soil, in fact, is just as good. In a few months, I think, I'll be in a position to present an offer. I try to guard against allowing hope to run away with reality, but in my mind's eye, I am already pacing if off and considering the daring notion of hard winter wheat. I'm not sure if this is determination, unwarranted optimism, or just trying to force my own luck.

I am plowing now. The smell of the sliced earth rises through the scent of engine oil and exhaust, as my tractor makes its turn and presents to me over its blunt nose another row of the field waiting for the polished blades hitched behind me. The sun is warm on my back, and I am content with my choice, happy with this morning and the expectation of the same tomorrow. Sometimes there are moments, late at night or standing by myself at the verge of the forest, when I wonder what my life would be like in a large city or distant country. But the thought fades; I don't mind these speculations. Perhaps you measure what you have by what you don't. I do not hear from Jola, but I know sometime I will; some card or letter will wend its way to me from Denmark or Sweden, South Africa or Australia. It will come with warmth, with fragments of information, and no return address. This is all right, too. She was, and is, a gift, memory's future, and I wish her well.

I am still in need of a wife, but not for much longer. The bride I will take resides, as my mother imagined, in the country, two villages away. Though she was not reared on a farm, she has never been far from them. She teaches school. She reads, she has ideas. She likes to talk, and I like to listen to her, to anticipate her flinty opinions, on books or world events or the people she knows. I like to watch her mouth move, her eyebrows dance and the way she can seem to fold herself, with sudden stillness, against the hollow of my shoulder. Her name is Anna, and I have grown to love her, for she is that rare thing, my luck and courage ascending together, the sun over the trees.